About the Authors

Sarah M. Anderson may live east of the Mississippi River, but her heart lies out west on the Great Plains. Sarah's book *A Man of Privilege* won a *RT Book Reviews* 2012 Reviewers' Choice Best Book Award. *The Nanny Plan* was a 2016 RITA® winner for Contemporary Romance: Short.

Sarah spends her days having conversations with imaginary cowboys and billionaires. Find out more about Sarah's heroes at www.sarahmanderson.com and sign up for the new-release newsletter at http://eepurl.com/nv39b

A fifth generation Californian, **Teresa Carpenter** lives in San Diego within miles of her extensive family and knows with their help she can accomplish anything. She takes particular joy and pride in her nieces and nephews who are all bright, fit, shining stars of the future. If she's not at a family event, you'll usually find her at home reading or writing her next grand romance.

USA TODAY bestseller **Michelle Celmer** is the author of more than forty books for Mills & Boon. You can usually find her in her office with her laptop loving the fact that she gets to work in her pyjamas.

Michelle loves to hear from her readers! Visit Michelle on Facebook at Michelle Celmer Author, or email at michelle@michellecelmer.com

The Bosses
COLLECTION

Taming
the Boss

SARAH M. ANDERSON

TERESA CARPENTER

MICHELLE CELMER

MILLS & BOON

First Published in Great Britain 2020
By Mills & Boon, an imprint of HarperCollins*Publishers*
1 London Bridge Street, London, SE1 9GF

TAMING THE BOSS © 2020 Harlequin Books S.A.

Twins for the Billionaire © 2017 Sarah M. Anderson
The Boss's Surprise Son © 2011 Teresa Carpenter
The Secretary's Secret © 2007 Michelle Celmer

ISBN: 978-0-263-28108-8

MIX
Paper from
responsible sources

FSC www.fsc.org

FSC™ C007454

This book is produced from independently certified FSC™ paper to ensure responsible forest management.

For more information visit: www.harpercollins.co.uk/green

Printed and bound in Spain
by CPI, Barcelona

TWINS FOR THE BILLIONAIRE

SARAH M. ANDERSON

To the real Adelina and Eduardo – thanks for all
your years of friendship and support with
my family!

Prologue

"So that's it?" Eric Jenner stared at the private investigator's report in his hand. The baby wasn't his. Somehow, he'd known this would be the answer.

Funny how it still hurt like hell.

"That's it." The investigator stood. "Unless there was something else you needed?"

Eric almost laughed. What did he need? He needed a happy ending to this whole mess. But it was clear he wasn't going to get one. Not today. Maybe not ever.

He gritted his teeth. Bad enough that he'd been stood up at the altar—literally. Six months later, the press was still having a field day with the photos of Eric looking stunned next to the priest. In front of six hundred wedding guests. In the Holy Name Cathedral.

But this? He knew he couldn't keep it quiet forever. Prudence had married less than two weeks after she'd left Eric at the altar. Apparently, it was true love. How else to explain Prudence running away with an accountant from her father's company? Who'd fathered Prudence's son and was, according to the PI's account, making her the happiest woman in the world.

Eric was thrilled for them. Really.

He breathed in slowly and exhaled even slower. "If I think of anything else, I'll let you know," he said to the investigator. The man nodded and left.

Eric read the report again. Oddly, he didn't miss Prudence. He didn't lie awake in bed at night, missing her touch. He didn't regret putting the condo he'd bought for her back on the market.

He'd clearly dodged a bullet. Except for one small detail.

That detail had been born at seven pounds, six ounces. He stared at the picture the investigator had included. The baby was bundled up in Prudence's arms, his eyes closed and a little smile on his face. She'd named him Aaron.

Something tightened in Eric's chest. No, Eric didn't miss Prudence at all. But…

Everywhere he went, people had babies. Suddenly, he couldn't avoid them. Even his oldest friend, Marcus Warren, had recently adopted a baby boy. After he'd married his assistant, of all people.

Eric and Marcus had always competed with each other—who had made the first million (Eric), the first billion (Marcus), who had the finest cars (it changed all the time) or the biggest boat. Eric always won that one, hands down.

It wasn't like the contest was over. But the rules had changed and Eric wasn't ready for this new game. He wasn't ready to stand by as his best friend cooed over his son while his wife looked at them both with love in her eyes.

It should have been nauseating.

Eric and Marcus's entire friendship was built on one-upmanship. But a loving wife and an adorable child?

And now this news from Prudence was the final blow.

One thing was clear. Eric had never lost this badly.

To hell with this.

He was Eric Jenner. He owned a quarter of the Chicago skyline, some of the most expensive properties in the world. He'd officially joined the exclusive ranks of billionaires. He was, he had been told, good-looking and good in bed. There wasn't anything he couldn't buy.

What he needed now was distraction. The kind he'd find in the arms of someone new who'd drive thoughts of happy families far from his mind. He hadn't lost anything. He was glad Prudence was gone—that marriage would have been a disaster. He'd gotten lucky. He wasn't tied down. He could do whatever he wanted—and what he wanted was *everything*.

The world was his for the taking. All he had to do was snap his fingers and whatever he wanted was his.

Abruptly, he slammed the report shut and jammed it in the bottom drawer of his desk.

Well.

Almost anything.

It turned out there were some things money couldn't buy.

One

Ten months later...

The elevator door dinged. Sofia Bingham waited for the rest of the crowd to exit first, nerves swirling in her stomach. She was really doing this—interviewing for the job of office manager at Jenner Properties.

Her breath caught in her throat as she stepped into the foyer of Eric Jenner's real estate empire. In her mind, this office had looked exactly the same as Eric's father's real estate office. Jenner and Associates had been a regal office located on the ground floor of a four-story building. John and Elise Jenner had run their exclusive agency on the Gold Coast of Chicago, catering to the rich and the ultrarich.

Her father, Emilio, had started as a janitor before moving up to staging houses for the Jenners and then starting his own company as a bilingual real estate agent. Sofia's mother, Rosa, had been the Jenners' housekeeper and Elise Jenner had had a soft spot for Sofia. Elise had showered Sofia with dresses and toys.

When Sofia had been growing up, the Jenners had seemed like the richest people in the world.

None of that had prepared her for *this*.

Jenner Properties took up the whole of the fortieth floor of the skyscraper at 310 South Wacker Drive. She could see Lake Michigan from here, the sun glittering off the water like a mirage come to life.

She smiled. It had been years since she had seen Eric Jenner, but she wasn't surprised he had a good view of the lake. He'd always loved the water. Not only had he taught her to swim in his family's pool but he'd even taught her how to sail his toy sailboats so they could race.

Around her, more elevators opened and more people poured out. Jenner and Associates had been run primarily by John and Elise Jenner and two other agents. But Jenner Properties was staffed by a small army of very serious-looking people, all of whom wore good suits and better shoes. Sofia looked down at her skirt and jacket combo, the nicest outfit she owned that didn't have baby food stains on it. It was cute—a black-and-white polka-dotted skirt with a white jacket over a black blouse with a bow at the neck—but it wasn't in the same class of clothing as the people rushing past her.

She stepped to the side and stared out at the lake. She was here for a job interview. The position of office manager had opened up and Sofia simply couldn't keep working as a real estate agent. She needed regular hours and a regular paycheck. It was easy to say that she needed both of those things for her twins, Adelina and Eduardo, but the truth was, she needed them for herself.

Yes, this job paid enough that she could hire a nanny to help Mom out. Sofia had been a real estate agent with her husband, David. She couldn't be one without him anymore.

There were other office manager jobs she could apply for, but this one paid more. That wasn't the only reason she was here, however...

Would Eric remember her?

There was no reason he should. She hadn't seen him since he'd turned sixteen and gone away to prep school in New York. Their paths hadn't crossed in the fifteen years since and Sofia was no longer a gangly thirteen-year-old with crooked teeth.

So he wouldn't recognize her. He probably wouldn't even remember her. After all, she'd just been the daughter of the family maid and the janitor.

But she'd never forgotten him. Time might have changed her but a girl never forgot her first kiss. Even if that kiss had been the result of a dare, it still counted.

Nervously, she watched Eric's employees file in. She needed this job, but she wanted to earn it on her own merits. She didn't want to have to rely on an old family connection that he'd probably forgotten.

But desperate times and all that.

There was a lull in people exiting the elevators as she stepped forward to the reception desk. She and David had worked in a perfectly respectable office serving northern Chicago, Skokie, Lincolnwood, Evanston and the surrounding areas. But even the receptionist here had a nicer desk than she'd had at the office.

"Hello," Sofia began, projecting more confidence than she felt right now. "My name is Sofia Bingham and I have a nine a.m. interview with Mr. Jenner."

The receptionist was young, blonde and gorgeous. Her eyebrows alone were works of art, to say nothing of the trendy patterned jacket she wore. Her eyes flicked over Sofia, but she didn't so much as frown, which had to count for something. "You're here for the office manager position?" Even her voice sounded trendy.

"Yes." Confident. That was Sofia. She could handle an interview. She could handle this office—although it didn't seem to need a lot of managing.

"One moment, please." The receptionist turned her attention to her computer screen.

Sofia's stomach tightened with anxiety. She'd been selling real estate for over seven years and before that, she'd been helping at her parents' agency. But managing an office like this?

This wasn't just real estate agents. Eric Jenner no longer bought and sold houses. He bought land and built things, like this skyscraper. He employed agents and architects and interior designers and lawyers. He built exclusive office spaces and luxury apartments. And he did it so well that he had become a billionaire. Sofia didn't stalk Eric online but it'd been hard to miss when he'd been left at the altar and then, just a few months later, been named one of Chicago's top five eligible bachelors, following the marriage and subsequent delisting of his friend, Marcus Warren.

What was she even doing here? She didn't know anything about billionaires. She knew how to sell houses and condos to families, not manage architects and negotiate tax breaks with municipalities. She was struggling to hold on to middle-class respectability, for crying out loud. She'd had to move back in with her parents because she couldn't afford house payments or daycare. This was not her world.

Her chest tightened and she had trouble breathing. *Oh, no.*

No, she could not have a panic attack. Not another one, not right now. She took a step back from the reception desk, the urge to flee so strong it was almost overwhelming. Two things stopped her. The first was the image of the twins in her mother's arms this morning, all waving bye-bye to Sofia as she went off for her big interview. Mom had been training Adelina and Eduardo to blow kisses and it was the cutest thing ever. The twins needed more than Sofia could give them right now. They needed stability and safety. They needed a mom who wasn't teetering on the edge, trying to keep everything together. To be that person for her children, she needed a steady job.

The other thing that halted her in her tracks was the sound of her name. "Ms. Bingham?"

She looked up and the air rushed out of her lungs. *There he was.* She'd seen pictures of him in those impossible-to-miss articles, but there was something unexpected about Eric Jenner in the flesh that shook her.

That smile, at least, hadn't changed. But the rest of him? Eric Jenner was now over six feet tall, moving with an easy grace that projected strength and confidence. He was simply breathtaking in a way she hadn't ever associated with him. His hair had deepened from bright copper to a rich burnished red, although his skin was still tanned. She almost grinned. Bronzed redheads were such a rare thing that it only made him all the more special.

One thing was certain—he was *not* the boy she remembered. His shoulders were broader, his legs more powerful as they closed the distance between them. And his eyes... When she lifted her gaze to his, he stumbled to a stop, his brow quirking and she knew he recognized her, even if he didn't know from where. Something in her chest loosened and she could breathe again because she knew it was going to be all right.

She hoped, anyway.

Then the realization broke over his face. *"Sofia?"* He took a step forward before pulling up short. "I'm sorry," he went on in a completely different voice. "You look like someone I used to know."

She became aware that they were standing in the middle of the reception area and that, while no one was openly staring at them, a lot of people were paying attention to this conversation. She clutched the strap of her handbag harder. "It's good to see you again, Mr. Jenner," she said because she did not want to presume anything at this point.

His face lit up and dang if that didn't make her smile. "What are you doing here? And when did you get married?" He paused and looked at her again. A warm heat flushed her cheeks. Great. Blushing.

It only got worse when he said, "Wow. You really grew up."

Her anxiety tried to wrestle control, but she powered through. "Actually, I'm your nine a.m. I'm here about the job." He blinked at her. "The opening for office manager?" she prompted him.

"Oh, oh—right." He glanced around, as if he was

also just becoming aware of how this conversation might look to his employees. "This office could definitely use some management. Come on back." He cast a critical eye around and people seemed to melt back into their offices but he did so with a faint smile on his face. Sofia caught the receptionist grinning and rolling her eyes. Eric saw it, too, and said, "All right, Heather—back to work."

"Of course, Mr. Jenner," Heather the receptionist said, still smiling. She had perfectly white, perfectly even teeth, which was almost enough to distract Sofia from the sly way she winked.

Eric winked back.

Sofia's heart began to pound again. What did she know about him, really? The boy he'd been had been someone privileged and wealthy but still kind to a little girl. He'd taught her how to swim and roller-skate and had, on more than one occasion, played tea with her and some of his mother's delicate china dolls.

But that didn't mean he was the same person now. Yes, he was rich, handsome—and single. Of course he would make eyes at the beautiful young receptionist. And the beautiful young receptionist—well, she wasn't stupid. Of course she would make eyes back.

Sofia had just begun to feel invisible when Eric turned back to her. "I had no idea you were applying for this job," he said, motioning for her to follow him. "Tell me about your husband. Who was lucky enough to land Sofia Cortés?"

He said it in a way that was almost believable, the kind of benign flirting a man like Eric no doubt excelled at. But, unfortunately, it wasn't run-of-the-mill small talk to Sofia. All she could do was keep breathing.

She didn't say anything until he led her back into his office. The room was huge, with leather couches and a massive mahogany desk, plus a wet bar. And behind it all was a wall of glass facing due east. He had an almost perfectly unobstructed view of Lake Michigan. She didn't sell downtown real estate, but even she knew this view was worth millions.

He closed the door behind her. For a moment, they stood with less than two feet separating them. Sofia became acutely aware of the heat of his body and it made her flush in a way that hadn't happened in months. Years.

"What an amazing vista," she said, striving for lighthearted—and willing him away from conversation about David. Willing away the heat she couldn't seem to ignore.

Eric Jenner was every inch the billionaire bachelor. There was no doubt in her mind that his suit was custom-made—everything he wore was probably custom-made, right down to his socks. He'd paired a bold royal blue suit with a light pink shirt and a silk tie that probably cost as much as her car payment. It all fit him like a second skin.

A forgotten feeling began to pulse through her body, a steady pounding that got louder with each beat. For a dazed moment, she didn't recognize it.

Desire. That's what this tight, hot heaviness was. *Want*. She'd forgotten she could feel this way anymore. She'd thought...well, she'd thought she'd buried her needs with her husband.

The realization that she could still feel raw attraction was startling enough. But the fact that her body was feeling desire for *Eric*? Her cheeks got hotter by the second and here in the privacy of his office, there weren't any winking receptionists or dinging elevators to distract his attention.

He stared at her, his eyes darkening. Her lungs refused to expand and she began to feel light-headed. She couldn't want Eric and he shouldn't be looking at her like that. That wasn't why she'd come.

"You've done well for yourself," she blurted out, making a conscious effort to look around the room. Photographs of him with famous people were mixed in with expensive-looking paintings and pictures of his buildings.

After a pause that was so quiet she was sure he could hear her pulse pounding, he said, "Was there any doubt?"

It sounded so cocky that she jerked back to look at him. He had a wolf's grin on his face, but then everything about him softened and she almost saw the boy she'd known. "I work hard for what I have, but let's be honest—I started from a place higher than almost everyone else, thanks to my parents."

A little bit of the anxiety loosened in her chest. Yes, he had always been the privileged son of privileged people. But the Eric she remembered had been almost embarrassed by that fact. His parents hadn't raised him to be an entitled, spoiled brat. How much of that boy still existed inside of him? Or was he the kind of man who hired a beautiful receptionist—or even a mildly attractive office manager—just to get her in bed?

She didn't want him to be like that. If he was, she wasn't sure she could destroy her fondest memories of him with reality. "How are your parents? I know they still exchange Christmas cards with my parents."

Eric sighed, an action of extreme exaggeration that made him look younger. "They're fine. They're disappointed I didn't manage to get married and start producing grandchildren, but they're fine." Before she could process that statement, he asked, "Your folks?"

"Doing well. I don't know how much your parents have shared with you, but after you went away to school, my father started selling houses. Your father opened the door for him," she added, always mindful of what the Jenners had done for her family. "It turned out there was a huge market for bilingual real estate agents and Dad was able to capitalize on that. He owns an agency in Wicker Park. Mom stays home with my children now. They spoil each other rotten."

His eyes widened before he turned away from her and strode toward his desk. Each step put physical distance between them—but there was no missing the emotional distance that went up like a wall around him.

This was all casual small talk, every bit of it. But there was something else going on that Sofia couldn't put her finger on. When he'd complained about his parents wanting grandbabies, it hadn't sounded quite right. And the look in his eyes when she'd mentioned her kids? On anyone else it would've been longing. She couldn't believe that someone like Eric Jenner, who literally had the world at his feet, would be interested in an old acquaintance's babies.

He didn't sit at the desk, didn't turn around. Instead, he stared out at the lake. Although it was still early, she could see a few boats out on the water, ready to enjoy the beautiful summer day. "I hadn't heard that you'd gotten married. Congratulations." His voice was level—unfeeling, almost.

"Oh." She couldn't help the dejected noise that escaped. Eric half turned, his silhouette outlined in sunshine. "I'm not. I mean, I was. But he…he died." No matter how long it'd been, her voice caught every time she had to state that fact out loud. "Seventeen months ago." Not that she was counting the days—the hours—since the worst day of her life.

She took a deep breath and lifted her chin. If she did this quickly, it wouldn't hurt so badly. That was the theory, anyway. "I don't know if you'd ever heard of him—David Bingham? We worked at a real estate agency up in Evanston."

He turned and took a step toward her and for a second, she thought he was going to fold her into his arms and she was going to let him. But he pulled up short. "Sofia," he said, his tone gentle. "I'm sorry. I had no idea. How are you doing?"

That wasn't small talk. That was an honest question from one of her oldest friends. God, she'd missed Eric.

It was so tempting to lie and smooth over the awkward moment with platitudes. Lord knew Eric was probably looking for an easy answer.

But none of her answers were easy. "That's why I'm here. My twins are—"

"Twins?" he cut her off, his eyes bugging out of his head. "How old?"

"Fifteen months."

He let out a low whistle of appreciation as his gaze traveled the length of her body. Her cheeks warmed at his leisurely inspection but then his face shuttered again. "I can't even imagine how difficult that must have been for you. I'm so sorry for your loss."

"I…thank you. It's been hard. Which," she went on

before he could distract her from her purpose again with his kind eyes and kinder words, "is why I'm here. David and I sold houses together and since he passed I just… can't. I need a job with regular hours and a steady paycheck to provide for my children." There. She'd gotten her spiel out and it'd only hurt a little.

"What are their names?"

"Adelina and Eduardo, although I call them Addy and Eddy—which my mom hates." She pulled her phone out of her handbag and called up the most recent picture, of the twins in the bath with matching grins, wet hair sticking straight up. "They're officially toddlers now. Mom watches them but I think she's outnumbered most days. I'd love to hire a nanny to help out." And pay off the bills that were piling up and put a little away for the kids' college funds and…

The list of problems money would solve for her was long. Even at the best of times, real estate involved odd hours and an unpredictable income. But if an agent couldn't sell a house without sobbing in the car, then the income got very predictable. Zero.

Eric took the phone. She watched him carefully as he tilted the screen and studied their little faces. "They look like you," he said. "Beautiful."

Her face flushed at the sincere compliment. "Thank you. They've kept me going."

Because if she hadn't had two helpless little babies that needed to be fed and rocked and loved, she might've curled into a ball and given up. The numbing depression and crushing panic attacks were never far, but Addy and Eddy were more than just her children. They were David's children—all she had left of him. She couldn't let him down. She couldn't let herself down.

So she'd kept moving forward—one day, one hour, sometimes even just one minute at a time. It'd gotten easier. That didn't make it easy, though.

Eric stared at the shot of her babies for a long moment before finally motioning Sofia to one of the plush leather seats before his desk. "And you want to try your hand at office management? This isn't a typical real estate office."

She lifted her chin again. "Mr. Jenner—"

"Eric, Sofia. We know each other too well for formalities, don't you think?" It was a challenge, the way he said it. "I'm not sure I could think of you as Mrs. Bingham, anyway. You'll always be Sofia Cortés to me."

She understood because she wanted to keep him as that fun, sweet boy in her mind forever. But she couldn't afford to romanticize the potential billionaire employer sitting behind his executive desk and she couldn't afford to let him romanticize her.

"That's who I was," she said, her words coming out more gently than she meant for them to. "But that's not who I am now. We've grown up, you and I. We're not the same kids splashing in the pool we used to be and I *need* this job."

His gaze met hers and she saw something there that she didn't want to think too deeply about. "Then it's yours."

Two

This was a mistake. Eric knew it before the words had left his mouth. But by then, it was too late.

He had just offered the position of office manager to a woman he wasn't entirely sure was qualified.

That was true, but it wasn't the whole truth. Because it wasn't some random woman off the street. It was Sofia Cortés. He'd practically grown up with her.

But this wasn't the little girl he remembered from his childhood. The woman before him was—well, she was all grown up. Despite the suit jacket and skirt she wore, Eric couldn't help but notice her body. Sofia was a woman in every sense. She came almost to his chin, her thick black hair pulled away from her face. Eric had an unreasonable urge to sink his fingers into her hair and tilt her head to the side, exposing the long line of her neck.

He shook that thought out of his head. Why hadn't his mother told him Sofia had gotten married and had twins, much less that her husband had died? Surely Mom knew. If nothing else, those were the sorts of things that tended to make a Christmas newsletter.

"Are you... Are you sure?" Sofia asked, looking stunned.

Eric felt much the same. He always did a thorough investigation of a candidate's skills. Even when he knew he wanted to hire them anyway, like Heather for the position of receptionist. Not only did she have the perfect look for the face of his company, but she was finishing her MBA on the company's dime. He hadn't hired her just because she was hot, although that never hurt. He'd hired her because she was brilliant and would transition into the contracts department. It was never too early to begin building loyalty and Eric's staff was beyond loyal.

That was something he'd learned from his father. Nurture the best talent and pay them well and they'd fight for you. Wasn't that why Sofia was here? Because the Jenner family had supported the Cortés family?

"Of course," he said with a certainty he wasn't sure was warranted. "Can you do the job?"

The color deepened along her cheeks. He was *not* going to notice how pretty it was on her. She didn't look like a widow with two adorable young children.

She looked...*lush.* And tempting.

He would not be tempted. One of his hard and fast rules was that he didn't hit on staff. Flirt, maybe. But he never put a valued employee in a position where they felt they couldn't say no because he was the boss.

What a shame he was hiring Sofia, then. Because that would put her completely out of reach. Which was fine. Good. She was undoubtedly still struggling with being a widow and a single mother. She didn't need the complications that seemed to follow Eric like shadows cast by the afternoon sun.

Sofia cleared her throat. "I'm a quick study. I helped run my dad's office when I was in school and staged homes part-time in college. I've been selling ever since I graduated." She dropped her gaze and cleared her throat. "Until…"

What had she said? Seventeen months since she had been left a widow. And her twins—two of the cutest babies he had ever seen—were fifteen months old.

Eric's world was one of logic and calculation. Real estate was a gamble on the best of days. But he always weighed the pros and cons of any option and he never bet more than he could afford to lose.

Of course, as a billionaire, he could afford to lose a lot.

Somehow, none of the usual checks and balances weighed much with this decision. Sofia was an old friend. Her family were good people. And those babies…

"The job is yours. There'll be a learning curve, I'm sure, but I'm confident you'll pick it up." Either Sofia would or she wouldn't. He had to give her that chance. And if she didn't, then he'd help her find a position that better fit her skill set. Something with regular hours and a paycheck that would help her raise her toddlers by herself. And if that happened…then she wouldn't work for him, would she? He could get to know her all over again. Every inch of her.

Hell. He was not thinking about Sofia—not like that.

Especially because he was still hiring her. It was the right thing to do.

Her eyes were huge, but she managed a smile. "That's…that's wonderful."

"We have a generous benefits package," he went on, pulling a number out of thin air. "The starting salary is a hundred and twenty thousand a year, with bonuses based on performance. Is it enough?"

Her mouth dropped open and she looked at him as if she'd never seen him before. He could afford to pay well because hiring the best people was worth it in the long run. But he honestly couldn't tell from her expression if she was insulted by that amount or flabbergasted.

"You can't be serious," she said in a strangled voice.

Eric raised an eyebrow at her. A couple extra thousand for him was nothing. Pocket change. "How about a hundred and forty-five?"

She got alarmingly pale. "Your negotiation skills are rusty," she finally croaked out, a hand pressed to her chest. "You're not supposed to go up, certainly not by twenty-five thousand. A hundred and twenty is enough. More than enough."

Eric cracked a grin at her. "And your negotiation skills…" He trailed off, shaking his head in mock disapproval. "That would've been the point to say make it one fifty and it's a deal. Are you sure you sold houses?" She got even paler and he realized teasing her was not the smartest thing to do. In fact, she looked like she was on the verge of fainting. "Are you all right?" He moved to the wet bar and grabbed a bottle of sparkling water. She was breathing heavily by the time he made his way back to her. "Sofia?"

He set the water on the desk and put his fingers on

the side of her neck. Her pulse fluttered weakly under his touch and her skin was clammy. "Breathe," he ordered, pushing her head down toward her knees. He crouched next to her. "Sofia? Honey, *breathe*."

They sat like that for several minutes while he rubbed her back and tried his best to sound soothing. What the hell had happened? Normally, when he offered people more money, they jumped to say yes.

But this woman had actually tried to say no.

He focused on smoothing her hair away from her forehead, on how her muscles tensed and relaxed along her spine as he rubbed her back. Even through her jacket, he could feel the warmth of her body. He couldn't imagine touching anyone else like this.

She was still struggling for air. Was this a medical crisis? He felt for her pulse again. It was steady enough. He needed to distract her. "Remember the sailboat races?" he asked. But he didn't pull his hand away from her. He stayed close.

"Yes," she said softly. "You let me win sometimes."

"Let you? Come on, Sofia. You beat me fair and square."

Her head popped up, a shaky grin on her face. "You're being kind," she said, her voice strangely quiet.

Eric realized there was less than a foot between them. If he wanted to kiss her, all he'd have to do was lean forward.

It came back to him in a rush—he'd kissed her once before, when they were kids. He'd had Marcus Warren over and Marcus had dared Eric to kiss her. So he had. And she'd let him.

Somehow, Eric knew that if he kissed her now, it wouldn't be a timid touching of lips. This time, he'd taste her, dipping his tongue into her mouth and savoring her sweetness. He'd take possession of her mouth and, God willing, she'd...

He jerked back so quickly he almost landed on his butt. "Here," he said gruffly, snagging the bottle of water off his desk and wrenching the cap off.

What the hell was wrong with him? He couldn't be thinking about Sofia Cortés like that. It didn't matter that she wasn't the same innocent little kid. It didn't even matter that she'd been married and had children. He couldn't think of her like that.

He'd just hired her.

She took the water but didn't look him in the eye. "I didn't realize how expensive those toy boats were until we sank the loser that one time. Which was me, of course."

"You were a worthy opponent but that avalanche was unavoidable," he replied. He barely remembered the boat. But he did remember the sheer glee when they'd hit the boat with a decorative stone so large it'd taken both of them to toss it. The splash had been *huge*. "You have to admit it was fun."

That got her to meet his gaze. "How old were we? I still remember the horror in my mom's eyes when she caught us."

"I was ten, I think. Old enough to know better, I was informed." His parents had been more than a little exasperated with him, but his dad hadn't been able to stop snickering when Eric had described the rockslide. "It was only a couple hundred dollars. No big deal."

Well, that and his parents had made him get every single rock out of the pool. His mother was of the opinion that they didn't need the pool boy to suffer for Eric's foolishness. Still, it had taken three people to get the boulder out of the deep end.

Sofia rolled her eyes at him, which made him grin. "Maybe to you. My mother was horrified that we'd have to pay it back somehow." She was talking to him now, sounding more like the Sofia he remembered. "There was no way we could have afforded that. Not then."

"That's why I took the blame." He leaned against the desk, his arms crossed over his chest. He wished they weren't in this office. He'd give anything to be out on the lake this morning. There, with the sun on his face and the wind in his hair, he'd be able to think clearly. Here, his mind was muddled.

She looked at him again. Her color was better and she seemed...well, not like the girl he'd known. But maybe someone he could still be friends with.

Friends who didn't kiss, that was.

"You always were," she murmured before she took another deep drink of the water.

"Were what?"

"Kind. One of the kindest people I'd ever known." She dropped her gaze. "You still are. This job..." She swallowed.

Kind? This wasn't kind. This was calculated. He was building loyalty and ensuring morale. This was keeping an eye on his business. And if it didn't work out, well—he'd show her *kind*. He'd have her out of her buttoned-up jacket and skirt so fast her head would spin.

He laughed at his own thoughts, a bitter sound. "I'm not. I'm ruthless. A coldhearted bastard of the first order. Don't you read the headlines?"

Three

Eric stared at her for a long moment, a dare in his eyes. Then he turned away and went to admire his view of the lake. The way he looked, silhouetted against the window, his shoulders broad and his hair curling gently just above the collar of his shirt—to say nothing of his backside in those custom-made pants…

She had seen the headlines, of course. He'd been left at the altar. He'd been named one of the "Top Five Billionaire Bachelors of Chicago." He'd been ruthless in his business dealings. But none of that was who he really was.

Was it?

Even if life had changed them both, she knew that deep down, they were still the same people they'd been back when they'd been kids. He wasn't a heartless bastard, no matter what people might say.

Heartless bastards wouldn't have rubbed her back when she'd had a panic attack. They wouldn't have gotten her water. They would have laughed her and her crippling anxiety right out of the office and slammed the door in her face.

Heartless bastards wouldn't have looked like they were going to kiss her and they most certainly wouldn't have stopped at just a look.

At least, Sofia thought that's what Eric had been thinking. She hadn't been kissed in a long time so she couldn't be sure. She and David had enjoyed a passionate four years together before she'd gotten pregnant. But after her body had begun to change, so had their love life. The intimacy had been deeper, richer—but at the cost of some of the heat.

She fanned herself. It was unnaturally warm in here.

"Are you sure you want me to work for you? Good office managers don't have panic attacks."

"Of course they do," he answered without turning around. "They just choose their locations wisely. I've always found it's best to have a panic attack safely behind closed doors. No one wants to pass out next to the coffeepot." He glanced back at her with a smirk. "Location, location, location—right?"

"Eric…"

A ripple of tension rolled over his shoulders. "Does that happen a lot?"

"It's…better." How to answer this question without making it sound like she was incapable of doing the job? "They started after David collapsed. One of them actually triggered early labor, but they got it stopped in time and I was on bed rest for five weeks. I hadn't had one in a few months, though. I just wasn't expecting any offer to be that…"

"Generous?"

"Insane." This was the first time an attack had been triggered by something positive. "Eric, I can't take that much money. The position was for seventy thousand. You can't just randomly double it because we used to be friends."

He made a scoffing sound and at that moment, he did sound a little ruthless. "First off, we're still friends and second off, I absolutely can. Who's going to stop me?"

A hundred and twenty was slightly more than she and David had earned together in a single year. The things she could do with that kind of money…but she didn't want to be Eric's charity case. "Most comparable positions are fifty to sixty thousand," she protested.

That made him snort. "Comparable to what, Sofia? If you're saying this position is just like running your suburban brokerage, you couldn't be more wrong. I can promise you regular hours most of the time, but I'll expect you to travel to potential sites occasionally. This isn't just ordering paper clips and deciding how ten agents divide them. I employ forty lawyers, architects, agents, tax specialists, lobbyists—"

"Lobbyists?" The fact that she had no idea why he would have lobbyists on staff was probably a sign that she was in over her head.

"To negotiate with municipalities and influence laws, of course. We're pursuing a project in St. Louis as we speak. If we play our cards right, we'll get tax breaks from the city, county and state." He grinned like he'd won the lottery.

"Of course," she mumbled, unsure what else she was supposed to say. He was right. She was vastly out of her league.

"Besides," he continued, sounding more than just a little cold as he turned his attention back out the window, "what's a spare fifty thousand or so to a guy like me?"

Nothing, probably. She could see how that wouldn't bankrupt a billionaire. Still, though. It was the principle of the matter. "But—"

"By the way," he went on, as if she hadn't spoken, "I have a better boat now. You should come with me sometime. I like to sail in the afternoons."

He still wasn't looking at her, but it was clear from the tone of his voice that the conversation about salary was finished.

"Is it a sailboat?" she asked.

"Nope. It's a yacht. And we won't sink this one with a rock, so don't worry. You could..." He paused and then continued, "You could even bring the kids. I bet they'd love being out on the water."

What was happening here? Eric was giving her a job and paying her way too much money. And now he was inviting her boating? With two rambunctious toddlers in tow? "Eric..."

"Never mind. I hear you've got a real bastard of a boss who won't let you take off work just to go jetting around." He turned and she barely recognized him at all—his face was that hard. "Come on. Let's find out what you've gotten yourself into, shall we?"

More than she could handle, she thought as she followed him to the door of his office and into the heart of Jenner Properties.

* * *

Three hours later, Sofia knew she was in over her head. She was reasonably confident Eric knew it, too—but it didn't seem to bother him. He would give her a look and say, "All right?" as if he were willing it to be true instead of asking a question.

He was putting a lot of faith in her and she didn't want to let him down. She didn't want to let her mom or her kids down, either. But most of all, she needed to do this for herself. This was the first big change she had undertaken on her own since her life had been thrown into upheaval a year and a half ago. She was tired of life happening to her. She was going to happen to her life. This job was the first step.

Even if that meant she would have to make it up as she went along.

"And here are Meryl and Steve Norton," Eric was saying as he knocked on the last door to the office closest to his. "Meryl is my chief negotiator for the St. Louis project and Steve is the project manager. It helps that they're married," he added in a stage whisper. "Guys, this is Sofia Bingham. She's our new office manager."

"Hello," Sofia said, smiling. Eric had stopped accidentally saying Cortés after only five or six introductions.

"Welcome," a tall, jovial man with thinning hair said as he rose from a desk on one side of the office. He was a little soft around the middle, but his smile was friendly and his eyes were warm. "To the madhouse," he went on, shaking her hand. "I'm Steve. I handle contractors."

As big as Steve was, an equally tiny woman hopped down off her desk chair from the other side of the room. Steve slid his arm around her shoulders as Meryl Norton said, "Don't listen to him. It's not that bad—as long as you can embrace the madness. I'm Meryl and I handle politicians. If you have any questions, don't hesitate to ask. I'm generally friendly." But she said it in such a way that Sofia couldn't help but grin in response.

Eric's wristwatch dinged and he said, "I've got to take this. Sofia, when you're done catching up with the Nortons, ask Heather to show you where all the supplies are. If I'm still here when you're done, stop in and see me. If not, check in with Tonya. She'll have your contract." With that, he was gone.

Sofia had done all right by his side because everyone in this building deferred to him. Eric seemed to understand his staff not just as employees but as people. Eric had given her a heads-up for the introverts who needed quiet to focus and the extroverts who needed someone to help them stay on task.

And Steve Norton clearly was an extrovert. "There's a rumor going around that you and the big boss used to know each other," he began with no other introduction, a slightly mischievous gleam in his eye.

"Honey," Meryl said, elbowing him. If she hadn't been so small, she would've elbowed him in the ribs. As it was, she more or less hit him in the hip bone. "Don't pry. He pries," she went on, giving Sofia a sympathetic look. "Did Mr. Jenner explain that there'll be times when travel is a part of the job?"

"He did—and," she added, before Steve could ask again, "we did know each other when we were little kids. His father gave my father his start in real estate." Normally, she might not have revealed that. But it was better to clarify up front that she and Eric had never dated or otherwise had any romantic entanglements.

In an office of this size, gossip could make her life a living hell. "Our parents still send Christmas cards to each other."

Steve looked amused by this. Meryl said to her husband, "There. Now you don't have to pry anymore. We're planning a trip to St. Louis next month," she went on, turning back to Sofia without pausing for breath. "They recently lost their football team and there's a section of the downtown that's depressed. We wouldn't expect you to be involved in negotiations, but planning trips like this would be your responsibility. So far, Heather and I have been handling this together, but I think it would be a good idea for you to join us. That way, in the future, you'll know how Mr. Jenner likes things done. You do have a background in real estate, correct?"

"I've been in real estate since I was fourteen. However, this is a different level," she admitted. Okay, she could handle a business trip with Eric. No problem.

"That's why the St. Louis trip will be good," Meryl said decisively. She definitely talked like a negotiator. "You get a chance to see what Mr. Jenner is trying to accomplish when he branches out into smaller markets and how you can help make that happen. Understanding the business is key to understanding how the office works."

Sofia glanced at Steve. For the project manager, he wasn't doing a lot of talking. He looked like he wanted to ask her something else that was probably personal, but Meryl plowed ahead. "I'll email you the current itinerary. We look forward to working with you, but no one expects you to manage Steve. That's my job," she added with a wink.

Steve protested loudly, although Sofia could tell it was all for show. Meryl waved Sofia away—but as she shut the door behind her, they were both laughing.

Sofia stood for a moment on the other side of the door, trying to get her bearings. She'd expected the interview to last an hour, if that—but she'd been here for almost four hours. Mom would worry, although the situation wouldn't get desperate until the twins got up from their naps. They had just come through a protracted period of clinginess and it was still touch and go when Addy and Eddy were waking up.

Eric's office was to the right of Steve and Meryl's. His door was closed. There was a window to the left. It didn't have a sweeping view of Lake Michigan, but it was no hardship to look at the Chicago skyline.

She stepped into a warm shaft of afternoon sunlight and checked her messages. Mom had texted a photo of the twins destroying their lunch. Sofia's heart clenched as she looked at her babies. When she and David had discovered they were having twins, she'd planned to take time off after their birth. She'd even entertained the notion of a maternity leave that lasted several years. But the life insurance policy had run out and honestly, as overwhelming as today had been, it'd been nice to have a conversation without someone screaming.

She replied to the text message with what time she thought she'd be home and then paused to look at the office.

It was spotless and gleaming. Eric's executive suite had been practically a temple to wealth and privilege, but even the carpet in the general areas was thick and plush. The office equipment she'd glanced at was state-of-the-art, and he provided snacks and beverages to everyone, not just coffee. Eric didn't cheap out on providing for his employees.

This office—this job—represented so much for her. There was more to her than life as a widow and mother of two babies.

Eric Jenner was giving her the opportunity to be more.

She worked her way around the front of the office, where trendy Heather was still behind the receptionist desk. "Um, hello. Mr. Jenner told me to—"

She cut Sofia off without even looking up. "One moment." Sofia swallowed. After a minute that felt painfully long, Heather finished whatever she was doing and stood, straightening her jacket. She had shimmering golden hair that fell halfway down her back. She was so young and effortlessly beautiful that Sofia couldn't help but feel old and fat by comparison.

"The supply closet is this way." Heather led Sofia back to a closet tucked behind the emergency stairwell. When they were inside with the door mostly shut behind them Heather turned to her. She cast a critical eye at Sofia's outfit again. "I don't know if anyone has said this to you yet," she began and Sofia braced herself. *Here it comes*, she thought. Heather went on, "But we're really glad you're here."

Sofia's mouth dropped open in shock. "I'm sorry?" Of all the things she'd expected Heather to say, an expression of welcome hadn't made the list. "You are?"

"Oh my gosh, yes. Stacy—the previous office manager? She got married and had a baby and decided she wanted to be a stay-at-home mom. Mr. Jenner offered me the job? But I'm almost done with my MBA and he's already promised me a job in the contracts department.

I've been doing this job *and* the receptionist job *and* training for the contracts department while finishing up my schooling and it's exhausting. I'm beyond thrilled to hand the reins over to you," she said and her smile seemed surprisingly genuine.

Sofia realized she had misjudged the young woman. Just because she was pretty and fashionable didn't mean Heather was catty or vain. "Do you like working for him?" Because Sofia had not forgotten those cheeky winks. "I mean, what kind of boss is he?"

"The best boss? I mean, really. The company is paying for my MBA. They already put my fiancée on the benefits package and we're not even married yet?" She had this habit of ending her statements on an up note, as if she were asking a question. "You'd think that a billionaire like him would be a total jerk, but he's actually really down-to-earth. The benefits package alone is worth this job? Everything else is just icing on the cake."

Fiancé. Sofia took a deep breath and smiled widely. "Congratulations on your engagement. What's his name?"

Heather slanted her a sly smile. "Her name is Suzanne."

Sofia felt her cheeks go bright red. "Oh, I'm sorry. I didn't mean to assume. It's just that..." Well, there had been those winks.

"Oh, no worries," Heather said, waving away Sofia's embarrassment. "It's a known fact that Mr. Jenner flirts with everyone. He's an equal opportunity flirt. But he keeps a hard line between flirting and hitting on someone." She leaned forward, her voice quieting to a whisper. "We're not supposed to talk about his former fiancée—and I don't recommend bringing it up—but there was a young woman who'd just started in the agent department when Mr. Jenner got dumped. She made a move."

It was wrong to gossip about Eric, both as an old friend and a new boss. That noble sentiment didn't stop Sofia from asking, "And?"

"And not only did he rebuff her advances, she was gone a month later."

"He *fired* her?"

"No, actually. That's the weird thing." Heather looked just as confused as Sofia felt. "She got 'a better offer' from one of his business rivals. The rumor is Mr. Jenner engineered it. I overheard him tell the Nortons that Wyatt got what he deserved out of the deal."

Wyatt—hadn't there been a kid named Robert Wyatt back when they were kids? If she was thinking of the same boy, then that was the kid who'd cornered her one time while Eric had been in the bathroom and tried to cop a feel.

Sofia remembered she'd done what her father had taught her and kneed Wyatt hard in the groin. Eric had found his so-called friend rolling on the ground and yelling bloody murder and Sofia had been terrified Wyatt would get her mom fired. But instead, Wyatt never came back over to play and Mrs. Jenner had bought Sofia a doll with a new set of clothes.

Heather was staring intently at her. "Well. That's… interesting, isn't it?" Sofia said numbly.

If she'd thought that would be the end of the conversation, she was wrong. "You two used to know each other?" Heather, Sofia realized, was the office gossip. Which meant that she was a good person to have on

Sofia's side. But that didn't mean she wanted to spread every childhood moment she and Eric had shared around the office. There was a fine line here and Sofia had to figure out how to walk it—quickly.

When she didn't answer right away, Heather pressed on. "I mean, that's what it sounded like. I've never heard him tell an interviewee—or anyone else, for that matter—that they 'grew up.'"

"We knew each other when we were little kids. His father gave my father a start in business." That line had worked well enough for the Nortons, but when Heather didn't respond immediately, Sofia decided she needed to steer the conversation away from the past. "It's good to hear that he's still the same kid he used to be. I was hoping being a billionaire hadn't changed him."

Heather exhaled heavily. "I don't think the money is what's changed him," she said quietly. Then she turned a too-bright smile to Sofia. "Okay? Here are the vendors that we use to order coffee…"

Sofia didn't get the chance to ask what Heather meant by that. And did it matter, really? No. What mattered was that Eric was giving her an incredible opportunity and putting a great deal of faith in her. What mattered was that his staff loved working for him. What mattered more than anything, she decided, was that he didn't sleep with his receptionist and he nurtured the talents of the people he hired.

She was going to make this work, she decided with renewed resolve.

So she better learn how to order the coffee.

Four

Normally, Eric would've been on the water by now. There was only one reason he was still at his desk today. *Sofia.* Somehow, he couldn't leave without making sure she'd take the job.

He was supposed to be reading her contract and non-disclosure agreement, but it wasn't going well. He was also supposed to be looking over the latest plans for the St. Louis trip, but he wasn't doing that, either.

Instead, he was thinking about Sofia. He couldn't remember the first time he'd seen her. She'd always been there. There hadn't been any big formal goodbyes, either. The Cortés family had not come to his farewell party when he'd gone away to school. He hadn't sought her out after the party. That had been that.

She'd always been a part of his life—until she wasn't anymore. He wanted to think he'd regretted not getting the closure of a goodbye, but honestly, he wasn't sure he had.

Now suddenly Sofia was back in his life. A mother with two little babies who depended on her.

She was taking the job, by God. That was final.

A soft knock on his door pulled him out of his messy thoughts. "Yes?"

The door opened and there she was. His breath caught in his throat as she stepped into his office. It didn't seem possible that she got lovelier every time he saw her.

But there was no denying it—she was simply prettier than she'd been an hour ago. Especially when her eyes lit up as she looked at him, her mouth softening into a kissable smile. "You're still here," she said, a touch of wonder in her voice. "I thought you'd be out on the lake by now."

He grinned. It didn't mean anything that she remembered how much he needed the water. Everyone else thought it was part of his eccentric charm, but Sofia had always understood that he needed the water like some people needed the air. "I'm still here," he told her. "Have a seat. I'm just going over your contract."

He watched her carefully as she crossed the room and sat in front of him. She looked a little bashful, but not like she was on the verge of another anxiety attack. "I don't suppose you made my salary something reasonable?"

"A hundred and twenty thousand is very reasonable, Sofia."

She laughed. "What if I'm not worth that much money?"

He was stunned by the words—and by how much

she seemed to mean them. Nervously, she glanced up at him. "I'm going to pretend you didn't say that," he said. "Stop acting like you don't belong here."

"I don't," she said, and he was impressed that she didn't sound cowed when she said it. "You're the one trying to make me fit into this world."

"You're the one who showed up for a job interview," he reminded her. At that, she opened her mouth to reply and then closed it with an audible snap. "There. We agree. You want the job and I'm giving it to you." He shoved the contract across the desk.

She reached for it, and he continued, "It's the standard contract, details on the benefit plan, bonus schedule and nondisclosure agreement. You're more than welcome to take it home and look it over. If you decide to accept the job, I'd like you to start next week. But Sofia?" She looked up at him again, the contract in her hand. "You're going to accept the job."

He braced for the worst—another panic attack—but it didn't happen. Instead, her brows furrowed and she twisted her lips. "I'm not going to win this argument, am I?"

"Of course not. I never lose arguments when I happen to be right."

"What are you going to tell your parents?"

He blinked once, then again. Of all the things she might have said—that wasn't what he'd expected. "I don't know that I need to tell them anything." Except that was a hedge and he knew it.

Because he wanted to know why his mother hadn't kept him up-to-date on what Sofia was doing and there was no way he could ask without revealing that Sofia now worked for him.

"I assume your parents know where you are?" he asked.

"They do." She dropped her gaze back to the contract and flipped the page. "They were worried."

"About?" Suddenly, he found himself hoping the Cortés family hadn't followed all the headlines—his abandonment on his wedding day or the subsequent re-sowing of his wild oats afterward.

"They want to see me succeed but…well, they knew this job was a stretch for me. I don't have the experience." She looked up at him and he saw the truth in her eyes. "I shouldn't even be telling you this," she went on in a rush. "Because the truth is that we're not friends anymore. We're old acquaintances who only knew each other because my parents worked for yours. Now you're my boss and I shouldn't be telling you about my family's hopes or that I suffered debilitating panic attacks after my husband died. You're not supposed to know these things about me."

She was almost shouting at him. The force of her emotion pushed him back in his chair.

"Oh, God," she said, slumping down. "And I definitely shouldn't be yelling at you. I couldn't be screwing this up more if I tried, could I?"

If it were anyone else, he'd agree. He'd show her the door and count himself lucky to have dodged a bullet.

So why wasn't he doing that right now?

When was the last time anyone had put him in his place? No one—with the obvious exception of his parents—talked to him like this. They all minced around him like he was a volatile chemical and they were afraid of the reaction he'd spark. Even Marcus Warren—who had no trouble telling anyone what he thought about anything—had been pulling his punches with Eric.

Sofia telling him off should have been infuriating. But...

All he could think about was how he'd missed her. And how he hoped she'd missed him, too. "You need a friend."

She looked at him, her eyes suspiciously shiny and a quirky smile on her face. "Maybe you do, too." Abruptly, she stood, grabbing her handbag and clutching the contract to her chest. "I'm going to take this job because you're right, I need it. But I won't be your object of pity. You don't owe me a larger salary. You don't owe me any special perks. I'm your employee. Try to remember that."

That was, hands down, one of the most effective set-downs he'd ever received in his life. It was so good that all he could do was smile as she walked out of the office.

"Mama!" Two small voices cried in unison when Sofia came through the door that evening. She still felt that she was moving in a daze but at least here, in the sanctuary of her parents' house, with her two children launching themselves at her, everything still felt the same.

"Babies!" she cried back, just like she did every time she had to be away from them. She opened her arms as they flung themselves at her, almost knocking her off balance in her heeled shoes. "Were you good for Abuelita today?" she asked over their heads as her mother slowly climbed to her feet from where she'd been sitting on the floor.

"Fine, fine," Mom said, waving away this concern.

"How about you? You got the job?" Then, after a moment's hesitation, she added, "Did he remember you?"

Sofia staggered over to the couch that was possibly older than she was with the children squirming in her arms, collapsing in a heap of happy baby sounds. Addy curled up in her lap and began humming contentedly while Eddy slid down and toddled over to a small set of table and chairs, where he picked up a piece of paper he'd made some very colorful lines on. He showed it to her proudly.

"Oh," Sofia said, touching the picture. "So pretty." Eddy began to chatter about whatever it was he'd drawn. She grinned. The twins weren't quite talking yet, but they sure had a lot to say.

As expected, Addy took all this attention for Eddy as a direct challenge to her artistic merits. She went to get her drawing, too. The twins were always competing like this and only occasionally did it result in tears.

After she had also complimented Addy's colorful lines, she leaned back, settling into the ancient cushions of the couch while the twins started coloring again. Even when her father had started selling houses and they'd moved into this small ranch home, the Cortéses hadn't wasted any money on new furniture.

Even though they were now respectably middle class, they still lived carefully and those were lessons Sofia had a hard time unlearning. It'd taken a long time to get used to the way David would decide he wanted a new phone or a new computer and just go buy it. Almost all of their fights had been about money. She'd never felt comfortable spending it but he couldn't understand why she didn't want a few nice things.

If anything, Eric was a million times worse than

David ever could have been. The craziest thing David had ever done with money—besides spending five thousand dollars on her engagement ring—had been buying a brand-new, top-of-the-line flat screen television that took up a huge chunk of wall in their living room. But that had only been seven thousand dollars.

Eric was throwing an extra *fifty* thousand dollars at her. Truly, he was being an idiot about it. But wasn't she being an idiot to try to give that cash back? It wasn't like she couldn't use the money. The life insurance money had run out and she'd moved back in with her parents because, well, she'd been in the grips of depression and the mother of two newborns. But it'd also been to save money.

She sighed. Eric was right. Fifty thousand was a year to her. To him, it couldn't be more than fifteen minutes of one day. And she had shown up for the job interview hoping that the Jenner kindness would help her get back on her feet. She was in no position to refuse that kindness.

Her mother appeared with a glass of lemonade and a worried smile on her face. "Well?"

"He remembered me. And I got the job." She took the lemonade and drank deeply. "He's paying me too much money."

At this, Mom smiled. "The Jenners—they always pay too much. They're very generous people."

Sofia looked up at her mother. Rosa Cortés had worked her entire life to take care of Sofia. But it wasn't until Sofia had unexpectedly become a widow with two infants that she had appreciated how her mother always kept her head up and hope in her heart.

Mom had given her everything. It was time for Sofia

to return the favor. "Listen, I'm going to start paying you to watch the kids. And hire someone to help out."

Her mother's eyes got wide and then immediately narrowed. Sofia braced herself. "You'll do no such thing," she snapped. "I love spending the day with my *nietos*. It's not a job."

"Yes, I will." Sofia was almost too tired to argue— but this was important. "You quit your job at the brokerage to stay home with us. You've kept me going more times than I can count. You've always taken care of me, Mom. Let me take care of you, too."

Her mother shook her head and stamped her foot, which was a show of temper for her. Rosa was so mild mannered as to be meek.

"Fine," Sofia said, knowing further debate would only make Mom dig in her heels even more. "I'll put the money in a retirement account for you. And I will hire someone to help out. That's nonnegotiable. You know Dad's going to be on my side about this."

Although he would never want to hurt Mom's feelings by suggesting she couldn't do everything, Dad had privately told Sofia he worried the twins might be too much for Mom.

Her mother looked like she was going to argue but just then, Addy flung her crayons to the side and stared at Sofia's glass, moving her hands in the way that meant she wanted some, too. Not to be outdone, Eddy plopped his bottom down on the rug and began to fuss. Mom clucked softly. "Oh, now—you two, it's time to wash our hands and have a snack." She picked up Eddy and Addy toddled along behind, the mention of a snack suddenly the most important thing in the world.

Sofia grinned after her babies. She had pictures of

David at that age and Eddy, especially, was going to look a lot like his father. Addy's hair was a little darker, her face a little more round—just like Sofia's had been.

She sank back into the old couch, grateful for the moment of silence. Maybe her mother was right. Maybe that's all there was to this insane salary. Eric was just being generous. Maybe it had nothing to do with her at all. To a guy like him, a Jenner, money was the easy, obvious solution. It would never run out.

It didn't feel like that, though. If anything, it felt… dangerous. More than just the way he'd talked her down from the panic attack, more than the heated way he looked at her whenever she pushed back against his dictates. Those things were bad enough, but easy to dismiss as old friends catching up or him flirting with her just like he flirted with everyone else.

No, what was dangerous to Sofia's mental well-being was the way he had matter-of-factly stated that he could somehow keep her safe.

It had been a sweet thing to say, but Sofia had recognized something else in his eyes when he said it, something lost. He had been left at the altar. Had he loved his ex-fiancée? Had his whole world changed in that one single moment and he still wasn't sure who he'd become in the aftermath?

How far had he fallen before he'd picked himself back up?

She shook her head. It didn't matter. She couldn't be that friend for him, not like in the old days. She was a professional. And besides, she didn't have much of a heart left to be broken.

"What am I supposed to do, David?" she whispered

in the quiet of the room. She got no answer, but she wasn't expecting one.

She had the job. She could take care of her outstanding bills, hire some help for her mom and start moving past living just one day at a time. And she could do all that without getting entangled in Eric's life again. She'd keep a tight handle on any behavior that might be construed as unprofessional, too. No more panic attacks—at least not in public. No more telling him she wasn't qualified for the job. She didn't belong in his world, but she could fake it until she made it.

The job was hers. She would do it for her children and her parents.

But most of all, she would do the job for herself. She needed the work and the salary.

She just had to remember that she didn't need Eric.

Five

"Darling!" Elise Jenner said from behind her desk in her office in the mansion. Dad's was connected to hers with a door, but they kept it firmly shut. Mom lived in mortal terror that John Jenner's clutter would spread like a contagion through the house.

His mother's office was best described as Louis XVI run amok. Rococo flourishes, gilt trim and pink upholstery made the place almost blinding to look at. Everything about Elise Jenner was overdone. Eric might not decorate with gold leaf, but his buildings had been described as over-the-top on more than one occasion. At least he came by it honestly.

"We weren't expecting you tonight." She studied him as he kicked off his shoes before stepping on the Persian rug. That had been a rule in this house for as long as he could remember. "What's wrong?"

"Why didn't you tell me that Sofia Cortés got married? Or widowed? Or had twins?"

His mother looked at him, surprised. "Why, dear—I didn't think you remembered her. You never asked about her." She sat back, looking perturbed. "What brought this on?"

"How could I forget her?" he replied, avoiding this second question. "She was practically my best friend when we were kids. Something I recall you encouraging," he added.

Elise tilted her head and stared at him. For all of her love of extravagant interior design, the woman wasn't soft. She cultivated a flamboyant image and then used it ruthlessly to her advantage. "What happened today, dear?"

Coming to visit his parents in this mood was a mistake. He wanted answers—not an interrogation. But the day with Sofia had muddled his thinking. "I hired her today. She's my new office manager."

"Oh?"

Eric glared at his mother. "And thanks to a lack of knowledge sharing on your behalf, I made an ass of myself three different times. If not more. I wasn't prepared for her to be a mother—to twins, no less."

"I see," she said in that slow, maddening way of hers. He could see the wheels turning in her head.

"When's Dad getting home?" he asked in a belated attempt to steer the conversation away from Sofia. He knew it was Mom sending Christmas cards to the Cortés family, not Dad. Plus Dad's office was cluttered and cozy. They could kick back, drink a beer and watch the Cubs. And not discuss other people's babies.

Elise waved her hand. "He's touring a condo on the

Gold Coast that hasn't been on the market for forty years. It's close to the pier you use, it's got amazing views and it's almost three thousand square feet—more than enough room for a family." She smiled prettily. "You should take a look at it. It'll need to be redone, obviously, but…"

His parents were semiretired, but to him, they still seemed as vibrant and active as ever. It helped that Mom had a really good plastic surgeon. She didn't look like she'd had work done but she certainly didn't look like she was in her sixties, either.

However, just because she didn't want to look like a grandmother didn't mean she didn't want grandbabies, because she did.

Oh, yeah—coming here had definitely been a mistake. "Mom, we're not getting into the topic of grandchildren again."

"We're not?" She sounded so innocent that he almost relaxed. Of course that was the exact moment she went for the kill. "Then why does it upset you that Sofia has children?"

"I'm not upset," he snapped. He began to pace. "It just surprised me. I didn't realize…"

"That she'd grown up and moved on with her life? Yes," his mother said in the caring voice that drove Eric nuts because she really did care. He had friends—Marcus Warren specifically—who had monsters dressed up as parents. Eric knew it was a rare and wonderful thing that he had two parents who not only loved each other but also him. They wanted to see him happy.

"I understand," his mother went on.

"Really, Mom? What do you understand?" He was aware that he was being a jerk—a fact confirmed by the pointed look she gave him. But he couldn't seem to help it.

He found himself thinking about Sofia's twins, Addy and Eddy. They'd been in a tub, their hair crazy and their smiles wide. They loved the water, it was clear. How much fun would they have in the pool? He'd taught Sofia to swim, after all. It would be hilarious to get those two paddling around.

And of course, if the twins were in the water, then Sofia would be with them. Which posed a very important question—bikini or one-piece? He'd love to see her curves in a bathing suit, water sheeting off her body as she pulled herself up the ladder, sun shining off her skin as she lay out under the summer sun to dry out...

He adjusted his trousers and tried to get his mind out of the gutter. It didn't do to fantasize about old friends in his mother's parlor. He should've gone out on his boat. In fact, he'd do that right now. He walked off the Persian rug and jammed his feet into his shoes.

"Things change whether you like it or not," his mother went on. "She changed—and you changed, honey. But you know what I've found?"

"What?" he asked as his mother gracefully rose from her chair and came to stand in front of him, her hands on his shoulders.

"The more things change, the more they stay the same." Even though he'd been nothing but surly to her, she hugged him and Eric hugged her back. "I hope she does well working in the office," Mom said when she leaned back. "She always was a bright, beautiful girl and a true friend to you."

He scowled at his mother. He hated it when she was

right. Everything *had* changed. Sofia had grown up into a gorgeous woman who'd loved and lost.

But for all that, Sofia was still bright and beautiful and no matter what she said, they were still friends.

Because some things never changed.

Eric wasn't in the office much. The weather was perfect, so most afternoons he was aboard the *Jennerosity*, speeding away from Chicago and out onto the lake. He could breathe out there, far away from prying eyes and the sounds and smells of the city. He had no trouble being the social playboy people expected one of the "Top Five Billionaire Bachelors of Chicago" to be, but he needed time to recharge.

A few times, he'd been on the verge of asking Sofia to come with him—hand on the doorknob, question on his lips. But how would that look, giving his brand-new office manager the afternoon off, just to take her boating? Bad, that's how it'd look. So he didn't.

Of course he worked, too. He made a quick trip down to St. Louis to get a look at the property alone. He thought he knew how the city would sell the development's benefits but he liked to check out every potential site unannounced, without anyone else offering their opinions. The property centered around the indoor football stadium that had been recently vacated when St. Louis lost its football team. Without crowds pouring in for weekend home games, whole blocks seemed to be boarded up. Much to Eric's advantage, an attempt to bring in a pro soccer team had recently failed. The city was no doubt growing desperate.

All of which meant he didn't see Sofia for several days. Which was fine. She didn't need him to babysit her. She'd made it plenty clear during their last conversation that the only relationship they could have going forward was a professional one.

That didn't mean he didn't think about her constantly. It took real work to make sure his thoughts stayed away from her body in a bikini and focused on her job performance. Heather reported that Sofia was naturally organized and seemed to be picking up the office systems quickly. "Thank God," she added, tapping her fingers on the desk nervously. "This final project for school is killing me, but she's taken over enough that I actually got a few hours of sleep last night."

Meryl and Steve had much the same report. Sofia was highly organized, detailed and neat. She asked good questions when she hit a stumbling block. "She's a little quiet," Meryl noted, "but you get the sense she's listening to everything."

"We don't need her to be loud," Steve countered. "That's my job."

Eric rolled his eyes and left his employees to squabble. There was a reason the two of them had their own office removed from everyone else. The Nortons deeply loved each other and they worked well together but their verbal gymnastics could wear on even the mellowest of cube workers.

Eric stood in his office, staring at the lake. Of course Sofia was an organized quick study. He remembered all those times she'd been in the house while he'd had friends over. She'd always hovered on the edge of the conversation until she'd been sure she was welcome to join in. She hadn't been quiet when it'd been just the two of them but for Sofia, at least, two had been company and three was always a crowd.

Were her children like her, quiet and watchful? Or were they handfuls?

He remembered so many things he hadn't thought about in such a long time. The sailboat, the kiss. Teaching her to swim, with her mother watching nervously from the kitchen window. He'd picked out a birthday present for her with his own money, a Barbie with dark hair, just like hers.

But she wasn't that girl, not anymore. Back then, she'd been a kid—and so had he. Now she was a woman and he wanted to get to know her again.

Without being aware of leaving his office, he found himself standing in front of her desk, located on the opposite side of the floor from his.

"Hi," he said, pointedly not staring at her.

Startled, she looked up at him, her dark eyes bright. She looked *amazing*, he realized, his breath catching in his throat. Her color was good and her breath came easily and everything about her radiated calm. In no way, shape or form did she look like she was struggling with the burdens of the job.

But that wasn't what had him unable to tear his gaze away. Somehow, she was even prettier than the last time he'd seen her. Today, she had on a wine-colored jacket over a patterned shirt and her hair was pulled back at the temples, the mass of dark waves spilling down her back. God, how he wanted to peel that jacket and shirt off her and sink his fingers into that silken hair and wind it around his fist so he could angle her head to the side and scrape his teeth over the delicate skin of her—

"Hi," she said, snapping him out of his insanity.

He couldn't respond for a moment as he fought to regain control of his body. Finally, he managed to croak out, "How's it going?"

She notched an eyebrow. "Fine. Haven't seen you for several days." He heard the challenge in her voice. She knew he'd been avoiding her.

But he hadn't been. Not intentionally. "Business waits for no man. I hear you're settling in."

"So far, so good." Her voice was perky and confident, but then she looked down at her desk. "Everyone's been really nice."

He almost heard a...*so far* at the end of that sentence. "But?"

A blush darkened her cheeks. "We're going to St. Louis next week, right?" She worried her lower lip with her teeth.

He almost leaned over to brush his thumb across her lip and soothe the worry away. Somehow, he just managed not to but his hand shook with the effort. She wore a shade of lipstick so deep a red it was almost brown. It looked great on her but God help him, he'd love to mess it up.

Then what she'd said penetrated his thoughts. She was worried about the trip. Was it the thought of traveling—or was it the thought of traveling with him? "Nervous about leaving your babies?" He leaned over and picked up the framed photo she'd put on her desk. This was a formal shot and, if he had to guess, he'd say it was for the twins' one-year birthday.

God, they were cute. Eddy, dressed in a tiny tie that was hilarious on him, was standing with his hands on a small stool. Addy, wearing a dress that almost swallowed her whole and bows on itty-bitty ponytails, sat on a blanket next to the stool. Both kids were grinning wildly and Addy was clapping. They looked... perfect. Something in his chest tightened as he stared at the picture.

He said a silent prayer for their father. What a damn shame that the man hadn't lived long enough to love his perfect family. If Eric had a wife like Sofia and kids like these babies, he wouldn't have done anything stupid like die. He'd spend the rest of his life making sure this family was happy and whole. He'd give them every opportunity he'd ever had and more.

His mind spun out a—well, a fantasy. Working with Sofia, then going home with her at the end of the day, doing all those things he'd watched Marcus do with his wife and son—messy dinners and playing in the park. Then, when the kids went to bed at night, Eric would pull Sofia into his arms and into bed, where he'd spend the better part of the night—and the next morning— getting lost in the pleasures of her body.

It was almost perfect, that little fantasy of his. But he couldn't just step into Sofia's life like that. He did not sleep with employees. Hell, he shouldn't even be fantasizing about them.

Belatedly, he realized Sofia hadn't answered his question. He glanced up and caught her staring at him staring at her picture. Trying to act casual, he set it back on the desk. "I'd miss them, too," he admitted, touching the frame with his finger. "How are they doing with you being at work?"

"It's been a little rough," she said quietly, as if she were afraid someone might overhear her admit to a weakness. She quickly added, "But it's not impacting my ability to do the job, Mr. Jenner."

It should have been the thing he wanted to hear. Yes,

he wanted his employees happy, but only because he wanted them to do their jobs to the best of their abilities.

So why did her words bother him so much?

He must have scowled because her eyes widened in what looked like alarm.

"Then what's bothering you?" he asked.

She didn't answer for a moment. Instead, her gaze lingered on his face before drifting down to his shoulders and the rest of his body.

Eric liked to think he wasn't a stupid man. He liked women on principle. He'd been enjoying them in one capacity or another since he'd gone away to school.

So he didn't think he was misinterpreting the way Sofia took in his body or the way the color on her cheeks deepened as her gaze met his again.

Interest. Attraction, even. Sofia looked at him as if he was a man she might just like to take a weekend trip with. And his body responded in a primal way. He heard his voice deepen when he said, "You can tell me, Sofia. You know that."

Her gaze jerked up to meet his. Her eyes were dark with desire and when she ran her tongue over her bottom lip, he went painfully hard. His body tilted toward hers of its own volition.

She glanced away, breaking the spell. "I was looking at the itinerary and it says we're having dinner with the lieutenant governor and a cocktail party with the mayor? I don't know what to wear…"

Ah, this was a problem he understood. "Is that all?"

"No," she said quietly. Her face turned bright red. "I mean, that's the only thing that I'm concerned I won't be prepared for. For the trip. The kids will be fine. We're only going to be gone two nights, right?"

"Right. We'll leave Friday morning and be back Sunday evening."

He knew what he needed to do. He'd have to give up his afternoon on the water but for some irrational reason, he found himself looking forward to it. Because this was one way to get her out of those stuffy jackets.

"Tell you what," he began. "We'll take the afternoon off and get you something to wear."

Limos, while practically a requirement for billionaires, were damned inconvenient to get around in downtown Chicago. Eric vastly preferred his Ferrari F60—one of only ten made—and he preferred driving himself.

Which meant Sofia was sitting next to him, clutching the door handle as if her life depended on it as he weaved through traffic on his way to Barneys. Her scent filled the car, warm and light. She smelled so good, like cookies fresh out of the oven. That had to be why he wanted to press his lips against the base of her neck and take a little bite.

"Macy's is fine. Even Nordstrom," she said for the sixth time.

To Eric's ears, she sounded almost desperate about it. Which was enough to keep him focused on the task at hand. Barely. "Come on, Sofia. I'm not exactly leading you to the gallows here. It's just a department store." They came to a screeching halt at a stoplight and he glanced over at her.

No, she wasn't happy. He had to be careful that he didn't accidentally push her too far. A cocktail dress was no reason to have a panic attack, in his opinion.

She snorted. "Eric," she began and he secretly

thrilled to hear her use his name again. It bothered him more than he'd realized that she'd called him Mr. Jenner. "Look. I can't afford anything in this store, okay?"

Yeah, but he was buying. "Don't worry about it."

The light turned green but, in true Chicago fashion, he had to wait for another four cars to blow through the red before he could go.

"No," she said, sounding stronger. "We're not ten anymore. And don't you dare turn into your mother, buying me frilly dresses that I'll never be able to wear again."

"First off, how dare you?" he said in mock outrage and she laughed. He grinned wildly at her. This was how he liked her—not cautious or worried, but ready and willing to give him hell. "I'm nothing like my mother, I'll have you know. Any dress I buy you won't be frilly." Even as he said it, his mind began to leap ahead. Sofia had the kind of body that called out for something slinky that cut close to her body, with a deep V in front so he could properly appreciate her...assets.

"You can't buy me clothes, Eric," she said in a quiet voice. "Would you buy Meryl clothes? Or Steve, for that matter?"

He scowled at a car that cut in front of him. "No, but they already know what's expected. Besides, if you think I'm going to let you walk into a situation where you're unprepared, you don't know me as well as you think you do."

But she was right. He wouldn't buy clothes for anyone else, wouldn't give anyone else the afternoon off and take them shopping. Just her.

He cleared his throat as the car came to a screeching halt outside Barneys. The valet was at Eric's door in an instant. "Mr. Jenner, good to see you again," the man said.

"Norman," Eric replied, handing over his keys. "Extra gentle with her, okay?" From the passenger seat, Sofia snorted.

He crossed around the front of the vehicle and opened Sofia's door. "It won't be that bad," he promised, holding out his hand to her. "It might even be fun."

Because, oddly, he was having fun. Sofia shot him a dirty look, which made him want to laugh. The few times he'd taken a woman shopping, they'd always simpered and smiled and were so effusive with gratitude that it had seemed less...real, somehow.

He didn't want things to be like that with Sofia. He was aware of her in a fundamental way that didn't make a lot of sense. He knew what she liked and, more than that, he knew what she needed.

Hell, he knew what he needed—but he was trying to be a better person. In the months since his ex had bailed on their wedding, he'd re-sowed a lot of his wild oats. But he wasn't a randy kid anymore and meaningless sex was just that—meaningless. He didn't want to chase a sexual relationship with Sofia if...

Well, if it didn't mean anything. Because even if this relationship never became sexual, Sofia meant something to him. More than an office manager, anyway. Much more.

Then she put her hand in his and the world stopped spinning. He didn't hear the noise of the streets or feel the heat of the summer sun on the back of his neck. He didn't see anything but her as she raised her gaze to his. All he saw was Sofia, her hand warm and light in his. Skin to skin, he swore he felt something pass between them. Something that maybe had tugged at his awareness when he'd touched her back through her jacket during her interview. Something that couldn't be ignored now.

"Come on," he said gruffly, pulling her to her feet and tucking her hand in the crook of his elbow. He didn't trust himself to say anything else.

Six

Sofia stared up at Eric in shock. What was happening? Really? Eric had been avoiding her since she'd scolded him—and she couldn't blame him. No one wanted to hang out with a harpy. But suddenly he'd appeared in front of her desk and not only asked thoughtful questions about her twins, but seemed genuinely interested in the answers. And then, when she broke her own rule about telling him she wasn't prepared for her job? He took her shopping.

At best, she might have expected him to send her out to Macy's with Heather, who no doubt knew exactly what kind of dress an office manager should wear to a cocktail party with the mayor of a midsize Midwestern city.

But that wasn't what was happening. Eric was going to take her shopping himself. At Barneys, of all places.

Even with her newly generous salary, Sofia couldn't afford to so much as walk through the doors here.

Well. This was a fine mess. She should refuse, absolutely. Except...

Except he really seemed to care about how her babies were doing now that she was back at work full-time. And sometimes, when he looked at her...she swore he was looking at her with new eyes. And she had nothing to wear and didn't want to show up at a semiformal event representing the company in the wrong kind of dress.

No, that wasn't the whole truth. It wasn't just that she didn't want to feel out of place at a fancy party. She didn't want to feel out of place when Eric looked at her.

She knew she didn't belong in his world. He was so far above her in terms of looks and money and power... That she was even considering this was a clear indication of how nuts she was. But was it wrong if, at least for a weekend, she wanted to pretend that she fit into his glamorous life? That they were equals?

That she was good enough for him?

It'd been so long since she'd felt attractive. Pregnancy had done a number on her self-esteem and then, after David's death, she hadn't exactly kept up her appearance. Who cared about under-eye concealer when she could barely force herself out of bed every morning? It'd only been in the last six months—coincidentally, about the same time the twins started sleeping through the night—that she'd been able to get past the fog and start putting herself on the list of people to take care of.

How was she supposed to do *this* with *Eric*? When he looked at her with his intense eyes, it made her want to do stupid, stupid things—like let him lavish her with the finest dresses money could buy. Like hope that he'd remove those fine dresses from her body and pull her into his arms and...

She cleared her throat, trying to get her pulse to stay at a steady rhythm. What was she going to do?

Apparently, she was going to let Eric buy her clothes. It was wildly inappropriate and completely beyond the normal boundaries of common sense. God only knew what the gossip at the office would be tomorrow or—worse—after the St. Louis trip.

But did she have a choice? She didn't even have a proper suit that fit anymore. She'd been making do with the cutest separates she could find. She'd gotten her first paycheck—with a number that was still stunning to her—but she hadn't had time to go buy some work clothes. She couldn't sacrifice any more time away from her babies for something as superficial as trousers.

Except for this damned cocktail party, that was. And heavens help her, she wanted to look good for him.

Her chest began to tighten in panic but she pushed back and made sure to count to four as she breathed in and then out.

"Mr. Jenner," a polished woman who might have been in her forties or her sixties said, coming forward to meet them. "How lovely to see you back at Barneys again."

"Clarice," Eric said, and Sofia heard a particular tone to his voice that he didn't use with her. Imperious, she might have called it. "This is Ms. Bingham."

Clarice turned her sharp gaze to Sofia. "Yes," she said, as if she'd just figured out that Sofia didn't belong here. "Ms. Bingham, if you'd come this way? I have some options already pulled, but of course I want to take your opinions under consideration."

"Wait—I thought..." Sofia looked dumbly at Eric. She'd assumed he'd be an active part of this. Was she wrong? She'd been nervous about him offering his opinion on each outfit. So how was the realization that he wouldn't somehow even *worse*?

His face softened with a smile and she almost sighed in relief. She didn't like him all imperious. Then he took her by the arm and led her a little away from Clarice, who immediately made it her business to focus anywhere but on them. "Surprise me," he said as he slid his hand down and pressed her palm against his. A silky warmth flowed between them.

Her body tightened with want because oh, how she wanted to surprise him. But want had nothing to do with this. It couldn't. "Eric, we can't do this," she murmured—which was true and also did nothing to explain why she couldn't seem to pull her hand away from his.

"Don't you dare accuse me of turning into my mother again," he said as his thumb charted a steady course along the base of hers.

"Your mother would never—" She barely managed to get her mouth shut before something really inappropriate, like "look at me like she wants to undress me," came tumbling out. "Bring me here," she finished weakly.

"Shows what you know." His grin faded and somehow, he got even closer to her. "I want to do this for you, Sofia. I want you to walk into that cocktail party looking beautiful and feeling like you've got the world at your feet because you are and you do. I can see it. I want everyone else—including you—to see it, too." His fingers laced with hers, pulling her in. She was power-less to let go of him. "What I don't want is for you to feel like you've lost control. If you start to panic, call me immediately, okay?" When she didn't answer right away, he said, "Let me take care of you," in an even softer voice.

It simply wasn't fair of him to make her fall a little in love with him in the middle of a damned upscale department store. But that's what happened. Eric Jenner was a sinfully rich, sinfully handsome bachelor and for some inexplicable reason, he cared about her. He understood her panic attacks. He gave her a chance. He made her smile. He made things better. How could she *not* fall for him? "All right." It came out husky and low and not at all like her normal voice. But then, there wasn't exactly anything normal about any of this.

His eyes darkened as his gaze dropped to her lips and without conscious choice, she licked them under his watchful eye. He inhaled sharply and then abruptly he stepped away from her, dropping her hand like it was hot. "I'll…" He cleared his throat and tried again. "I'll be in the menswear department."

And with that parting shot, he turned on his heel and strode off. All Sofia could do was watch him go. Her hand was still warm from where they'd been skin to skin and she had to fight the ridiculous urge to run after him.

Clarice appeared at her elbow. "Are you ready?" she asked, her voice crisp.

It took real effort to tear her gaze away from where Eric's back was disappearing down the stairs. Once again, he was putting a great deal of faith in her.

If he wanted to be surprised, then that's what she'd give him.

"I think so."

But when they made it back to a private fitting room, there were more than just a few cocktail dresses waiting. There were racks and racks of clothing, including business suits and shoes and even underwear. "What is all this?" Sofia asked, pressing her hand to her chest in alarm.

"When Mr. Jenner and I spoke on the phone, he made it clear that you would need to be outfitted for a cocktail party, business meetings and travel," Clarice said, smiling in a way that was probably supposed to be reassuring. "Isn't that what you two discussed?"

"Um…" He hadn't said anything about suits or traveling clothes. This was supposed to be a dress. One dress. Not an entire wardrobe. "How many outfits are we talking about here?"

Clarice didn't hesitate. "Two business suits, two evening outfits and two traveling outfits. Mr. Jenner made it clear that you were to be outfitted and accessorized from head to toe."

Sofia's heart began to hammer in her chest. This was too much. What part of six damned outfits that he hadn't even discussed with her was making sure she didn't feel like she was losing control?

She opened her mouth to refuse it all—the carte blanche, the outfits, Clarice's knowledgeable assistance—and then she remembered what Eric had said as he'd held her hand and leaned toward her. He wanted to do this for her because he knew she was beautiful and he wanted her to believe it, too.

She closed her eyes and made sure she was still

breathing. Oh, this was dangerous, that she was even considering this. She didn't just want to surprise him when she walked into that cocktail party and she didn't just want to look like she fit.

She wanted to feel pretty again.

She wanted to make Eric's brain stop functioning.

"Can you make me look great? Like, really great?"

Clarice's eyes lit up. "It would be my pleasure."

Seven

Sofia was a mess of nerves. She hadn't been able to eat breakfast and hadn't slept more than twenty or thirty minutes at a time last night. For once, it had nothing to do with the twins teething.

Her luggage, packed with five different outfits and three pairs of shoes for a three-day trip, stood by the front door, waiting. Eric was going to pick her up sometime in the next fifteen minutes and drive her to the airport. From there, he, Sofia and the Nortons would fly in Eric's private jet to St. Louis.

She was doing this. She was going away for a weekend with Eric. Business trip be damned. She had sexy lingerie in her bag, far too beautiful to keep hidden underneath clothes.

No, no—she wasn't nervous about that. Eric wasn't going to see her panties. She was just…nervous about flying. She'd been on an airplane exactly twice in her life, flying to and from Cancún for her honeymoon with David. She hadn't liked it then, and that had been a big plane. Eric's jet wasn't much more than a puddle jumper.

In fact, the only thing keeping her from a full-on panic attack was the fact that she was being mobbed by adorable babies.

"Are you going to miss me when I'm gone?" she asked, sitting on the floor with both Addy and Eddy on her lap. Eddy's lip began to tremble. "I'll come back," she promised. "I always come back, don't I? You'll have a lot of fun with Abuelita and Abuelito. Story time at the library, a trip to the park—"

"Pak!" Eddy yelled, flopping off her lap and toddling over to where his shoes were.

Sofia laughed. The boy would sell his sister for a swing set. "Later," she said. "When Miss Rita gets here, you can go to the park." Rita was a new addition to their routine, a young woman who reminded Sofia of what Rosa must've been like twenty or thirty years ago. Rita was a first-generation Mexican American, taking night classes, already working one part-time job and now helping out with the twins in the mornings.

Watching Rosa Cortés with Rita was a little like watching Mrs. Jenner buy dresses for Sofia when she had been a girl. Mom went out of her way to make extra food that Rita could take home because she wouldn't have time to get anything before class. Mom often had a sweater or a dress that she'd bought because she'd thought it would fit, but when she got it home it didn't—and it just happened to be in Rita's size.

Sofia was just glad Mom liked Rita and seemed to embrace her help with the twins. Sofia worried less about her parents now that there was backup.

That didn't make it any easier to leave her babies, though. Addy snuggled into Sofia's lap, her thumb in her mouth. Sofia stroked her daughter's hair, savoring this moment of closeness. God, she was going to miss them. But she wasn't going to cry. She swallowed hard a few times as she breathed in Addy's sweet baby smell. No crying allowed.

But was it wrong she was excited about this weekend trip? She was going to have a hotel room all to herself at the Chase Park Plaza, with room service and no one to wake her up in the middle of the night. She wouldn't have to cook or clean. She had two new dresses that made her feel beautiful and the company of a man who made her want more than she could even dream about.

She had no right to dream of him, but that hadn't stopped her from wondering if he'd wear a tux to this party. Or how he'd look if she reached up and tugged on that bow tie, unraveling the ends and pulling him toward her and—

The doorbell rang and Addy launched herself off Sofia's lap. She and Eddy ran to the door.

"That's the driver, Mom," Sofia called to her mother in the kitchen, her stomach doing a little flutter. She gathered the black pashmina wrap Clarice had insisted pulled the whole look together and her purse. That, at least, was still hers. She couldn't bring herself to let the accessorizing go so far as to include handbags. She knew exactly how expensive those things could be.

It was ridiculous that he was coming for her. He could've saved himself a lot of time if they'd met at the office.

But no. And he didn't even send a separate car. Instead, his driver was picking her up, even though it was way out of the way to drive from the Gold Coast where Eric lived down to the Pilsen neighborhood where she lived with her parents.

The Nortons lived close to the Chicago Executive Airport, where Eric kept his plane—which was on the far northern side of the city. So they'd meet them there. Which meant it would just be Eric and Sofia in the car. In the back seat. Hidden from the rest of the world.

Not that it mattered, because it didn't. This was a work-related trip. The brand-new clothes she was wearing were work clothes—although Sofia had not yet figured out in what alternative universe a silk georgette blouse and cropped white trousers constituted a "traveling outfit." In her world, white pants were a disaster waiting to happen. But she was wearing them anyway. The same went for the cocktail dresses. The outfits had nothing to do with the way Eric had held her hand in the store or told her to let him take care of her. Not a damned thing.

She might engage in some gentle flirting because that seemed unavoidable. But Eric flirted with everyone, so that was fine. Safe, even. As long as they kept it at flirting. No undressing, no lingerie.

The doorbell rang again. Sofia took hold of Addy as Mom hurried out of the kitchen to scoop up Eddy.

Sofia opened the door, saying, "My bag is—"

The man standing in the doorway was not the driver. Eric Jenner himself stood there, looking sinfully handsome in a brightly colored button-up shirt with a linen blazer over it. Her mouth fell open and all she could do was stare at him. His hair had more of a wave than normal and he looked so damn good she could feel her resolve crumbling like a cookie in a toddler's hands—and they hadn't even made it to the car yet.

She was going away with him for the weekend. And he wanted to take care of her.

Oh, God.

"Sofia," Eric began, but then his gaze was drawn to Addy, who'd curled against Sofia's shoulder. "Good heavens," he went on, sounding almost severe about it. "These children are even cuter in person than they are in pictures. I didn't think that was physically possible."

"Mr. Eric!" Mom said, struggling to hold on to Eddy. "Oh—we weren't expecting you! Oh!" she said again, her hand flying to her chest as she looked him over. "My, you've grown up so much!"

Eric took that as an invitation. He stepped inside and closed the door behind him. Then, before Sofia's eyes, he bowed. Bowed! "Mrs. Cortés, you haven't changed a bit. You are as lovely as I remember."

Mom blushed—which only made Sofia stare even more. When was the last time her mother had blushed? "Mr. Eric, we can't thank you enough for everything—"

Eric waved her off. "Sofia's doing a great job, just like I knew she would." Then he leaned forward and said, "May I?" Without waiting for an answer, he plucked Eddy from her mother's arms. "You must be Eduardo. I can tell—you're a very serious young man." As he said it, he tickled Eddy's tummy.

Eddy squealed with delight and kept right on squealing as Eric lifted the boy over his head a few times, saying, "Oh, yes—very serious indeed."

That got Addy's attention. Although she didn't fling herself at Eric, she sat up. She didn't have to wait long. Eric tucked Eddy into the crook of one arm and reached out for Addy. "Hello, Miss Adelina. Aren't you a good girl?"

"It's all right," Sofia reassured her and then Addy was lifted from her arms and cradled against Eric's chest.

"There we are," Eric said reassuringly, bouncing both children a little bit. Eddy seemed thrilled beyond words, but Addy was holding herself a little apart from him, still unsure about this strange man who'd just walked into their lives.

Next to her, Mom sighed—a noise that was part happiness, part relief and part…longing, maybe? Sofia could sympathize. The sight of her children in Eric's arms—if possible, this was even less fair than him tenderly telling her that he wanted her to feel as beautiful as she was.

Because he was holding her children, making silly sounds and getting Addy to smile while Eddy tried to copy his sounds, with varying degrees of success.

Eric was perfect.

"Oh, Mr. Eric—I have something for you," Mom said, hurrying off to the kitchen.

And leaving them alone. "Hi," he said over the heads of the twins. His eyes warmed as he looked her over. "It's good to see you."

Oh, Lord—the only thing worse than flirting right now was sincere compliments because there was no defense against sincerity. "Hi," she said back.

What was she supposed to say here? Because it simply wasn't fair how perfect he was. The least the universe could do would be to make him not like children. If he showed indifference or even open dislike of the twins, it would be so much easier to keep her attraction to him under control.

But no. He had to be perfect in every way. He was going to make her fall in love with him and it was going to break her heart.

"Hey, can you take a picture? I'll send it to my mom," he said. "Can we smile, kiddos?"

By the time she got the camera app open, they were all laughing. No, this wasn't fair at all. "Babies!" she said enthusiastically, which got both twins to focus on her. Eric looked up and grinned and she snapped several shots.

Then Eddy squirmed out of his arms and Sofia had to hide her smile at Eric trying to juggle the twins. But he didn't drop either toddler, so that counted for something. "What is it, big guy?"

Chattering excitedly, Eddy made his way over to the coloring table. "He wants to show you his drawings. Which means that, in about ten seconds, Addy will want to show you *her* drawings, too."

"A little friendly sibling rivalry?"

"You have no idea."

"Sofia?" Mom poked her head out of the kitchen. "Can you give me a hand before you leave?"

Sofia frowned at her mother. Normally the woman refused any and all offers of help. But Mom gave her *the look* and Sofia had no choice but to say to Eric, "Will you be all right for a minute?"

"Go on," he said, shooting her a grin that made her cheeks heat.

Mom had a small pile of food assembled on the counter. "Mom, what are you doing?"

"Mr. Eric—he always loved Jarritos. I think I have

another bottle of the *fresa* somewhere…" she said to herself, digging around one of the cabinets. "Ah, here it is." She pulled out the bottle of the red drink.

Strawberry had always been Sofia's favorite, too. "Did you call me in here just to help you find some soda?" Her heart began to pound faster, but it didn't feel like a panic attack waiting to happen.

"No, *cariño*." Her mom set the soda down by the other snacks—all Mexican brands. Bags of corn chips and pastries. The kind of snacks she'd loved growing up. She remembered how Eric had always treated Takis chips like a rare and special treat.

"I want you to promise me something," Mom said, her brow knit with worry.

What was this all about? It wasn't like her mother to be overly dramatic. "Okay, what?"

"I want you to have some fun this weekend." She said it in such a hushed, serious tone—like she was confessing to a sin.

"Fun?" Sofia shook her head from side to side, wondering when the world stopped making sense. Fun had always been low on her mother's priority list. "Mom, this is a business trip. We'll be working."

Her mother clucked and patted Sofia on the cheek and just like that, Sofia felt like she was seven again. "*Ayi*, it is—but this is the first time since David died that you've…" Her voice trailed off.

Sofia was suddenly terrified of what her mother might say. Because what it sounded like Mom was saying was that it might be a good idea if Sofia considered sleeping with her boss on a weekend getaway and that couldn't possibly be true. Especially not when Sofia had been daydreaming about doing just that.

"There's nothing going on here. We're just old friends who happen to work together now."

Her mother gave her another look, one that had Sofia's mouth snapping shut on any other protest. "It's been almost a year and a half. You need to move on with your life."

Sofia stared in disbelief, but Rosa Cortés didn't so much as blink. "I am moving on. I got a new job and some new clothes." Clothes that Eric had paid for. "There's nothing else I need from him." It didn't matter how much that might be a lie—she was sticking to it.

"Nothing?" Mom clucked again and dug out a bag to put the snacks in. "He grew up. So handsome. And thoughtful, to come get you himself." She sighed again and Sofia swore she could see stars in her mother's eyes. "The twins love him. You can just tell."

She could. Even Addy had warmed up to him in record time. "Mom…"

Because this was not the beginning of a new story. This was not a happily-ever-after in the making. And if Sofia allowed herself to buy into that delusion—that a hot, rich, thoughtful billionaire who cared for her and the children would somehow give her a perfect family and a storybook life—*no*. He was so far out of her league that she knew she'd fall if she tried to climb to his level. And she couldn't fall again. She wouldn't survive the bounce this time.

"It's just that you've been through so much—you deserve a little fun, don't you?" Mom nodded to herself as she bagged up the snacks. "It's time for you to smile again."

"I smile. I smile all the time." It was hard not to smile

and laugh when Addy and Eddy were being adorable—
or even when they were getting into trouble.

But even as she thought that, Sofia knew she was
being deliberately obtuse because that's not what Mom
was talking about and they both knew it.

Sorrow pulled at the corners of Mom's mouth. "Ah,
you smile for your children. You even smile for me and
your father, as if you think we can't see how you're
hiding behind it. But, *cariño*, when was the last time
you smiled for *yourself*?" With that parting shot, Mom
carried the overflowing bag of snacks and sodas out
to Eric.

Sofia stood there, struggling to breathe. Mom was
wrong. That's all there was to it. She smiled. She was
moving on and living her life. She…

Sofia dropped her head into her hands. She didn't
get enough sleep and every day was a new battle to be
waged against crushing depression and anxiety. Her
entire life had become faking it until she made it. Apparently, she wasn't faking it well enough to fool her
own mother.

And what, exactly, was that woman encouraging her to do? Seduce Eric? Have an affair with her
boss? It didn't make any sense. Although she had liked
David and approved of the marriage, Rosa Cortés had
been horrified when Sofia and David had moved in
together before the wedding. Mom was a very traditional woman. She would never do anything as risqué
as condone an affair.

But the moment the thoughts of seduction and Eric ran
headlong into each other in Sofia's head, her mind oh-
so-helpfully filled in the blanks. A big soft bed in a hotel
room, Eric looking at her with desire in his eyes as she

slipped the buttons free on his shirt and he slid down the zipper on her dress. Would he pounce on her, all masculine strength and raw lust? Or would it be a slow seduction, one that left her shaking and begging for release?

God, she missed sex.

"Wow—Takis? I haven't had these in years!" she heard Eric say. Sofia swung around to see him surge to his feet as Mom held out the snacks. "I can't believe you remembered how much I liked these!" He rummaged through the bag. "And Conchas? Oh, man—these are always such a special treat! Sofia always shared these."

Sofia watched as her mom ducked her head, another girlish blush on her cheeks. "We always brought extra for you. But not too much—we didn't want to make your mother mad."

"As long as we didn't get orange fingerprints on her office furniture…" They laughed, as if the passage of years had never happened.

Have fun. Maybe Sofia was reading too much into this.

It wasn't like she could just decide not to be anxious. It didn't work that way. But she could make a conscious choice to enjoy herself this weekend. She could continue to fake it until she made it because even if she'd still be forcing herself to smile, she might eventually make it to having a good time. To enjoying her time with Eric. Even if that just meant sharing a bag of fried corn chips.

Or even if it meant something…more.

God, it'd be so good to smile again. To be happy again. At least now, she could almost see happiness from where she stood. It wasn't a star hung too high in the sky that she'd never be able to reach, like it'd been in the first terrible months after David's death.

She'd never forget her husband—she didn't want to—but maybe it wasn't such a bad thing that Eric reminded her she'd been a happy, whole person before her marriage and she might be one again.

As she watched, Eric pulled Mom into an impulsive hug. "It's been so great to see you again, Mrs. Cortés. My parents always love to hear from you."

"Give my best to your mother." Just then, Eric's watch beeped. "Oh, you must go. You'll be late! I wouldn't want you to miss your flight."

Eric laughed. "Don't worry. They won't leave without me."

Eddy toddled over to him, holding up a sheet of paper. Eric bent down. "This is really nice, big guy. Did you make this for me?"

Eddy grinned widely and nodded. Not to be outdone, here came Addy, also brandishing a sheet of paper. "Oh, this is lovely," Eric said so seriously that Sofia couldn't help but laugh. "Can you write your name on it for me?"

Addy hurried to the table and then slashed a line in bright pink across the bottom.

"That's my girl," Eric said and another part of Sofia melted.

He would be *so* easy to fall for. She could fight against the fact that he was gorgeous and the fact that he had more money than most of the rest of the city put together. She could even work around the way he treated her with kindness. But this?

Because right now, he wasn't some unreachable fantasy. Right now, he was joking with her mother, making her babies smile—all while waiting to whisk her away for the weekend. She could almost pretend he fit in her world.

She only hoped she could pretend she fit in his. Just for a few days. Just to have a little fun.

Eddy signed his art, too—he chose a red crayon for his signature scribble. "I will treasure these always, guys," Eric said, folding the two sheets of paper and tucking them into an inside pocket. "I'll come back and see you again, okay? And maybe your mom will bring you out on the boat. We'll go swimming and everything."

Swimming didn't mean much to the twins—but *boat*? "Now you've done it," she told him as she came out of the kitchen, her resolve set. They were going to have a lovely weekend and that was final.

Sofia leaned down to give each of the twins another kiss on the head. "Be good," she told them. "I'll see you in a few days. Love you."

Eric put his hand in the small of Sofia's back. "Longer goodbyes only make it harder," he said, his voice low in her ear.

He guided her through the door and down the front steps, where a long black car was waiting. It wasn't quite a limousine, but it was close.

She looked back over her shoulder to see Mom holding the twins at the window, everyone waving. Sofia had to blink hard as she waved back and then Eric had the door open for her and she climbed into his luxury car.

He sat next to her and put the bag of snacks between them. "Ready to have some fun?"

She picked up one of the snacks. *Fun.* Nothing more and by God, nothing less. "Let's go wild."

Eight

Normally, Eric enjoyed everything about traveling to a site at the beginning of a new project. Of course he enjoyed making more money. Who didn't? But he actually loved buying a piece of property, whether it was vacant or the buildings were dilapidated or whatever, and seeing the possibilities. He loved choosing the best option from those possibilities and making it a reality. He was good at it, too. Every development was more successful than the last. Sometimes it seemed like there wasn't anything Eric couldn't turn to gold.

He glanced at the woman sitting across from him. She looked amazing today—but his awareness of her went deeper than just how her backside had looked in those white pants when she'd gotten into the car.

So many possibilities.

It didn't make any sense, how glad he was to see

her. He'd gone decades without Sofia in his life and suddenly, he was waking up early, thinking of ways he could make her laugh—or make her eyes deepen with desire, make her tongue flick over her lips in anticipation...

"Should I send that picture to you or your mother?" Sofia asked.

He jerked his gaze away from her lips. "Me." Because he wanted to hold on to that memory of Sofia's children in his arms, of Eddy's easy laughter, of Addy's slow but sweet smile.

He hadn't lied—those kids were even cuter in person. Eddy was outgoing and Addy was reserved, but they were two sides of the same coin. They weren't identical, in either their appearance or temperament, but they did little things together that tugged at his heartstrings, like tilting their heads the same way and smiling the same smile at the same time. They matched each other perfectly in every way.

He touched his jacket, right over where he'd tucked their drawings in his inside pocket. When he thought of those babies, all he saw was possibilities.

His reaction didn't make any sense, but he wanted to be there for them.

"There," Sofia said, seconds before his phone chimed. "You like strawberry best, right? I suppose it's not a great idea to load up on junk food before we get on the plane, though..." She fished out a bright red Jarritos soda from the overflowing bag Mrs. Cortés had packed.

"At least we won't starve to death anytime soon," he joked, twisting the cap off the soda. "I haven't had one of these in years." He took a long drink. And then immediately started coughing as the sugar hit his tongue like a tidal wave. "Was it always this sweet?" he choked out, his eyes watering.

Sofia laughed. He could see a little of the tension fading from around her eyes. "Yes, it was. You really haven't had one since we were kids?"

He shook his head and took a much smaller sip of the soda. All he could taste was sugar. It wasn't so much strawberry flavored, but damn if it didn't taste like his childhood and all the fun he used to have with Sofia. "I know you may find this hard to believe, but I don't exactly wander the aisles of grocery stores. I have a personal chef and I dine out a lot."

Her lips twisted into something that might've been a smile. Yes, he knew she didn't have personal chefs, but he didn't want to do a side-by-side comparison of their lifestyles.

"That's true, I suppose," she said.

"Hey, none of that." He held out his soda for her to taste. Mrs. Cortés had packed several bottles but he was possessed with the sudden urge to share with Sofia. They always had shared, back when they'd been kids, hiding from his mom's nutritionally conscious eyes. "We're going to have a good time this weekend and that's final. I don't know if I told you this yet, but you look very nice today."

She hesitated and then took the bottle from him. "Thank you. I can't take any credit for this outfit—or anything else. It's all Clarice."

"She may have picked it out," he said, his gaze drawn to the smooth expanse of her creamy skin revealed by the low-cut blouse, "but you're making it look good."

Sofia's cheeks shot bright pink and for a second, he

thought she was going to scold him. Instead, she lifted the bottle and placed it against her lips.

Suddenly, Eric couldn't do anything but watch her throat move as she swallowed. When she handed the bottle back to him, her tongue traced the path around her lips, capturing every drop of sweetness.

He went hard in a heartbeat and it only got worse when she looked up at him through her lashes. So many possibilities. How would she look, her hair undone and her lips swollen from kisses? Would she taste sweet or would she taste more complex, like a fine wine?

He shook back to himself. This was Sofia, for crying out loud. He had to stop thinking about kissing her at random times. About kissing her at all. Or about what she'd look like in a cocktail dress. Or even out of a cocktail dress.

Unfortunately, his thoughts went right back to her children. He dug out his phone and opened the picture and froze. Eddy was clapping, Addy was smiling and as for him?

He looked happy. Happier than he could ever remember looking.

This was bad. No, that wasn't true. *Bad* was wanting to strip her down to nothing and spending a long evening in a private hotel suite showing her how much better he'd gotten at kissing since he'd been a kid. He wanted to do bad, bad things to her. Repeatedly. Over the course of a long weekend.

Her babies weren't bad, because he now knew these twins and might very well keep on knowing them. He could visit them again or have Sofia bring them out on the boat. Hell, he could invite them to his parents' house because his mother would go crazy for these babies. He didn't have to cling to this one photo as if that was all he was going to get.

But it was worse, too—because how was he supposed to spend time with those babies and not want more? He could already see it all—the way they'd scream in delight as the boat roared across the lake. How much fun they'd have in the pool, splashing everywhere.

How was he supposed to spend time with *Sofia* and not think of stripping her down and covering her body with his every other second? How was he supposed to hold himself back from cupping her cheek in his palm, feeling the soft warmth of her skin against his?

He shifted in his seat. What was his problem? He was *not* thinking about seducing Sofia, damn it. And he couldn't be anything more to her children than an old family friend, either. As much as he cared for Sofia and her children, it wasn't like he could just snap his fingers and have a ready-made family come running to his side.

It was one thing to give Sofia a good salary to support her children—but another thing to think he could overcome the loss of her husband and the babies' father. All the money and power in the world couldn't replace David Bingham.

A happy ending for Sofia was one more thing he couldn't buy.

But if he could, he would. Because he did care for Sofia and he could very easily care for her children.

So many possibilities.

She opened a bag of Takis chips and held it out to him. "Thank you for being nice to the kids."

He snorted and took a chip. "You make it sound like I was forcing myself to endure their company and that couldn't be further from the truth. I'm only sorry we couldn't hang out more. And," he went on, cutting her off before she could argue with him, "I was serious about coming out on the boat. I'll get life preservers for them. Or maybe those little wet suits with the built-in floaties? Marcus had one for his son."

That set off another round of thoughts. Marcus had married his executive assistant—Liberty Reese, who Eric had tried to poach for his own office.

How had that worked out for the Warrens? They still ran Warren Capital together. They'd adopted a little baby and somehow made a family out of almost thin air.

He shook his head. Those were questions best left for later. "While it's a little cooler out toward the middle of the lake, the water's a lot cleaner," he went on. "The back of my boat opens out almost level with the water, so there wouldn't be a big jump for them. I think they'd love it." Then he popped the chip into his mouth.

And coughed again as his tongue caught on fire. "Were these always *this* spicy?" he spluttered, grabbing the soda and downing the rest of it in seconds. His eyes began to water as sweat popped out on his forehead.

Sofia laughed at him. "No, actually," she said, studying the bag. "These are a newer flavor. Too hot?"

"I wasn't prepared, that's all." But even as he said it, he swore he could see smoke curling out of his mouth. "I might never be prepared. Let's not take these out on the boat. I'd never forgive myself if one of the kids ate one by accident."

Her eyes narrowed as she studied him—although it was hard to look severe when eating corn chips. She didn't even seem to break a sweat eating those hellfire chips. "You're really serious? About the boat?"

"Sofia, when have I ever not been serious?"

She fought against a smile, he could tell. Her mouth twisted before she lost the battle and grinned at him. "Gosh," she said, taking a pastry from the bag. "I can't think of a time where you were never *not* serious."

He liked that smile on her. He didn't want to see worry crowding the corners of her eyes, drawing her full lips into a tight line. "Are you going to be okay this weekend?"

She looked out the window. "I think so. Yes. This is a whole different world for me, Eric. Private jets and expensive clothes and chauffeured cars…"

"Don't forget the boat."

She rolled her eyes, but she smiled again. "Who could forget the boat? I know we're going to be working. But I'm determined to have fun. I haven't had time away since…" She swallowed. "Since before," she finished decisively.

Although it probably wasn't a smart thing to do, Eric reached over and laced his fingers with hers. For a long moment, her hand was stiff in his and then, just when he'd decided this was another bad idea, her grip tightened around his. That spark flowed between them, but it was okay. Not a seduction. Here, in the car, they could hold hands and it would be all right.

"Sofia," he said softly, setting the bag of food on the floor and scooting over to her. "I'm so sorry."

Again, it was another long moment before she relaxed into him, her head against his shoulder. He closed his eyes and savored the feeling of her weight on his body. "It's…it's getting better. The job helps."

"Good." That was the most important thing, right? That he was giving her a way forward. That was the way he could help her best.

Her chest rose and fell as she took a deep breath and then, looking up at him, she said, "You help, Eric."

Up close, her eyes were a rich brown, shimmering and sweet, like the finest of brandies. He could get drunk on her, he realized.

He didn't know if she was leaning up to him or he was reaching down to her. Or both. He was only dimly aware of cupping her cheek with his hand and stroking his thumb over it. "I just want to make everything better for you," he murmured, staring in fascination as her eyes darkened. "That's what friends are for."

"Yes," she said, her voice little more than a whisper against his lips. "Friends."

Then she was kissing him and he was kissing her and it was intoxicating. She tasted sweet and spicy and hot. His temperature began to climb and it had nothing to do with artificial flavorings.

This wasn't like their first kiss. Not even close. Because this wasn't a tentative touching of lips with their eyes squeezed shut, both holding their breath.

This kiss was everything. He traced the scam of her lips with his tongue and Sofia sighed into his mouth, opening for him. He dipped his tongue into her mouth, searching for her taste underneath.

Sofia kissed him with a wild sort of abandon, like a woman starving for air who'd just surfaced above the waves. *Ah*, he thought, *there she was.* She tasted complex and sweet, just like the woman herself.

He shifted so he could wrap his arm around her shoulders and pull her in closer before he went back to kissing her. His blood hummed in his veins as the weight of her breasts pressed against his side. Shifting, he cupped one in his hand, the weight of her heavy and warm in his palm. Sofia moaned against his mouth as he stroked her. When her nipple went tight under his touch, he had to bite back his own groan. She was so responsive. God, she'd be amazing when she let go.

He wanted her to let go *now*. Still teasing her nipple, he sank his free hand into her hair, tilting her head so he could let his mouth drift down her neck until he found her pulse. It wasn't weak or irregular. Instead, her heart was beating hard and fast as a soft moan broke free of her lips. *"Eric."*

This was right, he realized. Sofia was right where she belonged, in his arms. He was hard for her and wanted nothing more than to sink into her softness and make her cry out with satisfaction.

The car lurched sharply around a corner, throwing them both off balance. He clutched her by the shoulders until they were both steady.

Or steadier, anyway. Her eyes were glazed with desire and he knew he wasn't in any better shape. All he could do was look down at her and think how much he wanted to do that again.

He didn't take the chance because just as he leaned forward, Sofia sat back. Her gaze cleared and that delicious desire was replaced with tight lines of worry. "Oh. Oh. That was…"

She touched her lips with the tips of her fingers and Eric had to resist the urge to replace her fingers with his lips. But he didn't get the chance because she retreated across from him. He had to drop his arm from around her shoulder, but he wasn't going to relinquish his hold on her that easily. He wrapped his fingers around hers again.

"A mistake," she finished weakly.

He managed not to scowl. "It didn't feel like a mistake to me." Why had he thought this would be easy? Because it wasn't going to be. "Is this the part where you tell me we can't do this?"

"We can't." But she didn't pull her hand away from his. "Eric, we really can't."

"Why not? I like you. More than like, actually," he admitted. "I haven't been able to stop thinking about you since you walked back into my office. Into my life."

"I can't fall again," she said, her voice breaking. She turned to look at him, her eyes bright with tears. "I have to…" She swallowed and looked away again. "I have a job to do. I don't want to risk that."

He rolled his eyes. "Your job has nothing to do with any of this."

That got him a sharp look. Funny how it made him want to smile. "Don't be intentionally dense, Eric. I need the job. I need to take care of my family. I need to keep moving forward. You're paying me too much money—"

"Not that again," he huffed.

"And I can't risk that. Not for something as selfish as…" She swallowed again. "As short-term as sex."

Eric gaped at her in confusion. "Sofia. Look at me."

She didn't. She could be stubborn, his Sofia. "This is exactly like the salary argument, Eric. You can afford to do whatever you want. But I can't. I don't have hundreds of thousands—millions—of dollars to fall back on when this doesn't work."

He thought about that for a moment. Really, her argument was sound. She worked for him and he had a hard-and-fast rule about relationships with his staff— he didn't have them, period.

But Sofia wasn't just his office manager. She was his friend. Their relationship had started long before she'd begun to work for him—and he was beginning to realize he wanted it to last long afterward. "When was the last time you had sex?"

"Really?" she snapped, jerking her hand from his. "You're going to ask me *that*?"

"After that kiss? You're damn right I'm going to ask that. When was the last time you put your needs first?" Because he was willing to bet money that Sofia was low on her own to-do list.

She squeezed her eyes shut, her lips trembling. "Don't."

He could read the truth on her face. She hadn't been with anyone since her husband had died. A year and a half was a long time to go without a little loving.

He wanted to crush her in his arms and tell her everything would be okay—but hell. She'd been widowed and he'd been left at the altar and he couldn't promise her that everything would work out just so.

That didn't mean he wasn't going to try, though. He wasn't promising her forever, after all. Just the weekend. "I'm trying to understand, babe. You need to take care of your family. I get that. But who takes care of you?" He knew her mother worried about her, too. But being mothered wasn't the same thing as putting herself first.

She swallowed hard. "You're not going to fight fair, are you?"

"Of course not." She almost smiled at that—but not quite. "This weekend—let me take care of you. Which," he added, stroking his thumb along the side of her hand, "I'm already doing. I can't wait to see what dresses you decided on."

"Not the same," she muttered, yet he couldn't help but notice that she was still holding his hand, still submitting to his touch.

"Let's have fun this weekend," he went on. "Just two old friends spending time together. No strings." He leaned over and nuzzled her hair with his nose. God, she smelled so good. He wanted to devour her. "Let me put you first, Sofia. You won't have to worry about anything."

She didn't answer for the longest time. "I don't know if I can do that. Not like you can."

That hurt more than he wanted it to. "Like me?"

"I can't be…casual." But she rested her head on his shoulder and it only made sense for him to tuck his arm around her again. "I mean… I don't know what I mean."

Eric let that thought roll around in his head. He assumed she knew about his ex-fiancée. Had she heard about the aftermath of the broken wedding? He'd gone through several high-profile, short-lived romances afterward before he'd burned himself out on meaningless sex. He hadn't exactly loved Prudence, but he'd at least cared for her, and sex without that caring wasn't the same. A physical release, yeah. But it hadn't been enough. He'd needed more.

Sofia in his arms felt like *more*.

His body ached for hers but for more than just a release—for both of them. He wanted to make her smile and laugh and…

He just wanted to make things right again. For her and maybe for him. For them both.

He kissed her head and did the right thing. "It's okay. We don't have to fool around." His body strained in protest but he ignored it. He wanted Sofia almost past the point of reason—but friends didn't pressure friends into sex.

She snorted in what he hoped was amusement.

"But," he went on, "if you change your mind, you let me know. Because I care about you, Sofia. I won't hurt you."

She was silent, but she let him hold her all the same. "Friends, right?"

"Right," he agreed. Friends were great. Friends with benefits were even better. But he managed to keep his mouth shut. "Always friends."

She sighed and leaned into him even more. "Thank you," she whispered.

And although it wasn't sex, there was something to just holding her that made Eric close his eyes and savor the moment.

He stroked Sofia's hair. She sighed again and even that small noise made him feel good. Great, even.

He needed this. He needed her and even if this was as far as it got, it was enough. For now.

The car bumped into a pothole and Sofia's cheek crinkled against the drawings her children had made for him. It was entirely possible, he realized, that he needed those babies, too. Their laughter, their hugs. Their joy. He needed that innocence in his life again. He was tired of being a cynic, holding himself apart from people because they'd disappoint him every single time.

He and Sofia stayed like that and Eric let himself enjoy the feel of her body pressed against his. Even this almost platonic touch felt right. She belonged in his arms.

How could he convince her of that?

Nine

"Almost there," Eric said, his voice low and close to her ear.

All Sofia could do was nod miserably as she leaned heavily on his arm.

"I can walk," Meryl protested weakly from just ahead of them.

"I know you can," Steve replied, sounding almost normal, "but no one needs to watch you bounce off the walls." With that, he swept his wife's legs out from underneath her and cradled her to his chest.

It wasn't much of a comfort that Sofia wasn't the only one who'd suffered mightily on the flight to St. Louis. The landing had been a terrifying exercise in flying during a storm and there'd been no way to push back against a panic attack. It'd been so bad that she'd forgotten how to breathe and had actually blacked out for a second.

Steve had gotten sick and Meryl looked like she needed a doctor. Even Eric, who was no doubt used to flying all over the place in that tiny aircraft as well as riding the waves on his boat, looked a little green around the gills.

Sofia's legs felt like rubber bands and her heart was still skipping at a weird rhythm—and they'd been on the ground for almost forty-five minutes. She hadn't had the strength to protest when Eric had slung his arm around her waist and held her up. She leaned into him, barely managing to keep hold of the bottle of ginger ale. She wasn't sure it was helping. She had no idea where her luggage was and she honestly didn't care.

"I know it's going to push us off schedule," Eric said loudly so Steve and Meryl could hear him, "but I think we all need a break. Can we afford two hours?"

"No," Meryl said, although she sounded like she was trying not to cry.

"Yes," Eric said more firmly. "Look at it this way, Meryl—no one would expect us to have landed during that storm, anyway. We had a flight delay, that's all. We still have all day tomorrow, too."

Meryl moaned pitifully, which made Steve croon to her.

The sound made Sofia's heart skip another beat, but not due to motion sickness. It was good, old-fashioned jealousy. God, she missed having someone who'd pick her up—literally or figuratively, it didn't much matter—when life knocked her sideways.

Just then, Eric leaned down to her, his arm tightening around her waist and his voice for her ears only. "There's your room, Sofia."

And even though it wasn't the same and Eric wasn't

hers, she leaned into him even more because she felt terrible and Eric was the strength she needed right now and whatever happened this weekend, they would always be friends. Even if she fell a little more in love with him, they were friends.

The Nortons' room was across the hall from hers. "Where's your room?" she asked as Eric fumbled with her key card.

"Next door." He got her door open and basically set her inside, one hand still around her waist. He pivoted back to where Steve had gotten his door open. "Take as long as you guys need," Eric said quietly, as if Meryl wasn't right there. "It's better to be late than be ill during the meetings."

"I'll be fine..." But Steve closed the door and cut off Meryl's weak protest.

Eric pivoted Sofia into her hotel room. "I'm so sorry I'm such a mess," she said, knowing it was pointless to apologize but apparently unable to help herself.

Eric snorted as he sat her on the bed. "I'm sorry the flight sucked. That was one of the roughest landings I've ever had. Wasn't entirely sure the plane was going to hold together."

Her breath caught in her throat. She'd wondered the same thing, right about the time she'd stopped breathing. "Maybe we can take the train home?" she said, trying to make a joke and failing.

"The weather is supposed to be clearer on Sunday," he promised. "If it looks bad, we can make alternative arrangements." Then he knelt before her and picked up one of her feet. Sofia was aware that her pretty new silk top was plastered to her back with sweat and the rain had done a number on her hair and she probably looked one step removed from a drowned rat. She certainly didn't feel much better than one.

But then Eric moved. Slowly, he slid the cuff of her trouser up and pulled her brand-new Stuart Weitzman flat off her foot. There wasn't anything strange about him seeing her bare leg. It was just a leg. God only knew he'd seen that and more back when they'd spent half a summer splashing in a pool.

But the fact that Eric was removing her shoes for her? Undressing her?

Heat flashed down her back again, which was just ridiculous. This was not a seduction. She looked like hell and felt worse and they were supposed to be getting ready for meetings with the mayor and the board of aldermen and she was not letting Eric distract her with all his tenderness and certainly not with these...

Eric's fingertips gently caressed her calf and stroked along the top of her foot. The touch sent sparks of heat arcing up her body, burning her with desire. Her eyes fluttered shut and she had to brace her arms against the bed to keep from toppling into him.

His hands moved over her ankles, up her calves again. He warmed her skin with his palms, a strong and steady touch, and she couldn't help but think back to that kiss in the car, the one that had managed to awaken every single sexual need and desire she'd locked away over the last year and a half.

With Eric kneading the muscles of her legs, slowly moving up higher and higher, she no longer felt clammy and sick. She felt...

Good. Warm and safe and cared for. God, she'd missed feeling this way.

"Sofia," he said, his voice soft.

She wasn't sure if it was a question or not. And honestly, it didn't matter. They were friends, weren't they? And friends helped each other out. They had fun together. They comforted each other when things went wrong—and that plane ride had been very, very wrong.

Friends didn't let something like a few billion dollars or a private jet or luxury clothing get in the way of a friendship.

And really, once the trappings of money were removed—weren't they just a man and a woman? Weren't they made to fit together?

God, how she wanted to be comforted. To be touched like Eric was touching her now. She wanted to be the one taking the attention and affection instead of giving them.

"Sofia?" he said again, his voice sending low flutters through her belly.

Really, no matter what the question was, the answer was simple. "Yes."

His hands slid to a stop on the curve of her calves. Funny how she'd never really thought of calves as being particularly sensual until now. "Will you lie down and rest for a bit?"

She looked at him then. One of the most powerful men in Chicago—and quite possibly the country, to say nothing of the world—was on his knees before her, waiting for her answer. She uncurled her fingers from where she'd fisted the bedclothes and reached out to stroke his cheek. It was still early—not even eleven yet—and his jaw was smooth. "Only if you join me."

His eyes widened as he sucked in air. "Give me a few." With that, he pushed back off his heels. She heard a door open and shut and then she was alone.

Sofia dropped her head in her hands. She could still feel his hands on her legs, stroking and caressing her. She could still feel his arm around her waist, refusing to let her stumble through the hotel. For that matter, she could still feel his hand surrounding hers, holding on through the turbulence. He'd refused to let go.

She could still feel his lips against hers, his tongue tracing the path of her lips, her name soft on his breath. Eric had kissed her like she was the air he couldn't breathe without.

He was taking care of her. He wanted her to rest.

He was going to come back in here.

And she still looked like hell.

That thought finally got her to move. She downed the rest of her ginger ale and took stock. This was a really nice hotel room—king-size bed with a plush duvet, a velvet-covered sofa next to a coffee table and a television almost as big as David had ever bought. She went to the bathroom—even the toiletries were top-of-the-line. Of course they were. Eric Jenner wouldn't settle for less.

She recoiled at her reflection. Her hair had come loose from the bun and her makeup was shot. And yet, Eric had still sat there, staring up at her as if she were the only woman in the world. The shirt was a total loss, so she stripped it off, leaving her in only her camisole. And she didn't want to nap—or do anything else—in these trousers. Quickly, she washed her face—but then she remembered she didn't have her toiletry kit. Her luggage was being delivered separately by a bellhop.

She'd never stayed in a hotel that had bellhops who carried up one danged suitcase before. It was probably a great thing—but she really needed her stuff now.

She was using the facilities when there was a knock

on the door. "One second," she called out, washing her hands quickly. But then she heard voices, both male.

Wait, what?

She cracked open the bathroom door to see Eric standing in an open door that…led to his room? Oh. *Oh.* Her room was connected to his. Of course it was. He had an executive suite. And her room was right next to his.

It shouldn't be a big deal, that he could walk into her room or she into his. It wasn't anything more intimate than removing her shoes, for God's sake. But it felt like the last barrier to truly spending the weekend in his arms had just been removed. They didn't have to walk out into the hall where Steve and Meryl might hear or see them.

Eric said, "Yes, that one goes in here. The other one goes in my room," as he looked up. When he saw her, his face softened as his gaze took in her face, her now-bare arms. He held up a finger to her, the universal sign for *hold on.*

She nodded and shut the door again, collapsing back against it. Their rooms connected. He wanted her. He'd already started to undress her.

She wanted him. Oh, how she wanted him.

But even as that thought occurred to her, she caught her reflection in the mirror. Her color was almost back to normal and she didn't look like she was on the verge of passing out again. Her hair wasn't great, though, so she unpinned it and combed it out with her fingers. She couldn't sleep with it pulled back like that, anyway.

She heard a door shut and then Eric said, "Do you need anything from your bag?"

"No," she fibbed. "I'll be right out."

"No rush."

Oh, but it felt like a rush. If she were going to throw herself at Eric—and that did look more and more likely—she would be jeopardizing her job and putting both of them in an awkward position. Steve and Meryl were right across the hall, so the risk of gossip spreading in the office was huge.

But damn it all, she needed him. She needed a weekend where she wasn't going through the motions of looking fine. She wanted to *be* fine and she knew Eric could give her that. He already had.

Sofia took one last look at her reflection. The hair was okay. She would prefer a little under-eye concealer, but the whole look wasn't too bad.

Have fun. Smile for yourself. That's what her mom had said. And Eric? He'd said nearly the same thing, adding in that he wanted to take care of her. And it was so clear from his actions in the last few hours that he didn't just mean a satisfying romp in bed. He really was taking care of her.

Her resolve set, she opened the door and stepped out.

The room was empty.

Ten

Sofia hesitated in the doorway of the suite. Not only was Eric's room much bigger than hers was, it was much grander. There was a dining room table set for four with fine china and crystal goblets. The kitchen—not a kitchenette, but a real kitchen with full-size stainless steel appliances and granite countertops—was off to the left. She took another step in, her feet sinking into the plush carpeting. The couches in the sitting area were similar to the one in her room, but they were longer and deeper and had luxurious-looking throw pillows on them. This place was far more spacious than the apartment she'd lived in growing up.

Okay, she thought. If she had to arrange travel for Eric in the future, this was the sort of room he needed. She'd do well to keep that in mind. She was trying to be a professional here. True, a barefoot professional in a camisole, but a professional nonetheless.

Then all thoughts of professionalism came to a screeching halt when Eric appeared in a doorway across the room. He'd unbuttoned his shirt and was working his cuff links loose. Even though he had on a white T-shirt underneath, there was something about seeing him unbuttoned that sent another shiver down Sofia's back.

Her nipples tightened underneath her camisole at the sight of him and that physical reaction had *nothing* to do with friendship.

She crossed her arms in front of her traitorous nipples. "So this is the kind of room you need when you travel?"

He notched an eyebrow at her, which made him look amused. "It is. In fact, when I come to St. Louis, I usually stay in this suite. I like the views of the park." He motioned to the windows over his shoulder. Sofia had a view of buildings, but Eric had a sweeping vista of a huge green park.

"The next best thing to a view of a lake?"

His smile deepened and she got the feeling that she'd pleased him. "It is."

They looked at each other for a moment. She wasn't sure what she was supposed to do in a situation like this. After all, they weren't acting in their capacity as boss and employee, but they weren't quite operating within the normal bounds prescribed by "old friends," either. She felt stuck. "I didn't realize our rooms connected," she said dumbly.

"I hope it's okay with you that I opened them up?" Then he began to slide his shirt off his shoulders. No, that was not the same body she remembered from all those years ago. Eric had filled out. His white T-shirt strained across his chest and his biceps. He wasn't overly muscled, but he wasn't lean and lanky anymore, either. She smiled as she looked at his biceps. There was an inch of paler skin showing just below the cuff of the sleeve before his arm turned a deep golden brown. She stared in fascination at that strip of skin. Redheads with a tan were so very rare.

He was so rare.

She had no right to be in this deluxe suite with him, no right to be staring at that strip of skin. She had no right to him—but she wanted him all the same. Just for the weekend. Just for herself.

Sofia took a deep breath and let her arms fall to her side. "Why wouldn't it be?"

His eyes darkened as his gaze fell to her breasts. Her nipples tightened even more, jutting out through the thin fabric of the camisole. She swore she heard him growl. But instead of pouncing, he said, "Feeling better?"

"A little."

He moved closer to her and she stepped into him. They stopped just short of each other and he lifted his hand to brush her hair away from her face. "Hi," he said softly, cupping her cheek in his palm.

She leaned into his touch. They'd spent the whole morning together, but this? She didn't feel like she was standing in front of Eric Jenner, eligible bachelor billionaire. Without his bespoke shirts and other trappings of wealth, she was just standing with Eric, her friend. She hesitated before she jumped into the gap, resting her hands on the narrow vee of his waist. His body radiated heat underneath her hands, all the hotter now because he wasn't wearing his jacket and shirt. "Were we going to lie down?"

"Absolutely." He stroked his thumb over the apple

of her cheek, his gaze on her lips. "Were we going to sleep?"

Heat flashed through her body, stronger and more insistent than what she'd felt in the car. Then, she'd been nervous about leaving the twins and the flight. All of that was behind her now—but the flight had left her drained. "We had a rough landing, Eric. And I don't get to nap very much. Let me just…" She stepped in closer, her breasts pressing against his chest. Her nipples ached as they brushed against him. She leaned her head on his shoulder. Dear God, she'd missed the feeling of a man. "Will you hold me?"

His arms did not come around her and for a paralyzing second, she thought he would say no. But before she could back away, Eric bent down and swept her legs out from under her, just like Steve had done to Meryl. "Eric!"

"I've got you," he said close to her ear. It was what she needed to hear. More than that, it was what she needed to believe.

And, as Eric cradled her lovingly, she did believe it. She relaxed into his arms and let him carry her weight. "Pick a room," he told her. "Mine or yours?"

She didn't have to think about it. "Yours." That way, if whatever this was didn't pan out, she could go back to her own room and not have to smell him on her pillows.

She should not be doing this but she seemed powerless to do anything but let him carry her to the very big bed. "Do you mind if I take my trousers off? I don't want to wrinkle them."

Such an innocent-sounding request, but there was no mistaking the fact that he'd be one step closer to naked. That didn't stop her from saying, "Go right ahead."

He sat her on the edge of the bed and stepped back. She looked up at him—and *not* at the buttons he was undoing. He paused and touched her cheek again.

She couldn't hold back the happy sigh. It'd been so long. She knew she was being dramatic but it almost felt like her first time again—and in a way, it was. Her first time with Eric.

Everything about her wanted to reach out for him, pull him in close and trust that he would be right there if she needed him, however she needed him.

Instead, she stood and undid her own button and zipper. The white trousers were more or less a total loss—the rain had seen to that. But she needed to be close to Eric right now, needed the comfort his body could provide. What she was feeling for him wasn't just about sex. Not entirely, anyway. It was about something more.

She tried not to stare at his bulge as he shucked his pants, but it wasn't easy because... Oh, my.

Grinning to herself, she kicked her trousers aside and gave thanks to Clarice, who had seen fit to include undergarments in her total wardrobe makeover. Instead of the serviceable cotton she normally wore Sofia had on a pair of high-cut silk panties with lace around the waist. They were a sheer nude color, all the better to be worn under a pair of white pants—and the first thong that she had ever owned. Clarice would hear of nothing else because she claimed that a visible panty line would just *ruin* the look.

Sofia felt exposed and vulnerable. But it wasn't a bad feeling, she realized. Instead of anxiety, tendrils of anticipation uncurled through her limbs, making her body feel heavy and needy.

For him. For the gorgeous man waiting for her in a

very large bed. He pulled the covers back and slid in first, patting the bed beside him. "Come here."

Sofia had not had a wild adolescence. She'd been raised in a fairly strict religious household that frowned upon casual dating and sex and besides, an accidental pregnancy would have made achieving her goals harder. She had been a virgin when she'd started dating David. She'd never been in bed with anyone else.

Except for now. Was there any turning back once she slid next to Eric and put her arms around his waist? Was there any hope of holding a part of herself back so she wouldn't fall in love with him all over again? Because if she were lucky, this…connection would last the weekend—and not a moment longer. A weekend was long enough to have some fun and reclaim her sexuality with Eric's help without it blowing up in her face. For a few days, she could pretend she belonged not only in his life, but in his bed.

A weekend would be enough. It had to be.

Eric's gaze drifted over her camisole, her bare legs. His eyes darkened and he held out his hand for her and she knew there was no turning back. She scooted over to him. He pulled the covers up over them and settled her in the curve of his arm. She wrapped her own arm around his waist and slung her leg over his. And then, for the first time in what felt like months, she exhaled. "Eric…"

"Shhh," he murmured, stroking her hair. "Just rest for a bit. I'll be here when you wake up." And although it didn't seem like she would be able to—not with their bare legs intertwined, not with his arms around her— Sofia closed her eyes and drifted off, feeling safe and, somehow, that everything was going to be all right.

* * *

Eric felt the moment Sofia slipped off to sleep. Her muscles relaxed and she sank into him, warm and soft. It was strange, how easy it was to hold her like this. His body hummed at a high pitch, attuned to everything about her. The softer she got, the harder he got.

Was he preparing for one of the biggest business meetings of his career? Was he looking toward the future at all? No. Instead, all he could think about—feel— was the curve of Sofia's breasts pressing against his side, her smooth leg thrown over his. She was wearing a see-through thong, which meant there was next to nothing between them. He could feel the heat of her body against his hip, smell the warmth of her skin.

This was torture, plain and simple. And he'd suffer it willingly because even with his dick throbbing, holding her was one of the most satisfying things he'd ever done.

How long had he told the Nortons? Two hours? It wasn't going to be enough. It'd never be enough time, not when he was tucked into bed with Sofia, his body straining for hers. And the hell of it was, he might just keep right on straining. Just because they were half-naked and wrapped around each other didn't mean that Sofia wanted anything else from him. She'd asked him to hold her and by God, that was what he was going to do.

Luckily, his watch was on the hand he could look at without disturbing her. Right before the bellhop had shown up with their luggage, he'd sent a quick message to the mayor's executive assistant, stating the weather had delayed them and he would be in touch when they were able to make it. But he figured that meant he and

Sofia only had an hour at most. Then they needed to get up and get changed and go back to being Mr. Jenner and Ms. Bingham, boss and office manager. And they had to stay that way until...

He mentally ran through the schedule. They had meetings with the mayor and the city planner this afternoon. This evening was a formal dinner with several members of the state government, including the lieutenant governor. Tomorrow was more meetings and site visits with negotiations. He needed Meryl to be his bulldog, Steve to convince everyone what they wanted was doable, and Sofia to be his eyes and ears. After all, this was a *huge* deal. St. Louis was ripe for the picking and if Eric played his cards right, he would be richer than his wildest dreams.

It was damned hard to care about that right now. He was already rich beyond his wildest dreams and following that carefully planned schedule meant he'd have to leave this room. He'd have to put distance between himself and Sofia and spend the afternoon and the next several days without holding her hand. Without touching her at all. He didn't know how he was supposed to do that.

If Meryl and Steve weren't here, Eric would claim the flu and cancel the whole weekend. But people depended on him. All of his employees, not to mention all of the locals he would hire for construction. He'd be sinking a lot of money into this project and it would do a lot of good. He couldn't blow that off for something as selfish as a weekend in Sofia's arms.

Besides, he was violating his own code of not getting involved with his employees. True, it was hard to remember that when he was with Sofia. But she did work for him. Technically, right now, they were on the clock. And mostly naked in bed together.

His last thought before he drifted off was that maybe he shouldn't have hired her.

Eric floated in the space between awake and asleep. He couldn't wait to get Eddy and Addy out on his boat. They might need to bring along a nanny to watch the kids. He wanted the kids to have fun, but he wanted Sofia to have a good time, too—and it might be hard to do that if she were constantly chasing after the twins. Because if the kids liked it and Sofia had a good time, then she'd come out boating with him again. And he wanted that.

How good would Sofia look on his boat, stretched out on a lounge chair, her body clad in a bikini, the sun kissing her skin like he wanted to? Instead of kissing her, he pulled her down into the cabin and stretched her out on the bed. She sighed as he put his hands on her body and the noise went straight through him. Her legs were long and shapely and he stroked his palm from her knees to her thigh and her hip and back down again. And again, and again. He couldn't get enough of her. Maybe he never would.

As he massaged her skin, she turned into him, her body almost on top of him. Now he could reach her backside. She had a woman's curves and all he could think was *lush*. Hopefully, when they woke up, he'd have a chance to do this in real life. He wanted his hands all over—not just stroking, but grabbing and feeling and knowing her, all of her.

His dream Sofia stretched against him and Eric half lifted, half rolled her onto his chest. Now he could grab her backside with both hands, filling his palms with her flesh. His fingertips grazed the lace edge of the barely there panties and he shifted her body so the hard length of his arousal was pressed against her very center.

His dream Sofia gasped, a noise that cut right through Eric's daze. He blinked and then blinked again. The bedroom cabin of his ship resolved into a familiar hotel room—but Sofia was still on top of him.

Holy crap, this wasn't a dream. Sofia was straddling him, staring down at him through heavy-lidded eyes. She pushed her hands through her hair and arched her back, driving her weight down onto his erection. Stunned, Eric was helpless to do anything but grind against her. She gasped again.

God, she felt so good, so damned right on top of him. He was afraid to say something, afraid to break the spell that would wake them both up from this dream. So he kept his mouth shut as he gripped her bottom in his hands and dragged her up along his erection again.

She moaned softly, so quietly he almost didn't hear it. She kept that little noise of satisfaction deep in her throat and he wanted to let it out. He wanted to swallow it and take it inside of himself and let it rattle around until it drove him past all reason.

She shifted and he shifted with her, pressing against her center again and again. Her back arched, thrusting her breasts out. He grabbed the hem of her camisole and yanked it over her head.

And his head fell back against the pillows as he stared at her body. *Lush* was still the only word he could think of. Soft and curved and wearing a sheer lace bra. He could see the wide dark circles of her nipples.

There was too much and not enough and it completely short-circuited his brain. He couldn't move, he couldn't think. All he could do was stare at her. Worship her.

He worshipped just a moment too long. Sofia dropped her gaze as she put one arm across her breasts, the other across her rounded stomach. "I know, I know. Having the twins changed me and I'm not—"

Eric didn't know what she was going to say, not exactly—but he knew he disagreed with it completely because she was perfect. He sat up and cut her off with a hard kiss. Sofia made a little squeaking noise, but then her arms came around his neck and she held on to him for balance as he slid his hands up and down her back. Then he began to work the catch of her bra, kissing her the entire time. She sank her fingers into his hair and refused to let go. He liked that she was a little aggressive and *very* sure of herself. The kiss in the car this morning had been a promise of things to come but this? This was a promise delivered.

The catch on her bra gave and he peeled the lace away. He didn't want to break the kiss, but he couldn't resist lowering his head to those beautiful breasts. They were full and heavy and he loved everything about them. Even the little white stretch marks along the sides—they were perfect because they were a part of Sofia. "Are these off-limits?" he asked as he kissed along the swells.

"No," she said, throwing her head back and giving him better access. "I only nursed for a year."

"You are the most beautiful woman I've ever seen," he murmured as he kissed the edge of her nipple and then swept his tongue over the tip. It went tight against his mouth and he couldn't help the rumble of satisfaction that built low in his chest. He was already drunk on her. He had no intention of jumping on the wagon now.

"Oh my God, Eric," she moaned, clutching his head to her breasts.

Her hips kept shifting back and forth, grinding down on his erection. With one hand steady on her backside, he slid his thumb down between her legs, over the silk of her panties until he found the center of her pleasure. She jolted as if he'd shocked her and he smiled against her skin before adding his teeth to her nipples.

"Oh, Eric," she gasped, letting her weight settle over his thumb.

He began to rub in small circles as he nipped and sucked at her breasts. They found a rhythm together as he worked her body. All he wanted to do was flip her over and drive into her heat over and over again until they were both spent and sated and then, once he'd caught his breath, he wanted to do it again.

But he wanted to give this to her first. No demands, just the gift of pleasure. Just her trusting him. Just him earning her trust.

Like he was doing right now. She was letting him love her and he was making the most of it. Dimly, in the back of his mind, he knew there were good reasons to not do this. But he couldn't come up with any of those reasons right now and besides, it was a little too late to keep his hands off her. That ship had definitely sailed.

As she shifted her hips back and forth, her warm heat stroked over his erection even as he stroked her body. The pressure was intense and amazing and when she pulled on his hair, forcing his face up so she could kiss him, he felt her entire body go tight and hard around his. "Let go, Sofia," he murmured against her lips.

And she did. Her thighs clamped around his waist and heat flooded her center as she came for him. The force of her climax was so strong that, amazingly, it triggered his own release. He hadn't been this excited, this eager, since he'd been a teenager discovering girls for the first time.

But that's what this felt like. He had just discovered something new and amazing.

He'd found Sofia.

Eleven

Sofia collapsed onto Eric's chest, breathing hard. His hand was still pressed between her legs and her stomach was damp where it rested against the waistband of his briefs. The orgasm ricocheted around her body like a bullet fired into a metal tank. She was hot and tight and loose all at the same time and it was *wonderful*. Simply amazing.

And that was when she realized that she might be completely in love with him. Damn his hide.

Her breathing was ragged and she couldn't seem to stop shaking. But in a good way. The best way. But it was different, too. She'd loved sex with her husband but that felt like a different life. She hadn't anticipated how different her body would feel straddling Eric as he brought her to completion. His mouth on hers, his teeth on her breasts?

She shuddered again. It hadn't been the same. Even that thought felt almost like a betrayal, though. She'd loved David with her whole heart and soul—and body.

But she might be in love with Eric.

God, her head was a mess. And the more those delicious little shivers of satisfaction faded away, the more her brain started to freak out. Good Lord—had she and Eric really just done *that*?

It'd all happened like a dream unfolding. She'd been asleep and then not quite asleep, Eric's warm body next to hers. Her body had filled with a languid warmth and the space between her legs had grown heavy and she had *wanted*. It'd been so long since she'd wanted. Desire and sensuality—they hadn't been a part of her life since David had died.

If it were anyone else, it wouldn't have happened. It wouldn't have gotten even close to happening because she never would've stripped down to her panties and climbed into bed with anyone else. But this wasn't some random stranger spouting stale pickup lines and vague promises he had no intention of keeping. This was Eric.

He'd held her children and made them laugh. He'd kissed her in the car. He'd promised that whatever happened in this bed was separate from them working together. He'd literally seen her at her worst—on multiple occasions—and yet he was still here, giving her a mind-blowing orgasm.

She didn't just want to get laid in the service of vague sexual frustration. She wanted *him*. And she could have him. So she had.

Sort of.

His arms came around her and he held her tightly.

"God, Sofia," he said, his chest still heaving from the climax. He sounded happy and...relieved? "I mean..." His voice trailed off and he kissed her head.

No, she didn't know what he meant. Other than he'd enjoyed it, too—which made her feel good. Although she hadn't done much.

Just straddled him. Just ground her hips down along his length—his very impressive length. Just cried out his name. Her body quivered, a reaction she couldn't control.

He shifted, somehow pulling her closer and that, at least, calmed her racing thoughts. She closed her eyes and ducked her chin against his shoulder and tried her hardest just to be in this moment. She hadn't had sex in so long, but she could still feel that passion, that need. And she could still be satisfied. That was the important thing here.

Not the fact that she had no idea what she was supposed to do next. Compliment him on his skills? Make some saucy comment about how she couldn't wait to do that and more this evening? Tell him how she felt about him? She and David had always said they loved each other afterward. Every single time.

Her mouth opened as if on automatic, but she snapped it back shut. Even if Eric had made her fall in love with him, she couldn't very well tell him that. Because he'd promised to take care of her, to have some fun with her. To keep this weekend separate from everything else. Love didn't figure into any of those things. In fact, it would probably ruin everything.

She didn't want to remind him that, outside of this room, they didn't belong together.

When she couldn't come up with anything reasonable to say, she felt Eric's arms tighten around her. "Babe? Are you okay?"

She let out a little laugh. No, she wasn't okay. Not even close. She couldn't even commit to a friends-with-benefits weekend without overthinking the whole danged thing. "Yeah. Just…"

"Been a while?"

She nodded, grateful to hide behind that half-truth. She *was* a little rusty, after all. "Now what?"

"I don't know about you, but I need a shower." Just then, his watch beeped. "Hang on." She tried to roll off him, but he put a hand on her lower back to keep her where she was before answering his watch. "Yes?"

"Eric? I've managed to get Meryl up and into the shower. She's arguing with me, so I think she's fine."

Sofia stayed very still as Steve spoke. Her face was burning. It wasn't as if Steve had walked in on them, but it felt like it.

Why couldn't she have decided to do this whole benefits thing when she wasn't on a business trip?

But then again, when else was she going to spend time with Eric?

Oh, what a mess.

"Are you guys sure you can make it through the afternoon?" Eric asked, sounding calm and professional and nothing like the man who had just brought her to orgasm with nothing more than his fingers.

"I think so. Give us another forty-five minutes and we should be ready."

"Sounds good," Eric agreed, but even as he said it, he lazily traced his fingertips up her bare back.

Then Steve asked, "Do you want me to tell Sofia?"

Eric still sounded perfectly normal when he said,

"I'll let her know. We'll see you in a few." He ended the call and let his head fall back against the mattress. "I guess that means we have to get up."

"I guess it does," she said. Eric's calm was contagious, almost. Her heart was slowing down to a steady, reliable beat and she was breathing normally.

But she still had no idea how she was supposed to face the afternoon schedule. Before, it had seemed daunting, but now it felt almost impossible. How was she supposed to handle herself now?

Eric tilted her face up so she had to look at him. "Are you sure you're all right?"

She tried a confident smile. Given the way he notched an eyebrow at her, she was pretty sure she failed. "I don't know what to do next. I mean, about us. About this." She let out a strangled laugh. "And also about having dinner with the lieutenant governor tonight. None of this is normal for me, Eric. I don't fit in this world."

He stroked his thumb over her cheek and gave her a smile that, if she'd been standing, would've made her knees wobble. "You're going back to your room to take a shower and get changed. I'm going to do the same here. We're going to some meetings where Meryl will negotiate until she's blue in the face, Steve will make friends with everyone and I'll make grand promises that sound too good to be true, except I'll have all the numbers to back them up. All you have to do for the rest of the evening is smile and listen. You're the best listener I've ever met. Take notes on what's being whispered, when people look nervous or whatever. I want to know what's not being said, okay?"

"Okay."

He stroked his thumb over her cheek again. "If you feel awkward, compliment someone on their tie or their presentation or whatever. Can't go wrong with compliments. You do that and we'll be fine."

He sounded so damned confident about it, as if he actually believed she could pull this off. Preparing for today's meetings and tonight's dinner—that was where all her focus should be. It didn't matter how easily he thought she could do this—she knew darned good and well that today would be hard and tonight would be harder. She had no experience in high-level meetings, even less experience at high-stakes cocktail parties. Eric could be confident because that sort of thing came naturally to him. He breathed it, lived it every single day.

God, she hoped she didn't embarrass herself. But more than that, she hoped she didn't embarrass him. There was a real risk that if she did something wrong, she might cost him this deal.

And if that happened, after what they'd shared?

She'd never be able to look him in the eye again.

But now, there was no escaping the fact that they were still lying in bed together, almost naked, the sweat on her back starting to cool. She wanted him to warm her up all over again. "And after that?"

He held her gaze for a moment before he said in a quiet voice, "That's up to you. But this is a big bed," he went on, giving her a playful grin. "Plenty of room." To emphasize this, he patted around. "I might get lonely. Just saying."

She should say no. She should walk away while she still could, before they crossed that final line. If she were strong enough, she'd sleep alone tonight.

But just then, Eric cupped her face and brushed a

tender kiss over her lips and she knew she wasn't going to be strong enough. She knew she'd be right back in his arms tonight.

"That would be tragic, wouldn't it?"

He leaned up to press a hard, quick kiss against her lips before he patted her bottom. "Devastating. But we've got a lot to do before then."

With a sigh, she rolled off him and out of bed. "Then we better get to it."

"Well," Eric said as the elevator doors closed behind them. "I think that went well."

It took almost everything Sofia had not to slump against the wall of the elevator. And frankly, she didn't have much left. Who would've thought that paying attention to conversations all day long with a smile plastered to her face would be so exhausting?

But that wasn't the only thing that had left her drained. The effort it took not to watch Eric, not to smile at him—not to show that she was aware of every single thing he did—had taken a lot out of her.

She hadn't wanted to look like a woman lusting after her boss. She had no idea if she'd made it.

Because she was *definitely* lusting after Eric.

She barely recognized the woman reflected in the mirrored walls of the elevator. The black-and-white lace patterned dress was working overtime, as was the strapless bra. She almost didn't look like the mother of twins, which was impressive.

If she threw a suit jacket over this dress, she could wear it to work. But for dinner tonight, she had tucked the pashmina shawl around her shoulders and left her arms bare.

Eric had noticed, too. She'd felt his gaze upon her all night long. Just like it was right now. He shifted closer to her so their shoulders were touching. In the reflection, he smiled at her and Sofia couldn't help but think, *We fit.*

Which was ridiculous. Just because his black suit and bright blue tie looked good with this dress absolutely did not mean that she fit with him. But it was enough to pretend for this weekend.

"Can we wait until morning to go over our notes?" Meryl asked, sounding drained.

Sofia startled. Were they supposed to be business professional after eight solid hours of meetings? Before she and Eric could pick up where they'd left off this afternoon?

Even throughout dinner—one of the finer meals she'd ever eaten—she'd been focused on listening. She was used to sleep deprivation. Anyone with small children was. But coloring with the kids required a much lower level of mental engagement than following along with a dinner conversation that encompassed state, federal and city ordinances.

But she hadn't made a fool of herself. She'd offered up a few compliments and paid attention and managed not to stare at Eric and think of nothing but his body against hers. Nothing tonight had come naturally to her, but she'd made it. It seemed that, for one weekend at least, she could pretend she belonged by Eric's side.

"Absolutely," Eric readily agreed. His fingertips brushed and then tangled with Sofia's. That simple contact went through her like a lightning bolt. Instantly, she was wide awake. "It's been a long day, but I'm so impressed at the way everyone recovered and I know that tomorrow, we'll be right back at it."

"Go, team," Steve said weakly, which made Meryl laugh.

Sofia managed a chuckle. Tomorrow would be another long day and she wasn't entirely sure she would be able to fake her way through it.

But tonight?

Tonight she would wrap her arms around Eric and be a little bit selfish. She could take what she needed instead of having to worry about what other people needed. It would be worth it, even if it were awkward tomorrow morning. She wanted to remember that she was Sofia, a woman with desires and needs.

She gave Eric's fingers a squeeze and felt a ripple of tension move up his arm. Then he let go of her hand as the elevator stopped at their floor. "What time is the first meeting tomorrow?" he asked as they filed out of the elevator and down the hall toward their rooms.

"Nine a.m." Sofia replied. And since everything had been pushed back today, there was no hoping for an extra hour tomorrow morning.

"Let's meet in my suite at eight for breakfast." He still sounded confident and alert, as if he could have lingered at the bar for another few hours.

She didn't want to linger at the bar. She wanted to linger in his bed, by God.

Meryl and Steve mumbled their agreements as they reached their room. Eric paused and looked back over his shoulder, making eye contact with Sofia. She bobbed her head, agreeing to the question he hadn't asked—at least not in words.

It didn't matter. The answer was still yes.

"Good night," she said to the hallway at large as she went into her room. She took a moment to use the bathroom and freshen up and then, still in her fancy dress, she opened the door on her side of the wall.

His side was already open. Quietly, she stepped into the room. Even that simple act had her pulse beating at a higher rhythm, which was still a new and exciting feeling to her. During that first year after David had passed, when she'd been struggling to care for her newborn twins, her sexuality had been in hibernation. She hadn't had the energy to miss it then, but when she'd begun to emerge from the fog of depression and sleep deprivation, she'd wondered if she would be capable of sexual desire again. It was almost like she'd forgotten how.

Then, this afternoon, Eric had made her shatter with nothing more than a well-placed touch and some passionate kisses. Which had been wonderful relief. She could still *feel*. That part of her hadn't died with David.

But she wanted more. She wanted it all.

She wanted Eric. And thank God, he was here for her.

This was just the weekend. On Monday, they'd go back to normal. She'd go to work and he'd go boating. No more clothes, no more kisses in the back of his car. No more pictures of Eric cuddling her children.

No one would know. Especially not her mother.

Eric came out of his bedroom and, without breaking stride, crossed the room and pulled her into his arms. His mouth came down over hers, a kiss so hot that suddenly she had on far too much clothing. Luckily for her, he was hell-bent on rectifying that situation.

"All night long," he murmured against the delicate skin of her neck, making her pulse flutter wildly, "I've been staring at you in this dress."

"I like this dress." The zipper moved down her back one notch at a time as his mouth drifted down her neck to her cleavage at the exact same pace. Luxurious warmth built low in her body and radiated out. For the first time in so long, she was warm. God, she hoped Eric heated her up.

She went on, "It makes me look…"

Well, it made her look like she fit in his world.

"Correction," he said as he tugged the zipper down the rest of the way. Cool air kissed her back and she shivered, her nipples going hard. "You make the dress look amazing, Sofia." He took a step back, and the dress gaped at her chest. He ran his fingers under the straps then pulled them off her shoulders. "But you know what's better than you in this dress?"

"What?"

"You out of this dress."

The dress puddled at her waist and he stepped into her again, working it over her hips.

"Oh, Sofia," he breathed as the dress fell to the floor and she was left in nothing but a strapless bra, underwear and her shoes. His eyes warmed as he stepped back to look her over. "I thought I was ready, but I'm not."

Twelve

"**Y**ou're not?" Anxiety began to twist in her stomach again. *Please,* please *don't let this be a mistake in the making.*

But Eric cupped her cheeks in his palms, lifting her face to his. "I may never be ready for you, babe. You're always going to take my breath away, aren't you?"

And before she could reply to that sincere compliment—damn him and his sincere compliments—he lowered his mouth to hers again.

She lost herself in the give-and-take of their kiss. Somehow, they were moving, although she wasn't aware of taking any steps. Eric kicked out of his shoes and then she was pushing his shirt off his shoulders. He lost his pants in the doorway to the bedroom and she pulled his undershirt off next to the bed. Now it was her turn to step back and admire him. It made her smile to see that he had on black boxer briefs. Black was de rigueur for the evening, apparently.

Hopping on one foot and then the other, he peeled off his socks. There was something familiar and comforting about it and yes, silly. She'd watched him peel off his socks and shoes countless times when they used to throw themselves into the pool as kids.

It was ridiculous that something as simple as taking off his socks could make her relax, but it did. This was okay. Better than okay. He was still Eric and somewhere, deep inside, she was still Sofia. No matter how much it changed, that would always be the same.

She started to take her strappy heeled sandals off, but Eric said, "No, wait." Before she could figure out what he meant, he fell to his knees and set his hands against the buckle of the sandal.

This was the second time today he had been on his knees before her, undressing her slowly. And she knew in all truthfulness that she might not ever be ready for him, either. It didn't make sense, why he was putting so much effort into this. He could've had his pick of any woman in the world. Why was he here with her?

He got her sandals off and then sat back on his heels, staring up at her. "You doing okay?" Before she could answer, he leaned forward and pressed a kiss against her thigh.

She laced her fingers in his hair to balance herself. "I think so," she answered honestly before she realized he might take it the wrong way.

He paused. "We can stop."

She stared down at him. Even from this angle, she could see his erection straining against the waistband of his briefs. She'd felt it grinding against her earlier, his body hot and heavy for her.

"I don't want to stop," she told him, raking her fingers through his hair. "I want to feel good, Eric. I want to be selfish." And, although she didn't say it, she knew he understood—she didn't want to regret this.

More than that, she didn't want this to be somber and quiet. She was so tired of being serious, of feeling like the fate of the world rested on every single decision she made.

"And I want to have fun," she said, unable to stop her voice from wavering. "I need to have fun. With you. Please."

"I would do anything for you, Sofia," he said and dammit all, his voice was serious. "Anything, that is, except eat one of those fire-hot Takis again."

She surprised herself by laughing and he grinned. "Those things took a year off of my life," he went on, somehow sounding serious and yet completely ridiculous at the same time. "And the fact that you could eat them without crying? I wonder about you sometimes."

He pulled her underwear, working them down slowly over her hips. It might've made her self-conscious, but for every inch he crossed, he leaned up and pressed a kiss. And even as he did that slow and sensual seduction, he kept cracking jokes.

Had she seen when the lieutenant governor's tie accidentally dipped into his soup? Had she heard the dirty jokes Steve had been telling to the owners of a local construction company? Had she caught it when Eric tripped over the threshold of the restaurant and nearly took out the hostess?

Of course she had. She hadn't missed any of it. But

she'd been afraid to laugh then, afraid to draw attention to herself.

But now? Her chest loosened as she was able to giggle at him, at the whole evening. People treated Eric like he was royalty, deigning to grace them with his presence, when he was just *Eric*. A man who occasionally threw boulders into a swimming pool and liked junk food and looked out for an old friend. He wasn't some high-and-mighty soulless billionaire.

Oh, God, she was completely in love with him, wasn't she?

No, this wasn't about love. This was about satisfaction and friendship and…and…sex. That's all. Nothing more. There couldn't be anything more.

"There," he said, coming to his feet and wrapping his arms around her, working the clasp of her bra. "There's that smile I wanted to see."

Then the bra gave and she was completely nude before him for the first time. Unlike this afternoon, she successfully fought the urge to cover herself with her hands. Instead of focusing on herself, she turned her attention to him. "Your turn."

"You know what I regret?" he asked as she hooked her fingers into the waistband of his briefs and began to pull down.

"No?" She really didn't want to bring regrets into this.

He slid a finger under her chin so that even as she pushed his briefs down, she had no choice but to look in his eyes. "I regret that I missed the moment you transformed from a kid I used to know into the woman I want."

She pushed the waistband over his lean hips and the shorts fell away. "You didn't miss it," she told him, her hands finding his erection. She didn't need to see it to know that he was impressive and powerful. She could feel it for herself. He sucked in air as she encircled his girth with her hands.

"I didn't?"

Somehow, it did her good to hear him on the edge like this, his voice unsteady, his eyes dark with desire.

"It was the moment I walked into your building. It never would've happened before that exact moment in time." She worked her hands up and down his erection, feeling him come alive under her touch.

"I'm so glad I didn't miss it," he said and then his mouth was on her, his hands pulling her hair loose from the updo she'd managed all by herself.

"Me, too," she said and then they were falling into bed together, his body covering hers. She touched him everywhere. He was so hot and smooth and hard against her, flexing his hips and dragging his erection over her very center. He was driving her wild and God, it felt so good.

This wasn't a dream, not like this afternoon. But the rest of the world fell away, anyway. She didn't think of funerals or hospital bills or babies or jobs. As Eric skimmed his teeth over the base of her neck, all she could think about was how he wanted to devour her. When he teased her nipples to tight, hard points, all she could think about was that she wanted to share them with him. And when he stroked his fingers between her legs, finding the center of her pleasure and working it until her hips bucked against his and she cried out with need, all she could think was that she'd found herself. She'd found herself again with him.

"One moment," he said, peeling himself off her. She shivered as the cold air touched her heated skin.

"What's the matter?"

"Nothing." He went back to the doorway, where his pants were still crumpled on the floor. He pulled a condom out of his pocket and then prowled back toward her.

She got her first good look at Eric's body. Oh, he had grown up well. She had felt all of those muscles and skin against her, cupped him with her hands—but seeing was believing and she wasn't sure she believed that he was all hers.

"Did I ever tell you I like your tan lines?" she asked as he kneeled back on the bed and climbed between her legs.

"No, you didn't." He rolled the condom on and then came against her.

"You should wear sunscreen," she told him, running her hands up and down his biceps. "But you're a redhead with a tan, Eric. Someone rare and special. There's no one else like you in the world and I can't believe I have you all to myself right now."

She could feel him at the entrance of her body. She desperately wanted to flex her hips up and take him inside of her. But he was staring down at her with such tenderness that it was almost alarming.

"Sofia…" he said, and something in his tone made her breath catch in her throat.

Then he began to thrust into her and she knew that no matter how much he made her laugh or how good he made her feel, this was about so much *more* than just a little bit of fun.

He went slow, filling her inch by inch. Her body

spasmed around his. Oh, it had been so long. And he felt so good that she wanted to cry with the relief.

He was breathing hard, his face buried against her neck and she thought he was shaking. For a long moment, they lay like that, joined but quiet in the intimacy of it all.

He said her name again softly. "Sofia."

"Yes," she whispered. It didn't really matter what the question was, after all. He was here with her and they were together and the answer was *yes*. Maybe it always would be.

He flexed his hips and she rose to meet him and together, they found a rhythm. Sofia wondered dimly if she should be doing more, trying harder. But there was something so freeing about laying back and letting him take care of everything. She didn't have to give and give and *give*, dammit, until there was nothing left for her. She could be selfish and greedy and take everything he had because right now, he was all hers.

"Tell me what you need, babe," Eric grunted, his breathing harsh. "Let me give it to you."

She needed so much—more than a night or even a weekend. She needed to make up for all the time she'd lost just getting by. She was tired of survival. She wanted to live.

She was finally going to. "Let's… Here. Lean back."

Eric did as she asked, sitting on his heels without pulling free of her body. "You feel so good," she told him, shifting her legs so that they were tucked up against him instead of locked behind his back.

Eric didn't immediately fall into a rhythm again. Instead, he sat back and looked at how she had arranged herself. "How about this?" Then, instead of tucking her knee under his arm—a position that worked well for her before—he instead tucked his arm behind her knee, lifting her leg over his shoulder. But just the one.

She felt her body tighten around him with this new angle and sucked in a quick breath. "Yeah," she said, adjusting to the different sensations. He felt larger, harder—and she felt closer to someone else than she'd been in so long. "Yeah, let's try that."

This time, his pace wasn't slow or measured. He wasn't taking his time, not anymore. This time, he buried himself inside of her over and over again and it couldn't have been more than a minute before her body tightened and the orgasm blazed through her. She cried out, "Eric!" And then she lost the ability to speak at all.

He didn't give her the chance to catch her breath. He didn't give her the time to come back down to earth from that beautiful orgasm. Instead, he drove her relentlessly, pushing her from that high peak to one even higher. This time, when she came, she thrashed against the bed, grabbed onto his shoulders and held tight. The cords of his neck stood out as he roared and then collapsed on her.

They were breathing heavily. She could still feel him inside of her, although he was already retreating. She shifted, trying to hold on to him even though she knew he couldn't stay.

She didn't want to let him go. Not now. Maybe not ever.

But she did, of course. She had to. There were practical considerations and cold hard facts that could not be ignored. So when Eric rolled off her, withdrawing completely, she had no choice but to let him go.

Not that he went far. He pulled her into his arms, shaping himself around her and whispering "My beautiful, beautiful Sofia" into her hair, and that was it.

She loved him.

What a shame she could never have him.

Thirteen

It was hard to think with his pulse pounding in his ears and his body vibrating at a pitch Eric wasn't sure he'd ever heard before. But one thought pushed its way through the collection of purely physical reactions to making love with Sofia.

He was in *so* much trouble.

Because he'd promised Sofia they could have some fun this weekend. He could make her feel good. She could have a break from being a mother and a widow and be… Well, not his significant other, but a woman with wants and needs that he could meet. And above all else, he'd promised her that no matter what happened, they would always be friends. Friends with benefits, yes. But friends first.

He wasn't sure he could be anything as trite as "just friends" with her ever again. Not after *that*. Jesus.

He hadn't had sex in over six months. Closer to ten,

now that he thought about it. It was possible this wave of possessive emotion was nothing more than a long-standing itch finally being scratched. He'd gotten lucky again and it was a relief.

Sofia kissed the hollow of his neck. "I'll be right back," she said softly, pulling away from him.

He fought the urge to pull her right back into his arms. Stupid urges. Instead, all he could say was "Okay," as if that were some brilliant pillow talk. He watched her cross in front of the bed and disappear into his bathroom and then he dropped his head back against the pillows.

His blood was still pounding in his veins like a call to arms. He should be good now. Tired. Ready to sleep. An evening of sexual anticipation had paid off for both of them. Now he could stop thinking about Sofia.

Yeah, *right*. Because one thing was clear—bedding Sofia was not an itch that had been scratched. This was something else. What he'd felt with her wasn't just satisfaction at a job well done.

Oh, he was in so much trouble.

He wasn't an impulsive person. He *wasn't*. But ever since she'd shown up in his office and his life again, he'd been making impulsive decisions. He'd hired her without running background checks or calling her references. He'd taken her shopping because she'd been worried about what she would wear this weekend.

He'd bedded her. Twice. She was his office manager and he'd been inside of her. And, God help him, if she gave him so much as a half smile and a long look, he'd be inside of her again. He wasn't sure he could control himself.

When he'd pulled himself together in those months

after discovering Prudence's son wasn't his, he'd been forced to make the adult, mature decision not to engage in any more casual sex. It scratched an itch but it never made him feel better, not in the long run. He'd needed something more in bed—and out of it.

This weekend was supposed to be casual. Just two friends helping each other out. Getting her back on her feet.

He dropped his head into his hands. God help him, nothing about this was casual. This was Sofia. He cared about her. And her children? Those two innocent little babies who didn't have a father and yet were so full of joy and laughter?

What was wrong with him? He was a thirty-one-year-old bachelor billionaire. The world was his playground. He could have anything he wanted. Anyone he wanted.

Why did he want Sofia? Not just a sexual relationship. He wanted it all. He wanted to be her family. A husband to her wife, a father to her children. He wanted the perfect ending to this story. He wanted the perfect life. One that he could only have with Sofia.

And dumbass that he was, he'd promised her that he could keep this casual. Just a weekend of letting off a little steam in between billion-dollar business negotiations.

He never should have hired her. He should have listened to his better instincts and immediately gotten her a good-paying job somewhere—anywhere—else and then asked her on a proper date. He'd been lying to himself from the very beginning about what he wanted from her.

He didn't want Sofia as his office manager. He wanted her as his everything.

He was the biggest idiot in the world.

Because he had promised. And trying to change the terms of the deal now could do more than just ruin the rest of his weekend. They worked together. She was still mourning her husband. She might never want to replace the father of her children. Not even with Eric.

The bathroom door opened and she walked out, her body on full display. She stood at the foot of the bed, her lips curved into a knowing smile as she looked down on him.

He was in *so* much damned trouble.

He had to get his head out of his ass. He got out of bed and kissed her. He could spend the rest of his life kissing her, he realized. Her warm body pressed against him and his body started to respond.

He stepped back. He wasn't some randy kid anymore, for God's sake. But there was no missing that blush high on Sofia's cheeks. "All right?"

She nodded. "I'm going to go get a few things from my room and check in with my mom."

"I'll be here." Once she was gone, Eric stared at his reflection in the mirror. He looked the same, but everything was different.

He liked sex. He'd always liked sex. But aside from maybe the first few times, where it was as if a whole new world had been opened up to him, he couldn't ever remember feeling this changed after making love with someone. Certainly not with his ex-fiancée. It hadn't been bad, sleeping with Prudence. They'd both enjoyed it. It just…

It hadn't left him a changed man. And he knew damned good and well that after Sofia, he'd never be the same again.

After he pulled on his shorts, he walked out to the kitchen and grabbed a sparkling water from the fridge. He never drank more than a glass or two of anything on a business trip. The last thing anyone needed was for him to get sloshed and torpedo a deal. So his rooms were always stocked with coffee, tea and sparkling water.

Frankly, he could use a drink right now. Something to help him get this wash of confusion under control. Because he wanted everything about Sofia—and he had no idea how to get it. Not without sending her running for the hills.

Sofia came back into the room. She'd dressed in a tank top and a pair of panties—he thought. He was sorely tempted to lift the hem on the shirt and double-check. She didn't seem the least bit self-conscious about walking around like that and Eric didn't feel the least bit self-conscious staring at her.

"Mom sent a picture—do you want to see?" she asked.

"Of course." Those two adorable children were sitting in matching high chairs, looking like they'd rolled around in a plate of spaghetti. Sauce and noodles were everywhere and they were grinning the same huge smile. Strangely, it was everything he needed and salt in the wound at the same time because they weren't his babies.

Somehow, he managed to chuckle. "I bet bath time is hilarious at your house."

"You have no idea," she said, sounding like a battle-scarred veteran instead of a young mother.

He handed her the water. He should be saying things,

he realized. Telling her how beautiful she was, how great the sex was. He'd never had any trouble coming up with those sorts of things before.

All of these easy words abandoned him. All he could say as he handed the phone back to her was, "Come to bed."

She looked up at him through her lashes and it took everything he had not to sweep her off her feet and make love to her all over again. "All right."

Hand in hand, they walked back to the bed. She was wearing panties, but a different pair than earlier. These were hers, not the ones Clarice had picked out for her. He liked them all the better for that.

He pulled the covers up over them and turned off the light. He didn't know if he would be able to sleep, but he hoped she would.

Long dark minutes passed before she said, "Eric?"

"Yeah, babe?"

She didn't answer for second, just flattened her hand against his chest. "I just want you to know—this really means a lot to me. I... I've never been with anyone else but my husband. Never even shared a bed with anyone else."

He swallowed hard. "I'm honored."

With a sigh, she burrowed deeper into him. God, she felt good there, her weight against his side. "Thank you for holding me. For being here for me. You've no idea how much it means to me."

Her trust was a gift. He honestly wasn't sure he was worthy of it. "I will always be here for you, Sofia," he said, because it was as close to the truth as he could get without changing the terms of their deal.

Sleep was a long time coming.

* * *

Even though he was forty feet away and there were probably thirty people standing in between them, Eric had not been able to stop looking at Sofia all night long. She was on the other side of the Starlight Room, a ballroom at the top of the Chase Park Plaza, listening to a conversation between the city planner's assistant and the wife of the contractor Steve preferred to use for the demolition.

Tonight, Sofia was wearing a cocktail dress of red lace. She was gorgeous in it and the low lighting in the room—supposedly starlight—made her practically glow. She was simply gorgeous, he decided. And he loved her in red.

Maybe he should get her some red lingerie—something lacy and tantalizing. Maybe with matching stockings and a garter belt. And a pair of black high heels. The vision of Sofia made it difficult for Eric to stand upright. All day long, he'd struggled to focus on the deal at hand. The effort it took not to moon over her was harder than he'd expected it to be.

She needed a strand of black pearls looped around her neck, he decided. She hadn't let Clarice add any jewelry to the outfits. Pearls nestled between her breasts, matching earrings dangling...

"The vision for the space..." someone was saying to him, but he wasn't paying attention. How much longer until he could pull her away from here? Until he could strip her out of that dress and lay her on his bed? The hours since he'd made love to her this morning felt like a lifetime. He wouldn't be able to hold out much longer.

But just then, Sofia stepped away from her conversation. Eric had to crane his neck, but he saw that she was staring down at her phone.

Instantly he went on alert. Something was wrong. He didn't know how he knew, but he did. That feeling only got stronger when she walked toward the hallway outside the ballroom, her phone already at her ear.

Eric followed her. His first thought went to the kids. Were they all right?

"Mr. Jenner," the mayor said, pulling him aside. "Have you met…"

"Ladies and gentlemen," Eric said, smiling broadly. He didn't have time to be the billionaire businessman right now. Sofia needed him. "If you would excuse me for a moment, there's something I need to see to."

He managed to get the rest of the way across the room without being intercepted by anyone else who wanted to shake his hand and welcome him to St. Louis. The details of the deal still had to be ironed out, but it looked like this development was going to happen and everyone was in a celebratory mood.

Everyone except for Sofia. He was all but running by the time he burst through the doors and into the hall. When Sofia jerked around to look at him, his heart dropped. He knew that look. She was on the verge of a full-on panic attack. Dammit, he hated being right sometimes. He walked up to her and put his hands on her shoulders, willing her to be strong. "What's wrong?"

Her words cut him like a knife. "The twins are sick."

For a moment, he couldn't do anything but stare down into her worried eyes as a feeling of complete and total helplessness swamped him. "How sick?"

He was not going to panic until he knew whether

this was a case of the sniffles run amok or something more serious.

"Mom said they started throwing up last night. She…" Sofia's lips trembled and she clutched Eric's arm. "Dad rushed Eddy to the hospital a few minutes ago. He wasn't responding. Eric, what are we going to do?" That last part came out as a sob.

He tried to make sense of what she was saying— but he wasn't coming up with anything. "They were fine last night. Your mom sent that picture, didn't she? Spaghetti?"

Sofia was taking in huge gulps of air, but for all that, Eric wasn't sure she was actually breathing. "She said Miss Rita was sick. And she didn't want to worry me today because I was working and I was supposed to be having fun. She said she kept hoping that the kids would work it out of their systems today, but Eddy kept getting worse and worse and Addy isn't much better and my baby is in the hospital and I'm in St. Louis! They need me and I'm not there!"

He didn't know anything about sick kids or hospitals but he knew that Sofia having a panic attack wouldn't help anyone right now. He had to keep her calm and get her moving. "I'm going to get you there," he promised. "We're leaving. Now."

The color left her face. "But your deal…"

He grabbed her hand and hauled her back into the hotel ballroom until he found Meryl and Steve. "Sofia's kids are sick," he said without any other introductions. "We're leaving. I want you guys to stay, make my apologies. I don't care how you get home. You can rent a car, take the train—charge it to the company credit card. I can send the plane back for you—"

"That won't be necessary," Steve said quickly.

"Go," Meryl said, giving Sofia a hug. "Take care of your kids. We've got this."

Sofia let out a little sob. Eric hooked her arm with his and guided her away from the party. While they waited for the elevator, he called his pilot and said, "I don't care how you do it, but we need to be in the air in an hour. If not sooner. Make it happen."

Finally, after what felt like a year, the elevator dinged and the doors opened. "It's going to be okay, babe," he said again as he guided Sofia into the elevator. Once the doors closed, he wrapped his arms around her shoulders and held her tight. She clung to him and it just about killed him. She was so worried and he couldn't snap his fingers and make it better.

All he could do was the next best thing. He could get her to her babies a hell of a lot faster than anyone else could. He could make sure Eddy had the very best care. And, God forbid, if anything happened, he'd be there for her. Because that's what friends were for.

But that wasn't true and he knew it. Because what he felt for Sofia went well beyond "friends" or even friends with benefits. What he felt for her wasn't casual and it wasn't friendly. She'd ignited a passion in his heart that he'd been missing for months. Years. Because he hadn't felt this way about Prudence. He hadn't fought for her.

But Sofia? Eddy and Addy? By God, he was going to fight for them. The truth hit him with a lurch.

Sofia and her children were his family. And he'd do anything for them.

And that started now.

He rubbed her back and said, "We'll be there in a

few hours. Everything's going to be fine," in his most reassuring voice.

She began to cry and all he could do was hold her. "I'm sorry," she blubbered, trying to get herself under control and, in Eric's opinion, failing miserably. "It's just that when David died…"

He crushed her to his chest. "That's not what's happening here," he said, even though he knew it wasn't a promise he could make. "Eddy's going to be fine. He's a tough little dude." He prayed. "Did your mom say where he was?"

"St. Anthony."

Dammit, he didn't know anyone there, at least not off the top of his head. If they could get Eddy to the Children's Hospital, then he knew some of the staff there. He donated a lot of money to the Children's Hospital.

Then it hit him—Robert Wyatt. The man was a doctor and the scion of the Wyatt Pharmaceuticals empire. Even if Wyatt didn't treat children—Eric wanted to think the man was a surgeon?—he'd be able to recommend the best for Eddy.

Normally Eric would never call in this favor. He had a friendly rivalry with Marcus Warren—but there was nothing friendly about his rivalry with Wyatt. The only reason the two men hadn't come to blows was that they were in different industries and even then, there'd been that one time…

No, he absolutely shouldn't call in this favor. But then Sofia looked up at him, tears in her eyes and he knew he had to. Eric would do anything he could to make Eddy better—even bring in Wyatt.

"I'll make some calls," he said. Wyatt wouldn't exactly jump at the chance to help Eric out, but frankly, he wasn't going to take no for an answer. The man owed him.

Sofia nodded tearfully and made a visible effort to pull herself together. Just then, the elevator slowed and the doors opened. "Let's go," she said, her jaw set.

They all but ran to their rooms. It took less than five minutes for them to grab their things and then they were running for the elevator again. Neither of them wasted time changing out of their party clothes. Eric stopped shoving his clothes into his bag only long enough to call down to the front desk and tell them to have a car ready to leave for the airport immediately. Any car would do.

He had to get Sofia to her son. Now.

Fourteen

Sofia hadn't noticed the landing. She couldn't have said if it was rough or smooth or perfect or a near-disaster. All she could think about was her children.

"Well?" Eric said when she hung up with her mom.

Sofia took a steadying breath, but it didn't steady anything. Eric's driver whipped the car around corners and ran red lights in true Chicago fashion and not even the seat belts could keep her from sliding all over the place. "She's home with Addy. She said Addy's drinking fluids from a bottle, which is good. She hasn't thrown up in two hours."

"Good," Eric said encouragingly, rubbing his thumb along the side of her hand. He hadn't let go of her since…well, since they'd gotten into the elevator to leave the hotel. She might not remember much about the flight or the middle-of-the-night landing, but she knew that Eric had been there.

Like he was right now. "And your dad's still at the hospital with Eddy?"

She nodded, her head feeling like lead. It was three in the morning and panic was exhausting. If it weren't for Eric, she had no idea how she would have made it.

"We're almost there," he said, all reassuring confidence. God, how she wished she could be reassured right now.

But she couldn't. All she could do was stare out the windows as familiar Chicago streets whipped by.

If she hadn't gone to St. Louis, then she would've been there when her babies got sick. She could've comforted them—and gotten them to the doctor sooner, at the very least. Her parents generally refused to go to the doctor unless things were dire because they didn't want to waste money on something like a cold.

She hadn't explained that to Eric because she wasn't sure he'd understand. But the fact that her parents had decided to take Eddy to the emergency room terrified Sofia because it meant something was really wrong with her baby.

God, she should have been here for her children. And instead, what had she been doing?

Sleeping with Eric.

For the first time since David's death, she had been a little bit selfish. She'd put herself first instead of putting her children first. And now?

Now she was racing to a hospital, hoping like hell she wasn't too late.

She was going to be ill. That's all there was to it. Because this was too familiar, this late-night mad dash to the hospital, hoping that she'd get there in time. Hoping no one would die.

"I found David," she heard herself say.

She didn't want to relive the worst day of her life, but the horrifying thought that it might not have been the worst day had her talking. "He got up. In the middle of the night. He'd had a headache all afternoon and it was getting worse, so he was going to take something. I was so pregnant I couldn't sleep so when he didn't come back to bed, I went looking for him. He was crumpled in the middle of the kitchen floor."

Eric lifted her hand to his mouth. "What happened?"

"They said it was an aneurysm. He…" Her breath caught in her throat. Would this ever get easier? "He was gone by the time they got him to the hospital. It was the worst day of my life."

"Oh, babe." Undoing his seat belt, Eric scooted over to her and wrapped his arms around her. "This isn't the same. Eddy's sick but he's not going to die. Not if I have anything to say about it."

"You don't," she said, willing herself to be numb. She couldn't take any more pain. *Please*, she thought, *please don't let* this *be the worst day of my life.* "No one does."

"Sofia." His tone was more commanding now and, when he cupped her cheek in the palm of his hand, she had no choice but to look him in the eye. Even in the dark car, she could see a fierceness to him that she hadn't seen before. "This isn't your fault."

Of course she knew that. But her eyes watered anyway as she said, "I should have been here, Eric. I should have been with my kids when they were sick instead…"

Instead of being with you.

She didn't say it out loud.

She didn't have to.

Something in Eric's eyes shifted and he looked like

he might cry. Which was ridiculous. Why would he be upset over a sick kid? She was overreacting, of course. Mom guilt was a thing.

But Eric had no claims to her or her kids. They were friends, yeah—friends with some benefits, at least. She'd pulled him away from a huge business deal, though. She was putting his business at risk. And for what?

Before she could finish that thought, the car came to a screeching halt. Eric pulled away from her as she looked dumbly out the window. They were in front of the hospital.

"Let's go."

He helped her out of the car and then held on to her hand as they ran inside. "Which floor?"

"Third."

When the elevator doors closed behind them, Eric turned to her and cupped her face. "Take a deep breath, Sofia," he said, his voice somewhere between soothing and commanding. Eric stroked her cheeks with his thumb. "In and out. Panic is contagious and we don't want to upset him, do we?"

Her lungs—she wasn't sure they'd worked right in hours. But she forced herself to breathe. It was a struggle, but Eric was right. If she rolled into that room hysterical and sobbing, it would only agitate Eddy. "I'm so sorry about the deal."

This was exactly what she'd been afraid of—somehow, she'd ruin the deal and show him why it was a mistake to pretend she fit by his side.

God, what a mess.

"Sofia," he said, laughter in his voice. "How could you think the deal means anything to me when you need me? When Eddy needs me? You and your children are so much more to me than that."

Sofia's breath caught in her throat. In any other circumstances, that would have been a statement so romantic it was practically a declaration. She mentally shook her head, though. He was just trying to make her feel better. Lord knew she needed all the help she could get right now.

The elevator dinged and they were on the pediatric floor. It took some doing but they found the right room and there was her father, sitting in the chair, looking tired and old. "Sofia," he said, coming to his feet and pulling her into a hug that threatened to undo her all over again. "Everything is fine. He's responding well but they're keeping him sedated so he doesn't pull out the IV. And there can only be one..."

She didn't hear what her father was saying as she collapsed in the chair next to Eddy's bed. The lump in her throat was huge and she was having trouble breathing again.

"There's my serious little man," Eric said, stepping around her. She saw him pull the blanket up and realized that he was covering the IV port in Eddy's arm so she wouldn't have to see it. Then she watched him smooth her baby's hair away from his tiny little face. Even though he was unconscious, Eddy's lips twitched into something that looked so much like a smile that it almost broke her heart.

Eric looked at her and she remembered she was supposed to be breathing. She held Eddy's little hand in hers and said, "Mommy's here, baby. Sorry it took so long, but I'm here now and you are doing such a good job."

She was aware of Eric squeezing her shoulder, aware that her father was saying something to her. She nodded, even though she didn't catch what he'd said. The room got quiet, except for the beeping of the machines and the roaring sound of her guilt.

Time lost all meaning as she watched his little chest rise and fall. Her son wore nothing but a diaper and he looked so small. So helpless.

She should have been here for him, not in Eric's bed. She'd let her baby down and for what? If something happened to Eddy, she didn't know how she'd ever forgive herself.

"Good morning," a deep male voice rumbled from the doorway. "Ms. Bingham, correct?"

Sofia startled and hurriedly wiped tears away from her face. When she looked at the doctor, she startled again. "Wyatt? Robert Wyatt?"

Because it sure as hell looked like the boy who'd tried to cop a feel twenty years ago—except all grown up. The man before her was tall and broad, with dashing dark hair and bright blue eyes.

And a white lab coat with a stethoscope hanging out of his pocket.

What was going on?

"Dr. Wyatt, actually. Do I know you?" he said, staring at her. "Wait…"

She scrubbed at her face. How could this day get any stranger? The last person she wanted to see was Robert Wyatt—especially when she was a mess. "I'm sorry. I'm Sofia. I was a friend of Eric's, back when we were kids."

His eyes bulged in his head. "You're the maid's daughter, right?"

Embarrassment flashed down the back of her neck.

Even after all this time, she was still the maid's daughter. This weekend it'd been fun to pretend she could live in Eric's world, but it was just that—pretend. Eric might not realize the truth but everyone else? All the other people who fit naturally into his world?

She'd always be *just* the maid's daughter. She'd be a liability to him.

She eyed Wyatt, wondering if she should kick him again. But Wyatt beat her to the punch. "I owe you an apology, then."

She was so surprised at that statement that all she could do was blink. "What?"

And Wyatt blushed. He blushed! Because of her! What the hell was going on? "Look, I know it was a long time ago and we were just kids and you probably don't even remember it—"

"I remember you cornered me," she said quietly.

He looked pained. "Like I said, I owe you an apology. What I did was wrong. I shouldn't have tried to grab you. Although," he added, shooting her a sheepish smile, "if I recall correctly, you got your revenge."

This was the weirdest conversation she'd ever had. "This is all very well and good, but why are you here?" Because she didn't want to rehash old memories with a boy she'd never liked. She just wanted her son to get better.

He looked at her in surprise. "Jenner called me. He said a friend's baby was sick and he asked me to check things over. I just didn't realize you were the friend in question." As he spoke, he headed toward the computer terminal and logged in.

"Excuse me," she said again, her head feeling heavy. "But are you even qualified to be in this room?"

"Hmm," he said, looking over the file. Then he answered her question. "In addition to Wyatt Pharmaceuticals, I'm a pediatric surgeon. That's why Jenner called me. Well," he added, shooting a quick smile in her direction, "that and I owed him one. Or, more specifically, I owed you one, so I guess I still owe him one." He chuckled. Sofia blinked, trying to follow that train of thought. Nope. She was still at the station.

"Now, about your son. Has anyone talked to you yet?" Wyatt asked. She shook her head slowly. "There has been a particularly nasty strain of the stomach flu going around. It hits hard but doesn't last long. He's responding well to treatment." He moved to Eddy's bedside, lightly touching his little body. "He's going to be fine," Wyatt said sympathetically. "There wasn't anything anyone could have done differently."

Now that was exactly the sort of bull line that was condescending and irritating. Of course she could have done things differently! She could have stayed home and taken care of her kids like she was supposed to and, in the process, not doomed Eric's deal! She could have made sure that things hadn't gotten to the point where *Wyatt* was offering her false platitudes of comfort!

"I never liked you," she blurted out and then, mortified, she added, "I'm sorry. I haven't slept and I'm very worried."

Wyatt snorted. He didn't even look offended. "I had that coming. But you don't have to like me. You just have to trust me when I say that your son is going to make a full and—knowing kids—*fast* recovery. I'll confer with the resident on duty before I leave but I'd be willing to bet he goes home tomorrow."

Sofia tried to say something, but her words got

blocked up in her throat as she stared down at Eddy. *Please, please let Wyatt be right.*

"Thank you for coming," she finally got out. "I appreciate it."

Wyatt didn't reply for a long moment, which made her look up at him. "Thank you for accepting my apology. I must say, Jenner doesn't call in favors for just anyone." His smile warmed. "But I can see why he did. Take care, Sofia."

And just like that, he was gone.

Sofia sat there in a state of shock for a long time. Alone. What the heck had Wyatt meant when he'd said he could see why Eric had called in a favor?

She wished Eric were here. She wanted him right then. He had risked so much for her. It didn't make any sense because he was a billionaire and powerful and sexy and freaking great in bed and wonderful with her kids and apparently stupid enough to put huge deals in danger just for...

For *her*?

Idiot man.

She wanted to apologize for costing him the deal and making him waste his favors on her but she also wanted to bury her face against his chest and have him tell her it would be all right.

Hell, she didn't know what she wanted. Not anymore. She'd gone into this wanting a good job to take care of her family. Nothing more.

But even that was a lie. Because she could have applied for any number of jobs. Instead, she'd shot for the moon. And why?

Because of Eric. Because she'd wanted something more. And for a glorious day and a half, she'd had it.

He'd made her feel things, *want* things that she'd forgotten she'd even dreamed of. Love. Satisfaction.

Happiness.

For the first time since her husband had died, Sofia had dared to be a little selfish. And what had it gotten her?

Eddy was hooked up to an IV in the hospital. Addy was also sick at home and Sofia couldn't even be there for her daughter because she was with Eddy. She might have done permanent damage to Eric's business.

And Eric wasn't here. Sofia wasn't sure she'd ever felt so alone.

Where was he?

Fifteen

By the time Eddy woke up, hungry and cranky and so perfectly normal that Sofia could barely hold it together, her mom had shown up at the hospital. Sofia did manage to ask how Addy was doing, to which her mother replied, "Much better. She's been sleeping and—" but that was when the nurse and the doctor came in and began unhooking Eddy from his IV and Sofia didn't get to finish her conversation with her mother.

She knew she looked like hell and felt worse. She'd managed to snatch a few hours of broken rest after Wyatt's mysterious appearance, but nobody slept well in a hospital, least of all a worried mother.

By the time Sofia and Mom left with Eddy, it was two in the afternoon and Sofia was still wearing the same pair of shapewear she'd had on for the last thirty-some-odd hours. Her dress was no longer pretty but wilted and wrinkled, just like Sofia.

The funny thing was that they didn't take a cab home. Eric's car and driver were waiting for them, complete with a car seat for Eddy in the back. It was the sort of thoughtful gesture that made Sofia realize she couldn't be upset with Eric. He might have disappeared at some point in the middle of the night, but it was thoughtful of him to send the car. Besides, it wasn't like she expected him to hang out in the hospital waiting room. There hadn't been space for him in Eddy's small room and he wasn't the boy's father.

She had no idea what was going to happen at work tomorrow. Or even if she was going to work tomorrow. How was she supposed to do her job now that she and Eric had fallen into bed together? Would she even be able to walk into his office without thinking of him moving over her? Or would he conveniently "find" another job for her, one that removed her from the office, like he'd done for the last employee who'd tried to seduce him? And sleeping with him didn't even count the damage she might have done to his deal. If he lost the St. Louis development, would he blame her? Her stomach turned at the thought.

It'd been a mistake, she'd realized at some point in the middle of the night. She never should've mixed business and pleasure. It had been a mistake to leave her children for the weekend and that mistake had been compounded by sleeping with Eric.

He would be upset, she knew. But the plain truth was that she did not have the time or energy to start a relationship. Her children had to come first and Eric was a bachelor. A gorgeous billionaire bachelor. Frankly, she'd never figured out why he was interested in her in the first place. Not when he could have his pick of anyone—and they both knew he could. He was the very highest of the high and she was...

Well, she was more than just the maid's daughter. But she was a single mom, an office manager. She didn't fit with him. That's all there was to it.

Still, she thought as she sank back into the luxurious leather seating of Eric's car, being with Eric had been a gift in and of itself. A misguided one, but still. She had not died when her husband had. She had struggled and mourned, but she hadn't given up and she still had the capacity to open her heart to someone else. She still needed love. She still wanted to share her heart—and her body—with someone.

It just couldn't be Eric. A weekend's wardrobe of couture clothing didn't change the differences between them. Billionaire bachelors didn't get involved with widowed office managers with twin toddlers. They didn't deal with dirty diapers and barfing and the constant messes and sleepless nights. They jetted around the country with supermodels on their arms and partied with the rich and famous.

Her head hurt just thinking about Eric in the arms of another woman, which was, again, not logical. She couldn't have him and she had no right to be jealous of someone else having him.

Eddy fussed mightily as they pulled up in front of the house and Sofia unbuckled him. She was suddenly desperate to see Addy. It wasn't fair to her daughter that she hadn't been able to get home and see her yet.

Sofia followed her mom inside, dragging hard. She needed to change and she couldn't remember the last time she ate something. But she had to see her baby girl first. "Addy? Honey, Mommy's home," she called out softly.

"She's in the living room," Mom said as she headed for the kitchen. "With—"

Sofia came to a stumbling halt as she turned the corner. Because Addy was, indeed, in the living room—fast asleep on Eric's chest. Eric was sprawled out on the ancient family couch. He'd lost both his jacket and his button-up shirt at some point and was wearing nothing but a T-shirt that, even at this distance, Sofia could see was stained. Addy had a blanket draped around her, and Eric was holding her, one hand under her bottom, the other across her back.

Oh, God. Had he been here with her daughter the entire night?

She must've gasped or something because just then, Eric's eyes fluttered open. He blinked and then focused on her. "Hey," he said, smiling sleepily. "You guys are home. That's wonderful. Addy and I have been holding down the couch for you."

And it wasn't fair, damn it all, that he was here with Addy while she had been at the hospital with Eddy. It wasn't fair that, even in a stained T-shirt, he was still the most handsome man she'd ever seen. And it wasn't fair that, just when she'd realized she could never be right for him, he went and made her fall in love with him all over again.

"How long have you been here?"

"What time is it?" he asked, stretching carefully so that he didn't jostle the baby girl.

"Two thirty." It was naptime, she realized. Eric and Addy had been napping together and it was so perfectly sweet it was going to break her heart.

He yawned. "I think I left the hospital a little before four? Addy was pretty fussy, but she seemed calmer when I held her, so I stayed. Sorry I didn't get back to check on you and Eddy. How are you doing, big guy?" he asked when Eddy swiveled his head around at the sound of his name.

At the same time, Addy jolted awake. She looked up and saw Sofia. Instantly, her lips began to quiver.

Eric sat up and kissed Addy's head and it wasn't fair because Sofia wanted him so much and it simply wouldn't work. There were reasons she couldn't have this. Good reasons. That she couldn't think of right now.

Eric stood and came toward her and her breath caught in her throat. "Trade you," he said, as Addy leaned toward Sofia and Eddy pitched toward Eric because even her son was happy to see him. Eric caught the little boy in his arms and Sofia knew she wasn't imagining that the man was happy to see her baby boy.

She caught Addy in her arms and hugged the little girl to her chest, trying to find her balance. But before that happened, Eric leaned over and kissed Sofia's forehead. "I'm so glad you're home, babe. I hated leaving you there, but I figured you'd want me to be with Addy."

"I..." She blinked at him. His jaw was scruffy and he was rumpled and he was still the sexiest man she'd ever seen.

"Listen," Eric said, his voice low as he rubbed Eddy's back. "I was thinking—your parents are great, but this is a super small house and the kids need room to grow. My dad was touring a condo on the Gold Coast that would be perfect for us."

"Us?" He hadn't said *us*, had he? No, she was just hearing things. She was tired and—

"Three thousand square feet, a great view of the lake—plenty of room for the kids. Closer to everything. And we could get a better couch," he joked, stretching like a cat.

"Eric…" Maybe she was still dreaming. She'd fallen asleep in the hospital and was hallucinating that a man like Eric Jenner had spent the last God-only-knew-how-many hours taking care of a sick baby.

And waiting on her. Waiting to—to what? To ask her to move in with him? Or just… "I can't afford a Gold Coast condo, Eric."

He had the nerve to snort in amusement. "I wouldn't expect you to split the cost with me, babe. It's a gift for you. For us."

There was that word again. *Us.* And Eric was saying it while soothing a clingy Eddy.

But Sofia was not feeling calm. "What are you talking about? Because it sounds like…" Like he wanted her to move her whole family in with him. How did that make any sense?

It didn't.

"Not today, of course," he said, completely oblivious to her confusion. "The condo needs to be remodeled. But I can buy it and when it's ready, we can move in together."

Her mouth flopped open. She wasn't dreaming this, was she? He was asking her to move in with him.

"I'd hope," he went on, stepping in closer and shifting so he could cup her cheek in his palm without disrupting Eddy, "that you'd consider getting married before that point, though. I'll take you any way I can get you, but if you'll have me, I'd consider it the greatest honor of my life if you'd marry me, Sofia. I promised I'd take care of you and I meant it. For the rest of our lives, let me take care of you."

His thumb stroked over her cheek and Addy sighed in what felt like happiness and Eddy smiled at her from where he was tucked against Eric's chest and Sofia almost, *almost* said yes. This was every fantasy come to life—a hot, rich, single billionaire who liked small children and was great in bed and was promising to give her the world on a silver platter.

But when she opened her mouth, *yes* wasn't what came out. Because she did love him and she did want him and her babies loved him…but how on earth could he think she could fit into his world?

How much would it cost him if she said yes? Not just this deal. There was always something with kids.

She couldn't do this to him. She couldn't saddle him with her life, her problems, couldn't expect him to step into the role of father to someone else's children.

Oh, this hurt. But it was the right thing to do. He'd see that soon enough.

"Eric, no."

Sixteen

Eric stared down in confusion at Sofia, who was clutching Addy to her chest as if the toddler was a shield. "No *what*?"

Because it seemed like there should be an additional thought there. No, she didn't like the Gold Coast. No, she didn't want to wait to get married.

Not *no thank you*. She couldn't mean that. He forged ahead. "We don't have to live on the Gold Coast. We can look around. I want you to be happy with whatever place we choose."

Her eyes bugged out of her head and she stepped away from him. Eric had no choice but to let his hand fall away. "Eric, *no*," she repeated with more force. "I can't marry you. What the hell—heck," she quickly corrected, glancing at her children, "are you even thinking, talking like this?"

He could understand that she was upset. It had been an upsetting couple of days. But this was different.

"I was thinking I care for you. And your children. I was thinking…" He swallowed nervously as her eyes opened even wider. "I was thinking we could be a family."

All the blood drained out of her face and he wasn't sure she was breathing. She took another jerky step away from him before he could wrap his free arm around her.

"I can't do this, Eric," she said, her voice breaking. "What happened this weekend… I can't. When they needed me I wasn't here. I was with you and it was fine when we were alone but I don't know how to live in your world and I don't want to damage your business and…"

"What are you talking about?"

She swallowed hard a couple of times, squeezing her eyes shut. That didn't stop the tears from trickling down her cheeks. "I can't be with you. I have to put my children first. Always."

He opened his mouth, closed it and then tried again. How did that make any sense? It didn't. He wasn't trying to get rid of her kids. He loved these babies. He wanted to give her children a father. He wanted to be her husband. "Babe, you're tired. You're upset. You're not thinking clearly right—"

He knew the moment the words left his mouth that they were wrong. Her eyes flashed with anger and she reached out and plucked Eddy from his chest. Even though he'd known the babies such a short time, Eric felt almost lost without a twin in his arms. "I *am* thinking clearly, Eric. What happened this weekend risked everything. I shouldn't have left my kids. I shouldn't have been with you. I shouldn't have been so stupid, so damned selfish."

"Sofia," he managed to get out. "Slow down. Kids get sick, don't they? And you didn't cost me a deal. I promise you—even if it falls through, it's not going to bankrupt me."

She stared at him and then barked out a bitter laugh. "No, of course not. Of course you could afford to lose a deal this huge. Don't you see, Eric? I don't fit in your world. How could I? I'm just the office manager. The maid's daughter. A widowed single mom. I'll never belong and every time you try to make me fit, something bad will happen." She choked out a rough sob. "And I can't let anything else bad happen. I couldn't take it if something bad happened to you."

Both babies began to cry and her parents appeared in the doorway behind her, looking frantic.

"Sofia," he said softly, holding up his hands in the universal sign of surrender. "You do fit. I thought this weekend proved that."

"Oh, please," she said and he honestly couldn't tell if she was being sarcastic or if she was begging him.

Timing was everything, however, and there was no mistaking that his timing sucked. She was still in her cocktail dress and she probably hadn't slept and she'd been in a state of constant panic for the last day. "We can talk about this after you've gotten some—"

But she cut him off. "No, Eric—we can't. I…" She swallowed, apparently realizing they had an audience. She turned and handed the fussing babies over to her folks. "Can you give us a minute?" When her parents didn't move except to exchange worried glances, Sofia added "Please?" with more force.

"We'll be in the kitchen if you need us," her father said. Then he shot a look that Eric hoped was encouraging over Sofia's head.

Sofia glared at Eric until her parents were gone. And all he could do was stare back at her in surprise. "Babe," he began again, but she cut him off.

"No, Eric. I don't know what you're thinking, but *no*."

"I care for you," he got out before she could launch into another denial. "That's what I'm thinking. And I thought that, after what we shared this weekend, you cared for me, too."

Her throat worked and he got the feeling she was trying not to cry. "Damn you," she whispered, her voice hoarse. "Of course I do. Of course I care for you."

"Then why won't you let me take care of you?"

"You really think it's that easy? That you just snap your fingers and the world falls all over itself to meet your high expectations?" She snapped for emphasis. "That I meet your high expectations? For God's sake, Eric—look at me! I live with my parents because I can barely function on my own! I'm struggling to put one foot in front of the other!" She choked on the words again, curling into herself.

It about broke his heart because she wouldn't see reason. How was he supposed to comfort her if she wouldn't even let him touch her?

"Sofia," he said quietly. "What did Wyatt say to you?" Because yeah, she'd been worried about his deal before he'd left her at the hospital—but she hadn't been this frantic. And Eddy was doing so much better—so where was the disconnect?

It had to be Wyatt. Damn that man.

"He didn't say anything, Eric—except to tell me that Eddy would be fine." Her eyes were shiny and her voice wobbled as she spoke. "But don't you see? You're a man who can fly me home at a moment's notice and call in favors from the heads of pharmaceutical companies and—"

"To make sure you're okay? And your kids are okay? You're damn right I'm going to do that—that and more," he cut in, trying not to yell. The maddening woman wasn't making any sense!

Which only made her look sadder. "But that's not my world, Eric."

"I don't care." Yeah, he was yelling. "I wouldn't care if you lived in a box! You're beautiful and intelligent and the bravest woman I've ever met! And I..." His throat caught but he pushed on. "You were my best friend when we were kids and that hasn't changed. I still love you—but now I love you more. And for the life of me, I can't figure out why that makes me the bad guy here!"

She began to shake and he tried to pull her into his arms and make sure she was all right. But she moved—away from him. "I think you need to leave."

"Babe," he said, his voice gruff. "It never mattered to me. How diffcrent our lives have been."

But again, she dodged his grasp, turning and all but fleeing from the room. "It matters," he heard her mutter. In seconds, she was gone.

He heard a door slam from somewhere deeper in the house and then her father was back, looking apologetic. "Eric, I am sorry. It's been a long weekend and she's upset and..."

"I know." Eric scrubbed at the back of his neck. "My

timing was crap. I was just so glad to see her and Eddy, you know?"

Emilio nodded. "I understand." He held out Eric's shirt and jacket. "I, ah, I do not think she will be in to-morrow."

The way the older man said it made Eric's stomach drop. "Of course not," he quickly agreed. "She's worn ragged and she'll want to make sure the kids are fully on the mend." He shrugged into his jacket. "But tell her I hope to see her on Tuesday, okay?"

Emilio nodded, but he didn't look convinced and Eric's stomach dropped another two notches.

He'd just found Sofia and her family.

He wasn't going to walk away from them all.

Sofia didn't come to work on Monday, which Eric expected. She also didn't show on Tuesday. "Her son was released from the hospital," he told Meryl and Steve when they came in to work on Tuesday. Sofia wasn't the only one who needed to recover from the weekend.

"Thank goodness for that," Steve said.

"Let us know if there's anything we can do to help," Meryl added.

But Eric just nodded and smiled and, when he got back to his desk, ordered two dozen roses delivered to Sofia's house.

She didn't come to work on Wednesday, either.

By Thursday, he was feeling frantic. Where was she? She hadn't quit. He was pretty sure he'd remember that. And it wasn't like Sofia to hide. Back when they'd been kids...

Eric slumped behind his desk. They weren't kids anymore. They couldn't go back to that easy friendship. He couldn't be just friends with her anymore. Or even friends with benefits.

He wanted to be with her through good and bad. He wanted to see her children grow up. He wanted children of his own. God, to see Sofia's body change and grow with his child—the longing was physically painful.

He wanted everything. With her—only with her—he could have it.

By God, he was Eric Jenner.

He was going to get it.

Seventeen

They didn't talk about the business trip. Or Eric. Or about the fact that Sofia hadn't gone back to work.

Suddenly, Sofia's household was quiet and tense, everyone walking around on eggshells. And, after Tuesday, they couldn't even hide behind the lie that it was because the twins were sick because they weren't. Dr. Robert Wyatt had been correct—Eddy and Addy bounced back as if they'd never been sick at all.

And Sofia couldn't even say she was moving through life in a fog—certainly not like she'd been after David died. She was tired, of course. It'd been a rough week. But sorrow wasn't the overarching emotion that kept her awake at night.

No, it was anger. Clear, bright anger that burned without flickering.

How dare Eric propose marriage just like *that*? What gave him the right to talk about love and marriage and condos, as if he could wave a magic wand and make everything perfect? Why couldn't he see that she didn't belong with him? All this talk of love was great but she wasn't a girl anymore. There was no avoiding the realities of her life. What would happen if she said yes? If she let herself get swept away? She'd spend the rest of her life trying to prove she belonged with him. Had she thought that dinner with the lieutenant governor or the cocktail party was draining? Ha! She'd have to achieve that level of acting every second of every day just to keep people like Dr. Robert Wyatt from sneering at her. And honestly, even if she did everything right and was the model wife—which wasn't going to happen in this life or the next—they'd still sneer.

The only person who didn't seem to realize this was Eric. Idiot man.

She got mad all over again every time she walked past the bouquet of flowers in the middle of the dining room table. Because those flowers were hard to miss. Two dozen of the biggest, reddest roses she'd ever seen—the house smelled like a florist's shop. It was ridiculous.

The anger burned for days.

She tried to forget it, though. Addy and Eddy were okay. Better than okay. They spent long afternoons at the park, the twins toddling all over. They didn't understand that the reason they got all this extra Mom time was that Sofia couldn't bring herself to go back to work. How was she supposed to face Eric?

When they made it home for lunch and then naptime, Sofia collapsed on the couch. She couldn't continue to ignore Eric in the hopes that he'd go away. The roses screamed loud and clear that they weren't done.

Five long days had passed since she'd brought Eddy home from the hospital and told Eric to leave. Five days since he'd told her he loved her and she'd—what? Told him it wouldn't work?

She was right. She lived in a cramped three-bedroom house with her parents. She was sitting on the same sofa she'd sat on her entire life. She didn't fit with him. In all honesty, she'd barely fit with David.

David hadn't died on purpose. Just like Miss Rita hadn't gotten the kids sick on purpose. Bad things happened.

She just wanted bad things to stop happening to *her*.

She dropped her head into her hands. Eric had been a good thing. A wonderful, amazing, fun thing. He'd made her feel safe and happy and…

And loved.

He'd made love to her and protected her and she…

God, she'd fallen completely in love with him. She'd always cared for him—but the dratted man was right. They weren't kids anymore and what she felt for him wasn't anything so simple as friendship.

And he'd said he loved her, too. He loved her and she loved him and he wanted to marry her and she'd—what? Said *no*?

That was the whole problem, wasn't it?

There was a quiet knock on the front door, which made Sofia startle. She threw herself off the couch before the visitor could ring the doorbell and wake up the twins.

She gasped when she looked through the glass, because there was Eric. Her first thought was, *Shouldn't he be on the water?* It was a beautiful Friday afternoon, after all.

She opened the door cautiously. "Eric? What are you doing here?"

The look of relief on his face when he saw her almost took her breath away. "Sofia," he said and just the sound of her name on his lips was almost enough to undo her. "I need to talk to you."

"Why?"

He gave her a look, one so familiar and comfortable that she smiled in spite of herself. "You know, when we were kids and we'd have a fight, your mom always had us apologize and make up."

"True." They hadn't argued much, but all children bickered. "But we're not kids anymore."

"No, we're not."

"Is that Eric?" Mom appeared behind Sofia, all but shoving her out of the house. "I'll keep an eye on the kids. Go on, now." The way she said it made Sofia instantly suspicious.

"What's going on?" But that was as far as she got before Mom shoved Sofia's purse into her hands and closed the door behind her. Sofia turned to glare at Eric, who didn't even have the decency to look guilty. "What did you do?"

"Your mom wants us to make up," he said, tucking her hand into the crook of his arm and leading her down the steps. His car was waiting. "You know, it's true— the more things change, the more they stay the same."

She came to a stop. "Eric..."

"I hope you've gotten some rest," he went on, as if small talk was why he was here when they both knew it wasn't. "I've been worried sick about you."

"You can't say things like that," she scolded gently.

But even as she said it, her heart felt like it was going to break again.

He'd been worried about her. He'd done everything in his power to take care of her babies. He'd said he loved her.

And, fool that she was, she loved him back. Hopelessly.

"Listen, you stubborn woman," he began, but he was smiling as he said it.

"Great start, that," she muttered.

He cut her a look and she closed her mouth. "I don't think we can be friends anymore."

Her breath froze in her lungs, despite the summer heat. "What?" Because of all the things she'd thought he might say right then, that hadn't even made the list.

"Because I wasn't a very good friend," he went on. "I guess I was an out-of-sight, out-of-mind person. I left home and grew up and wasn't there for you, good times or bad."

She suddenly had to swallow several times. "Don't do this, Eric. It won't end well."

"Don't do what? Tell you I love you? Ask you to marry me again? Try to do it better than I did last time, when we were both exhausted and frantic?"

"You can't be with me," she reminded him.

"I'm Eric Jenner," he said, sounding cocky and imperious. "I can do whatever the hell I want because who's going to stop me? If I want to spend every afternoon aboard my boat, who'll say no? If I want to build luxury condos on the moon, all I have to do is snap my fingers and the best, brightest minds will make it happen. If I want to walk around in a duck outfit—"

"A duck outfit?" she gasped.

"I'd set off a new feathered fashion craze," he went on, ignoring her. "And if I want to fall in love with my office manager and her twin babies, who'd dare tell me it's a bad idea? You? I hope not, Sofia. Because you're smarter than that."

Oh, Lord. He wasn't really going to do this on the sidewalk, was he? "But others will."

He had the nerve to look dangerous. And dang it all if it didn't send a thrill down her spine. "I can't stop them," he said, his voice low. Another part of her heart broke. "But if anyone dares insult you? How can you think that I'd care what people like Wyatt would say? How could you think that I'd care what anyone but you and I think?"

"But our lives are so different…" But even to her own ears, that sounded weak.

"Do you know why we were friends?" Oh, he looked so dangerous right now. "Because you treated me like any other kid. And I hope I did the same to you. You were never just the maid's daughter to me, babe. You were always Sofia. And I hope I was never just a rich boy to you. I…" He swallowed, looking suddenly nervous. "I was Eric to you. Wasn't I?"

"Of course you were—are," she sobbed. "But I can't ask this of you, Eric. My kids and I are not your responsibility."

"You're not asking—I am." He pressed a kiss to her forehead and despite everything, she felt it all the way down to her toes. "Aren't you listening? I never do anything I don't want to. I'm here with you, babe. I was here last week and I'll be here next week. You mean too much to me for one bad moment to make me walk away from you."

He was making too much sense. Way, way too much sense. There were objections, she knew there were. But darned if she could remember them right now. "But…"

"And I'm not trying to replace David," he said. "He'll always be a part of you and he'll always be a part of the twins. But you didn't die with him, Sofia. And I believe, deep in my heart, that he wouldn't want you to face raising those children by yourself." Her mouth opened to reply, but he cut her off. "Nothing against your parents, babe. They love you and the twins and they're wonderful people. But they can't be a father to your children." His voice dropped and he took a step closer to her. "They can't be a husband to you."

"That was low," she choked out, losing the battle to her tears. She didn't want to cry because if she started, she wasn't sure she'd be able to stop. Because the infuriating man was right. David wouldn't have wanted Sofia to feel like she was completely alone right now.

He would have wanted her to smile again.

Eric pulled her into his arms and it was as if a weight was lifted off her chest. For the first time in days, she could breathe again. "Then quit making me fight dirty and just accept that I'm not going anywhere." He stroked her hair as he said it and damn it, she was comforted. "I missed you," he said into her hair. "You didn't come to work this week."

"I needed a few days," she admitted. "So much happened so quickly and I just…" She hadn't been able to deal with it.

"I know. And I made it worse, didn't I? I sprung the idea of the condo and living together on you and you…"

She choked out a little laugh. "And I felt horribly guilty. I still do."

That got him to lean back. "Guilty? Why?"

"My babies were sick and I wasn't there for them. I was with…" She swallowed hard. "I was with you."

He stared down at her in surprise. "But they were with your parents. It's not like you left them all alone."

She had no idea how she was even supposed to explain mommy guilt to him. "But I have to focus on them. I… I love you, too. But I have to put them first, don't you see?"

Hope flared in his eyes but it quickly turned into something fiercer. "So you're going to what—martyr yourself for them?"

"No, of course not." But even as she said it, she wondered if maybe there wasn't a little truth to that. "But they need me. They're only babies, Eric. I'm all they've got."

He took a step away from her and then spun to fix her with a glare. "Get in the car."

"What?"

"I have to tell you something and I'd rather not do it in public." He opened the car door and motioned. "In, Sofia."

Feeling nervous, she climbed in. He slid in after her and slammed the door. For a tense moment, they sat there. Then he pressed a button and said, "Drive."

Instantly, the car began to move. "Eric?"

"My fiancée was three months pregnant with another man's baby," he blurted out. "When she stood me up. We hadn't had sex in six months because she said it would make our wedding night more 'special' and you know what? I didn't fight for her. I let her slip away."

Sofia gasped and covered her mouth with her hand. "And the baby…"

"Paternity tests confirmed it—not mine. Do you want to know what's funny, Sofia? I don't miss Prudence at all. Not the sex, not the silence that always existed between us, not her. But when I found out about the baby…"

He stared out the window. "I was ready and willing to fight for that baby. But he wasn't mine and Prudence married his father less than two weeks after she left me."

"Eric, I had no idea."

"No one does, outside of Prudence's family and the private investigators. So far, I've kept it quiet."

She reached over and wrapped her fingers around his. "I'm sorry."

"I only tell you this now because I want you to understand—when I say I love your kids, I don't just mean in that generic, all-babies-are-cute kind of way." He took a deep breath and turned wet eyes in her direction. "I can buy anything, do anything I want."

"You mentioned a duck costume," she murmured.

"Anything," he repeated with more force. "Except I can't buy the love of a good woman and a family. I didn't mourn losing Prudence because she was never mine to lose. But I mourned that little boy. I had no idea how much I wanted to be a father until I thought I might be one. That was taken away from me, too. Then you showed up, an old friend who was much too easy to love, with a pair of toddlers who needed a father and…"

He blinked hard and Sofia's eyes watered. "I'm not trying to replace David, Sofia. But you're more than I'd ever thought I'd find because I don't just love you. You're my friend. You're my everything."

Oh, hell. How was she supposed to argue with that?

"You've given me a reason to smile again," she told him through her tears. "I didn't know I could still smile for myself. But I didn't want you to think that the only reason I took the job or the clothes or the weekend together was because I was trying to snag you. I didn't want you to think I was like that."

He laughed. "The more things change, Sofia, the more they stay the same and you were never like that. You've always fit with me. It never mattered who you were when we were kids—you were just my friend. It's the same now, except that I love you. None of the other stuff matters except for this." He took both of her hands in his. "Marry me, babe. Let me be your family. And when you stumble, let me be there to make sure you don't fall again."

"You're sure it can work?" But even as she asked the question, she knew she was being ridiculous.

"I'm Eric Jenner," he reminded her, as if she could forget. "I can make anything work. Even twin toddlers."

She laughed and threw her arms around him. "Yes. You make me happy. You make me smile," she told him. And she'd missed smiling.

"Babe, I'm going to make you smile every day for the rest of our lives."

"Promise?"

He lowered his mouth to hers. "Oh, yeah—that's a promise I'm looking forward to keeping."

Epilogue

"**O**n three," Eric said, treading water. The lake was cool and crisp—which, given that the temperature was close to one hundred, was a welcome relief.

"One," Eddy Jenner said in a very serious tone. Eric couldn't fight the smile as he held up his fingers to count off. "Two…three!" And then the boy launched himself into the air.

Eric hurriedly paddled backward, barely getting his arms up in time to catch Eddy before they both plunged under the surface of the lake. When they resurfaced seconds later, Eddy was squealing with delight and Eric was laughing.

"My turn, Daddy—my turn!" Addy insisted, stamping her little foot on the deck of his boat. Both of the kids wore wet suits with built-in floaties and what wasn't covered by fabric was slathered with the highest SPF known to womankind.

Sofia insisted and who was Eric to say no to his wife? Besides, it was no hardship to have her rub sunscreen all over his back. And chest. And arms. Lord knew he enjoyed returning the favor. Sun protection was *sexy*.

Eric pushed Eddy back toward the boat and swam alongside him to make sure that the three-year-old wasn't struggling, but he didn't need to worry. The kids took to water like ducks. When they were in the pool at his parents' house, Eric didn't even put them in floaties. He just made sure they stayed in the shallow end, where he could get to them at all times.

Sofia was waiting for Eddy by the ladder. "You're going to be doing this all day long, you know that?" she asked Eric with that smile he loved.

"If you want a turn, I'll catch you, babe," he said, waggling his eyebrows at her.

She laughed and then leaned forward suggestively, her breasts practically spilling out of the bikini top. "You can catch me later."

Eric flopped back in the water, pretending to faint. She killed him every single day. It was a crime, how good his wife looked in that bikini. Especially now that she was four months pregnant. While she always looked good in a bikini—red, forever red—the way her body had changed so far was nothing short of a revelation. And it went far beyond her stunning breasts. He found the gentle swell of her stomach to be unbelievably erotic. After a rough three months, Sofia had promised him that the second trimester was the fun one and they were just getting started.

She was a wonder, his Sofia.

"Daddy!" Addy said, scolding his lack of attention. Sofia winked at him as Addy said, "Catch me!"

"Count to three," he told his daughter.

She pushed her hair out of her face and counted very solemnly before screaming her way out onto the water. Eric caught her and they laughed as they bobbed together.

As he helped Addy back to the ladder, Eric looked up at his wife and smiled again. This was his life now. He loved his wife. What he and Sofia had was a bright, passionate love that got stronger over time, not weaker. It was no joke to say that she was his best friend and every day, he worked hard making sure he was her best friend, too.

In another hour, the twins would be worn out from all of this jumping. He and Sofia would put them down for a nap in their room in the yacht and then he and his wife would steal half an hour to themselves in their own cabin. Warm from the sun and relaxed by the water, Eric was never happier than when he was making love to his wife on this boat. Then, she would rest while he piloted them back to the pier. Tonight, they'd have dinner at his parents' house. Sofia's parents were coming, too—one big happy family.

Finally, he had everything he wanted. And the more things changed—the twins growing up, the new baby, maybe a bigger boat—the more they would stay the same.

Sofia had his heart and he had hers.

He'd earned the one thing money couldn't buy.

* * * * *

THE BOSS'S
SURPRISE SON

TERESA CARPENTER

For my beautiful niece Erika Beasley and
her handsome groom, Aaron Miller.
Congratulations, Mr. and Mrs. Miller.
Welcome to the family, Aaron.

CHAPTER ONE

RICK SULLIVAN left his office on the hunt for food. He'd been wrapped up in meetings with his department managers all morning going over end-of-year goals. They looked as if they would exceed projected sales. A good thing as he hoped to take Sullivans' Jewels into the international market next year to celebrate their centennial.

Not the best timing for his personal assistant to be out for knee surgery.

He noticed with relief that his new assistant Savannah Jones wasn't at her desk and moved over to flip the hourglass she kept on the corner. One end was white marble, the other black, and she'd asked him to place it black-side-up whenever he left the building. Apparently it was a pressing question when people saw his door was open.

When he got closer he saw he'd been both right and wrong. Ms. Jones wasn't *at* her desk, she was *under* it.

He slowly shook his head. He had two weaknesses: chocolate and his paternal grandmother. Both had the potential to get him in trouble, but where he could muster the discipline to say no to chocolate chip cookies, he'd never mastered the art of denying Gram's pleading blue eyes.

Which explained his current view of his new assistant's backside as she delved under her desk.

Temporary assistant, he reminded himself. His regular assistant, the highly efficient Miss Molly Green would be back in six months, two weeks, five days and—he glanced at his watch—three hours and forty-five minutes.

Damn right he was counting. And it was all Gram's fault. She'd convinced him to hire Ms. Jones, a bit of fluff with little practical work experience and a penchant for chatter. Gram knew the Jones family, and when Rick blew through three assistants in the first three weeks of Molly's leave, Gram took advantage of his guilt and frustration to refer her friend and to insist he keep Ms. Jones on until Molly's return.

Though Ms. Jones's head burrowed out of view, he had no problem recognizing the half on display. Her bent position caused the gray fabric of her pants to pull taut, intimately framing the lush jut of her derriere.

Suddenly warm, he shrugged out of his jacket and without conscious thought walked around the side of her desk to get a better view.

His cheeks heated when he realized what he'd done. Annoyed at himself and her, he snapped, "Ms. Jones, what do you think you're doing?"

She started and a muffled "Ouch!" followed the sound of her head hitting the underside of the desk.

"I'm...trying to..." She tugged on something out of sight, the motion causing her hips to wiggle enticingly. "...plug in my new electric stapler. But...the cord is... stuck."

More tugging, more wiggling, and he saw a bulky gray object shift on her desk.

Honestly, did he deserve this? It wasn't as if he expected his assistant to wait on him. He took care of his own coffee, dry cleaning and personal business. Were competent, efficient and prompt too much to ask for?

And okay, to be fair, in the four weeks she'd been here Ms. Jones had shown she understood instructions and could successfully proof her own work, which was better than the misfits he'd gone through in the first three weeks. But her methods were all over the place, much like her shifting hips.

"Ms. Jones, surely you could have called maintenance to handle this for you?" he asked impatiently.

"Gracious, I'm not going to call maintenance just for a plug-in. The cord is just a little short, that's all. I'll be finished here in a moment. Did you need something?"

Wiggle, bend, wiggle.

Rick groaned as heat flared through him once again, and he almost strangled on his own breath.

Did he need something? Was she kidding? He'd be lucky to remember his own name at the moment. He should walk away, just end the torment. Yet, everything in him denied him the option of leaving her vulnerable to another man's approach. He glanced around sharply to make sure no male neared the vicinity. They were alone—both a blessing and a curse.

"Ms. Jones, I insist you remove yourself from under there this instant," he bit out.

"I've almost got it, but it's stuck. Can you push the cord through from that side?" she asked.

Anything to bring this scene to a close. He moved behind the desk and bent forward to shove the electric stapler closer to the opening for cords. Unfortunately the hole was full and the cord buckled up instead of dropping down.

He hesitated. He'd have to step between her legs to get the leverage he needed and somehow that seemed too intimate.

"Rick?"

"Just a blasted minute. You have too many cords in here." Manning up, he carefully placed his foot in the narrow opening between her shins and leaned over her to reach the tangle of cords. He shoved at the stubborn cord and his weight shifted, bringing his knee in contact with the soft cushion of her butt.

"Aha!" she exclaimed.

He nearly jumped out of his skin in his hurry to retreat to safety.

"That did it." Triumph rang in her voice.

He kept his gaze carefully plastered to her screen saver, a picture of her with her brother and sister, as she backed out and dusted off her hands.

"Thanks for the help." Her leaf-green eyes smiled as she ran a hand down the length of her mahogany ponytail to check it was smooth. "What can I do for you?"

His mind went blank. Why had he stopped at her desk?

"You can stay out from under your desk. We have maintenance on site for a reason. Next time use them," he ordered. Turning on his heel, he returned to his office.

His stomach growled as he sat behind his desk, reminding him of his original mission. He ignored it. He'd rather go hungry than wander out that door again.

The corner of Savannah Jones's lip curled upward in perplexed amusement as she watched her boss disappear into his office. What had that been about? He'd never even said what he wanted.

And for the first time the look in his piercing blue eyes sent a tingle zinging down her spine.

She shook it off and took her seat.

His high-handed attitude was nothing new. Nor was his gruffness—truly, the man could teach grim to the reaper—but his agitation and the fact he couldn't hold her gaze was.

Hmm. It was almost as if she'd made him nervous.

How interesting.

At six-one with thick dark hair, broad shoulders, narrow hips and piercing blue eyes Rick Sullivan had it all over Dr. McDreamy. And, oh, Savannah had it bad for Dr. McDreamy.

Wait. Wait. Wait. What was she thinking?

Rick made her tingle? She made him nervous? Neither emotion belonged in the workplace. And neither was good when there was no future for them except as colleagues.

She loved her new job, the challenge, the diversity, the responsibility. Executive assistant to the CEO of Sullivans' Jewels, a family-owned jewelry chain, was more than she'd ever dreamed of. More than she'd ever dared to hope for. Especially with her varied work history, from waitress to floral delivery to two years as a temp in corporate San Diego, she felt like she'd done it all.

She was determined to do a great job. She owed the Sullivans so much, especially Mrs. Sullivan, Rick's grandmother, not only for this opportunity but also for all they'd done for her sister. The Sullivan family donated two five-thousand-dollar scholarships a year to Paradise Pines students for their college education, renewable each year if the students maintained certain grade levels and continued to give back to the Paradise Pines community.

Savannah's sister, Claudia, had benefited from their generosity for the past four years. She'd be graduating with honors later this year.

Savannah hadn't gone to college, and she'd been well into her twenties before she got her first job. Her high-school years had been spent caring for her mom. She'd been seventeen when the cancer eventually took her mom, and her dad had just disappeared into his work, leaving Savannah to raise her younger brother and sister.

So, yeah, she'd already done the family thing, but now Daniel was a cop in La Mesa with a beautiful wife and daughter and Claudia was about to graduate college. It was time for Savannah to think about her own career. She was done playing around, hopping from job to job. This might not be teaching, which she'd dreamed of doing long ago, but it was a career to be proud of, and she wasn't going to screw it up.

Even if Rick didn't have an aversion to a workplace romance—and he'd made it more than clear he did— she had an aversion to workaholics. Been there. Done that.

Never again.

Rick worked, worked and worked some more. He was an expert at ignoring personal interaction on the job, to the point where he was considered positively antisocial by most of the staff.

He wasn't much of a talker, and, the Lord help her, she felt compelled to fill the quiet. So, while he read over reports and letters, she filled him in on all the office gossip. Nothing harmful, just birthdays, anniversaries, family events and such.

He probably didn't even hear her, though occasionally he'd hold up a finger for silence. So maybe he took in more than she thought.

Taking her seat, she noticed he'd flipped the hour-glass black-side-up, which meant he'd been headed out of the office. She didn't know of any appointments, but he'd been tied up with his managers all day so he'd probably been heading for some lunch.

So why had he retreated to his office instead?

Hmm. Perhaps because she'd made him nervous?

With a grin she reached for the phone to order him a sandwich from a local deli that delivered.

The two of them might not have a future together, but it still felt good to send a man as hot and strong-willed as Rick Sullivan into an agitated retreat. Her self-esteem appreciated the boost.

After placing the order, she reached for her mirror and refreshed her lipstick, suddenly feeling very female and proud of it.

Being executive assistant to the president and CEO of Sullivans' Jewels demanded a professional appearance. Unfortunately, she'd spent too many years at home not worrying about her makeup or the need to tame her thick mass of hair.

Now a check in the morning and pop-up reminders in her email program kept her from becoming too frayed around the edges throughout the day.

Happily, she noted that there was nothing caught in her straight white teeth, which she considered one of her best features, thanks to Dr. Stevens and three years in braces, though she'd hated them when she was twelve, both Dr. Stevens and the braces.

Now she thanked the beauty gods for her straight teeth and plump lips, which she felt made up for her average features.

When the sandwich arrived, she knocked on Rick's

door and got a finger wave to enter. He eyed her suspiciously as she crossed the room. Tickled by his reaction, she gave him a huge smile as she set the bag on his desk, causing his eyes to narrow even more.

"I thought you might be hungry."

"Thanks," he muttered.

"No problem," she said cheerfully.

She didn't linger but turned to leave and, because a girl had to find her fun where she could, added a little wiggle to her walk.

A strange sound, kind of a muffled groan, followed her exit. With a wicked grin she settled behind her desk suddenly energized to tackle the afternoon.

The next morning Savannah entered the conference room for her first monthly sales meeting juggling two boxes, a cup of coffee, her notebook and a pile of copies.

Of course Rick already sat at the head of the table. He glanced up at her with a pained look as she dropped her load on the table.

"You're late, Ms. Jones. What is all that?"

"Copies of the reports you requested plus doughnuts and a few bran muffins for the healthy-minded." She set her work and coffee aside and opened one of the boxes. "I hope that's okay. You forgot to tell me if you wanted bagels or doughnuts for the meeting, and I have a Donut Stop near my place so I just ran through there."

"I didn't forget anything," he corrected her. "This is a meeting, not a social event."

"Oh." Savannah blinked at him. No food at a morning

meeting? The man was Scrooge. Seemed she couldn't do anything to please him. "I always thought it was a show of appreciation for valued employees." She set the box in the middle of the table toward the far end. "It'll be my treat today."

He scowled at that.

Undeterred—she'd learned while nursing her mother not to let someone else's mood bring her down—she opened the second box and pulled out napkins and plates, spacing them out over the table. And then she took the box to him, because he might be stiff, but she really did want to impress him and earn a permanent position in his company. "Would you like one?"

She expected him to refuse, but he surprised her by taking a chocolate cake doughnut and placing it on the plate she offered.

"Thank you."

"Doughnuts! Now you're talking." Rett Sullivan, Rick's twin and a co-owner of Sullivans' Jewels, along with their four brothers, walked through the door, snagging a cinnamon roll on the way to his seat next to Rick. "You should have done this years ago."

"You can thank Ms. Jones," Rick advised.

"Ms. Jones." Rett toasted her with his coffee mug. "Not only beautiful but sharp and generous, too. When I see you later, I'll have to thank you properly."

"I'm sure she got the message," Rick stated pointedly in a clear signal for his twin to desist.

In response, Rett winked at Savannah.

As identical twins, the two men obviously shared the

same height, same build, same coloring. But Rett carried his weight leaner, meaner, his hair longer. Vice President of Design and Purchasing, Rett spurned what he described as the boring, restrictive suits Rick wore, stating they stifled his creativity. Instead, he chose matching dress pants and shirts in solid colors and rich fabrics. Today he wore a dark chocolate brown. The chain of his St. Christopher medal gleamed gold against his neck.

He was a charming flirt, easy to be with and easy to resist. They'd become friends when she asked him to teach her how to work with precious gems to design a gift for her sister's college graduation.

Rick's scowl landed on her again, and she quickly reached for the stack of copies and began putting one set at each seat around the table.

The doughnuts were a big hit as sales managers and associates began to fill the room. There was friendly chatter as everyone helped themselves. When she regained her seat, she slid a sideways glance at Rick. He was watching those in the room as if seeing them for the first time.

She wondered if that was a good thing. He began the meeting promptly at eight-thirty and kept to the agenda, moving smoothly from topic to topic while encouraging input from everyone at the table. He had her taking notes, but she noticed he also jotted down items when someone made a good point.

At the end of the meeting the room quickly emptied out, except for Rick. Savannah began clearing the debris.

"Ms. Jones?" He waited until she glanced up to meet his gaze. "What do you have going on with Rett?"

Savannah groaned internally. Just great. Because of Rett's playful comments Rick now had the wrong impression about them. She could tell him about the lessons; they weren't a secret. But she wasn't entirely sure he'd approve or believe she didn't have a thing for his brother. So she decided to prevaricate.

Avoiding his gaze, she dumped a load of trash and then picked up the wastebasket and brought it back to the table to finish the cleanup.

"I don't have anything with him today, but you wanted me to sit in on the meeting for the security upgrade and that's tomorrow."

He blinked, and then crossed his arms over his chest. "I *meant* are you seeing him?"

"I see him every day." She smiled and blinked, playing confused.

Should she just tell him? After all, it wasn't the office romance he feared. No, best not open a can of worms. The lessons were important to her and she didn't want to mess things up.

What if he wanted to see her work as proof? With two weeks of lessons under her belt she was thrilled at how well she was doing, but she was still new at the craft and by no means ready to go public with her efforts. Especially not to a professional jeweler.

"It sounded like he expected to see you later. As if you had a date," he stated baldly.

"Gracious no. That's just Rett." She waved a careless

hand, her comment true, yet not an outright denial, a fact that didn't slip past Rick if his narrowed gaze was any indication. "He's a bit of a flirt, you know," she confided as if sharing a secret.

And then she just continued to smile and waited for him to move on.

And waited. He stood, hands in his pockets, staring at her.

"Or maybe I misunderstood," she said guilelessly. "Did you want me to find him and ask him something?"

"No. I—" He glanced at his watch, clearly still suspicious, but mindful of his schedule. "Never mind. Can you stop by the legal department on your way back to your desk? I want to know if we've received the signed contracts from Emerson for the international deal. We should have received them by now."

"Of course." Savannah dumped the last of the trash, glad to have avoided the confrontation. For now. He'd find out eventually. But she hoped to be indispensable by then.

Her lessons were important to her. But private. For years the classes she took at night and online had been her only freedom, her bid for independence from too much responsibility at home.

She still took courses that interested her or furthered her career. She just didn't talk about them much. Somehow, they'd always been too important to share. The knowledge, yes, but the classes, she kept to herself.

Nobody could steal the joy from her if they didn't know about it.

Rick turned to leave, and then paused. "The doughnuts were a nice touch. Be sure to put in an expense voucher."

Savannah watched him go. Not so stiff after all.

Deciding he needed a break later that afternoon, Rick dropped by Rett's workshop to see if he wanted to go kayaking.

"Man that sounds so good." Rett didn't lift his head from the piece he was faceting. "But I have a client consult in twenty minutes. Can you wait an hour?"

"No. I only have about an hour. I'm going to go ahead and go. I really need to work off some tension," Rick said.

"Okay, we'll connect later in the week. Call me when you get back, so I don't send the Coast Guard out looking for you," Rett replied.

As he hopped into his kayak and began paddling against the waves, Rick realized he'd really needed the fresh air and exercise. Pitting himself against the ocean, using his mind and muscles to beat the elements gave him a sense of freedom he got nowhere else.

Unfortunately, the rhythmic lift, dip and pull of paddling, first one side and then the other, left room for thoughts of Savannah to invade his mind. Darn it. Too often thoughts of her occupied him when he should be concentrating on business.

The idea of her spending private time with Rett nagged at him. And not just because of Rick's policy against interoffice relationships—Rett followed his own rules in that regard and was much less strict in his personal interaction with colleagues.

But Savannah was Rick's. Oh, not romantically, but still, he realized he didn't want to share her with anybody.

He dug in deeper, pulled back harder, causing water to roll over the sides of the shallow boat.

Okay, he'd noticed her soft curves and her great legs. Of course he'd noticed; he was a man after all. But he had no business noticing. She was his administrative assistant, not his girlfriend.

His inappropriate thoughts served as a reminder of why he never mixed business with pleasure. It was a bad practice. It definitely led to trouble and, for him, it had no future.

His muscles burned and the chill, salt-laden air felt good against his sweaty brow.

Marriage wasn't for him. In his experience love was always followed by pain. Better to keep his relationships light and put his energies into the business.

As for Savannah, he wished her gone, not hanging out with Rett.

Turning the kayak, Rick firmly put thoughts of Savannah's body, dating and marriage aside and headed back to shore. He had a business to tend to.

CHAPTER TWO

RICK HAD STEPPED OUT FOR LUNCH the next afternoon when a pretty redhead toting a baby carrier stopped by Savannah's desk.

"Hi, I'm Rick's sister-in-law, Jesse," the woman introduced herself. "His brother Brock's wife. Is he in?"

"I'm sorry, no. I'm his new assistant, Savannah. Can I help you with something?" she offered.

"Right, Savannah." The woman offered her hand with a genuine smile. "Gram speaks very highly of you. She mentioned something about you working with Rick."

"Mrs. Sullivan is a doll," Savannah enthused. "I really appreciate her putting in a good word for me with Rick. I'm very excited to have this opportunity."

A fussy cry came from the carrier, and Jesse grimaced at Savannah before cooing at her baby. Once the fussing quieted, she looked up again.

"I have an appointment with Rett to discuss a gift for Gram for her eighty-fifth birthday. The guys are throwing a big surprise party, so they want it to be something spectacular."

"She'll love that. When is her birthday? I'd love to get her a little something to show my appreciation."

"Oh it's not for another few months." Jesse rolled her eyes at herself. "I know, I'm way anal, but I like to start early. And we want a really spectacular gift so it's only fair to give Rett plenty of time to work. But Troy is awake and alert now and wants attention. I was hoping Rick would take him for a few minutes while I consult with Rett."

"Oh, well..." Watching a baby, even his own nephew, didn't sound like a Rick activity, but Jesse must know her brother-in-law better than Savannah did. "How long do you expect to be?"

"Only about twenty minutes. That's all Rett could squeeze in today, but we wanted to get started and at least discuss what we want to do." She bounced the carrier when another cry sounded. "Never mind. I know Rett won't mind—he loves the kids. We just won't get as much done as we'd hoped."

Savannah glanced at the hourglass; most of the sand had already fallen to the bottom half. Rick rarely took a full hour for lunch. "He should be back soon. If you like, you can leave Troy here with me and I'll watch him until Rick gets back."

"Really? That's so nice of you." Relief brightened Jesse's features. "He's fed and newly changed, so he shouldn't be any trouble." She set the carrier on Savannah's desk. "Thank you so much."

"No problem. How old is he?" Savannah asked.

"Five months." Jesse handed over Troy's diaper bag. "I'll be as quick as I can." With a wave, she rushed off.

"We'll be here, won't we, baby?" Savannah talked to Troy, smiling gently. Babies liked her. She figured they had her number. She was mush in their tiny hands and they knew it.

She spent a few minutes getting acquainted before lifting the little boy from the carrier. She cuddled him and then settled him in her lap, bouncing him lightly while she went back to the numbers.

That worked for ten full seconds. Troy's tiny fingers wrinkled the paper. She just got that away from him and he knocked her pen to the floor. Rescuing that as well, she turned him around and sat him on the desk facing her.

"You're a busy boy. Are you trying to be like your uncle Rick and work, work, work?"

Troy grinned at her and then promptly burped up.

"Oh, baby." She reached into his bag and pulled out a cloth to clean him up. "That's better, but let's see if we can get you rinsed off."

She lifted Troy to her shoulder before setting the diaper bag in the carrier and carrying both into Rick's office. He had a private bathroom. She set the carrier in his empty in-basket and took Troy into the bathroom to clean him up.

Rick strolled into his office after lunch and froze in shock just inside the door. A baby carrier sat in his in-basket. With a frown he glanced back at Savannah's desk. It was empty.

What was going on? He moved to his desk, but the carrier was empty, too.

What was Savannah up to now? Babysitting no doubt. People here already had her pegged as an easy mark. Well, he'd put a stop to this. There was a limit to his patience. And babies topped the list. His brothers popped them out on a regular basis; well, their wives did, and more power to them.

Rick preferred to keep his distance. Not that he was nervous or anything, it was just that babies were complicated. You had to hold them just so, bounce them a certain way, make sure they didn't touch things. Feed them, change them, burp them. Yes, definitely complicated.

A baby's cry shot tension straight up his spine. There was no ignoring that wail of displeasure. A moment later Savannah walked out of his bathroom with a baby boy in her arms.

"So there *is* a baby here," he said, looking from her to the boy in her arms, ready to take her to task for wasting time. Wait, the kid looked familiar. "Does it belong to one of my brothers?"

"Yes, *he* is your nephew, Troy." She bounced the boy gently. "Do you think five months is too young for an apprenticeship?"

"Oh, yeah, we'll just put a nanny on staff." He opened his top drawer and tossed his wallet inside. "Where are Brock and Jesse?"

"Jesse is downstairs going over preliminary designs

for your grandmother's birthday gift with Rett." She shifted the baby. "Do you want to hold him?"

"No." He took an involuntary step back.

Savannah lifted both brows at his reaction. "No? With your large family I'd think you'd be used to kids."

"Yeah, well, kids aren't really my thing."

"Really?" His answer shocked Savannah. "How can you resist such a charmer?" She turned Troy to face him. "He's adorable. And babies are so easy to reach, all you have to do is smile and coo."

To show him, she smiled at the five-month-old.

Troy shyly smiled back.

"See?" She glanced up at Rick and got caught in his watchful gaze.

"Pull yourself together Ms. Jones. I never coo," he said firmly.

"Well, that's a shame." The baby squealed and bobbed in her arms. She felt bad for Rick, that his icy reserve prevented him from finding joy in his infant nephew. "Maybe you should try it sometime. Babies love unconditionally, you know. It's kind of a win-win situation."

He cocked a dark brow, reminding her silently that she was speaking to the boss.

"Right. What was I thinking?" She backpedaled a bit. She needed to leave the room before she said something she'd regret. She knew she talked too much. Her sister, Claudia, said it was Savannah's biggest weakness and her biggest strength; she tended to say too much, but she also had the power to put people at ease.

Rick tolerated her chatter fairly well, though he rarely

spoke himself. Rather he observed and directed, often without saying a word. He orchestrated her comings and goings with the crook or staying motion of a finger. For the first week she'd felt as though she danced to the tune of the puppet master. Now she appreciated the efficiency of their system.

She just wished he could connect with his nephew, who was so lovable and accepting. Maybe if he held Troy, he'd be swayed by the baby's sweetness.

When the phone rang, she grabbed her chance.

"I should get that. Here, take Troy for just a minute." She plopped the boy into Rick's arms and reached for the phone, carefully keeping an eye on the pair as she spoke.

He skewered her with a glare. Though he seemed uncertain, he instinctively cradled Troy against his shoulder, looking more as if he held a fragile piece of spun glass than a living, breathing child.

Why did a single man holding a baby always look so sexy?

Of course, Rick always looked good. Her first week of work she'd had a serious talk with herself about keeping her eyes off the boss.

Yeah, right. The man was serious eye candy so that didn't work.

But she wanted this job and that did. So yeah, her ambition helped her keep her hormones in check. That and Rick's workaholic habits and stern demeanor.

Today none of that seemed to matter. Not when he

looked so vulnerable, strong yet gentle, with the baby cuddled in his arms.

Not wanting to press her luck, she wrapped up the call. "Sorry about that." Savannah took a step toward Rick. "I'll just take him back—oh, baby!"

Troy burped up, all down the front of himself. And Rick.

"Sh—" Rick broke off a curse. His reflexes in holding the baby out and away had not been quite fast enough to save himself from a nasty dousing, including on his shiny black loafers.

Troy's brow puckered up, and Savannah grabbed the wet cloth from his seat and rushed forward to clean him up before he started to cry.

"It's okay, sweet thing, you're fine, you're good." Once she had the baby all mopped up, she turned to Rick and swiped at his white shirt. After she got the worst of the mess off the front of him, she lifted her gaze and met his blue eyes, which were much closer than she had anticipated, and were focused on her with a mixture of irritation and awareness.

"Sorry, that's the best I can do," she said, her voice huskier than normal.

"Thank you," he said, his voice calm and controlled, his gaze holding hers. "I think you should take him until Jesse returns."

"Of course." She hastily stepped forward, almost tripping over her own feet as her nerves tingled. A ring sounded through the open door and she paused. "Oh, there's the phone on my desk."

"Let it go to voice mail," Rick ordered. "I need you to take Troy while I change my shirt." Without waiting for her response, he passed the baby into her care.

The phone on her desk stopped, and his began to ring.

Even as he picked up the receiver the other hand went to the top button of his shirt. He made quick work of both the call and stripping to the waist.

Savannah swallowed hard, tempted by the sight of bronze skin and hard muscles. A taut, lean torso supported broad shoulders and narrowed to lean hips. The ocean-kayaking he did with his twin showed in the defined muscles of his arms.

"Savannah." Her name was a buzz in her ears until he thrust the phone into her hand. "Take down the details of this conference call for me. I'll be back in a minute."

"Of course." She watched his strong back disappear into his private bathroom before turning her attention to the task. Easily juggling baby and receiver she jotted down the information from the manager of the San Francisco branch.

When Rick returned a few minutes later retucked and retied she pushed the memo slip into his hand and, carrying Troy, began to back toward the door.

"I'll just go find Jesse." She made her escape.

At the door she snuck a quick peek back. Rick sat behind his desk. Once again at work, once again in control.

The sight sent a longing through her she couldn't

explain. And couldn't afford. Not when she still tingled from the tempting view of his hot body.

She loved her new job; the work interested and challenged her. And she'd learned a lot. But suddenly she looked forward to Rick's upcoming trip to Europe. Thank goodness for the international deal he'd closed.

After the moment of heated awareness between them, having a full continent and an ocean dividing them for a week seemed like a really good idea.

Troy smirked at Rick over Savannah's shoulder as if happy to have her to himself. That drew a reluctant grin out of Rick. The boy was a true Sullivan.

Savannah was another matter. Rick had never known the irrepressible Ms. Jones to be so skittish.

Why he found her quick retreat so fascinating he couldn't say. Maybe he just liked seeing her flustered. She deserved it after tossing the baby at him and then standing so close that the sweet scent of her hair teased him even over the stink of baby burp, sending a spark of awareness streaming through his blood.

The shock of watching the gold flecks sparkle in her green eyes triggered an inappropriate physical response inside him he had no intention of acting on.

The last thing Rick wanted or needed were lascivious thoughts about his assistant. What a train wreck that would be.

Better to be annoyed than aroused by her.

The best thing would be if she quit. Hmm, he

mulled the idea over. He saw two problems with that option. Gram would blame him, citing his promise, and Savannah wouldn't be so easy to get rid of. She actually seemed to like her job.

She might talk too much, but she didn't jump if he said a sharp word, unlike the temps before her. And she didn't squeak at the long hours unless there was a conflict with a family event.

He understood family obligation. One of six brothers, Rick had a large, close-knit family that liked to get together on a regular basis. He participated because of Gram and because it was expected, but he often felt isolated even when he was part of the crowd. It'd been that way since he was a kid.

He loved his brothers, but he'd never found it easy to share, except with Rett, of course. That had always been enough for him. Especially after his broken engagement in college.

Losing people hurt. In his opinion, loneliness was a small price to pay for peace.

"Hey, Rick." Jesse strolled in, her baby in her arms. "I really appreciate you and Savannah helping with Troy. Rett and I came up with some great ideas for Gram."

"I'm glad." They exchanged a few pleasantries as she efficiently strapped Troy into his carrier.

"I'm sorry to have to run off, but I have to get Allie from preschool," Jesse explained.

"No problem. I'll walk you out." Rick saw Jesse into the elevator across the hall from his and Savannah's offices. "See you later."

"Oh, I almost forgot." Jesse stopped the doors from closing. "Do you know your grandfather's birthday? We need to know his birthstone for Gram's gift."

Rick frowned as he raked his mind. "No. Sometime in the summer, but I don't remember when."

"I have it," Savannah said, and he turned to her in surprise. "It's in Molly's history file. There are biographies on all the past presidents, including dates of birth and dates of death." Her fingers clicked at the keys of her computer as she talked. "Charles Sullivan was born July 23. Do you need the year?"

"No. This is wonderful." Jesse beamed. "You've saved me. I thought I was going to have to pump Gram without tipping her off about the party. Can you let Rett know?"

"Sure. I'll send it to his email."

"Thanks. And thanks again for watching Tr—" The elevator door cut off Jesse's words.

Blessed silence descended on the office.

Rick sighed and met Savannah's gaze to see an understanding gleam of amusement.

"Yeah," Savannah agreed as she went back to the papers in front of her. "You love to see them. And you love to see them go."

"Huh." She'd nailed it on the head.

It felt strange to have her read him so well. Strange for anyone to make the effort with him. People tended to avoid rather than interact with him. Generally that suited him fine, but the moment of connection warmed him in an odd way. Turning back to his office, he rubbed absently at his chest.

She still talked too much.

The next afternoon the ringing of the phone summoned Savannah as she approached her cubicle after a late lunch. Rushing to answer, she expected the call to be business-related but was surprised to find her sister, Claudia, on the other end.

A very excited Claudia.

"Oh, my God, Savannah. I love you. I love Mrs. Sullivan. I love Rick Sullivan. I love *all* the Sullivans."

"Hold on, slow down." Still catching her breath, Savannah struggled to understand her sister's chatter. "What are you talking about? What has Rick done?"

"I just heard that because I'm going back to Paradise Pines after I graduate, they're going to give me a bonus scholarship to help me get settled as I start my new job. That means—"

"Wait a minute." Savannah sat down, setting her purse on the desk. "You're telling me the Sullivans gave you *more* money?"

"Yes. Savannah, I'll be able to get my own apartment, and a new computer. And a new wardrobe. I need to thank a Sullivan. I need to thank them all. Mrs. Sullivan didn't answer her phone so I thought of Rick. Is he in?"

"I don't understand." Savannah felt thick-headed, but this was so huge. "You mean even though you'll be out of school, they're giving you *another* five thousand?"

"Yes!" Claudia's excitement reached squeal proportions, dimmed only slightly by the distance of the phone. "This is so amazing! Can you believe it?"

Yeah, Savannah could, when she got past the shock enough to take it all in. One of the things she admired most about the Sullivans—including Rick, the whole doughnut incident notwithstanding—was their generosity.

"You deserve it. You've worked really hard these last four years," she told Claudia.

"I'm overwhelmed. Thank you."

"Don't thank me. Thank Rick." Just when she had him pegged as all work and no play, Rick did this. Something so thoughtful and sweet it showed what a truly decent man he was. And she knew he was involved because Mrs. Sullivan had told her he had the final say over the scholarships.

"I do thank you. You've always been there for me. And of course, Rick, too. Is he there?"

Savannah glanced up at his closed door. "He's on a conference call. But I'll tell him you called."

"Oh, okay. I know you're busy so I won't keep you. Promise you'll give Rick a big kiss from me. Love you lots. Bye."

"Claudia!" Savannah protested.

But her sister hung up, leaving Savannah with the image of kissing Rick. A visual she really didn't need. After the incident with Troy yesterday it was easy, way too easy, to imagine how he'd taste, how he'd feel against her.

She'd never known a man like him, so physically fit, so stern in demeanor. All male, he made the men she'd dated seem like boys in comparison. Not that there'd been that many boys. Her high-school years had been spent caring for her mother instead of flirting.

Savannah never quite recaptured those flirty, experimental years. And, ever since, she'd felt one step behind in the game of love.

Unfortunately, Rick really made her wonder what she'd been missing.

A few minutes after Rick's conference call wrapped up a knock sounded at his door. He looked up as Savannah peeked around the edge.

"Good, you're free," she said, stepping into his office. Her fitted skirt showed her legs to advantage as she made her way toward her usual chair in front of his desk.

Even then she didn't stop. She kept coming, clear around the desk.

At the determined look in her eyes, he surged to his feet. When she leaned toward him, he leaned away. But she kept on coming, lifting onto her toes to touch her lips to his cheek. Instead of pulling away, he bent over her, breathing in the soft scent of honeysuckle.

Now why hadn't he guessed she'd start the afternoon with a kiss?

"That's from Claudia," she said, now intent on avoiding his gaze as she rose on her toes again and her lips caressed his other cheek. "And that's from me."

Her hair brushed his cheek as she moved back. He clenched his fist to keep from pulling her closer.

"You Sullivans have been incredibly good to her. She's over the top about the bonus money for returning to Paradise Pines."

Ahh. Rick resisted the urge to shift restlessly as he resumed his seat. "The scholarships are my grandmother's purview."

"And *she* told me you always participate in the final decision," she countered.

Caught, he shrugged. "Paradise Pines needs young professionals. We're just doing what's good for the community."

"Claudia will be great for the community and she'd be returning to Paradise without the incentive, but thank you." She hesitated, as if she might say something more. Or kiss him again. Instead, she nodded and turned to return to her desk.

Today she was calm, collected, with no sign of the flustered woman from yesterday.

Perfect. Cool and distant were good.

He could use a little indifference himself. Watching her long-legged retreat on red-hot heels, he fought the urge to loosen his tie, the airy room feeling suddenly overly warm.

He should be happy to be back on a professional footing, but for some reason he wasn't.

"Savannah."

"Yes." She stopped at the door to look back at him, her leaf-green gaze wary.

Right. No point in embarrassing them both. Which meant no more inappropriate thoughts of Savannah, short skirts and his desktop…

He pulled a legal pad toward himself. "I'm glad your sister is happy."

CHAPTER THREE

"YOUR DESIGN IS LOVELY."

The next Monday after work, Savannah stood in Rett's pristine workshop for their regularly scheduled lesson, watching as he held her sketch, turning it this way and that to view it from all angles.

"The setting will look great in gold, intertwined but independent with the classic emerald anchoring the middle. The symmetry is aesthetically beautiful. Your sister is going to love this piece," he told her.

"Thank you." Satisfaction and excitement made her giddy. But anxiety kept her grounded. She intended the pendant and earrings as a gift for Claudia's graduation, so Savannah needed it to be perfect. "You don't think it's too ambitious?"

He hit her with amused blue eyes. "You passed ambitious when you decided to design the pieces in the first place, so don't get wimpy on me now."

"I'm not." His approval of her design only made her more determined to finish the project. "But my skills are pretty new. I played around with beading when I was younger but this is the first time I've worked with precious gems."

"Relax, you're a natural. Your designs are busy enough to have interest but simple enough to have classic appeal. Plus I'll be doing the actual gem work."

"I know and I really appreciate it." She smiled sheepishly at him; it was strange relying on someone else's opinion of her work. His praise felt good, but at the same time it was hard being judged. She focused on the positive. "Someday I want to learn to facet, too."

"Why don't you take it one step at a time? Here, let me show you something." He walked across his workroom and unlocked a drawer under the counter running the length of the wall. He pulled out a small, clear box and brought it over to her.

"Open it." He placed the box in her hands.

Through the clear container she saw a brilliant green. Curious, she flipped the lid. Inside nestled a set of emerald earrings. Round cuts in an intricate swirl of yellow gold.

"This is my design!" Her gaze flew up to meet his.

He nodded. "You left your drawing on the counter last week."

"You made my design into real jewelry?" she demanded, both surprised and proud.

"That is what we do here at Sullivans' Jewels," he reminded her with a smile.

"Yeah, but I'm an amateur."

"Yes, it is, and yes, you are," a deep voice said from the doorway. Rick wove his way around the worktables in the middle of the workshop to reach them. "You're working with novices now?" he asked his brother in disbelief.

"We all start somewhere. But don't worry. She's good. See for yourself." Rett handed Rick the earrings. Turning back to Savannah he assured her, "This is a great design, but you may want to wait to make a decision on which design you use until after we've had a few more lessons."

"Good idea." Chewing her bottom lip, she watched Rick as he inspected her work. Talk about being judged. Rett, at least, was an artist, but Rick was all business, he'd look at her work from an entirely different perspective. She told herself she respected his knowledge and his taste.

And still she held her breath.

"These are nice, very elegant. I'm impressed," Rick said. He pinned Savannah with a pointed stare. "So this is what you two have been up to."

Ignoring his comment, she focused on his approval: Rick's words of praise made her feel like a diamond, valuable and brilliant.

"Why are you down here, Rick?" Rett asked, taking the earrings back.

"I received some news. The Emerson Group is pulling out of our international deal."

"What the heck?" Rett exclaimed, his hands going to his hips in an automatic, challenging stance.

She understood his confusion. She'd heard how long

and hard they'd worked on the international anniversary event and suddenly it was null and void?

"What happened?" Rett asked. "Jack Emerson seemed excited by the alliance. I can't believe he changed his mind."

"Jack suffered a heart attack last week. That's why we hadn't received the final documents. His board of directors invoked the rescission clause," Rick said heavily.

"Oh, my God." Savannah had talked to Emerson a couple of times; she'd liked the older man, finding his bluntness and honesty refreshing. "Is he okay?"

"He had triple bypass surgery. He's home and doing fine, but he has some recovery ahead of him."

"Man, I'm sorry." Rett shook his head, showing his support with a clap on Rick's shoulder. "You've worked so hard on this deal."

Savannah knew months had gone into Rick's plans to lease international sites for Sullivans' Jewels. In the last ten years, he'd taken the family-owned company national by opening stores in Beverly Hills, San Francisco, Las Vegas, Dallas, Chicago and New York. To celebrate the company's one-hundredth anniversary, he intended to take the company international. That plan might be in jeopardy now.

"Too hard to give up now," Rick answered grimly. "I've gone through the notes on our alternative choices. I like Crosse International as a close second. Albert Crosse has agreed to meet with me next Tuesday. That gives us a week to regroup and put together a new plan. Savannah, I need you to pull the notes from our earlier negotiations. I want a list of our points of agreement and dispute."

"Of course. Rick, you know I'll work over the weekend if necessary to be ready for the meeting."

"Thanks." Even distracted he sent her a brief glance of appreciation. "But we'll be traveling over the weekend. Our meeting with Crosse is in London. Since I had the trip planned, he's offered us a suite at his London hotel. You'll need to cancel the other reservations."

"We?" she exclaimed.

"Yes, I'll need you to go with me."

"London." Stunned, Savannah sank onto a nearby stool, pictures of Big Ben, Buckingham Palace and Westminster Abbey flowing through her mind.

"Savannah?" Rick brought her back to the moment.

Everything was moving so quickly she had to stop and clarify. "You want me to come with you to England?"

"I'll need you there, yes." He leaned back against the work counter, his gaze running over her. Not that he saw her; his mind was clearly on business strategy.

"I can handle the change in reservations, but I'm not sure I can get on the same flight as you." The thought of traveling with him gave Savannah mixed feelings. A trip to Europe thrilled her. Being alone with him really didn't.

"Then change my flight." Rick glanced at his watch. "Can you stay? I want you working on the Crosse deal full-time. If we're going to meet our deadline of opening the first international store by November next year, this deal has to close by the end of December." Leading the way out of the workshop, he outlined their timeline. "That gives us two weeks to finalize the negotiations and site the European stores."

"I'll get started right away," she said.

Savannah couldn't believe her luck. Being involved in these new negotiations really gave her a chance to prove herself in the job. And it would look really good on her résumé. Not to mention the exciting trip to England.

Okay so she'd be sharing a suite with Rick. But with so much on the line, surely she could control her hormones for a week?

Thursday night Rick sat brooding in his office. He'd had one ambition when he took over as CEO of Sullivans' Jewels: to make the family business so strong it would never be vulnerable again.

As it had been under his father's control.

The store almost went under after his parents' death. Gram held it together with grit and sheer determination. Rick and his brothers had helped where they could. He and Rett had only been ten, but they'd gone into the store with her on weekends. And when they got older they put in more time. He'd helped Gram while Rett hung out in the design workshop.

And when Gram announced her retirement and handed the company over to him, he'd made the hard choice to put family first. He'd sacrificed his engagement in order to stay in San Diego and take over Sullivans' Jewels.

Maybe when they celebrated the company's one-hundredth anniversary in their first international store, he'd feel he'd finally succeeded where good old Dad had failed.

By rescinding their offer, Emerson had cost Rick six months toward the completion of his goal. Now, in order to meet his December deadline, he needed to hit the floor running.

Savannah had really come through for him these past few days. With her help he'd restructured the package for Crosse International, including acceptable concessions for being second choice. When they touched down in England, they'd take Crosse by siege.

A knock sounded at the open door as Savannah entered the room. He watched as she strolled toward him across the office floor.

"Here are the profit and loss statements for the past two years. Accounting is still working on the amended projections for this year. I set up an appointment with the CFO for tomorrow morning." She handed him the files then sat and crossed her legs, waiting for a response.

With determined professionalism he looked away from the tempting sight of her navy skirt inching over her knees onto her thighs.

After reviewing the documents, he tossed the file on his desk. The action startled Savannah, catching her in the middle of a yawn. Sometime during the day she'd removed her jacket, but otherwise she looked as fresh and serene as when she'd walked through the door this morning.

He winced when a glance at the clock revealed that had been close to thirteen hours ago.

The overhead light cast fiery highlights in her dark red hair, drawing his attention. She wore the mahogany mass up on her head but this late in the day escaping tendrils cascaded over her neck and brow. Maybe not so fresh after all, but sexy.

Way too sexy. And touchable.

He definitely had no business wanting to touch her.

He needed to give the woman a dress code, he thought with an inward groan, one that included oversized jackets and buttoned-up shirts. Looking at all the toned, creamy-white skin revealed by the light gold, sleeveless, scoop-necked blouse, he knew he needed to change the course of his thoughts or risk embarrassing himself.

They'd been working together since before seven this morning and it was after eight at night now. A repeat of the past two days. What he needed, what they both needed, was a break.

As if on cue, Rett strolled through the door. "You guys still working? I thought you said you had the proposal pretty much wrapped."

Rick leaned back in his chair.

"We do. The attorney has it. We'll get his comments in the morning and go through it one last time. I was just going to suggest we call it a night and start out fresh tomorrow." That was good, that should end the torment of the day.

Except Rett had other ideas. "Hey, you have a fifteen-hour flight on Saturday. You'll be begging for something to do to fill the time. Save your review for then and give Savannah tomorrow off."

"Wait a minute," Rick protested.

"Come on." Rett dropped into the second visitor's chair. "I bet she's already put in over forty hours. With all the overtime she probably hasn't even had a chance to pack. Have you?" He directed the question to Savannah.

"What?" Her eyes grew big as the attention centered on her. "Oh, well actually—"

"See." Rett waved a triumphant hand. "Think about it," he tossed at Rick. "In the meantime, why don't I call and make reservations for the three of us for dinner. You both deserve a decent break."

"I really should head home." With a weary sigh Savannah rose to her feet, drawing Rick's attention once again to her blouse, and the way sunshine clung to her breasts. Much as he strived for professional detachment, yellow had just become his new favorite color.

"No, join us," Rett insisted. "You've worked hard. Let us treat you to dinner."

She hesitated for a moment and then smiled. "Okay, you only have to ask me twice. Why don't I meet you at the restaurant? Then I can just leave from there."

They finalized plans and Rick insisted on walking her to her car. Then he followed her to his favorite steak house, silently cursing his brother's interference.

Rick disliked mixing business with pleasure, and dinner with Savannah definitely blurred the edges of personal and professional. Her performance this week had surprised him; he could admit that. And despite the occasional distraction of her stunning legs or the sweet scent of her shampoo, they'd accomplished an amazing amount of work. She'd stayed calm and often anticipated him, providing reports and stats before he could ask.

Dinner should be innocent enough with Rett along.

Yeah, strictly business. In fact, he'd use dinner to discuss options on where they should open the first international store.

Unfortunately just as he reached the restaurant Rett called to say he couldn't make it after all. Rick couldn't help but curse.

Savannah waited just inside the door, buttoned into her jacket, her hair once again neat and tidy.

"Rett blew us off for a date, so I guess that leaves just you and me," Rick said bluntly.

She bit her lip, drawing his attention to the plump, pink perfection of her mouth. "Maybe I should just go home. It's been a long day."

He should grab the offer, but the weariness in her sea-green eyes got to him. "No, stay. You have to eat and this will be better than some fast food you pick up on the way home." Not waiting for an answer, he settled his hand in the small of her back and indicated to the maître d' they needed a table for two.

She quickly stepped ahead of him, leaving him with a view of her gently swaying hips as he followed her to their table. Telling himself the hunger clawing at his gut was for food, he ordered a rib eye.

"I want something I can sink my teeth into," he declared with a smile.

Rick's words caused a fluttering in Savannah's insides. She'd like to dismiss the response as a symptom of hunger, but unfortunately she was too self-aware for the flimsy excuse. Really, she should have headed straight home and avoided any chance of an intimate dinner with Rick. But the thought of having to cook after the long day—days—she'd put in held as little or less appeal than a plastic drive-through meal. And she'd thought she'd be safe with Rett along, too.

The waiter delivered their drink order. Rick placed both arms on the table and leaned forward. "I've pretty much narrowed the choice of location for the first store to London or Paris. I know you put together a list of properties earlier this week. What are your impressions?"

Okay, she knew the key to maintaining an emotional distance from him hinged on concentrating on work, and she appreciated being asked for her opinion. But she couldn't take any more today. Her brain couldn't hold another fact.

She inhaled a bracing breath, and then met his gaze. "Can we talk about something besides business?"

For a moment shock stole his voice. "What?" he managed to croak.

"My brain is fried. No more shop talk." She outlined her rules in clear, concise terms.

Rick stared at her, clearly speechless. Yet after a moment he relaxed back into his seat and opened his hands, palms out to her. "Sure. We'll talk about whatever you want."

"Try to hold back your enthusiasm," she said with a wry smile as she reached for a roll. Tearing it in half, she put the remaining half back in the bread basket.

Totally at ease in his habitual black suit and white shirt, Rick exuded elegance and class, putting most of the other men in the room to shame. The broad stretch of his shoulders and confident tilt of his dark head added to his sense of presence.

He looked good, really good. He always did, but tonight she found it hard to look away. She should be leery, especially when his gaze revealed he liked looking at her, too, but she didn't have the energy. Instead she enjoyed the delicious tingle of excitement zipping along her nerves.

A sensation common sense promptly squashed.

She didn't want the situation to change. She valued this job too much to risk it on the unsteady influence of romance.

"Okay." Rick picked up the half roll, took a bite. "Where'd you learn to speak French?"

"High school. I took it instead of Spanish. And then I took an advanced class in night school. After the class ended a bunch of us would get together for dinner at a French restaurant once a month and only speak French. It helped to cement the language. Especially if others in the restaurant joined in." She popped the last bite of roll in her mouth then licked a smudge of butter from her finger. "I sign up for classes and seminars all the time."

"Seminars?" he asked, his interest caught. "What topics interest you?"

Lifting one shoulder in a half shrug, she said, "All kinds of things, child development, business courses, design, some self-help classes where you learn how to end clutter in your life or build up your psyche with daily affirmations. That kind of thing."

"Ah." He nodded in understanding. "Sounds…boring."

His honesty surprised a laugh from her. "Some of it, yes. Some are ridiculous. Some are definitely more helpful than others. I just enjoy getting out, learning something new."

"Like jewelry design and faceting?" he said.

"Exactly."

The waiter arrived with their salads and to top up their water.

"Share something ridiculous," Rick demanded as soon as the waiter left.

Ridiculous? That shouldn't be hard. The man had a master's degree in Business Administration; he'd probably find most of what she went for ridiculous. Actually, she knew just the thing to tickle his fancy.

"In Strengthening Your Relationships, to get into your partner's point of view, you're supposed to strip completely naked, lie down on the bed and imagine yourself as a man."

"I *am* a man." No hesitation. No apology.

Oh, yeah. As if she needed to be reminded of his male factor.

"*You* would be imagining yourself as a woman."

His dark eyebrows spiked up. "That *is* ridiculous. Who thinks these things up?"

"Doctors, therapists." She speared a bite of lettuce, dipped it in her dressing. "The point is to see, to feel, to react from the aspect of your mate."

"Sensitivity training." The corner of his sensual mouth curled down, indicating what he thought of the idea. "You almost make it sound interesting."

"Thanks. I think," she said, defiant, though in truth his comment pleased her. She liked the thought of engaging his interest. But she wasn't sure she didn't agree with his obvious disdain of the topic. In fact, her imagination was working overtime, putting *naked*, *bed* and *man* together, and not just any man, but Rick.

Heat rose in her cheeks, and she reached for her ice water to cool off.

Rick's gaze narrowed then became intense as he slowly chewed and swallowed. "Why relationship seminars? You haven't mentioned a man in your life."

She wished she had a name to give him, that in truth she had a man in her life. If she were involved, Rick would be easier to resist. But there hadn't been a man in her life in close to seven months. And then it had been more of a friendship than anything else.

She demanded a lot when it came to love. She wanted what her younger brother had found with his wife, Kathy, what her mother and father had had before her mother died and her father buried himself in work. A loving partner to spend her life with.

"I'm ready for a new relationship," she admitted slowly.

"With a man who pretends he's a woman?"

"No." Amused, she shook her finger at him. "You're trying to mess with me, but it's not going to work. The sensitivity training was just a class. And I admit I got more out of the seminar on clutter control." She swirled her glass on the table. "Have you tried to patch things up with Diana?"

He'd broken up with the woman just after Savannah had started at Sullivans' Jewels. Diana had called several times over the past couple of weeks. Rick had taken the calls but they'd been very brief.

The waiter appeared, holding steaming plates of fragrant food. He stepped aside so the busboy could take the salad dishes, Rick's empty, hers half-eaten.

"Careful, the plates are hot," the waiter said as he set the dishes down, asked if they had everything they needed and then discreetly disappeared.

Rick frowned as he picked up his knife and fork. "It's over. We had some good times, but she was looking to change the rules, so it was time to end it."

"Of course, you have relationship rules." She shook her head as she took a bite of her fish. "I'm curious, what do you have against marriage? Most of your brothers are happily married. From what I've heard your parents and grandparents were happily married, yet you seem to be dead-set against it. Why?"

"I'm not against marriage," he denied. "I wish my brothers and their beautiful wives all the best. It's just not for me."

"Why not?" she pressed, trying to understand his position. "I'm focused on my career right now, but in the future I want a family, a partner and a couple of kids. Don't you see that for yourself someday?"

"I have a huge family, lots of nieces and nephews. I don't need kids of my own. My work gives me more satisfaction than any relationship I've ever been in."

Although Rick was not normally a man to be pitied, Savannah felt sorry for the lonely future he outlined.

"I love my job. Thirteen-hour days notwithstanding." She sent him a telling glance through thick lashes, and then smiled. "But I can't see it being enough for me. I need family in my life."

He nodded, his features expressionless as he focused on cutting his steak. "So you'd choose family over work?"

"Probably." Time to turn the tables. "What about you?"

"I love my job, too." Laughter brightening his blue eyes, he toasted her. "Thirteen-hour days notwithstanding."

Appreciating his comeback, she raised her glass and clicked rims with him. Still, his evasion challenged her. He didn't often open up like this—okay he *never* opened up like this—and she perversely welcomed the chance to get to know more about him.

Perversely because she knew better than to open herself to him.

"I meant, don't you want love in your life?" she asked curiously.

"No." He didn't even hesitate. "I'm not getting married," he reminded her. "Love isn't worth the pain."

He'd been hurt. The sharpness of his tone revealed a depth of emotion he kept carefully buried. He'd lost his parents when he was so young. She knew how tough that was, knew how every subsequent loss to the heart compounded the pain, leaving you feeling raw and exposed. Those were not emotions that would sit easily with Rick.

It saddened her to see such a strong man give up.

"I'm sorry for your pain, but love hurts because it's important." She gently covered his hand with her own. "It doesn't mean you have to give up on having a family of your own."

His openness closed down in a blink as he pulled his hand free of her touch and disappeared behind a facade of indifference.

"It's not a loss if it's not what you want."

Or if you told yourself you didn't want it so the hurting stopped. Kind of what she'd done with her dream of going to college.

"You're right." Common sense returned on a wave of self-preservation. Why let his attitude bother her when she had self-deceptions of her own? Suddenly uncomfortable with the topic, she sought a change. "Who started this conversation anyway?"

"You did," he reminded her as he pushed his plate aside. "You said you wanted to settle down someday and have a family."

"Right. Well that's a long way in the future." Nodding to the waiter's offer of coffee, she dismissed the serious conversation with a careless wave of her hand. "I'm not looking for anything permanent right now." She met his gaze over her mug. "So maybe I need to know more about those rules you were talking about."

CHAPTER FOUR

"I'M THINKING OF GOING BACK to school for a teacher's degree," Savannah announced to her sister the next afternoon. When Claudia had learned Savannah was traveling to London, she'd insisted on a shopping trip to update Savannah's wardrobe.

Claudia rounded the rack of dresses in a stylish boutique at the mall and gave Savannah a once-over and then, totally serious, nodded her head and said, "I think you'd make a really good teacher."

"Really?" Savannah couldn't hide her wistfulness. "You're not just saying that because you know it's what I want to hear?"

"Dude, you know that's not me. I don't do pretty little lies. And in this case I don't have to. You're smart, patient and creative, all great traits for a teacher. I think you should go for it."

"You don't feel I'm too old to bother now?" Savannah asked.

"Phff. There are people of all ages at State, but if it bothers you, try online classes. These days you can practically get your degree without ever going to the classroom." Claudia absently pushed a few hangers along the rack. "But isn't this kind of sudden? What brought this idea on?"

"I've always wanted to go to college, but I didn't really know what I wanted to study. Something Rick said last night really started me thinking. Teaching feels right. But it's been so long since I was in school."

"What did he say?" Of course, Claudia snagged on the Rick element.

"I was telling him about some of the seminars I've attended at dinner last night, and he said I made something ridiculous sound interesting."

"At dinner you say?" Claudia wiggled her dark brows.

"Oh, stop. It was a reward for putting in a long day."

"It sounds like you had a good time."

"Yes. I mean, no. It wasn't like that. And believe me, I put my foot in my mouth before I was through." She went on to tell her sister how she'd tried to change the subject when it got too uncomfortable.

"You asked him about his dating rules?" Claudia smirked at Savannah over a rack of cocktail dresses. "How brave of you."

"The conversation was getting heavy." Savannah shook her head at the red mini dress Claudia held up. The color would clash with the red in her hair. "I was trying to lighten things up."

"Right." Claudia eyed the red dress, shrugged and draped it over her arm. The color would be stunning with her own coffee-brown hair, green eyes and pale skin.

"Ohh, look at this." Claudia held up a black dress and the breath caught in the back of Savannah's throat. It was fitted from the hips up, with wide bands of material that wrapped the dress, crisscrossing each other over the breasts and then flaring out to create short, off-the-shoulder sleeves. A full, flirty skirt would swirl several inches above the knee.

"It's beautiful, but I can't. This is a business trip. I'll have no occasion to wear a cocktail dress."

"You never know. It's always good to have a little black dress along on a trip just in case. And this material will travel really well. Come on, at least try it on."

Giving in to temptation, Savannah disappeared into the fitting room. Of course, she loved the dress. It fitted like a dream, making her feel pretty and special.

She stepped out to show Claudia.

"Oh my." Her sister circled Savannah, practically purring. "You *have* to buy it. If you don't, I'll buy it for you, and I can't afford it."

Savannah did want it. "It has no sleeves. It'll be too cold to wear in England."

"My roommate is from New York. She has a beautiful black wool overcoat you can borrow."

"I can't borrow your roommate's coat."

"Sure you can. She never wears it unless she's going home. Come on, Savannah, you know you want it."

Savannah grinned. "Yeah, I do. But probably not for England."

"Please. Wear this to dinner and Rick will forget all about his rules."

"Oh, no. No." She shook her finger at her sister. "He can keep his rules. I just didn't want him thinking I was looking to get married and leave Sullivans', or that I was desperate for a man."

Claudia laughed as she went back to shopping. "Instead he probably thinks you were hitting on him."

"Oh, my God." Appalled, Savannah rounded the rack and caught Claudia's arm. "Is that what it sounded like to you?"

"Calm down." Claudia pried Savannah's fingers loose. "I was just kidding."

"No, you're right." Weak as the events of last night replayed through her head, Savannah sank into a chair outside the fitting room. "I was trying for light and sophisticated, but it sounded like a proposition." She mimicked a stab to the heart. "Just kill me now."

"Such drama. That's more me than you." Claudia squeezed Savannah's shoulder. "Sister mine, I love you, but we both know the flirting gene skipped you."

Tragic, but true. Still Savannah shook her head. "He doesn't know that."

"Okay, so what did he say? What are these famous rules?"

"He didn't answer. The waiter came with the check and the moment was lost. And that was the end of dinner."

"He just left?" The notion clearly outraged her younger sister, who'd been wrapping men around her little finger since infancy. Even their father responded to Claudia. Of course she was the shining image of their mother, which helped.

"No. Rick is too much of a gentleman to do that. He walked me to my car. Oh, gosh, and then told me I could have today off and he'd see me at the airport. Oh, this is bad. First the kiss and now I've propositioned him. I'll probably get home and find a message telling me I've been traded with Tammy from accounting."

"Whoa, whoa, whoa! Stop right there." Claudia dropped to the floor to sit cross-legged in front of Savannah. "You never mentioned a kiss. Spill! I want all the details."

Heat rose in a tide from Savannah's chest to her hairline. "It's *your* fault. *You* told me to thank him for the extra money from the scholarship."

"You actually *kissed* him?" Claudia demanded. "On the *mouth?*"

Savannah blinked at her. "Of course not, on the cheek, but you're missing the point here."

"Right, right. I see the problem. In the last two days you've kissed him *and* hit on him."

Savannah groaned. "That's it. I've cost myself the perfect job. And a trip to Europe."

"He's really got you twisted up. I've never seen you so flustered over a man."

"He's not a man. He's my boss."

"Oh, sweetie," Claudia admonished her. "He's *all* man and if you're trying to ignore that, no wonder you're in trouble."

"You're not helping," Savannah said.

"Helping? Right, you want to know if he realized you were hitting on him."

Savannah gritted her teeth.

"Hmm." Claudia tapped her lip while she thought. "Did he revert back to business?"

"No." Savannah perked up, seeing where her sister was going. Work would be an instinctive barrier for Rick to throw between them if he felt she'd gotten too familiar. "He asked how the plans were going for his grandmother's birthday. That's good, right?"

"Yeah, I think you're safe. He'd have played the work card if he wanted to shut you down. He probably just didn't want to talk about his love life."

"There's no love in his relationships." With a relieved breath Savannah pushed to her feet, helped Claudia to hers. "That's what the rules are about."

"Another reason for him not to answer you. Nobody that knows you could see you in a loveless relationship."

Savannah's plan as she strapped herself into her business-class seat on the airplane was to act as if it were business as usual when Rick arrived. No talk of rules or relationships. Or anything else. She'd guard her tongue if she had to bite it off.

This was one time when his lack of talking would be welcome.

Where was he anyway? She leaned over the aisle seat to glance up the companionway but there was no sign of her stalwart boss. She'd been surprised when he wasn't waiting for her in the departure area, but as the boarding passengers began to dwindle, she began to worry.

There shouldn't be any traffic at this time of night. They were taking the red-eye to New York and would catch an international flight out of JFK in the morning.

Frowning, she looked at her watch. Oh, God, what if he didn't show? Did she fly or get off the plane?

Just as she reached to ring the flight attendant to ask if he'd checked in, he strolled through the door.

And—*oh my*.

Rick in a business suit was controlled elegance, a man who knew what he wanted and how to get it. Rick in jeans and a navy T-shirt was big and broad and just a little rough around the edges, a man who took what he wanted and enjoyed the challenge.

She couldn't take her eyes off him the whole time he stowed his gear and took his seat.

When he met her stare with his take-no-prisoners blue eyes, she blurted, "I was about to flip a coin to see if I should fly without you or get off the plane."

He didn't apologize, simply said, "Rett drove me to the airport."

"Oh. And he was late?"

"He wouldn't think so." Rick grimly stated what sounded like an age-old argument between the brothers. He tucked a newspaper in the seat back in front of him. "Rett and I have a difference of opinion about how much lead time you need when you're flying."

"Why do you let him drive you then?"

"As he pointed out, I haven't missed a plane yet."

"Well, this wasn't the one to start with," she informed him, still a little on edge at the close call, a feeling that nudged up a few notches when the plane door closed.

"Settle down, Ms. Jones. I'm here safe and sound."

"Let's hope you stay that way," she muttered under her breath.

"What does that mean?" Of course he'd heard her.

"Nothing," she evaded, her attention focused out the window at the city lights as the plane began to roll.

Now Rick had arrived, there was nothing to distract her from the fact she'd soon be taking to the air in a very heavy object. Biting on her lower lip, she reminded herself thousands of people flew across the country every day.

Suddenly a strong, warm hand closed over hers on the armrest, stilling her tapping fingers.

She followed the reverse angle from hand to hair-dusted forearm, to muscular biceps, to strong neck, stubborn chin and eyes narrowed in suspicion.

"Don't tell me you're a nervous flyer," he accused.

"I don't know." She pulled her hand free. "This is my first time flying. I'm sure I'll be fine, but right at the moment, yes, I'm a little nervous."

"Huh." The suspicion backed down to mild irritation. "Don't you have a Valium or something you can take?"

Now that was just rude.

"I don't need to be medicated. I need a distraction." She almost changed her mind about that as the plane picked up speed rushing down the runway and she felt the wheels lift.

Okay, oblivion may not be such a bad thing.

She cleared her throat and concentrated on the conversation. "Don't worry. I'm not going to jump into your lap or anything."

"That's good to know," he said as he dug her nails out of his arm.

"Sorry." She smiled weakly, and, reclaiming her hand, she sought her own distraction in her carry-on. The first thing she pulled out was a plastic zip bag of home-baked chocolate chip cookies—nothing distracted or soothed as well as chocolate—and the second thing was the newest novel by one of her favorite authors. Rick had his paper so she didn't need to feel bad about reading her book. And once she started reading, she'd get caught up in the characters, mystery and romance.

After tucking her tote back under the seat in front of her, she dug out a chocolate chip cookie. Taking a healthy bite, she settled back in her seat and sighed, feeling the tension leave her body as she chewed.

Next to her she heard Rick sniff the air. From the corner of her eye she saw him slowly turn in her direction.

"Are those chocolate chip cookies?"

"Yes. But you wouldn't hold my hand so you can't have any."

"A tad cranky tonight, aren't you?"

"It's the nerves. I want to fix it, but I just have to get

through it." Because she wasn't mean, she turned the open bag of cookies toward him. "Peace offering?"

He took a cookie. "You still can't jump in my lap."

She grinned. "Spoilsport."

"But I suppose I can sacrifice a hand occasionally if you feel the need."

Her insides warmed at the offer, evidence the grouch did have a heart. But, oh, not good. Warm feelings for Rick were too much of a distraction. She'd better stick to the chocolate.

"Thanks." She held up a second cookie. "But I'm feeling better already."

"Good. Because it's a long flight. Do you think you'll be able to sleep?" He licked a smear of chocolate off his finger, a sensuous move she followed with her eyes.

This relaxed Rick fascinated her, which made him very dangerous indeed.

"Savannah?"

"Huh?"

"Do you think you'll sleep?" he repeated.

"Oh. Eventually. I can sleep anywhere." She zipped the bag of cookies and tucked it in the seat back in front of her. "How about you?"

"I'll doze."

"Maybe *you* need the Valium."

He laughed. A hearty sound she realized she'd not heard from him before.

How sad, she'd worked closely with the man for close to two months and had never heard him laugh. She immediately wanted to make him laugh again. He really needed lightness in his life, but this was another thing she couldn't fix, not without putting herself on the line emotionally, something she couldn't risk. And it didn't even have to do with the job.

She couldn't risk opening her heart to a man obsessed with work.

The loneliness, the lack of support, the disappointments—she wouldn't, couldn't go through that again.

So, instead of continuing the conversation and coaxing another laugh from him, she said, "Do you mind if I read for a while? I think it'll relax me."

The laughter faded from his eyes and he shook his head. "Go ahead. Will it bother you if I work?"

"Not at all."

With a curious sense of letdown, she lowered her tray table and opened the hardback to page one. Luckily, the characters soon drew her into the action and before long she was caught up. Flying, Rick, the sound of him typing all faded to the background as she outright giggled at what she was reading.

Rick couldn't sleep. Not with the soft scent of honeysuckle tickling his senses, a constant reminder of the woman occupying his companion seat.

At least she finally slept. She'd read for a while, and had a great time of it, too, if the musical sound of her laughter was any indication.

He glanced at the book, wondering again what she found so amusing. Since she appeared dead to the world, he reached for the book and read the front blurb—and then the first page.

An enjoyable hour had passed when he next looked at his watch. Stifling a yawn, he returned the book to where she'd had it stowed.

To stretch his legs he walked to the restroom at the far end of the plane. When he got back, he stood looking down on Savannah.

She sat half-turned toward him, a hand tucked under her cheek, so young, so sweet, so lovely. Cinnamon curls caressed creamy-white skin while dark lashes fanned over her cheeks. She shifted in her sleep and a pretty pink tongue swept over full, bare lips leaving them damp and as inviting as the smudge of chocolate above the corner of her mouth.

Fatigue must be getting to him because he wanted to lick her, first to eat the chocolate beckoning to him and next to taste the plump line of her lips, to sink inside and share the treat with her.

What on earth?

He rubbed his eyes. Pull it together, man.

To escape further temptation he slid into his seat and stared at the boring weave of the blue-and-gray fabric of the seat in front of him.

What had possessed him to bring her on this trip? He'd have been better off with someone from legal, someone fifty and comfortably thick.

Okay, so she'd been a great help prepping for the upcoming meeting, but she was still more optimistic than organized, totally unpredictable and distressingly unafraid of anything. A little healthy trepidation would make her so much easier to control.

She had yet to meet a stranger. The woman made friends wherever she went.

When was the last time a woman had made him laugh? He couldn't remember. More importantly, when had he become such a staid old man? So he cared about the business, cared about providing for his family. Did that have to mean he gave up on fun, gave up chasing all the enjoyable pursuits life had to offer?

Of course not. He determined to broaden his horizons when he got back. Spend more time with his brothers, read for pleasure and find a new woman friend.

Right. He closed his eyes and hoped by the time he got home—with the international deal sealed—the idea would hold more appeal.

The plane suddenly shook and then dropped, startling Rick out of a light doze. Instinctively, he grabbed the armrest before he even opened his eyes. His fingers closed around flesh and bone rather than hard plastic.

Savannah. Concerned, he glanced her way. She slept on but a slight furrow creased the fine porcelain of her brow. He pulled his hand back, granting her use of the armrest. She immediately became restless and the frown deepened.

He covered her hand again, twining his fingers with hers and she stilled and settled back into slumber.

She was as soft as he'd known she would be. Not that he allowed himself thoughts of her.

Another shake, a lift and then a sharp drop. Someone

screamed and Savannah came awake with a start. She blinked at him.

"What happened?" Husky from sleep, her voice stroked along fine nerves, causing the hair on the back of his neck to tingle in aroused awareness.

"Just a little turbulence."

"So I didn't dream a scream or that the plane was shaking?"

"Ladies and gentlemen." A calm voice came over the public-announcement system. "We are experiencing some heavy turbulence and the pilot has turned on the seat-belt light. Please remain buckled in your seats until he turns off the seat-belt light. Thank you."

Savannah's trembling fingers tightened on his. "Are we going to be okay?"

"I've heard no plane has ever gone down because of turbulence."

"Really?"

"That's what I've heard," he said reassuringly.

"Right. Oh, gosh." They were thrown back in their seats as the aircraft dipped and swayed.

"It shouldn't last long." He sought to relieve her distress. "The pilot will try to get either above or below the problem area."

"That would be good." Her agitation showed in the rapid rise and fall of her breasts. "That would be really good."

She fell silent as the plane continued to rock and roll. And he watched her to make sure she didn't hyperventilate. White knuckles defined the clasp of their hands, but neither fought to ease the hold one had on the other. He didn't expect the plane to crash, but he wouldn't deny he took comfort from the connection.

The flight evened out for about ten minutes, just long enough for everyone to begin to relax, when the shaking began again.

The drastic drop in altitude got to him, but the distressed whimper from the seat next to him was like a fist to the gut. Acting on impulse, he lifted the armrest between them and pulled her into his arms.

She clung to him and, lifting tearful eyes to his, pleaded, "Can't you make it stop?"

In that moment he'd give anything to fix it, to bring the laughter back to her eyes. He couldn't stop the turbulence, but perhaps he could take her mind off it.

"You have some chocolate on your face."

She blinked. "Huh?"

"Right here." He lowered his head and licked the corner of her mouth, sweeping the chocolate up with a flick of his tongue.

CHAPTER FIVE

SAVANNAH FELT AS IF the plane had done a loop-the-loop, turning her world upside down. She went still as Rick's mouth teased her, his tongue swirling over her skin.

Snug in the warm clasp of his arms, her existence narrowed to just the two of them. Strong and solid, he made her feel safe, protected. The scent of him, familiar and all male, surrounded her. And she wanted more of him; she wanted that mobile mouth on hers. But he continued to flick and nibble at the edge of her lips, close but not close enough.

With a low growl of need she turned her head and found his mouth with hers. Yum.

As if he'd been waiting for just that, he opened his mouth over hers and took control of the kiss, plundering her mouth with deft finesse, stealing her ability to think.

Sensation took over. Chocolate, hot and sweet, exploded over her tastebuds. She hummed with approval and met his tongue in a passionate tango of thrust and retreat. He lifted her, half pulling her into his lap, only her seat belt hampering him from completing the action.

Oh, better. Looping her arms around his neck, she threaded her fingers through his short, mink-soft hair, holding him to her, drawing his essence in and giving herself back.

"Ladies and gentlemen, the pilot has turned off the seat-belt sign. You are now free to move about the cabin."

The announcement washed over them like a bucket of cold water. They broke apart, and Savannah buried her face against Rick's chest.

The world came rushing back—the plane, other passengers, the near-death experience. For a while none of it had mattered; now it all did.

She bit back a groan as her brain reengaged and she realized where she was. In the boss's arms. This was not good, not good at all. It helped only slightly that Rick's heartbeat matched the racing pace of her own.

How to extricate herself?

"Restroom." She fumbled for her seat belt. "I've got to go." Once she found the release, she bolted to her feet and escaped down the aisle. Luckily, there was a line of people waiting. Maybe it would last until they reached New York.

Five people and two hours to kill? Not even she was that optimistic. Which meant she'd have to sit next to him with the blood still speeding way too fast through her system. Thank goodness her jacket hid the aroused state of her nipples because if it was cold in here, she didn't feel it.

All too soon she was sitting in her seat again, her jacket wrapped around her, staring at the gray hair of the man seated in front of her while Rick focused his attention on the ceiling.

Not comfortable with being uncomfortable, she said, "Thank you. I was scared and you…helped me. It was very kind of you."

He made a choking sound. "Don't mention it. Please."

"I wasn't propositioning you."

He turned his head slowly and pinned her with an intense stare. "What are you going on about now?"

"The other night at dinner when I asked about your dating rules. I wasn't propositioning you." She cleared her throat and dropped her eyes. "In case you think I've been throwing myself at you."

"I didn't." He went back to his contemplation of the ceiling. "I don't."

Instead of reassuring Savannah, his simple dismissal struck a contrary chord. It wasn't as if there was no chemistry between them. The last few minutes had proved that conclusively.

"Well, all right then." She let silence fall between them, telling herself she should be glad to have that worry gone. But she couldn't help herself. "Why not?"

Her pique must have sounded in her voice because he sighed.

"I know when I'm being propositioned. And flirting isn't your style. You're too straightforward."

"Then why didn't you tell me the rules?"

"Because there isn't a hope in hell you'd ever abide by them."

"I don't know how you can know that," she retorted, stung.

"The rules are about establishing personal boundaries to prevent expectations of a deeper relationship from forming. You have personal relationships with everyone."

"Not everyone."

"Everyone," he insisted. "Including the mail boy."

"He goes to State, which is where my sister attends college. So yeah, we've chatted a few times."

"What's his girlfriend's name?"

"Amber."

"I rest my case."

"That only proves I'm a good listener."

"I've worked with Molly for twelve years and I don't even know her daughter's name."

"Oh. Well." His confession stunned her so she had no argument for him. "What was your point again?"

"That my rules aren't meant for you."

For a moment it sounded as if he meant that his rules didn't apply to her, and a wild rush of pleasure bloomed in her. She quickly squashed it, first because she knew how he intended what he'd said, and second because he wasn't for her.

Anyone who worked with someone for twelve years

and didn't know something as intimate as her daughter's name was too impersonal for Savannah.

She could never be with someone who believed that work was more important than people. And that described Rick to a T.

"You're right," she conceded. "Your rules aren't for me."

To Savannah's relief the trip concluded without further incident and they arrived in London exhausted but ready for the upcoming meeting. After spending fifteen hours practically joined at the thigh with Rick, she was ready to retreat to her own room.

"Beautiful hotel," she commented on the way to the elevator, admiring the large leather furnishings and dark woods amidst marble and crystal. "I see now why you were drawn to Crosse International."

"What do you mean?" he asked as they boarded the elevator.

"The ambience. A modern feel in a traditional setting. You know, kind of a comfortable chic."

Rick simply nodded and she wondered if he was even listening. Except for business, he'd kept conversation between them to a minimum ever since the embrace on the flight to New York.

Savannah closed her eyes and sighed at the thought of stretching out in a bed. She was *so* ready for some alone time.

"It reminds me of the store back home," she muttered.

"What does?" Rick held the elevator door for her to exit.

"The hotel. Oh, we're right here." Savannah had never been so happy to reach a destination. She slid her key card into the slot. "See you in the morning."

As she closed her bedroom door, she almost had herself convinced she was pleased by his impersonal attitude.

Almost.

So call her crazy. She wanted to have her cake and to eat it, too. Working so closely with Rick these last few days had twisted her emotions in a knot. His drive and dedication challenged her while his intelligence and dry sense of humor made the long hours speed by.

Not to mention every little touch tested her ability to remain unaffected, from the accidental brush of skin against skin to the warmth of his breath on her cheek as they bent over the proposed contract.

All in all, her feelings for him weren't as easy to ignore as she'd hoped. And the awareness growing between them buzzed like static in the air.

But if he could pretend indifference to the passionate kiss they'd shared, so could she.

Right.

Savannah slept like the dead, waking only when her alarm went off. She showered and dressed in her navy suit with the gold scoop-neck blouse. She wanted to look good and the outfit made her feel confident and professional.

When she entered the parlor suite connecting her room to Rick's, she found him already sitting at the dining table reading the paper. He'd ordered coffee along with an array of muffins, yogurt and fruit.

"Good morning," he greeted her, his glance up from the paper slightly leery as if he feared what she might say, or perhaps it was that she might start chattering.

He needn't worry; she liked to ease her way into the day. After helping herself to coffee and fruit, she took a discarded section of his paper and enjoyed the quiet and the view.

Having the meeting with Crosse in the hotel was convenient, allowing them to leave their room at ten to ten and simply ride the elevator down. But that was the end of her peaceful morning.

The meeting was the crash and burn they had narrowly missed the day before, or it would be if Savannah didn't act fast.

True to form, Rick masterfully presented the numbers and projections, but his confidence and all-business approach came across as arrogant. Albert Crosse, a fit man in his early sixties, flanked by his two sons, listened but seemed restless. And the more Rick pushed, the further apart the two got.

She tried to catch Rick's eye more than once, but he ignored her, so she took matters into her own hands.

"Mr. Crosse." She spoke into a tense silence. "I was wondering which property you would suggest for the joint venture?"

Rick shot her a repressive glance. "Ms. Jones, this isn't the time—"

"Please." Crosse waved Rick off. "I don't mind, though you must remember to call me Albert."

"Of course, Albert."

Short and compact, Crosse exuded a charm and charisma that exceeded his stature. His presence demanded attention, and, though his sons were present, it was obvious Crosse ruled.

He leaned forward and clasped his hands on the table. "Actually, I believe this property would be spot-on for your purposes. This location runs at seventy-five percent or more capacity for most of the year. We've already converted first-level offices into retail space and have leases with a full-service day spa and a coffeehouse. There are two more spaces available."

Perfect. This was better than she'd hoped for when she'd taken the discussion off topic. A field trip would change the current dynamic and, she hoped, get the negotiations flowing again.

"Gracious, right here in the hotel? Can we go see the space? After the long flight yesterday and sitting most of the morning I'm a bit stiff and would welcome a chance to stretch my legs."

"Ms. Jones—"

Savannah turned so only Rick could see her and silently mouthed, "We're losing him." Aloud, she said, "I know we have an appointment with the property manager later, but I'm sure Albert will be an excellent guide."

"Splendid idea. It would be my pleasure." Crosse talked right over Rick's objections. "I'll have the property manager meet us there. I was scheduled to inspect the conversions today, but agreed to take this meeting instead."

"Will we have an opportunity to finish our meeting?" Rick asked as everyone stood.

"I have some thinking to do tonight," Crosse advised him stiffly. "I'll have my assistant call you with a time for tomorrow."

When they reached the lobby, Crosse stopped to talk briefly with his sons who were taking this opportunity to break away.

"What do you think you're doing?" Rick demanded, pulling Savannah aside.

"We were losing him." She moved to watch the Crosses so Albert couldn't walk up on their conversation. "We needed a distraction."

"That's ludicrous." He dismissed her claim. "This is a solid proposition."

"Yes, but he was already sold on the numbers—you sold him on those before. And then you chose to go with someone else. Now he's wondering what's to keep you from jumping again if a better deal comes along."

"Sullivans' Jewels has a solid reputation. And we made concessions."

"On paper." How could such a brilliant man be so dense? "You are an exceptional business strategist, but in this instance you need to read the man. It's a matter of loyalty, of pride. Think how you'd feel if the situation were reversed."

He frowned, but she'd caught his attention. Seeing Crosse's conversation was breaking up, she stepped closer to Rick and lowered her voice. "You said I relate to everyone. Well, trust me on this. Let him know he can trust you." Hooking her arm through his, she turned him toward Crosse. "And when we tour the space, don't bring up the deal. Business is fine but stay away from anything personal. Connect with him on another level."

She felt him stiffen before pulling away. "I think I know how to conduct myself with a business colleague."

"Of course." She stepped away, feeling awkward. What had she been thinking linking arms with him like that? She was his assistant, not his girlfriend. "Sorry. Go do your magic."

Rick hated to admit it, but Savannah was right.

A good thing for her, because if she'd blown this deal she'd be gone, promise to Gram or no promise.

He'd known Crosse was antsy. Yet, instead of stopping to think it through and adapt to the situation, he'd let the man's stoic response cause him to push harder.

Rick didn't like being in this position. He was used to being the one making decisions, not the one waiting for the nod.

But more importantly, Savannah had hit the biggest issue on the mark. If the situation were reversed he'd want more than facts and figures thrown at him.

Despite any concessions tossed his way, he'd want to know Sullivans' Jewels was more than a second choice. After all, they weren't just talking about the lease of space; they were talking about partnering brands to broaden their demographics.

The insight made him stop and question himself. Had his goal become more important than the process? Was he rushing his decisions to meet his self-imposed deadline? If that were the case, he needed to stop now and reassess.

He kept his mind open to the possibilities as they toured the space with Crosse. His first impression was of the size. It was smaller than any of their other stores. But the prime location, right on the lobby, and accessibility to the old vault one story down were strong factors in its favor.

Because he agreed with the strategy, he heeded Savannah's advice to avoid talk of the proposal except for renovations and contractors in general because Crosse brought them up. By the time they completed the tour, including visits to the spa and coffee store, he'd made a decision. The process and the goal were both right-on.

"Albert, thank you for your time." He shook Crosse's hand. "They say all things happen for a reason and in this case I need to agree. I originally went with Emerson because I thought their traditional image was a closer match for Sullivans' Jewels. After staying here and talking with you and your sons, I see I was wrong.

"We're both family-owned and family-run companies.

And our styles are very similar—'comfortable chic,' Savannah called it last night."

With nothing to lose, Rick spoke from the heart. "I know you're hesitant about going forward with the project, but I hope you decide in our favor. The fact is we fit very well indeed. And I'm excited about the prospect of working together. I think I can learn a lot from you."

"Hmm." Albert stood with his arms crossed, nodding. They were totally mixed signals: one said he was closed off, the other that he was listening. He turned to Savannah, who had drifted to the background during the tour. She'd asked a few questions but had mostly followed quietly as the men wandered and talked.

"Beautiful lady, what am I to make of this bloke? Upstairs he is cold and calculating, so serious with the numbers. But down here he comes alive, and shows passion and heart. Which is the true man?" Albert asked.

Savannah smiled. "Both, of course. Upstairs he's looking forward to what could be. He knows his business and the numbers tell of the possibilities. Here—" she spread her arms to indicate the vacant space they'd returned to "—it becomes real. He can see his store, feel it, breathe it. And, yes, he's serious about his business. He is the heart of Sullivans' Jewels."

Crosse angled his head at Rick. "Beautiful and loyal. You are lucky, Rick, to have someone who believes in you so strongly."

"Yes." Truthfully her response had surprised Rick. He knew he'd been tough on her from the beginning, yet she'd nailed him with that comment. He found it more than a little disconcerting.

"I have much to think about," Albert stated. "I'll have my assistant contact you regarding a time when we can meet tomorrow."

"Is it all right if we view the other London properties as time allows?" Rick requested.

"I see no harm in that," Crosse agreed.

Rick inclined his head. "We'll be waiting for your call."

Happy to be out of the snow and cold, Savannah crawled into the back of a taxi, scooting over to allow room for Rick. As she settled into the worn leather seat, her relief at being out of the weather shattered as her hand came to rest against Rick's muscular thigh on the bench seat.

Immediately the heat of his body warmed the backs of her icy fingers. For the thousandth time that day she rued forgetting her gloves at home.

Rick's head whipped around. It took every ounce of poise she possessed to meet the awareness in his blue gaze with a semblance of calm professionalism.

Unfair. Unfair. What a cosmic joke if she had to fight him as well as herself to keep their relationship on a business level.

She racked her mind for something to distract his attention from her. A street sign caught her attention. "Buckingham Palace. It must be close, can we drive by?"

He looked over his shoulder at her with lifted brows, but he leaned forward and spoke to the driver.

"Thank you." She'd seen some lovely sights as they made their way through town to the Crosse properties— St. Paul's Cathedral, the Millennium Bridge. Seen but not experienced.

"I know we're here on business, but please tell me we'll get some free time to actually visit some of these beautiful sights."

She saw him looking at her out of the corner of his eye. "I suppose you deserve something for your interference today," Rick conceded. "You were right about Crosse. He needed reassurance. You saw that and quite possibly saved the deal."

"I hope so." She shifted so she faced him. Watched as he lifted a hand to smother a yawn. The muscles in his throat worked and her mouth watered. "I liked Crosse."

"He liked you, too." That was the second time in two days he'd said a man liked her. Knowing she shouldn't go there, she couldn't prevent the question from popping out.

"Do you?" she asked.

"Yes. I was being honest with him. I really do think I can learn from him."

"No," she corrected, "do you like *me?*"

His profile froze before he slowly turned and shot her a harassed glare. "What do you mean?"

"Never mind, it doesn't matter." What was she thinking asking such a personal question? Other than that somehow his answer mattered a great deal to her.

"What are you talking about?" he asked, genuine puzzlement in his tone. "Everyone likes you."

"So you seem to think." Stop this now, she pleaded with herself. But she didn't care about everyone; she cared about him. "But what about *you?* I know you think I talk too much."

"You do," he said with casual ease. "But I'm getting used to it. I even learn things, like 'comfortable chic.'"

She grinned. His announcement had both surprised and pleased her. "I noticed how you used that." And how he'd skipped over her question.

"I meant what I said. You changed the direction of the meeting today. Thank you."

"I'm sure you would have noticed before it was too late."

"Don't start lying to me now, Savannah. I like to think I would have caught on eventually, but you don't think so or you wouldn't have interrupted."

"Well, you were overexcited—"

He laughed. "Now that's something I've never been accused of before."

"It's not a bad thing. And you're entitled. Oh look, it's the guards with the bearskin hats. And, oh, the palace."

The view was out Rick's window and she had to lean forward and toward him to catch sight of the grand palace. Even in her excitement she noticed how good he smelled, clean with a hint of spice. It made her want to snuggle close, and she'd already practically climbed in his lap in order to see better.

"Savannah." He ground out the throaty protest.

And, of course, he was right. The one time under extreme conditions on the plane could be excused; twice and it was getting to be a bad habit.

"Sorry." She eased back into her own space and lost all sight of the palace. "Driver, please stop," she called.

"What are you doing?" Rick demanded.

"I'm getting out. I can't come to London and not see the palace. I'll find my own way back."

"It's freezing out there. Literally."

"I'll be fine. I may even find a shop to buy some gloves."

She reached for her purse and when she looked up she saw an odd flash of emotion cross Rick's face. The vulnerability in his hooded gaze stunned her, brought a lump to her throat. For a moment, the strong, confident man looked lonely.

"You should come with me," she heard herself say. "We can find a pub and have some fish and chips."

He hesitated, then surprised her by nodding. "Sure. I could eat."

CHAPTER SIX

AS A DISTRACTION, Buckingham Palace ranked right up there with chocolate and shopping in Savannah's estimation. In fact, having a studly companion as she strolled the block fronting the majestic building and grounds didn't suck either.

The snow-drenched grounds were well-lit, as was the massive building with majestic columns and row upon row of windows. And, of course, the beautiful Nash statue of Queen Victoria. It was awe-inspiring to consider the longevity and history incorporated in this palace. She definitely needed to come back for a tour.

"Thanks," she said to Rick, blowing on her hands to warm them as the cold finally drove her to leave. "Ready for the fish and chips now?"

"You bet." Rick stopped a local to ask after a good pub, and minutes later they were seated at a scarred wooden table in a room crowded with tables and people. Soccer and rugby equipment along with player jerseys lined the walls while a rugby game played on several mounted TVs. In a back room a rowdy group erupted with cheers and groans.

"Dart tournament tonight, folks," a dark-haired waitress said as she stopped by the table. In her mid-forties, she was comfortably lush in a green T-shirt and blue jeans. "It'll be pretty loud."

"It's perfect." Savannah grinned at her. "I flat-out confess to being a tourist, so it's all part of the experience for me."

"Aye, and my guess is you'll be wanting some fish and chips and a pint. Where do you come to us from?"

"San Diego." Savannah rubbed her hands together. "Where it's much warmer this time of year. And yes, I'm going to be totally typical and get the fish and chips. And what the heck, I'll try the pint, too."

"You got it, doll. I'll bring you something pale." She turned her attention to Rick. Friendly when she spoke to Savannah, her gaze turned downright predatory as it ran over his body. "How about you, sweet thing?"

Savannah hid a smile behind her hand as red color flooded his cheeks.

He cleared his throat. "I'll have the same."

"Aye, and I'll bring you something dark." She shifted closer to him with a roll of well-rounded hips. "You look man enough to handle it."

With a lingering backward glance she disappeared into the crowd.

"Oh, she likes you," Savannah teased him. "Just let me know if you need me to make myself scarce."

"That woman just ate me alive with her eyes." He shook his finger at Savannah. "Under no circumstances are you to leave me alone with that cougar."

"Cougar?" She laughed. "Oh my, does she scare you?"

"I'm an intelligent man, so hell yeah."

She grinned. "Don't worry, I'll protect your virtue—or should I say manhood? I mean really, what if we were a couple?"

He pinned her with an intent stare. "Sweetheart, for the next hour, we are."

"What? You don't think she'd play by your *rules?*" How dangerous to play with him like this, but she couldn't resist.

"The rules are there so no one gets hurt." He defended his system with a flick of his eyes toward the bar and the woman under discussion. "She doesn't look like she's afraid of pain."

"It hurts so good?" she teased provocatively.

His gaze flashed back to her. "You're shocking me, Ms. Jones."

Yeah, she'd rather shocked herself. "You brought it up. Besides, I'm not as innocent as you seem to think."

"Sure you are," he assured her, certainty clear as crystal in his tone, "and it has nothing to do with how many lovers you've had. You're caring and giving. Genuine. You bring everyone around you to a higher level."

"Wow," she breathed, inordinately pleased by his assessment. She knew she got on his nerves sometimes and she was nowhere near his intellectual equal, so his comment touched her deeply. About to gush, she pulled herself back. He'd hate that. Instead she blessed him with a cheeky smile. "So you *do* like me."

He grinned and shook his head. "Sometimes."

"Uh-uh, be nice. Here comes the waitress with our food."

He lifted one dark brow. "Maybe you're not so innocent after all. You've got a mean streak."

"Oh, I bet I'm just a kitten next to the cougar."

"Just stay close."

"I will, I promise." She scooted back her chair. "As soon as I get back from the restroom."

"What?" he demanded in mock outrage. "Some friend you are."

"Come on, we both know you can handle her. Be right back."

She made quick work of her trip to the bathroom, not because she was worried about Rick—he could take care of himself. But she was having fun and didn't want to miss a minute of the adventure.

Over fish and chips they got involved in the rugby game, she rooting for Ireland while he cheered for Wales. The dart tournament got louder still, the waitress flirted some more and Savannah had a ball.

The game ended and they donned their coats and walked down the street toward Buckingham Palace to catch a cab. It amazed her that some of the shops were still open, but when she glanced at her watch it was only seven.

"Wait. In here." Rick caught her hand. Startled by the searing touch she stopped in her tracks. He pulled her toward a leather and coat shop. "We can get you some gloves."

"Oh, no," She held back. "I'll find some closer to the hotel."

"Come on. Let's at least see what they have." He opened the door and ushered her inside.

The rich scent of leather pleasantly filled the small store. Savannah reluctantly followed Rick to the accessory section where he selected several pairs for her to try on. She did so, marveling at the suppleness and warmth. She particularly enjoyed a pair made of leather with a fleece lining; the quality and fit were exquisite. They were so soft, so warm she didn't want to take them off. But she must.

"Those are a nice fit," Rick said.

"Yes." A little sad, a little embarrassed, she pulled them off. "Rick, it's so nice of you to stop here, but, really, I can't afford these."

"But you like them?"

"Of course." She placed them back on the rack. "But that's not the point."

"It's exactly the point." He retrieved the gloves and handed them to the hovering clerk along with a pair of men's gloves. "We'll take both."

"Rick, no," Savannah protested. "I can't get these."

"You're not. I'm getting them."

Touched, she still shook her head. "I can't let you do that."

"You have no choice. They're a gift for your help today." He handed the clerk his credit card.

"Rick, this isn't necessary."

"I know. I want to get them for you." After pocketing

his wallet he placed the bag in her hands. "Thank you."

"No, thank *you*." Letting the fun and ease of the evening direct her, she gave in to impulse and lifted onto her toes to kiss his cheek.

Desire flared in his eyes. He appeared to struggle with himself for a moment, then he lowered his head and covered her mouth with his. For one glorious minute he consumed her, drawing a response from her that met his passionate demand.

When he pulled back, she'd all but forgotten where she was.

While she regrouped, he ran a finger down her cheek. "My apologies. That's the last time that can happen."

Not quite able to wrap her tongue around words, she nodded mutely.

With a return to his stoic expression, he stepped back. "We should head back to the hotel."

Rick stared hard at his reflection in the mirror the next morning as he finished shaving. He didn't look any different. Didn't really feel different, but something was off.

Maybe it was jet lag or something in the water here in England, but there had to be an explanation for his uncharacteristic behavior. Playing tourist, flirting, kissing his assistant: Was he insane? He had no business having fun.

Okay, that was wrong. He deserved to have fun as much as the next guy. But not with Savannah. He had no business having fun with his assistant. The next time she wanted to play tourist she was on her own.

Huh, that thought certainly took the punch out of his day. He attributed the curious sense of letdown to delayed jet lag rather than to the disquieting notion of Savannah being out and about on her own. Not that she'd hesitate. The woman was fearless, which wasn't the same as being safe. Though the Lord knew she made friends wherever she went. Take the cougar last night. Propositioning him in the hallway one moment and laughing like old friends with Savannah the next.

He tossed down the towel and reached for his deodorant.

The problem was, he'd had a great time last night.

Watching the game, sharing the camaraderie of the crowd, eating the simple but good food. And with Savannah seated across from him making him laugh.

Swish and rinse. Finished, he dropped his toothbrush in a cup and set his shaving kit aside.

Again she'd made him laugh. He enjoyed the company of women, but they didn't engage him. He didn't let them. But Savannah slid under his guard and challenged him in so many ways.

But it had to stop. No more laughing, no more flirting, no more giving her gifts, and certainly no more nibbling on her plump bottom lip.

Now he felt downright deflated. Yes, it was definitely jet lag.

The phone was ringing when he entered the parlor suite. Savannah sat at the table eating muffins for breakfast.

She began to rise, but he waved her off and answered the phone himself.

It was Crosse calling to set up an appointment for four that afternoon.

"His attorneys are going over the changes and they'll have a counteroffer to us within the next couple of days," Rick told Savannah after hanging up the phone. "We'll have two days to review and respond. He's hoping we'll be able to celebrate with dinner before we leave."

"That's great news," she enthused. "Did he say what the changes were?"

"No, but he said they were minor. I'm not expecting anything too shocking."

He was right. When the contract arrived and they reviewed the noted changes, most were in areas where Rick had already built in room for negotiation. Only one required him to get on the phone to the company attorney.

He and Savannah made a good team, taking care of the details and wrapping up loose ends. He felt great going into the meeting the next day.

His confidence was rewarded when an agreement was reached and the contracts were signed. The relief and satisfaction were huge, even more so than when he'd closed the deal with Emerson. Maybe because he'd come close to failing this time, something he wasn't used to, but he didn't think so; this fit felt right. He respected Crosse and they actually hit it off once they began to communicate properly.

He spent the rest of the week viewing properties and interviewing local contractors and vendors. He was so pleased with their progress he gave in to Savannah's wishes for some tourist time on their last day as long as she was back in time for dinner with the Crosses.

"I don't know where to start." All smiles, she headed straight for the stack of brochures she'd been collecting. Fanning them in front of her, she invited, "You choose."

He really wanted to—he'd had the best time at the pub with her their first night in London, and knew he'd have a blast jetting around town with her.

But… "You go on without me," he declined. "I have some loose ends to tie up here first." It was better this way. He'd already relaxed his standards around her more than with any other employee. He needed to rein himself in, which might be more boring but was safer all around.

He finished the bit of business he wanted to do and then wandered over to the Tower of London. A jeweler could hardly come to town without viewing the Crown Jewels. The Imperial State Crown was a marvel in itself. Over three thousand precious jewels—diamonds, emeralds, sapphires and rubies—manifested the majesty of the headpiece.

Yeah. "You are what you wear" was by no means a modern edict. A thought that proved true when he moved over to the display of royal armory. Fascinating stuff, but the third time he found himself turning to draw

Savannah's attention to something and being frustrated when she wasn't there, he decided it was time to go.

Back at the hotel he freshened up and changed into a suit and tie and then opened his laptop to go through his emails while he waited for Savannah.

He'd been at it thirty minutes when the door to Savannah's room opened and she entered the room.

"I'm ready."

Rick glanced from the report he was reading to the clock in the corner of the screen. Excellent. They had fifteen minutes to get downstairs, where Crosse and his wife would pick them up.

Things were definitely looking up.

Until he glanced over and saw Savannah in a hot little black dress that made his mouth literally water. The dark color showcased her pale skin, while the swirl of the skirt and her spiked heels made her legs look as though they went on forever. And the shimmering peach lipstick painted on her lush lips tempted him to take a bite.

He was in *so* much trouble.

The Crosses had reservations for them at the Criterion restaurant, a jewel of Piccadilly Square since 1873. Stunned to be in one of London's finest restaurants, Savannah felt truly a part of this historic city. The glamour, sophistication and elegance made her feel special. The gilded ceilings, magnificent grand windows and towering arches were awe-inspiring. Gold and marble oozed lavishness from every angle, an excellent example of old-world grandeur and timeless elegance.

Crossing her ankles under the table, Savannah silently thanked Claudia for insisting she bring the little black dress on her trip. The silky slide of the material over her body gave her confidence, something she desperately needed with Albert's wife, Paulette, sitting across from her.

Beautiful, elegant and well-spoken, the woman epitomized everything Savannah wanted to be and fell short of.

Feeling out of her depth she was prepared to slide into the background but Paulette, both gracious and friendly, drew her into the conversation. Savannah held her own, and she soon relaxed, enjoying a glass of wine while laughing and chatting as the meal progressed.

The men had ordered brandy when the conversation turned to the properties they'd toured. Savannah switched to coffee and listened. As they talked, it became clear Rick had narrowed his choice down to two.

She watched as he lifted a snifter to his mouth. The muscles in his throat worked as he swallowed. Her mouth watered.

"Rett would like the property at our hotel best," Savannah blurted out, to distract her thoughts from the deliciousness that was her boss.

Mention of his twin brought a frown to Rick's brow. She'd never known two men closer than the brothers, but they had very different business styles.

"My twin brother," he clarified for the Crosses. "He's in charge of purchasing and design."

Paulette touched the diamond choker at her neck. "I'm familiar with his work."

"Is that one of Rett's pieces?" Savannah asked. "I've been admiring it all night."

"I love it." Paulette affectionately patted Crosse's hand on the table. "Albert picked it up for me when he was in San Diego for the discussions last spring. Why do you say Rett would prefer the Knightsbridge property?"

"It's smaller than the other property, but it has more character and more windows, which allows for more natural lighting, plus more display space."

"Security is more important than setting." Rick stated the age-old argument between the brothers.

"Not to Rett," she said simply.

He half turned toward her, hooking an elbow on the back of his chair "You're *my* assistant—your loyalty should be to me."

"But he's teaching me design." She shifted so she faced him. "And he's not here to represent his view."

"If he asks again, tell him I've got it covered," Rick suggested. "He'll listen to you, since obviously he likes you."

"Oh, no, you're not using me to misdirect him."

"How delightful." Paulette clapped her hands, drawing Savannah and Rick's attention.

Both the Crosses smiled at them. Paulette shared a laughing glance with Albert. "Don't they make a lovely couple? Remember when we used to bicker like that? Oh, you loved to give me a bad time."

Crosse winked at his wife. "Spot-on. You rose so beautifully to the bait." Nodding to Savannah and Rick, Albert said, "She still does."

"Oh, no." Savannah jumped in to correct the wrong impression. "I'm just Rick's assistant."

"And I was in the secretarial queue when Albert found me," Paulette said.

Startled by that revelation, Savannah blurted, "But you went to college, right?"

Paulette shook her blond head. "I started in reception right out of school. My family had no funds for university. But that didn't matter to Albert."

"I never went to university. Why should it matter to me if she did? After our boys were out of nappies, she got her degree in art history. Now she's assistant curator at the Museum of Modern Art."

"Albert, stop." Paulette flushed with pleasure. "They're not interested in hearing about me."

Actually, Savannah found it very intriguing. She'd been thinking of going back to school, and here was a beautiful, intelligent woman who had got her degree after she began her family. It motivated Savannah to act on her dream.

Working at Sullivans' with Rick gave her a sense of confidence she'd lacked for a long time. It had brought her to this fabulous restaurant with these gracious, sophisticated people. How much further could it take her?

"It's an amazing accomplishment." She smiled at Paulette. "Was it hard?"

The older woman winced, but there was pride in her expression, as well. "It was worth it," she said. "But we were talking about you two."

"No, really—"

"It's obvious you have feelings for each other." Albert patted his wife's hand fondly. "We've been together for thirty-two years. Good years. The heart of your family comes from your commitment to each other. But I'm here to tell you the key to any successful relationship is compromise."

"It's true," Paulette confirmed softly. "The love you share creates the core of your family. The heart comes from working together, supporting each other."

They were so sweet, so earnest, Savannah bit her lip to keep from blurting out the truth. Or laughing out loud at their mistake. She wasn't sure which would come out if she let go. She didn't dare meet Rick's gaze.

"Don't be fooled—it takes work. Sometimes it's really difficult, but the kids, and always having someone there for you, make the journey worth it." Dignified and proud, Albert stood and helped his wife to her feet. "And I know what hard workers you are, so you're halfway there."

Savannah shook her head.

"There's no use denying it, dear." Paulette graced both Savannah and Rick with a smile as she joined her husband. "I can see you're meant for each other."

Albert glanced between the two of them and nodded.

"She's rarely wrong about these things." He reached for his wife's hand. "Rick, I know you have something planned, so we'll leave you here." The men shook hands. "I look forward to working with you both."

"It was lovely meeting you." Savannah stood to give Paulette a friendly hug. "Thank you for coming out to celebrate with us."

"My pleasure. You're such a charming couple. I'm sure we will all work well together."

"Paulette—"

"We're grateful for your well wishes. Aren't we, darling?" Rick picked her hand up from the table and carried it to his mouth. The heat of his breath on her skin, then the touch of his lips caused her mouth to go dry.

Vaguely, she heard Paulette giggle in delight as she walked away.

Savannah cleared her throat, made a tentative effort to pull her hand free. "Why?"

He retained his grip on her; in fact, he turned her hand over and pressed his lips to the sensitive skin of her wrist.

Oh my.

Unprepared for his sensual assault, she yanked her hand away and buried it along with her other hand in her lap. "What are you doing?"

Happy with life, no doubt helped along by the wine and brandy, he grinned. "Come on, we made her day."

Enough already. She found the constant buzz of sexual tension between her and Rick exhausting. And he thought it would be amusing to play sensual games?

He wanted to play? Well, she'd show him she knew how to throw a hardball.

"I understand." She drained the last sip of wine. "You were just flirting for your audience."

He inclined his head, the overhead light gleaming in the dark sheen of his hair. Humor lit his blue eyes, inviting her to enjoy the moment. "They wanted lovers, I gave them lovers. It ends things on a positive note."

"I see." Beyond being amused, she stood and slowly leaned toward him. The closer she got, the more wary his gaze became.

Wise man.

The kiss they'd shared on the plane never strayed far from her mind, and her inner diva demanded she remind him exactly why it was dangerous to play with fire. Standing over him, she cupped his face in her hands and pressed her lips to his.

Slowly, softly, she kissed him.

Oh my, indeed.

When she raised her head, desire burned in his eyes. He reached for her. She stepped back, then licked her lips.

Yeah, she'd shown him.

She turned to find the whole room watching. She literally felt the pink rush to her face. Passion made her movements sluggish as she picked up her purse and jacket. "Good night. *Darling.*"

CHAPTER SEVEN

OF COURSE, HE RUINED her great exit by following her. Savannah dodged him by stepping into the restroom. *Good night. Darling.* Right. What had she been thinking?

Obviously, she hadn't thought. She'd reacted.

He'd looked so pleased with himself. Sitting there so calm and composed with no hint that his outrageous gesture had shaken him at all when it had rocked her to the very core. Now she just felt foolish.

But she couldn't hide forever.

She left the restroom. Rick stood in the lobby, holding her coat and scarf.

"That was a miserable end to an otherwise delightful dinner." Even to her it sounded like an accusation. She cocked her head and decided that suited her just fine.

"Don't you think you're overreacting?" he countered.

"No. What did Crosse mean you have something planned? Should I make my own way back to the hotel?" she asked, changing the subject.

"I have a surprise for our last night here." He helped her into her coat.

She scowled, in no mood to go anywhere with him. "I don't like surprises."

"Really? I thought you'd love surprises." Undeterred, he swept her along, ushering her outside into the crisp night air.

"I used to."

"You'll like this one," he insisted as he hailed a taxi.

A short while later she slowly climbed out of the car, her gaze locked on the huge Millennium Wheel. "Okay, I'm surprised."

"They say at night it's like you're right in the middle of the stars," he said, excitement obvious in his voice.

It caused her to stop and really look at him. He'd removed his jacket and stood there looking a little rumpled, his hair slightly disheveled, his eyes shining with anticipation.

"I've rented a private flight for us." Rubbing his hands together, he led the way into the terminal.

With a sigh, she put aside her embarrassment and annoyance, unable to deflate his rare show of enthusiasm.

Still, nerves got the better of her as the time came to board. "Oh, Rick. I don't know. I'm not sure I'm this brave."

He simply held out his hand for hers. "If there's one thing I've learned about you, Savannah, it's that you're fearless."

She looked at his outstretched hand. Did he really believe that? How she wished it were true. She wasn't fear-*less*; she just didn't let her fears stop her. Except when it came to school—maybe because she wanted it so badly? Another hint it was time to stop procrastinating.

She bit her lip. Not so fearless when it came to flying either.

"Do you trust me?" he asked softly.

"Oh." She released her pent-up breath in a resigned sigh. "Yes, of course."

"Then let me give you the stars."

Oh, man. How did she resist that?

"Okay, but if you have to carry me around tomorrow because of my shattered knees, just remember you insisted."

"I'll keep you safe."

The promise issued in his forthright manner was enough to cause her knees to melt, so maybe she wouldn't have any problems after all.

The trip more than lived up to his claims. An attendant accompanied them yet stayed discreetly in the background. Champagne and strawberries immediately helped to lighten her tension.

Rick stood directly behind her, close enough to touch yet always at a distance. Quietly keeping his word.

"It's so quiet," she observed.

"That's probably because there are no other people around," he said dryly.

She flicked him a reproachful gaze. "It's not that. There's a stillness up here."

He moved to her side. "Yeah. I feel it, too."

"The view is magnificent." Watching the lights of the city expand outward made the gradual rise into the dark an exciting adventure. "It's like we're flying among the stars."

"When I promise a woman the stars, I deliver."

"Yes, you do." She laughed up into his blue eyes. "Thank you for insisting."

Desire flared between them, practically sizzling in the air.

A finger under her chin lifted her head up to his, and he fitted his mouth to hers. Closing her eyes she saw more stars as he made her world twirl in wild abandon.

This night was a dream come true even while she knew it was too good to be true. She knew she should question his uncharacteristic change of attitude. But it felt too wonderful standing in the middle of the heavens with her head on his chest.

So she wouldn't ask, wouldn't question. She'd simply hold on tight and live in the moment. And when they left England tomorrow, she'd have an unbelievable memory of more than this fabulous city that had captured her heart.

He spun her around so her back snugged against his front and they both faced the view.

"So, what put you off surprises?" he asked huskily.

Oh. The question brought up painful memories of promises made and broken, of surprises dangled but never coming to fruition. She loved her father, but she'd been disappointed so many times she'd lost her faith in him, and she didn't know if she'd ever get it back, which saddened her. She refused to be sad tonight; she'd just vowed to live in the moment. And this was where it had taken her.

"Experience," she answered softly. "When they don't come off, it's more painful and disappointing than if you'd never gotten your hopes up in the first place."

"Ouch. Your dad?"

She nodded. "When my mom got sick my dad disappeared from our lives. Not literally—he came home each night, but emotionally he was disconnected." She lifted her eyes to meet his. "Actually I give him credit—he was there for Mom right through to the end. But it took all he had. He shut the rest of us out."

"Rough times. I know from Gram your mom has been gone for a while. You must have been very young."

"Fourteen when she got sick, seventeen when she passed. Dad didn't even make my high-school graduation. He just buried himself in work."

His arms tightened around her. "The workaholic you once mentioned."

"Yes. Claudia and Daniel were younger, four and five years younger than me, but it didn't take them long to figure out Dad was unavailable."

"It was different for them. They had you. I know what a difference that makes because we had Gram."

"Thank you, that helps a lot."

Tonight was turning into so much more than she'd ever anticipated. She felt closer to Rick than ever before.

They talked about everything and nothing. He made her laugh, he made her want, and when he talked of his father, he nearly made her cry.

"We went fishing and he played ball with us. He came to our games when he could. I thought he was the best dad in the world."

"Sure sounds like it." It made her remember the early days, when her own father made time to be with the family.

"Yeah, I only learned the truth about the business failing when I watched Gram pick up the pieces after he and my mom died. If she weren't such a cagey old gal, we would have lost everything."

"So you're complaining because he spent time with you?"

"He should have taken care of business instead. Sure, it was fun to play catch. It wouldn't have been fun to lose our house." He released her to grab them two glasses of champagne. "We were two payments behind on the mortgage payments when he died. We went to live with Gram and she sold the house, put the money into the business. It saved us."

And changed him forever. At the age of nine or ten he'd lost the man he'd worshipped and learned that he'd been a dreamer rather than a businessman. The worst of all possible sins to Rick. No wonder he worked so hard. It was in compensation for the damage done by his father, and a tribute to the sacrifices made by his grandmother.

"He loved you. Chose you and your brothers over his job." She laid a hand over his. "That says a lot."

"It says he was weak."

"No," she said softly, "it says you were more important to him than a store."

"It was our livelihood. And the store had been in my family for over seventy years. Built on the sweat of my father's father, grandfather and great-grandfather." He turned his hand over to lace his fingers with hers. "You're too easy to talk to, and I've revealed too much. No one knows about the late mortgage but Gram and I."

"Your secret is safe with me." She focused on her wineglass, circling the rim with a fingertip. "Divided loyalties—that's a hard lesson to learn so young. Have you never wanted more from life then? Never believed you could fall in love *and* run a successful business?"

Rick took the question on the chin. He should have known when he took the conversation to a personal level that Savannah would draw more from him than he found comfortable. For some reason he felt compelled to know more about her, to ferret out her secrets. It was only fair to give up some of his own in return.

He knew love; his family abounded in it. Yet he'd always felt apart from the closeness that held them all together. Perhaps his resentment for their father had something to do with it. Or maybe he just feared losing anyone else.

"No. I haven't always been so resistant to relationships. In college a pretty little blonde from Boston caught my attention enough that I asked her to marry me. She accepted, but in the end she missed her family and chose to return east."

Savannah turned in his arms to look up at him. He saw a hundred more questions in her eyes and braced himself.

"Did you consider going after her?"

"I thought about it. But it came down to this—she didn't love me enough to stay. I didn't love her enough to follow. The breakup still hurt, though."

"I'm sure it did. If there's one thing I've learned about you, Rick, it's that you feel things deeper than you let on."

How could she possibly know that? It was something he'd buried long ago. Feelings were messy and distracting. He preferred things simple and straightforward and that's how he'd built his life.

"I'm sorry you gave up on love. I think you have a lot to offer."

"Sir." The attendant stood a few feet away. "The flight will be docking in a few minutes. We'll need you to be ready to exit."

Rick nodded and the man returned to his station. They'd been so intent on each other, they hadn't noticed the flight was over. And so was their time alone.

Tomorrow it would be back to business.

Back in the hotel suite, Savannah pulled off her gloves and scarf. She glanced at Rick through her lashes. He was much closer than she'd expected and she had to run her gaze over his broad chest to reach his eyes.

"Thank you for the lovely surprise. I'll never forget tonight."

"I'm not ready for it to end." He caught her hand and pulled her to him. Slowly, he lowered his head, his lips settling softly against hers.

Oh my. She held still, afraid to move, not because she feared him, but because she didn't want him to stop. Giving in to the temptation of his mouth on hers, she touched the tip of her tongue to his bottom lip. Immediately he angled his head and took the kiss to a new level. He tasted of man and champagne, an intoxicating mix.

And a potent reminder of the alcohol he'd consumed through dinner and the flight. That they'd both consumed.

Regretfully, she turned her head, breaking off contact. "We should stop."

"Do you want to stop?" His breath heated the skin of her temple.

No, not at all, her heart cried, though her head said different. "You won't be happy about this in the morning."

"Define *happy*. Life is mostly the same old, same old with rare moments of extreme pleasure." He traced the shell of her ear with his tongue. "I think we can reach new levels of extreme."

As skillful fingers played down her sides, she fully

believed him. He whispered in her ear that he had protection.

"This is so wrong." But she lifted her mouth to his, meeting him halfway, threading her fingers through the short strands of his dark hair.

"Yeah, but it feels so right." He sealed his mouth over hers, ending the conversation.

Opening her mouth under his, she let him in, let him sweep away her protests. She held him to her, breathing in his scent, man and soap with a hint of spice. He smelled as good as he tasted.

He demanded and she gave willingly, lifting onto her toes to get closer. He nibbled her lower lip then soothed the bite with a swipe of his tongue. She moaned as he worked his way down her jaw and then her neck, to her shoulder and lower. She shivered at each bite, sighed with each soothing caress.

Passion eclipsed common sense as she practically climbed him to deepen the embrace, and he helped by circling her waist with one strong arm and lifting her against him, her feet several inches off the ground. She wrapped her arms around his neck and let him carry her to his room. One high heel fell off and she kicked away the other.

"Business is over for the day."

Once she gained her feet again, she took delight in removing his tie, pulling hand over hand until it hung loose in her fingers. Feeling wicked she tossed it over her shoulder and reached for the buttons of his shirt.

For each one she released, she kissed the warm skin

revealed until he lost patience and stripped off the shirt himself. Next he made short work of sliding down her zipper and the little black dress pooled on the floor.

They sank to the bed where the tension smoldering below the surface exploded in sizzling passion.

Some called him cold, unfeeling, but she'd always seen his intensity, his deep sense of duty. It drove his ambition and dedication, which, in turn, fueled his isolation. But cold and unfeeling? Not by a long shot. By turns tender and demanding, he fanned the flames of her desire hotter and hotter.

He was in the shower when she woke up. With mixed feelings, she escaped to her room to shower, dress and complete her packing. And then they were in a taxi on the way to the airport.

In a blink they were back on a plane on the last leg of the flight home. Another red-eye flight. She hoped they didn't encounter turbulence as bad as on her first flight.

Tired but anxious, she shifted in her seat.

"You've been quiet," Rick said. "Do you think you'll be able to sleep?"

She blinked at him. "Wow. Déjà vu. I hope that doesn't mean we'll have bad turbulence."

He looked away, and she rolled her eyes in rueful amusement, not surprised by his avoidance of emotional discourse.

"Don't worry. I'm not going to get clingy," she reassured him. "In fact, I want to thank you for an awesome trip. I had a great time."

"Yes. It was a very successful trip. Even Rett should be happy."

"I'm glad it worked out for the company, but I was talking about us. I do understand that it all ends when we touch down in San Diego."

He turned back to her, relief clear in his eyes. "Oh, I think I can see you to your door."

"Such a gentleman." She smiled, careful to keep the growing sorrow from showing. He would have done that anyway. "Your grandmother would be proud of you."

He flinched slightly, just a quick narrowing of the eyes and she wondered at the moment of vulnerability. Maybe he wasn't as unmoved by the end of their fling as he wanted her to think.

"I'm going to miss you," she said softly.

His gaze flicked to hers. "We'll be working together every day."

"Of course." And the proximity would make things harder not easier.

"Are you going to be all right with that?" he pressed.

"Yes." She nodded, emphatically. "Last night was indescribable, but I'm not really the kind of girl to enjoy flings. And when I find the right man I want to know I'm number one for him. That when it comes to priorities and split loyalties, I come first. I told you about how my father turned to work for solace so maybe you can understand that. I know he loves me. It just doesn't always feel like it."

"And you think that's how I treat the women in my life?" he asked thoughtfully.

"Yes," she answered honestly and saw that flash of vulnerability in him again. "But it's okay, because that's the life you've chosen. You've said you don't plan to get married. I respect that. But I also hope you find someone who'll fulfill you more than well-balanced profit statements."

"Thanks. I think."

She forced another smile and lowered her gaze to their hands, separated by several inches on the console between their first-class seats, and thought, *That's the way it has to be.* But she closed her eyes, shutting out the sight.

"I think I will try to sleep."

He said nothing, but a moment later his hand covered hers.

CHAPTER EIGHT

"SAVANNAH, I'LL BE AT the downtown branch for a few hours, and then I'm off the clock until four." Rick stopped at her desk to give her his schedule. "Call me if you need me."

"I thought you were attending the meeting with human resources for the proposal from the independent health-care provider this afternoon."

"I changed my mind."

"Really?" she blurted in surprise and then quickly tried to recoup. "I mean did you want me to sit in on the meeting and take notes?"

"No. The manager can handle it." Instead of leaving he stood jiggling the change in his pocket. "Aren't you having lunch with Jesse today?"

"Yes. How did you know about that?"

He lifted a dark brow, silently reminding her Jesse was family. "Are you going to talk to her about her teacher's certification?"

"Maybe."

"You are."

She looked at him from under her lashes. "Don't push me."

"You should talk to human resources. We pay for continuing education for our employees."

Okay, she just shook her head at that. "I'm a temp, remember? And teaching is not continuing ed for jewelry-making, consumer marketing or retail sales."

He inclined his head. "There's design. You have a real talent in that direction."

"I thought of that, but I want to teach. Plus, I'm still only a temp."

The man was driving her insane. The stoic, distancing man from before their trip to England had returned with a vengeance upon touchdown in San Diego a month ago. Which she'd expected, of course. And she'd prepared herself for his reappearance. Not that it had been easy to switch gears from lover to assistant when she was suffering from jet lag.

But on odd occasions this solicitous man popped up, and she truly didn't know what to make of him.

"Unless you're offering me a permanent position here at Sullivans'?" she prompted.

"A permanent position?" he drawled in speculation.

The expressions fleeting across his face reflected the way she felt, a combination of horror followed by hope replaced by resignation. Which told her his customary cold shoulder was as much a facade as her daily display of disinterest.

The chemistry between them blazed as strongly

now as it had in England. And before that if she was honest.

Honest? Who was she kidding? If he were to offer her a permanent job, she'd probably jump on it even though she told herself nightly she'd be out of here and away from the temptation of Rick Sullivan in a heartbeat if it weren't for her obligation to Mrs. Sullivan to see the job assignment through to the end.

Yep, that's what she told herself. And at night she meant it, but during the day she longed for the sight of him, shivered at the sound of his deep voice. More than once she'd caught herself leaning closer to get a whiff of his cologne and the underlying scent of man.

When he was around, that is. Since their return to the States, he'd hit the road to visit all the branch offices. This was his second trip downtown.

"I don't get you, Rick." Frustration made her speak up. "I can't tell if you want me to stay or you're trying to get rid of me."

He pinned her with an intense, unreadable gaze. "Good question. When I figure it out, you'll be the first to know." And flipping the marble hourglass, he turned and walked out of the office.

She glared after his retreating back. No mixed signals there.

And lunch with Jesse only added to her confusion. For all his recent travels, it seemed Rick had made time to spend time with his family.

"I don't know what happened in England." Jesse

flashed Savannah a knowing glance. "But Rick is like a new man."

"Really?" Savannah twisted her iced-tea glass on the table, avoiding eye contact. "In what way?"

"He's more visible, more available. This afternoon he's playing handball with Brock. And it's been great to have him at Sunday dinners again. I can tell you Gram's thrilled."

"Family means a lot to him." Savannah thought of his willingness to sacrifice a family of his own to protect the interests of the whole. "That's not new."

"No, but he's always been a little aloof. I mean, he makes the big events, but usually only gets to Sunday dinner three or four times a year." Jesse sat back, allowing the waiter room to deliver her meal. "Something definitely happened to shake him up in England."

"He's very excited about the international deal." Feeling a tad nauseous, Savannah pushed the club salad around on her plate. "It was an important goal for him."

"Hmm." Jesse nodded over a bite of Chinese chicken salad. "He's invited everyone to the London opening in November. I can hardly wait. But enough about Rick, except to say keep on doing whatever you're doing. Let's talk about you. I love to teach, so I'm happy to share anything you want to know. Do you have a field of study you want to specialize in?"

The talk turned to education, both learning and teaching, but in the back of Savannah's mind lurked the thought that his trip to Europe may well have changed

Rick. She knew he'd been impressed with Crosse and his style of doing business.

She'd certainly come back a different person, both in heart and spirit. Paulette's story had inspired Savannah to act on her desire to go back to school. And in giving herself to Rick she'd opened herself to him more than to any other man she'd known.

Too bad she was a woman who needed to know she came first in her man's life, and he was a man driven by ghosts to see his company succeed.

When it came down to essentials those were two things that weren't going to change.

She'd be a fool to believe anything else. No matter how much she wished things were different.

Feeling totally sick, she pushed her plate away.

Dazed and confused took on new meaning as Savannah stared at the plus sign on the little white stick. Equally excited and horrified she finally acknowledged her suspicions were correct. Still carrying the stick she moved into her bedroom.

"I'm pregnant." She tested the words and found they made her knees weak.

"Oh, Savannah." Claudia was right there lending Savannah strength, walking her to the bed to sit. "It's going to be okay."

She sank to the edge of the mattress when she'd rather crawl into the middle and hide her head under the covers.

"I'm expecting the boss's baby. That's really *not* okay," she said in a strangled voice.

"Don't panic. That was only one test. Maybe it's wrong. We'll get another one, or two. We'll get three more tests and try again. I'm sure it's just a mistake."

"It's not a mistake. I've been sick in the afternoons, and I'm constantly tired. I have to stop pretending it's not real."

"The flu is going around. I've heard a lot of people misread these tests—"

"Claudia, this is the third test I've taken."

She'd been in denial for nearly a month before buying the first test. She'd honestly thought she had the flu. As Claudia said, there were some nasty ones going around. Plus Savannah had kept reminding herself they'd used protection, and she was on the pill, so she couldn't be pregnant.

"Oh." Claudia took in Savannah's announcement. Then the questions began. "But how? You're on the pill right?"

"Yes, but I've thought about that. I'm usually very good about taking the pills at the same time every day, because the doctor said that was most effective, but with the long flights and time change I figure I missed a whole day and then I was on London time. I'm sure it got messed up."

"But you said you used protection."

Savannah bit her lip and looked at Claudia through her lashes. "We talked about using protection. It definitely got mentioned at one point. But I just don't know."

She rubbed at her temples as if trying to massage the memories back. "After we moved to the bedroom I don't remember anything but the really hot sex."

"Now you're just bragging." Claudia grinned.

"Really. Hot. Sex. Three times."

"Savannah!" Claudia exclaimed, happily scandalized. "You're a red-hot mama. I'm so proud of you."

"Not exactly the reaction I'm looking for."

"Sweetie, you're a bit of a prude, probably because you had to take on the mother's role with Daniel and me. And we both know you stink at flirting. I'm just happy you found someone that saw beyond all that. You deserve to have fun."

"I guess I can't even do fun right, because it sure seems like it comes at a high price." Savannah swiped a tear from the corner of her eye.

"Well, I see this as a blessing." Claudia rubbed a soothing hand up and down Savannah's back. "No one will make a better mother than you."

"You're so sweet." She mustered a smile for her sister. "But I need to get through the panic stage before I can start seeing blessings. I just enrolled at National University. I finally make the decision to go back to school and suddenly I'm back to raising a family again. Oh, God." Savannah wrung her hands. "How am I going to tell Rick? He is going to freak out."

"Come on, he's a stand-up guy. I'm sure he'll handle this with integrity."

"Phff," Savannah huffed. "You got that right. He's

strong on duty and responsibility. I see a marriage proposal coming, and I so don't want that."

"Wait. I thought you were worried you'd have to do the whole single-parent thing on your own? You just said you want to continue your schooling. The man has money, looks, and ethics and you don't want to marry him?" Claudia waved the little stick. "You obviously have chemistry and motivation, so what's the problem?"

"The problem is I deserve to be *loved,* to have an equal partner in the marriage. I don't want to settle for less."

"No, and you shouldn't. But do you want to raise this baby alone?" Hearing how that sounded, Claudia quickly added. "I mean, of course, I'll be there to help."

"Stop, I know what you mean. The problem is Rick's sense of duty might prompt him to propose, but I don't see him being a lot of help. He has issues and work is his coping mechanism. Jesse says he's changed, but I haven't seen it. He makes our dad look like a happy homemaker."

"Don't you think you're being a little harsh?"

"No."

"You're scared."

Now there was an understatement. "I really am."

Claudia leaned her head on Savannah's shoulder. "What are you going to do?"

Good question. Much as she might want to there'd be no burying her head in the covers, no hiding from this.

She may not have chosen to have a child, but a life beat within her. It was time to man up.

Savannah patted her belly. "I'm going to have a baby. But first I'm going to quit my job."

Savannah felt sick to her stomach. She'd been nauseous all morning. Neither crackers nor soda had helped. Nor had the meager bites of sandwich she'd managed to eat at lunch.

Today she intended to give Rick her notice of resignation. In fact, she'd already printed it out; she just needed to find it. She'd been scatterbrained all morning, stressing over the upcoming confrontation.

In the past month she'd chosen a doctor and had the pregnancy confirmed. And she'd looked for and accepted a new job as a department assistant for a private school.

She'd miss Sullivans' Jewels, but she felt it best to get out from under Rick's authority before she told him about the baby. He could be ruthless, and she wanted to be in a position of strength, to show him she was capable of providing for her child. Maybe not to the level his money would allow, but then she didn't intend cutting him out of the child's life. He could be as involved as he wanted to be.

From a distance.

Not that they'd be having that discussion today. She'd decided to wait to tell him about the baby until she was further along. Yes, it was a selfish decision, but she was the one carrying this baby. In this instance she needed to put herself first.

A baby's cry gave her an odd sense of déjà vu. The sound came again as she reached Rick's open door.

He stood at his desk in his shirtsleeves, hands on hips, staring with bemused frustration at the baby kicking in the carrier on his desk.

He looked up as she appeared in the doorway. "Good, you're back."

"Is Jesse with Rett again?" she asked.

"Yes. And thanks to you, she seems to think I welcome these opportunities to spend time with Troy."

"And so you should." She ventured a step into the room. Considering her current situation, she found the circumstances fascinating. "He's your nephew and the new addition to the family. How long has he been here?"

"Twenty minutes. He just woke up. And as for being new to the family, now most of my brothers are married new additions pop out on a regular basis."

She frowned at his cavalier comment. "That doesn't mean each child isn't special in his or her own right."

"No, but they're all pretty much the same at this age. I usually don't engage with them until they're able to talk."

"You're wrong. They're individuals from the moment they're born." She rounded the desk to smile down at Troy, who continued to kick at his carrier. "It's amazing to watch their personalities develop right before your eyes."

"Huh." He cocked his head as if acknowledging the info and then stepped back and gestured her forward. "All Troy appears to be developing is a fit."

"Oh, no." Savannah caught Rick's arm and drew him back in front of the baby, the first voluntary contact she'd had with him since returning to the States two and a half months ago. The flex of muscle under her fingers revealed his awareness of the moment. She ignored her reaction and his.

"This is the perfect time to get better acquainted. He just wants up."

"Up?" Rick scowled, the gaze he flicked her way revealing an uncharacteristic uncertainty.

"He wants out of the carrier."

He glanced back at the baby. "He's locked in."

"It's not locked." Amused, she rolled her eyes at him. "It's just a few buckles. I'm sure you can figure it out."

Challenged, he made quick work of releasing the buckles. Troy squealed and kicked harder, excited by the signs of freedom. But Rick froze once he had the belts loosened.

"He won't break," Savannah reassured him. "Just hold him with confidence."

"I really don't have time for this. I have a meeting with Anderson."

"It's not for another hour."

Still he hesitated.

"Coward."

His blue eyes flashed a warning. She didn't care.

What could he do, fire her? Not a big threat with her letter of resignation waiting to be found somewhere on her desk.

Her stomach churned at the thought of the coming discussion.

The goading worked. Rick bent and carefully lifted Troy out of his seat. Clearly uncomfortable, Rick held the boy with both hands away from his body.

Thrilled by his new position, Troy kicked his feet and reached for Rick, connecting with his nose.

"See. He likes you."

"Yeah." Removing the little hand from his nose, Rick placed a strong hand under the baby's butt and bounced the little one up and down.

Troy squealed and giggled and Rick shot her a look of triumph, his smile almost as big as Troy's.

"Very nice. I'll just leave you two to get to know each other." Seeing him with the baby, watching him find joy in the child's delight, threw her into an emotional retreat.

"No," he ordered, his tone just short of panicked.

Troy frowned at the sharp bark of Rick's command.

"Don't go." Rick smiled and bounced the baby, quickly gaining control of himself. The sheepish look he sent Savannah held a plea. "We're not ready to fly solo yet."

Even more than before she longed to flee to the safety of her desk, his vulnerability touching her in ways that weakened her resolve, making him more approachable than he'd been in months.

She didn't want to see the warm, funny man she'd gotten to know in Europe. Far easier to walk away from the stern taskmaster she knew outside of their trip.

Though it cost her, she stayed while he and Troy got accustomed to each other. He knew the basics, having watched others handle the babies in the family, and he had good instincts. He didn't really need her, which unaccountably hurt.

And when Jesse called to say she'd be up in a minute to fetch Troy, Savannah made good her escape.

Angry at the irrational emotions warring within her, she began an extensive search for the missing letter of resignation. The sooner she got away from Rick, the better.

Jesse came and went with a cheerful wave. Savannah absently smiled and wished her well while pawing through the files piled on her desk. The letter had to be here somewhere.

A few minutes later a familiar paper landed in front of her. "You want to explain this?" a deep male voice demanded.

Savannah jumped, her elbow connected with a folder and papers flew every which way.

With an arched brow, Rick bent to gather the loose papers, which he carefully handed her. She reached for them, but he held firm until she raised her eyes to meet his. Determination deepened the blue in his. "Is there something you want to tell me?"

"Obviously you read the letter. It's pretty clear." Her stomach roiled as she realized this was it, no more delaying the inevitable.

"Don't play dumb, Savannah. It doesn't become you."

True. It didn't sit well either. So she'd go on the offense. "You had to see this coming."

"You're leaving for 'personal reasons.'" A storm brewed in his eyes. "How convenient."

"No, actually, it's quite inconvenient," she denied with more vehemence than she knew she harbored. "It wasn't an easy decision to leave. I've enjoyed working for Sullivans'. And working on the international deal. I've learned a lot from you. So no, none of this has been convenient for me at all."

"Your personal reasons being you're uncomfortable spending time with me?" he asked in a deceptively conversational tone.

She wasn't fooled. The more reasonable he appeared, the more upset he was. And how like him to go right to the heart of the problem.

"Yes."

"I thought we were handling the situation just fine."

"You barely speak to me." She rubbed at an ache forming behind her right eye. "We communicate by email, voice mail and the occasional sticky note," she said dryly.

"It's working."

"It is so *not* working. What's happening is you're

doing more than usual, which leaves me twiddling my thumbs and you cranky."

"I haven't been cranky."

She lifted her brows at him and folded her hands on her desk. "Believe me, you've been cranky."

She'd dreaded the conversation because it skirted the issue of their night of passion, a topic she wanted to avoid if possible to keep him from suspecting the news she wanted to keep hidden.

What she hadn't expected was for him to argue with her.

She sat back in her chair and folded her arms over her chest. "Why are you fighting me on this?"

"I don't want to have to train another assistant. Especially when there's no valid reason for you to leave."

Frustrated and feeling sick, she said through clenched teeth, "You aren't listening to me."

"You haven't said anything worth listening to."

"Right." She finally gave in, realizing there'd be no relenting until he got his answers. She stood and walked past him into his office where she turned and confronted him after he closed the door. "Here's the truth. You may have been able to erase the time we spent together from your memory, but I haven't been so successful. So I felt it best to move on."

"Just like that?" he demanded. "Two weeks' notice and you're gone?"

"It's for the best. Training a new assistant will be better than continuing to fight the attraction we have no intention of acting on." She sighed, torn. But she wouldn't lie to him. "You know I'm right."

He frowned, his internal struggle obvious. "Do you want an apology?"

Confused, she cocked her head. "For what?"

"London—"

"No," she abruptly cut him off, and then swallowed against a wave of sickness. "I don't want an apology."

"Then what do you want?"

"Nothing. Oh, no." Suddenly the nerves and nausea got to her and she felt her stomach protesting. She breathed deeply, hoping it would settle. No such luck.

"No, no, no." She clapped a hand over her mouth and flew to his executive bathroom where she tossed up the meager contents of her stomach.

Embarrassed on top of being sick, she reached new levels of mortification when Rick's black loafers appeared at the edge of the toilet.

"Go away," she implored him.

"Shh." He smoothed a hand down her back and then held the hair away from her face when she bent forward again.

Sweat broke out on her forehead at the same time chills racked her body. Retching turned to dry heaves and she welcomed the strength of his hold as she shuddered under the assault on her system.

Finally she straightened, and he handed her a glass of water, which she accepted gratefully.

"I'm okay. Thank you." She braced her hands on the

counter, carefully avoiding her reflection in the mirror. "Can I have a few minutes alone?"

"Sure." With a soft stroke of his fingers, he tucked her hair behind her ear. "Take your time."

"Oh, Mama." Savannah moaned once the door closed behind him. That last gentle touch had almost undone all her resolve. And it had reminded her of just how tender and caring he'd been in England.

She very much feared she'd given away a part of her heart she might never get back.

In the cupboard she found toothpaste and a new toothbrush and used both. She didn't even try to save her makeup. A damp cloth felt good on her clammy skin, but the lack of cosmetics left her feeling doubly exposed when she returned to Rick's office.

He wasn't at his desk. She sighed in relief at the momentary reprieve.

"You're pregnant, aren't you?"

"Ahh!" She jumped, screamed and twisted all at the same time.

Rick leaned against the wall to the left of the bathroom, arms crossed over his chest. She'd walked right past him without seeing him. Was he standing guard in case she needed him, or so she couldn't escape?

"My God, you scared me." She pressed a hand to her racing heart. She ignored his question for the moment. Damn him for being so astute.

She hadn't planned to tell him, but she wouldn't lie to him either.

"This isn't the first time you've been sick in the last

couple of weeks. You're pale as fine porcelain, you've lost weight and you're constantly tired. All symptoms of pregnancy. And now you want to leave Sullivans'." He dropped his arms and straightened away from the wall. "Talk to me, Savannah."

She shrugged helplessly. "I don't know what to say, or how to explain—"

"I don't need explanations." He cut her off. "I know how babies are made and we took a few chances. What I need is confirmation. Are you pregnant?"

She slowly nodded.

His corresponding nod was much sharper. "We'll get married then."

Savannah swallowed hard. She'd expected the proposal, yet it still touched her, as did his acceptance of his participation in their circumstances. Some men would be looking to place blame or find a way out of the situation.

Tears welled up and a warmth grew ever bigger in her chest, spreading from her heart outward.

Oh, no. Oh, Lord. She loved him. In that moment she realized she'd been deluding herself. She'd thought knowledge would protect her, that making love to him with her eyes open and her expectations curtailed would prevent her from losing her heart to him.

Wrong.

The heart couldn't be controlled. Wouldn't be dictated to.

She went to him and, wrapping her arms around him, held him tight. His arms enveloped her, and where her head rested on his chest she heard his heartbeat accelerate. The instant chemistry almost convinced her to change her mind. How simple it would be to accept his proposal; she'd have great sex and financial security, and she'd inherit a whole family. All important factors, but not enough.

She wouldn't give up on her dream of love.

"Thank you." She stepped back and wiped at a stray tear. "But that's not necessary."

"It is, actually," he said, no give in his words or his stance. "My baby, my responsibility."

He couldn't have said anything more designed to put her back up. Or to tell her she'd made the right decision.

"No," she said, equally firm. "You've made it clear you have no intention of getting married or of having kids. I respect that and I'm prepared to raise this child alone."

"My decision not to marry or have children was a choice I made. Now the choice is gone. I'll do my duty." He went to his desk and began flipping through his calendar.

"We should get married as soon as possible. If we go with a civil ceremony, we could get it done by the end of the week." The look on her face must have warned him how off he was because he closed the calendar. "I suppose you want a church wedding with all the trimmings?"

"Yes." She crossed her arms over her chest. "When I get married that's what I'll want. But we're not getting married and rushing me isn't going to change my mind."

"I want to do right by you, by the child."

"If you want to be a part of your child's life, I'm not going to stop you, but it won't be as my husband."

"This is about your dad, isn't it?"

"This is about *me,* and the fact I deserve a partner who loves me, someone who wants to be with me for myself and not just because it's convenient or because duty demands it."

"That's nice, but you have a child to think of now."

"The best thing I can do for my child is put him or her in a loving, nurturing environment. *Duty* can't provide that. And I can't put myself in that situation again. I don't think my self-esteem could survive it."

He stepped close, tenderly pushing her hair behind her ear in a simple caress. "It doesn't have to be that way. I care about you. It won't be like it was with your dad. I've already started to delegate and give more authority to my managers. I didn't plan to have a child, but now one is here, I'll do whatever it takes to be a good father."

"I'm sure you'd try. And I appreciate that you want to." She backed away, creating necessary distance between them. "But I can't take the chance. The child and I will both be better off if you're a visitor in our lives. Then we won't expect too much from you."

"Don't you think you should give yourself time to consider my offer, to make sure you're making the right decision?"

He just didn't get it. "Can you say you love me?"

Silence greeted her question.

"Then I'm making the right decision. But you made the offer so your duty is met. Consider yourself off the hook." Holding herself tightly, she turned and walked to the door.

"Savannah." He stopped her before she cleared the entrance. "You *were* going to tell me, right?"

She bit her lip as she faced him. "Eventually," she admitted and then backed out the door.

CHAPTER NINE

SHORTLY BEFORE FIVE, the door to Rick's office opened and his brother Rett entered. Rick waved him in while he listened to the vendor on the other end of the phone make excuses for an error in accounting.

Rett dropped into a visitor's chair facing the desk and crossed one leg over the other. Today he wore a navy so midnight-dark only the sheen showed blue. The gold of his St. Christopher medal gleamed in the open neck of his shirt.

Rick wrapped up the call after gaining a promise of reimbursement. He leaned back and met his brother's identical blue eyes. "Hey."

Rett grinned. "Congratulations, Daddy."

Unable to sit still, Rick rose to get a bottle of water from his mini refrigerator. "Thanks."

"What's wrong?" Rett waved off an offer of a drink, making no effort to hide his interest. "You're going to be a dad. You should be off-the-hook happy."

"Yeah, not so much." Rick scowled, still upset by Savannah's refusal to marry him. She talked about letting him off the hook, but that wasn't who he was.

Rett's raised brows reflected his puzzlement. "Trouble in paradise already? After your call I thought we'd be celebrating."

"No paradise. I proposed. She turned me down." Using succinct sentences, Rick explained the situation.

Rett contemplated Rick over steepled fingers pressed against compressed lips. After a tense study, Rett shook his head. "You need to woo her. It should be easy enough—you spend all day together."

"Not anymore. She quit. She took a job as a department assistant at a school. And I don't know when I'll have time to woo her. She's decided she wants to teach so she's going back to school."

"You're joking."

"Do I look like I'm joking?"

Rett lifted a dark brow. "You look constipated."

Startled by the off comment, a chuckle started low in Rick's throat, erupting in a full-body laugh. He threw back his head and enjoyed the freeing moment. Count on Rett to give it to him straight.

Drawing in a deep breath, Rick released the air along with a wealth of tension. He'd needed a serious reality check, and Rett hadn't hesitated to give it to him. Thank God for his twin.

"When you're right, you're right. Rett, I can't just let her go."

"You let Diana walk away, and you loved her," his twin pointed out.

The memory of that time had always had the ability to upset Rick. But the pain of that loss paled in comparison to having Savannah deny him a permanent place in his child's life.

"That was fifteen years ago. I was young and an idealist. This is different. Savannah is expecting my child. I'm just going to have to change her mind."

"Good luck with that." Amusement gleamed unrepentantly in Rett's direct gaze. "I hope it happens soon. I wouldn't want to be you if Gram hears you're going to be a father and there's no engagement."

"I'm driving out to see her tomorrow. Maybe it won't be so bad. She's been after me to meet a nice woman and start a family."

"Yeah. I don't think this is quite what she had in mind." Rett laughed.

Rick pulled in to the long drive of his grandmother's Victorian home in Paradise Pines. The large white house still felt like home because of the woman who'd given up so much to help raise him and his brothers. Gram deserved to hear the news in person. He was going to be a father. The concept still rocked him to the core.

Him, a father.

Funny, the thought didn't freak him out as much as he'd expected, considering he'd given up all expectation of ever having a family of his own. He should be upset. Instead, he was having a hard time suppressing a rising excitement.

It didn't make breaking the news to Gram any easier, not when she'd sent Savannah to him. That would not sit well with her. Nor would Savannah's refusal to marry him, because he and his brothers had been raised to take responsibility for their actions.

No surprise, she took the first part of his announcement really well.

"You're going to be a father?" Joy lit up Gram's aged features as she rose from her floral sofa to give him a hug.

He stood to return the embrace and she tugged him over to join her on the sofa.

"Tell me everything. I'd almost given up hope of you finding a nice young woman to change your mind from the lonely future you had planned for yourself."

Now came the hard part.

"You know her actually. The mother is Savannah Jones."

"I had a feeling about her." Gram clapped her hands. "Such a sweet child but with a lively spirit."

Yeah, that was Savannah. "Hardly a child or we wouldn't be in this situation."

"Situation?" A stern expression replaced the excitement on her face. "Derrick Francis Sullivan, you *are* going to marry this girl, aren't you?"

He cringed at the use of his full name, not only because he hated it, but because she only used it in moments of extreme upset. Not that he didn't agree with her. Savannah's refusal to marry him still stung.

"I placed that woman in your care," she stated with regal dignity. "I cannot believe you'd take advantage of her, get her with child and not marry her. Explain yourself."

"Of course I asked her to marry me. She turned me down."

"Hmm." Gram gave him her I-know-you look. "Are you sure you *asked* her and it wasn't just a statement of intent?"

Feeling his cheeks heat guiltily, he scowled. "What difference does it make? I'm willing to marry her—isn't that enough?"

"Well, with that kind of enthusiasm I don't know how the girl could turn you down."

"We have a child to consider. We don't get to just think of ourselves."

She inclined her curly gray head. "What reason did she give for turning you down?"

"She said she wants to marry for love, and that she doesn't want a husband who's a workaholic like her dad."

"Ah." Gram nodded while compassion came into the blue eyes she'd passed on to her grandsons. "I don't know the whole history there, but Savannah practically raised her younger brother and sister. And she was barely more than a child herself."

"He skipped out on them emotionally after her mom was diagnosed with cancer. Sank into his work and never really came back out."

Gram tsked. "It must have been very hard on her."

"Right. She should marry me so I can make it easier for her this time."

"I don't know." Gram settled back in her corner of the sofa and eyed him seriously. "Maybe she's right."

Outraged, he shot to his feet. "How can you say that? I'm *nothing* like her father."

"Savannah is your assistant, Rick," Gram reminded him. "I think she knows your work habits. Which were fine when you didn't intend to marry, as you often said you wouldn't. But those habits are hard to break."

"Taking care of the company *is* me providing for my family."

"A woman needs more than a paycheck in a partner," she pointed out.

"Of course I know that." He paced the floral area rug he'd crawled on as a baby. "I can cut back on my hours."

"It'll take more than a change in schedule." His grandmother folded her hands in her lap. "It'll take a change in mind-set. I've tried to talk to you about your father before, but you weren't willing to listen."

No, he didn't want to hear. What was the point of hearing the details of failure?

"He ran the company into the ground," he stated grimly. "That's all I need to know."

"Life is rarely so simple. You should have learned that by now. You think of your father as weak because he chose to spend his time with his family over the business."

"He had a duty to provide for us. Dad was your son. I understand you don't want to hear anything bad about him, but what would we have done if the company had gone bankrupt?"

"It wouldn't have gotten to that point." Gram patted

the sofa beside her. "Come sit with me. Let me tell you how it was."

"Gram—"

"Sit!"

Rick sat and hung his hands between his knees. He'd listen, but it wasn't going to change anything.

"Did you know your mother once left your father?" she asked.

"*What?*" Startled, he turned his head and nailed his grandmother with a glare. "No way."

"Oh, she did." Gram nodded emphatically. "Business was never in your father's heart. He preferred archaeology. He actually met your mother on a dig. They settled down when you kids started to come along, though they stole away to a dig every year or so. But they went through a bad patch after you and Rett were born. Your grandfather passed away that year and your dad stepped up to run the store. You two were a lot to handle, but your dad had to put in a lot of time to run the business."

Rick shook his head. He'd never heard any of this.

Gram placed a hand on his thigh. "Just listen. When your mom got pregnant with Ford she told your father he needed to help out more at home or she was leaving. He promised he would, and I believe he had good intentions."

Rick's grandmother stopped to reach for a tissue from the box on the coffee table. Her hand trembled, and he realized how hard this was for her.

"Gram," he said painfully.

"I'm fine." She waved off his concern. "And you need to hear this." She drew in a steadying breath. "Your dad didn't make enough of a change, so your mom packed you kids up and went home to her parents. It killed your dad to be without his family. Eventually he convinced her he'd change. And he did. It took a while for the toll to show at the store, and when it did, he hired a manager. But by then we were in the middle of a recession, and then shortly afterward your parents were gone. It was my decision to let the manager go and run the store myself, which probably wasn't fair to you boys."

"Stop," he demanded, unwilling to listen to her speak ill of herself when he remembered how hard she'd worked to hold home and store together. "You did the best you could."

Her blue eyes teared up as she nodded. "That's what I'm trying to tell you. We can only ever do our best. Sometimes it pays off. Sometimes you have to adjust and try again. Your father changed because he had a lot to lose. Promising to change and not really making an effort hurts everyone involved. So be careful what you promise."

CHAPTER TEN

TWO MONTHS LATER Rick sat in a doctor's office with Savannah and watched the screen as the doctor moved a ball in jelly across Savannah's abdomen.

"See, here's the baby's head and the feet. And here—" the doctor, a white-haired man with wire-rimmed glasses, pointed at a blip on the screen "—you can see the heart beat."

Rick squinted at the spot indicated and then he saw it, the pulsing beat of his child's heart. And yes, there was the head, and the arms and legs and the tiny feet.

"Rick, do you see?" Savannah fumbled for his hand.

"Yeah." Awe filled him to overflowing. Not taking his eyes from the small heartbeat, he wrapped his fingers around hers and squeezed. "Our baby. It's beautiful."

In an instant his world changed beyond anything he'd ever known. The sense of duty and responsibility increased a hundredfold, but added to that was an emotion so profound it filled his soul.

This was a love like nothing he'd ever known.

"No, not an *it* anymore." Savannah stared at the

screen, turning her head this way and that to try and work out what she was seeing. "Dr. Wilcox, are we having a boy or a girl?"

Rick found himself holding his breath. Not that it mattered. Boy or girl, he just hoped for a healthy baby, knew Savannah felt the same.

"You are having a baby boy."

A son. For the first time ever he had an inkling of what his father must have felt. Was it possible to feel six times this much love? Rick couldn't imagine it.

"Ouch. Rick!" Savannah exclaimed.

He blinked at her and then looked down to where he felt a yanking on his hand to find he was crushing her fingers in his.

"Oh, sorry." He immediately loosened his grip.

She grinned at him. "Pretty intense, huh, Daddy?"

"It's the biggest thing I've ever done."

"Me, too." The look in her green eyes softened and when she turned back to the monitor and tears welled, he understood exactly how she felt.

He leaned down to kiss her just behind her left ear.

She smiled and turned her hand in his to thread their fingers together.

"Marry me," he whispered. "Let's be a family."

She went totally still. When she came to life again she flicked him an unreadable look from the corner of her eye. A moment later she was focused on the screen again, even white teeth torturing her plump bottom lip.

But she just shook her head silently.

* * *

After the appointment Savannah sat at a traffic light tapping the steering wheel with nails painted in Pixie Dust Pink waiting for Claudia to answer her cell. Savannah's mind churned with thoughts of the doctor's appointment she'd just left. Of the second marriage proposal from Rick she'd turned down.

That did not get easier with practice.

"Hello." Claudia finally picked up.

"It's a boy," Savannah announced to the hands-free kit attached to the dash. She grinned and patted her bulge, a boy.

"A nephew! Woohoo!" Claudia whooped. "I knew it. I told Daniel you were having a boy. Have you told Rick?"

"I didn't have to. He was there. And yes, he's thrilled." Not that he'd made a big show of it, but she knew he was pleased.

Though, like her, he'd be happy whatever the gender as long as the baby was healthy. She always breathed easier after hearing the doctor say everything looked good.

"He showed up at your appointment again?"

"He wanted to drive me, but I have a meeting back at the school so I insisted on driving myself."

The fact Rick had been at all her appointments still surprised her. She saw almost as much of him now as she had when she'd worked for him. Especially during those last couple of months when he'd been avoiding her.

Who knew that by quitting she'd be freeing him to

pursue her? On the days she didn't have her college classes, he'd stop by her home bringing dinner with him or charming—okay, bullying—her to go out with him. A few times she hadn't felt like going out, so she'd cooked.

She could tell he liked those times best, though he never expected it. And she realized that for all his bluster about staying single he was as much a family man at heart as any of his brothers.

No question she'd have more distance and privacy if she'd continued to work for him.

"Hey, I wanted to give you the news. Now I need to call and tell Daniel you were right. I'll see you on Saturday."

The light turned green, and Savannah pulled forward. The squeal of brakes gave her little warning. She looked up, saw an SUV barreling for her. Sheer instinct had her slamming both feet down on the brakes.

She screamed.

Claudia frantically called out her name.

And then everything went black.

Savannah lay in the hospital bed cradling the bulge that was her baby and fighting back tears. She was bleeding and the doctors were worried.

She was terrified. And alone.

She remembered talking to Claudia. Everything after the call blurred in a kaleidoscope of scary, painful events. The SUV had run a red light and hit the front of her sedan broadside. The police had told her if she hadn't stood on her brakes it would have hit her right in the driver's side door.

She could be dead right now.

Gulping back a sob she rubbed her belly. Instead her baby might die.

"Sir, you can't go in there. You need to check in with admissions. *Sir!*"

A large, bronzed hand pushed the curtain aside and suddenly Rick was there. In the next instant he held her in his arms. He didn't lift her but came down to her. She wrapped her arms around him, hung on tight and let the tears flow.

"I'm here, Savannah," he crooned against her ear. "Everything is going to be fine."

Oh, he lied. But it was exactly what she needed to hear.

"The baby," she choked out.

"Our boy is strong," he assured her. "He'll make it through this. How are you? Are you hurt? They wouldn't tell me anything."

"Shook up, a little bruised. The air bag saved me. But it was like a punch to the gut, and the baby..." She buried her face in his chest. "I'm bleeding. I'm so sorry."

"Stop. It's not your fault. None of this is your fault." He repeated it again and again until she almost believed it.

He stayed with her and eventually she calmed enough to tell him what she knew. A nurse came along to say the doctor had ordered an ultrasound and they'd be moving her in a few minutes.

Through the next hours she clung to Rick's hand. He stood by her side, his presence lending her strength, his touch giving her hope, especially when the doctors said they wanted to keep her and the baby under observation overnight and reevaluate the situation in the morning.

"Placental abruption is the separation of the placenta from the uterine lining," Doctor Wilcox stated the next afternoon. "I believe you have a partial separation caused by the trauma to the abdomen."

"That sounds serious." Heart beating frantically, Savannah squeezed Rick's hand.

"It is," the doctor confirmed. "The placenta is part of your baby's life-support system. When the placenta separates from your uterine lining, it can interrupt the transportation of oxygen and nutrients to your baby."

"Rick."

He circled her hand with both of his and held on tight. "Are you saying she's going to lose the baby?" he asked.

"She hasn't yet—that's a good sign. Plus his heartbeat is strong, which is an excellent indication of his chances. But you have to be cautious. I'm going to order complete bed rest for the next month and then we'll see. I want to monitor the baby carefully, at least once a week."

He went on to outline the limitations of bed rest and to caution her against overdoing things. She wondered how she was going to manage, especially when he mentioned she should have someone with her day and night.

A few minutes later Rett arrived and the doctor took his leave. Savannah tried to hold it together as family came and went through the evening, as the prognosis was repeated again and again.

Even her dad came by, which touched Savannah, but she was so emotionally overwrought she didn't know how to act. Rick saw the toll it was all taking on her and chased everyone on their way.

And then he held her while she cried herself to sleep.

"Are you ready to marry me now?" Rick asked from where he stood by the window.

Head bowed, she frowned down at the serviceable blue blanket covering her to the waist. Stupid, rough, ugly blanket.

"You're seriously taking advantage of a pregnant woman when she's down?" she exclaimed.

"I'll do whatever it takes." He crossed his arms over his chest, the gesture a wordless statement of his determination. "It's the practical solution to the situation."

Flicking him an irritated glance she said, "You might want to try something more romantic next time."

"Will that work?" Speculation lit up his eyes.

"No, but it'll mix it up for me."

Suddenly he was next to the bed, and she was framed by the magnificent columns of his muscular arms. And then his mouth was on hers, hard, hot, urgent, a demand

and a declaration. When he lifted his head, resolve burned in his gorgeous blue eyes.

"Be warned. I'm not going to stop asking until I get the answer I want."

Savannah licked her lips as she stared up into all that heated intensity. Okay, what he lacked in romance, he definitely made up for in tenacity.

"You're not supposed to rile the sick lady. Just because I've been ordered to undergo bed rest doesn't mean I get to do anything interesting while I'm there." Turning sullen again, she plucked at the ugly blanket. "Over four months in bed. I'm going to go nuts."

Rick kissed her again, this time slow and sweet. "Don't get ahead of yourself. Take it one day at a time. Plus I know you. You'll find a way to fill the time."

"That'll be hard to do from a hospital room." The doctor had ordered complete bed rest for the first month with a possible move to moderate bed rest for the rest of her term, depending on how the baby was doing at the end of the first month.

The problem was complete bed rest meant no cooking, no chores, no moving around her apartment. If she didn't have someone to help her at home, they wanted to put her in a long-term facility. The thought of that made her want to cry.

But she wasn't willing to marry Rick just to keep from being bored. And she told him so.

"I have a proposition," he said, dropping into his customary chair beside the bed. "Come live with me. I talked to my housekeeper last night. She's willing to extend her hours and work from eight to four. That means you'll only be alone a couple of hours a day."

"Really?" It sounded perfect. Except it probably came with a ring attached. "Even though I'm not going to marry you?"

He lifted a dark brow. "My proposal stands. But, no, a marriage ceremony is not necessary for you to stay with me."

She eyed him suspiciously. "What's the catch?"

"You sleep with me."

Oh, no, not a good idea. "The doctor said no sex."

"Yeah, I was sitting here when he said it. This isn't about that. I'm not going to do anything to hurt the baby."

"Then why?" she asked.

"Because I won't be able to sleep at night worrying about you."

"Oh, come on." She just kept herself from snorting.

"I'm serious. What if you start having pains or fall while going to the bathroom? Anything could happen and I might not hear you if you call out. I need you where I can see you, hear you, reach out and touch you."

His intensity was back. Stronger, more stark. Yeah, he was serious. But could she do as he asked, sleep beside him every night for the next month, and probably more? Close enough to see, to hear, to touch.

What was the alternative? A sterile room with an antiseptic smell, and rough, ugly, blue blankets? And inevitable, eternal boredom? Sure, family and friends would call and visit, but there were so many hours in the day, and too many during the night. Usually a positive person, Savannah felt lonely just thinking about it.

Inside her a tiny movement stirred. She caught her breath and went completely still.

"What is it?" Concerned, Rick returned to her bedside and reached for her hand. "Are you in pain? Is it the baby?"

The flutter came again and she grinned through the tears blooming in her eyes. Pushing aside the blanket, she moved his hand to her belly, covered only by her thin nightshirt.

"It *is* the baby, but it's all good. He's moving." She pressed her hand over Rick's right where the tiny sensation stirred. "Do you feel him?"

He shook his head, and she saw that overwhelmed by emotion, words had failed him.

"I do. He's moving. He's going to be okay," she said and believed it. For the first time since the accident, she felt encouraged, the small movement of her child the medicine she needed to look forward again.

Rick sank into the chair and laid his head in her lap. She wished she could see his face but he was turned away from her. Threading her fingers through his chocolate-brown hair, she gave him a moment. When she felt her nightshirt grow slightly damp, she swallowed the lump in her throat and made a decision.

"Do you promise not to harass me about getting married?"

"I won't ask more than once a day."

She shook her head. Stubborn man.

"Okay. I'll come live with you."

Savannah moved in on Saturday. Rick saw it as a triumph. Now if only she looked happy about it.

With great satisfaction he got her settled in his bed and then propped his hands on his hips and surveyed her. A small frown puckering between her russet eyebrows, she looked around the room.

He followed her gaze, seeing his space through her eyes. His style ran to traditional comfort. A king-size black leather sleigh bed with a burnished nutmeg finish dominated the room with accompanying nightstands and bureau. Light flooded in through ceiling-to-floor multipaneled windows, reflecting off the beige suede comforter and showcasing the brown-and-beige medallion rug. Lush green plants added color and a sense of luxury.

"Do you like it?" he asked.

"It's lovely." Nice words but they held no feeling.

She was depressed, and it wasn't because she'd officially started her bed rest. At least not entirely. Today was Claudia's graduation and Savannah was missing it.

He knew how much she'd been looking forward to this day, how proud she was of her sister. For that reason he had a surprise for her.

"Let me show you what I've got set up for you." He went to the closet and pulled out a hospital table, one of those that swung over the bed. On it sat her laptop computer. "Your link with the world."

"Rick." She fingered the laptop and forced a smile for him. "You're too good to me."

Wanting a real smile, he angled the computer toward him, hit a couple of keys to bring up the live stream from San Diego State, and then turned the screen back to her.

"What's this?" She blinked and focused on the video feed. She pulled the laptop closer. "Is that State?" Turning gleaming eyes up to him, she demanded, "Claudia's graduation?"

"I know how much you wanted to go. But you're doing everything you can to take care of our baby, so I got the IT department to show me how to set up the live feed and Daniel agreed to video it. I wanted to surprise you."

"You have." There was the genuine smile he sought. Beaming, she patted the bed beside her. "Come watch with me."

Nodding, he walked around the bed, climbed in next to her and leaned back against the black leather head-board to watch the ceremony.

"Once you see her get her diploma, you have to rest, because your family is coming back here after the ceremony."

"Really?" She turned hopeful eyes toward him. "They're coming here?"

"Straight from the graduation. Including your dad.

Are you going to be okay with that? I don't want you getting upset."

"I was glad he came to the hospital. Too much of an emotional mess to show it, but I was really glad he came. And Daniel said Dad's been dropping by his place quite a bit recently, getting to know his granddaughter."

Tears welled in her eyes, but her smile never dimmed. It felt good to have her here, to know she and the baby were in his care. He was glad to give her this after all she'd been through.

"You can personally give Claudia her gift."

"Thanks to you." She snuggled closer to him. "This is the best surprise ever."

CHAPTER ELEVEN

SAVANNAH TIED OFF THE large black bow on the silver gift-wrapped package, pleased that it looked striking yet masculine. A week ago Jesse had mentioned today was Rick and Rett's birthday. Knowing Rick wouldn't go along with any fuss, Savannah had planned a surprise for him.

He'd given her several beautiful surprises so she owed him.

She grinned. It felt good to be in control of something again, nothing elaborate as she was still mostly stuck in bed and had to rely on others to do the work for her. But she had a plan and she was putting it into action.

With the package wrapped and the smell of baking chocolate cake drifting from the kitchen, she made a call to Rick's favorite Italian restaurant and ordered a meal of lasagna, salad and bread.

At three-thirty she showered and washed her hair, scrunching in mousse and leaving it to air-dry in long, loose curls while the housekeeper went through the closet to find her something besides sweatpants to wear.

"This is nice." Sybille showed her a black knit halter dress. Braided material criss-crossed the bodice before tying behind the neck and the hem fell all the way to the floor.

"Oh my. That must be one of the pieces Jesse picked up for me." Rick had insisted Savannah have some new comfortable clothes to celebrate the move to moderate bed rest. She'd protested because it turned out not to be that big a difference, which meant there was little motivation to get dressed in anything beyond sweats and pajamas.

But if this was a sample of what she now owned, she might need to make an effort. And now she thought of it, Rick might enjoy seeing her in something more appealing than sweats.

"Thanks, Sybille. It's perfect."

"It'll look stunning with your pale skin and vivid hair." Sybille laid the dress on the end of the bed.

"You don't think it'll wash me out?"

"Not if you put a pop of color on your lips."

Savannah pawed through her cosmetic case and chose a tube of lipstick. She rolled it up for Sybille to see the deep bronze color.

The German woman shook her head. "Scarlet, to bring out the red in your hair."

Frowning down at the contents of her case, Savannah chewed her bottom lip. "I don't think I have anything like that."

"I do." Lushly round and eternally blonde, though easily in her fifties, Sybille hurried out and came back a few minutes later with her purse in hand. But she held back. "Would you allow me to redo your makeup?"

Savannah hesitated for just a moment and then nodded. What the heck? Sybille obviously knew makeup secrets. She always looked great even though she came to cook, clean and to keep Savannah company. She suspected the woman had a bit of the cougar in her.

With a glint in her eyes that made Savannah nervous, the older woman placed the mirror out of Savannah's reach and then suggested she change first. A few minutes later Sybille sat beside her on the bed and reached into the cosmetic bag.

"The cake is iced and ready," Sybille said as she wielded a shadow brush over Savannah's eyelids. "Do you want me to set up a table in here?"

"No. I was thinking the living room. Can you organize two place settings on the coffee table? The food should arrive just after he gets home, and everything will be ready."

"He's going to be very surprised."

"Happily, I hope."

"Open." Sybille held up the lipstick, then applied it when Savannah complied. "Ah, yes. When he sees you, he will be happy."

Taking the proffered mirror, Savannah sighed at her reflection. The colors were subtle, her creamy skin softly highlighted with a warm blusher and the pop of scarlet on her lips was actually more of a lush dark cherry. "Sybille, you've made me beautiful."

"The beauty was already there. I just brought it to the surface."

"Thank you. For everything."

"It is my pleasure. Now, what more can I do?"

"That's it. Once the table is set, I just need five o'clock to roll around for Rick to get home."

But instead of greeting Rick at five, she got a phone call that he'd be an hour late as Rett wanted to go for a beer. He didn't mention it was their birthday but she understood, so she assured him she'd be fine for another hour.

She wasn't so fine an hour and a half later when the door opened and it was Sybille returning with the message Rick had been detained even further.

Savannah tried to fight the resulting depression. After all he hadn't known she'd planned a surprise. But the scene was too familiar, the disappointment too sharp for her to be gracious.

Why wasn't she important enough to come first once in a while?

He hadn't even called her himself, but had rung the housekeeper to come babysit. Could the message be any clearer?

"I'm so sorry, Savannah." Sybille sat on the couch and gave her a hug. "I know how important this was to you."

"I'm fine." Savannah pasted on a smile. No reason to bring Sybille down with her. "Good idea, bad timing. Can you freeze the lasagna? I'm not really very hungry."

"I was going to tell him—"

"No," Savannah said, a little too loudly. How mortifying would that be? "Let him enjoy his dinner with his brothers. We'll have our cake tomorrow."

"Okay. Except you have to eat. Let me heat some of this up for you."

The thought made her ill. "I don't think I can."

"Some soup then, or a salad. What would you like?"

"Whatever's easy. I'm going to go change."

"Oh, not yet. You look so pretty. Let me enjoy my handiwork a little longer." At her reluctant nod, Sybille smiled. "Lovely. Now I'll go make our dinner."

Laughter broke out as Ford, Rick's youngest brother and a navy SEAL, ribbed Rett over his fashion sense.

"You're just jealous because I don't have to wear a uniform," Rett shot back.

Rick looked at the faces of his brothers grouped around the table. They'd all come out to surprise him and Rett. And it was fun. But all he'd really wanted for his birthday was a quiet night at home with Savannah.

He'd gotten used to having her around. For all he hadn't planned to marry, he'd learned a bit about what he'd chosen to give up: the companionship, the laughter, the support and concern for his happiness. She made it all so easy.

And that's what he wanted tonight.

"Sorry, guys." He stood up. "Thanks for coming out. I love you all, but I'm going to go home."

"What?" Rett demanded. "I thought you were staying for dinner?"

"I was, but Savannah is at home alone. She's stuck there every day. It doesn't feel right to be out having a good time without her."

"But you already made arrangements to stay."

Rick shrugged. "Then it'll be a surprise when I show up."

"A surprise? Cool." Ford knocked knuckles with Cole. "Let's go. We can call our ladies and have them meet us at your place."

"No." Rick threw a credit card on the table. "Stay and enjoy dinner. My treat. I'll see you all at Sunday dinner." With a sense of deep satisfaction, he turned and headed home.

A short drive later he opened the door to find Savannah, sexy in wild curls and a hot black number, sitting on the couch. On the table were place settings for two and a huge chocolate cake.

"Oh man. On sh—" Rick bit off the curse. He watched her duck her head, but not before he saw the sheen of her tears.

His heart sank. "I'm so sorry."

Obviously she'd meant to surprise him. And he'd ruined it by staying out with the boys. He cringed inside, remembering how she'd told him she'd stopped believing in surprises because it hurt too much when they didn't come off as planned.

"I thought you were having dinner with your brothers," she said to the hands in her lap.

"I couldn't stay." He lifted her chin to look into her flooded green eyes. "I wanted to spend my birthday with you."

"Really?" she whispered.

"Yes. And I'm glad I did. You look amazing." He leaned in to nibble her ear. "Good enough to eat."

That earned him a small smile. "There's lasagna from San Fillipio's."

"I'm sorry I wasn't here for your surprise."

Her gaze was back on her hands. "You called a ba-a-bysitter for me."

He flinched at the catch in her voice and the pain it revealed.

"That was thoughtless of me," he admitted. "I just didn't want you to be alone. And then I realized what I really wanted was to come home to you."

She leaned her head on his shoulder, and he felt her relax against him. "I'm glad."

Relieved at her acceptance, he stole a quick kiss.

"I hope there's plenty of cake, because I have a feeling the surprises aren't over yet. I tried to dissuade my brothers from following me home when I left early, but my guess is they'll be here shortly," he said wryly.

She cupped his cheek. "They love you and want to spend time with you. How could I object to that?"

A particularly rambunctious kick woke Savannah from a sound sleep. She smiled in the dark, pleased by Derrick Charles's hearty kick. Or Adam Joseph's, depending on who won the name game. She and Rick were still negotiating. Charles was to honor Rick's grandfather, as was Joseph. But she'd liked Derrick as soon as she heard it was Rick's full name.

Who knew? And Rett's full name was Everett. He was so *not* an Everett, which showed how important a name was.

She rubbed her bulge, pleased by the baby's vigorous activity, evidence of his continued growth.

Rick rolled over, his warmth blanketing her back as he cradled her to him, his hand coming to rest on her belly next to hers. He'd been on the phone with England when she went to sleep. They were having trouble with the installation of the new vault. She'd missed him. In the past couple of months she'd come to relish the nights when she got to languish in his arms.

"Adam is active tonight," he murmured.

"You mean *Derrick* is active tonight."

She felt him smile against her hair.

"The doctor is pleased with his progress. He's well within the growth rate for this point in your term."

"Yes, I was excited by his optimism today."

Rick kissed her behind the ear. "You're not disappointed to continue the bed rest? I know you were hoping for a little freedom."

"Some, but the baby's growth is more important. If Dr. Wilcox believes it'll make a difference, I'm not going to argue."

"Has it been that bad?" The total lack of emotion in his voice spoke volumes.

Needing to see him, Savannah slowly rolled over

to face him and he gently helped her get resituated by arranging the pillows that helped support her.

"Not at night, not when I'm with you," she assured him and he relaxed. She traced the dark shadow of his jaw, visible because of the light he insisted on leaving on in the bathroom.

"But the days are so long. Jesse has been a lifesaver. She drafted me to help with Gram's party. She brings Troy and sometimes Allie and comes over almost every day with something for me to take care of or just to talk over the status of everything. I know that she could handle it all alone, but still the work and the company have helped to keep me sane."

"What about your online classes? I thought those were keeping you occupied?"

She loved her classes, loved the sense of accomplishment they gave her. Pursuing a degree in education gave her a whole new sense of self-worth. She couldn't learn fast enough.

"They do. And I shouldn't complain because I have such great support from my family and from your family. I'm not lonely, just antsy. And I should stop whining."

"You're allowed." He brought her hand to his mouth and kissed her palm. "Better to vent than to let the feelings fester. I can take it and the stress wouldn't be good for you or Adam."

"How can you be so good to me when I look like a beached whale?"

"You couldn't be anything but beautiful if you tried."

She smiled. "Ahh, and they say Rett is supposed to be the charming twin."

"It's not charm when it's true."

"Oh, Rick, you leave me breathless." Literally. The lack of flattery only made the rare compliments more poignant.

"Does that mean you're ready to marry me?"

Yes. The word almost sprang off her tongue. Every time he asked it got harder to say no.

He took such exquisite care of her. Every night he arrived home by five-thirty and promptly came in to see how her day had gone and to share the events in his before hitting the kitchen to heat up whatever meal Sybille had made for them.

Not once had he lost his patience with her, not even when she got snappy with him out of boredom, fear or just from whacked-out hormones. And he made the bedroom as much his prison as hers even when he didn't have to, spending most of his time either beside her in bed reading or watching TV or at the desk he'd set up in the corner so he could keep her company while he worked.

And no matter how big she got, he made her feel wanted.

He was constantly touching her, never missing an opportunity to hold her or kiss her, yet he always kept a tight rein on his desire, never allowing them to get too carried away. She'd offered to please him in ways that wouldn't hurt the baby, but he'd refused to take a chance by overstimulating her.

"No fair," she whispered, "you already asked today."

"That was technically yesterday. I'm just asking early today."

"Too early. My defenses are down."

"Good." He settled his lips on hers, taking her mouth in a slow and tender seduction that made her sigh, made her yearn. "Say yes."

"Oh, you do tempt me."

"Then take a chance," he urged and she heard the tension in his voice when he usually restrained himself from pushing.

"I can't." Because she loved him, and no one knew better than her how much it hurt when you loved someone more than they loved you.

Yes, Rick had surprised her by supporting her, by being physically present and an emotional rock. But it would be a huge error to mistake support for love.

"You've spoiled me so, it's already going to hurt to leave."

"So don't leave."

Could she stay? Could she give them a chance? Not counting the whole bed-rest thing and fearing for her baby's health, the past two months had been nearly perfect. Although she turned him down daily, she felt as though she was part of a couple.

Yet she couldn't forget the pain of living with a workaholic. The highs and lows, the disappointments, the loss of hope, of self, took over your life no matter how hard you tried to disassociate it from everything else. She didn't like who she became then—impatient, moody, needy. It wasn't a good place to be.

Not even for Rick would she go back there. Her son—their son—deserved better from his mother than watching her become a shadow to his father.

"I've been thinking like a dad." He rolled to his back, propped his head on his hands and spoke to the ceiling. "Delegating more, cutting back my hours. I've tried to be here for you. Haven't I proved how important you and the baby are to me?"

She longed to tell him she loved him, yet feared doing so. He had to say it first and through his own initiative. And then she wasn't sure she'd actually believe him. Hadn't he said he'd do anything to get her to marry him?

"I see the effort you're making." She plucked at the sheet between them. "But it's only been a couple of months."

He pinned her with a hard gaze, his eyes navy in the darkened room. "I'm not your father, Savannah. Don't punish me for his sins."

"I'm trying not to. But my father's shadow isn't the only problem. There's your father's ghost haunting us, as well."

"What do you mean?" he demanded.

"I'm sure you loved your father, but you also resent him. It sounds like he valued his time with his family above everything, yet you blame him for nearly destroying Sullivans'. I don't know if you can put family first, and I need to know you will."

"Taking care of the business *is* taking care of my family," he insisted.

"Sometimes." She'd give him that.

"Most of the time."

"The question is, will you know when it's not?"

He had no answer for that, and, for the first time since she'd moved in with him, they went to sleep without touching.

"This is such a lovely party. I love the mix of casual seating along with the banquet and cocktail tables. It invites people to mix and mingle between trips to the dance floor."

Stunning in a silver evening suit with an asymmetrical collar and long skirt, Mrs. Sullivan regally lowered herself into the opposite corner of the couch from Savannah.

"I understand you helped with a lot of the arrangements." She patted Savannah's hand where it rested between them on the leather cushion. "Thank you."

"Jesse did most of the work." Savannah gave credit where it was due. "Really, it was a blessing to have something to keep me occupied. And the idea for the couches and chairs is courtesy of Rick. He insisted I have a comfortable place to sit all night, and I didn't want to be the only one, so I created the mix. It seems to be working out well."

"It's wonderful. My feet thank you. And Rick. Careful, dear." She caught Savannah in the middle of a yawn.

"I have strict instructions to notify Rick immediately if you show signs of weariness or fatigue."

"Oh...your hair is lovely in that sleek French knot." Savannah sought to distract Mrs. Sullivan with a compliment. She was too excited at being a part of the music and revelry of the matriarch's grand party to leave so early.

She glanced to Rick, who stood surrounded by his brothers at the bar. With a wink at Savannah, Rett and the others had dragged Rick away. As she watched, they all laughed while Rett pretended to be stabbed in the heart. It made her happy to see Rick happy.

No, she wasn't ready to make an exit just yet, so she continued to praise her friend. "You're truly the queen of the ball tonight."

Mrs. Sullivan shook a finger at Savannah. "Flattery will not save you. I value my life and that of my great-grandson too much to thwart Rick."

"Oh, please don't tell him, Mrs. Sullivan," Savannah begged. "He'll banish me upstairs, and I'm having too much fun. And it wasn't flattery—you look so sophisticated and vibrant you glow tonight. And way too young to be celebrating your eighty-fifth birthday."

"Bless you, child, the secret is in the dim lighting, a good girdle and a really expensive face powder. But a woman does what she must when she's the star of the show."

Savannah laughed and patted her prominent belly. "There's no tucking this guy out of sight. He likes the music. He's been dancing all night."

Delighted, Mrs. Sullivan put out her hand. "May I?"

"Of course." Savannah held the older woman's hand over the baby's movements.

"You need to call me Gram." Tears welled in Mrs. Sullivan's vivid blue eyes when the baby bucked against their fingers. "You are family now. Because of this little guy. But even more for the happiness I see in my grandson's eyes. Thank you for bringing him back to us."

Gram placed her other hand over Savannah's and squeezed her fingers. "That's better than any birthday present anyone could ever give me."

"You're welcome. But Rick hasn't really gone anywhere."

"Dear, he's been distancing himself a little bit at a time for years. Making it to fewer Sunday dinners or just making an appearance at bigger events."

"Always too busy?" Savannah bit her lower lip. This was exactly the behavior she feared from Rick. But now she was hearing about it, surprisingly, it didn't feel right.

"That was his excuse, yes. But that changed after your trip to England. I was very excited when he had the family to his place for Sunday dinner. That was a first and it was all because of you."

"He's always looking for ways to keep me entertained," Savannah confirmed.

"It's more than that. He's made it clear to everyone in the family that you're his wife whether you decide to make it official or not. I'm hoping you will. I've been dodging Father John all night."

"Mrs. Sullivan!" Savannah giggled.

"Gram," the older woman insisted.

"Gram." Savannah's throat tightened on the word. This family's generous welcome touched her deeply. Rick's grandmother deserved to know the truth. "You shouldn't get your hopes up. Rick has been wonderful, but this child, me, we're only a duty to him. He'd treat anyone in his care the same way."

"You're too smart not to see how he feels about you. You're just afraid to believe it."

"You think I'm smart?"

"Of course, especially at reading people. I wouldn't have recommended you to Rick as an assistant otherwise. You're too close to this situation if you can't see that he loves you."

Hope bloomed in her heart at Gram's declaration, but she quickly squashed the feeling. Better not to delude herself.

"I think you're mistaking concern for something more," she said.

"And I think you're letting fear color your judgment. He's calmer, more contented than I've ever seen him. And you've brought laughter back into his life. I can see his effect on you, as well. You two belong together."

Savannah blinked back tears. "I wish I could believe that. But I can't afford to spin dreams out of hopes. I lived that way for years and all I got in return was indifference and disappointments. I can't do that to myself again. And I won't do it to my child."

Avoiding Gram's gaze, Savannah pleated folds into

the skirt of her navy dress. "Rick has been married to the business too long to change now. With the baby at threat his strong sense of duty and responsibility are motivating his actions. When the baby gets here, he'll start putting in more time at the office again. And it's okay, because that's what makes him happy. But I need more from the man I marry."

"Oh, child, you're wrong. I wonder how long he has to prove himself to you before you believe in him. A year? Five years? How fair is that? Rick deserves a chance to make his own mistakes, not his father's or your father's."

Stricken by this stark truth, Savannah watched Gram stand and smooth down her skirts.

"I'm fond of you, Savannah. You survived a tough childhood. And there's no denying you're right—you deserve a man who loves and adores you. But I'm going to leave you with one thought. The only thing worse than the lack of trust in a relationship is the lack of faith."

CHAPTER TWELVE

SUNDAY MORNING Rick zipped his suitcase and lifted
it to the floor. His flight to London left in two hours.
Rett would be here in a few minutes to drive him to
the airport.

He didn't want to go, didn't want to leave Savannah,
but the security issues with the vault needed to be addressed. With no one on-site to oversee the work, the
renovations were moving too slowly. Rick planned to
hire a manager while he was in the area.

Looking up, he met Savannah's gaze from where she
was propped up on the bed watching him. She wore
white shorts and a pink tank top that matched the color
on her toes. But her complexion was wan, the skin
around her eyes drawn tight in fatigue from a restless
night.

"You look pale," he said with concern. "I let you
overdo it at Gram's party."

"I had a ball. And I'm fine." She smiled and held out
a hand to him. "I miss you already."

He sat and, cupping her face in his hand, swept

his thumb over her cheek, tracing the shadow under her eye.

"Say the word and I'll send Rett in my place."

"Please, we both know you're chomping at the bit to get there and whip everyone into shape."

"Maybe," he allowed, because part of him did. The total businessman he used to be would demand it. That man would have been on a plane when the company installing the new vault had first called about the problem.

But he'd changed.

"You know it's true." She took his hand and laced their fingers together.

"I know I'll miss you," he admitted.

"Then maybe you'll hurry home—ahh." She flinched and caught her breath.

"What is it?" he demanded. "Are you okay?"

"Yeah." She rubbed her belly. "It's just your son the baseball player getting in some practice."

"That must be your son. My son plays football."

No, he wasn't just a businessman anymore. He was a family man, too. It amazed him how his priorities had changed. How something that affected the store had always been his first consideration when it came to making plans and decisions.

Not anymore.

Savannah and the baby came first. It was clear to him now that they always would. Which was exactly what she'd asked of him—to put her first.

He loved her.

The truth of his feelings hit him in a rush. It was so simple, so clear, so deep he wanted to shout it from the mountaintops.

He opened his mouth to tell her just as a pounding sounded at the door. Damn, he'd have to wait until he got back. Better to do that anyway, as he wouldn't be rushing off halfway across the world. He'd be able to hold her, kiss her and finally convince her to be his wife.

There was a knock on the bedroom door and then Claudia stuck her head inside. "Rett is here."

"Thanks," Rick said, and she retreated, giving them a chance to say goodbye.

"Kiss me before he takes you away."

"First," he said, reaching for the baby monitor on the night table, "don't forget to give Claudia the monitor while she's staying here with you. I want her to be able to hear you at all times. I'll tell Rett, for when he takes over on Tuesday night. I'll be back Friday."

She completely ignored his instructions but pinned him with a suspicious gaze.

"I notice you didn't come up with the baby monitor idea before you insisted I sleep with you."

Caught.

He leaned over her and claimed her mouth in a lingering caress, dragging the kiss out as passion surged between them. Finally he lifted his head and met her desire-drenched eyes.

"I wanted you in my bed."

"But we couldn't do anything."

"Didn't matter."

She swallowed hard. "Oh."

He kissed her again, short and urgent.

"We have to talk when I get home."

"About what?" Her hand tightened on his.

He shook his head, stepped back and grabbed his suitcase. "When I get back." He needed to go while he still could. "Be good, and try not to have the baby while I'm gone."

"Claudia!" Savannah yelled for her sister and then went back to her breathing exercises. She'd been having little aches and pains all morning, so, after Rick left with Rett, it didn't take Savannah long to realize there was more to the pains than a little discomfort.

"You called?" Claudia strolled into the room.

"Can you get my overnight bag and put a few things in it for me?"

"Sure. I've heard they advise you to have it ready early, just in case. I can do it after we eat. I'm making chicken salad and there's some mango, yogurt and sweet rolls. Something should spark your appetite. I thought we'd eat out on the back deck, if you think the chaise will be comfortable enough."

Savannah blinked at her sister, realized the misunderstanding and fought the urge to snap back.

"No, no, no. No chicken salad. Not just in case." She swung her feet over the side of the bed. "Now!"

Fear, uncertainty, anticipation and a hundred other emotions raked at her nerves, pulling her in a hundred directions. In, out, she continued her breathing; as long as she remained calm everything would be okay.

"I called Dr. Wilcox." She gasped at a sharp pain. "He's meeting us at the hospital."

"What?" Claudia's eyes popped wide. "Now? You're having the baby now?" She dropped the dish towel she'd carried into the room and dashed to the closet. "You called Rick, right? Luckily the plane won't have left yet. He can meet us at the hospital, too."

"I'm not calling Rick."

She wanted Rick, needed him by her side. Yet she couldn't call him. The glitch with the security in the vault was a big deal; if it couldn't be fixed soon, they wouldn't be able to complete the remodel in time for the planned opening. And Rick wouldn't meet his goal of making Sullivans' Jewels international during their centennial year.

She hadn't told him because she couldn't stand to see him choose the business over her. It would break her heart.

"His flight doesn't leave for forty-five minutes." Claudia stepped out of the closet carrying an overnight bag. "If you call now, you can still catch him before he gets on the plane."

Shaking her head, Savannah said, "It's best if he goes."

Claudia looked confused. "You're not going to tell Rick you're in labor?"

"No." Savannah swallowed back tears. "And I don't want you calling him either."

This was the way it had to be. She could have this baby on her own, but not if she were agonizing over Rick's absence.

"Savannah." Obviously sensing something was wrong Claudia spoke very gently. "He has a right to be here."

"I'm the one having this baby, and I said *no*." Savannah didn't care that she was being unreasonable. She needed to do what was best for the baby. And right now that meant thinking of herself first.

Dr. Wilcox was waiting at the hospital. Savannah was admitted quickly and, after a brief exam, he ordered the nurse to prep her for a cesarean delivery. Then he left to get ready for the procedure.

Claudia agreed to go with Savannah into the delivery room and was led away to get suited up.

Momentarily alone, Savannah lay staring at the ceiling, thinking Rick's plane was probably taking off over San Diego as she waited to go into surgery. At least twenty times she'd looked for him or reached out a hand, expecting his to wrap around hers in a show of support. So many times these last few months he'd been her strength, her rock, holding her steady when her nerves became shredded, keeping her company when frustration shortened her temper.

Each time she reached for him and he wasn't there was a reminder of every time she'd reached for him over the past months and he *had* been. Not at the office, at a meeting or away on business. But here for her. In so many ways he'd demonstrated his commitment to her and their child, but she'd been too blind to see, too afraid to believe.

Oh, Lord, he was going to be so angry she hadn't called him.

He should be here. More, he'd want to be here.

Her insecurities had cost her big this time, but, worse, they'd robbed Rick of the opportunity to be at his son's birth.

Gram's words about trust and faith echoed in Savannah's head and a new fear enveloped her. What if he couldn't forgive her?

She could lose him and it would be all her fault.

The nurse would be back in a minute. Savannah glanced toward the door but only saw the curtain guarding her privacy. She needed to act now. Maybe his flight had been delayed. Hands shaking, she dialed his cell. She needed to tell him about the baby, needed to tell him how wrong she'd been.

His voice mail came on. Disappointment crashed through her. Too late. She swiped at tears and almost hung up, but he deserved to hear about the baby from her.

"Rick, oh, Rick, I'm so sorry. I should have called sooner, should have had faith in you, but I was stupid." The door opened, but Savannah rushed on, hoping the nurse would give her a few minutes to finish. "So stupid. I was afraid you'd leave me to do this alone. But that was my fear talking. In my heart I knew better. Know better. You are the best man I've ever known. I love you so much—"

The curtain was pushed back and Rick stood there. She blinked at him, unable to believe her eyes.

"That better be me you're talking to." He stepped over, gently took the phone from her and set it on the bedside table.

"Rick." She threw herself into his arms. They instantly closed around her and tightened, giving her a sense of wholeness and strength. "Claudia called you. Thank God."

"It should have been you." She heard the hurt in his voice and cringed.

"I know." She pulled back and framed his precious face in her hands. "I'm sorry. You've been so patient with me, so giving and all I've done is doubt you and hold back. I love you."

She ran her fingers down his cheeks, but looked at his hair, his lips, his chin, anywhere but his eyes.

"I was afraid to tell you, because it would give you too much power over me. But love isn't something you can harness or control. Hiding my feelings only weakened me and diminished us." She smiled through her tears. "I know you don't love me—"

"But I do."

She blinked. "What?"

"I love you." The declaration was all the more powerful for its simplicity. "I wanted to tell you before I left but I ran out of time."

"You love me?" Hope and joy sent warmth flowing through her. "Really?"

"Savannah." Rick cradled her hand in his, brought it

to his mouth and kissed her palm. "Claudia caught me at the airport, but I'd already exchanged my reservation on the plane with Rett. I kept remembering how pale you looked, how active the baby was and I couldn't leave you. I love you. I love our child. I want to live the rest of my life with you."

"So you forgive me?"

"Of course I do. We're together now, and that's what matters." Still holding her hand he shifted so he stood beside the bed. "I'd go down on one knee, but I wouldn't be able to see you. Savannah Jones, I love you. Will you marry me?"

A contraction hit.

Her breath caught in her throat and she clamped down on his fingers. Before the contraction finished and she could accept his proposal, Rick went into panic mode, which was really interesting to see for the thirty seconds it lasted.

He turned white while his gaze darted wildly around the room as if he might find the doctor hiding in the corner. He barked out questions and concerns that she had no breath to respond to.

Finally he caught himself, inhaled and gathered his control.

"Stay right there. I'm going to find the nurse."

She nodded between panting breaths. Right. She'd stay right here.

The nurse returned without Rick, declaring he was being prepped to join Savannah in the birthing room.

From that point on there was no opportunity to speak to him alone. She was too busy having their baby.

A few hours later Rick stood at Savannah's bedside, his arm draped over her pillow, their fingers linked near her shoulder, watching his grandmother cradle his son in her arms. It was a sight he'd thought he'd never see.

What a waste it would have been.

The room was packed with people, with more waiting in the lobby for their chance to admire the newest addition to the family.

Savannah pulled on his hand and he looked down. Exhausted but euphoric, she'd never been more beautiful to him. Bending, he kissed her gently.

"You are amazing." He praised her. "Thank you for my son."

"Charles Joseph after your grandfathers. Gram is pleased."

"Gram is ecstatic. Little Joey will be the apple of her eye." He didn't know how life could get any better, except maybe being alone with Savannah and his son.

"Yes," she said softly.

"Yes?"

She smiled into his eyes. "I love you. And yes, I'll marry you."

His heart melted. Finally.

Life had just gotten better.

THE SECRETARY'S SECRET

MICHELLE CELMER

This book is in honour of the dedicated volunteers at Regap of Michigan (Retired Greyhounds as Pets), www.rescuedgreyhound.org

It has been a pleasure and a privilege to be a part of something so special

One

Nick Bateman lay in bed in the honeymoon suite of the hotel, pretending to be asleep, wondering what the hell he'd just done.

Instead of spending his wedding night with the woman who was supposed to be his new wife—the one he'd left at the altar halfway through their vows—he'd slept with Zoë, his office manager.

He would have liked to blame the champagne for what had happened, but two shared bottles wasn't exactly enough to get him rip roaring drunk. He'd been too intoxicated to drive, no question, but sober enough to know it was a really bad idea to sleep with an employee.

And even worse, he considered Zoë one of his best friends.

He rubbed a hand across the opposite side of the mattress and could feel lingering traces of heat. The scent of sex and pheromones and her spicy perfume clung to his skin and the sheets.

He heard a thump and a softly muttered curse from somewhere across the room. She had been slinking through the darkness for several minutes now, probably looking for her clothes.

His only excuse for what he'd let happen, even if it was a lame one, was that on the night of his failed wedding he'd been discouraged and depressed and obviously not thinking straight.

Instead of saying *I do*, he'd said *I don't* and skipped out on his fiancée. His second, in fact. Could he help it if it had only occurred to him just then the terrible mistake he was making? That his desire for a wife and family was clouding his judgment? That after a month of courtship he barely knew the woman standing beside him, and she was in fact—as his friends had tried to warn him—only after his money.

What a nightmare.

He would never forget the look of stunned indignation on Lynn's face when, halfway through their vows, he had turned to her and said, "I'm sorry, I can't do this." He could still feel the sting of her fist where it had connected solidly with his jaw.

He'd deserved it. Despite being a lying, blood-sucking vampire, she didn't deserve to be humiliated that way. Why was it that he couldn't seem to find the right woman? It had been five years since he decided he was ready to settle down. He'd figured by now he would be happily married with at least one baby and another on the way.

Nothing in his life was going the way it was supposed to. The way he'd planned.

After the abrupt end of the service, Zoë had driven him to the hotel where the honeymoon suite awaited and the champagne was already chilling. He'd been in no mood to drink alone, so he'd invited her in. She'd ordered room service—even though he hadn't been particularly hungry—and made him an ice pack for his jaw.

She always took care of him. And damn, had she taken care of him last night.

He wasn't even sure how it started. One minute they were sitting there talking, then she gave him this look, and the next thing he knew his tongue was in her mouth and they were tearing each other's clothes off.

Her mouth had been so hot and sweet, her body soft and warm and responsive. And the sex? It had been freaking fantastic. He'd never been with a woman quite so...*vocal* in bed. He'd never once had to guess what she wanted because she wasn't shy about asking.

God, he'd really slept with Zoë.

It's not that he'd never looked at her in a sexual way. He'd always been attracted to her. She wasn't the kind of woman who hypnotized a man with her dazzling good looks—not that she wasn't pretty—but Zoë's beauty was subtle. It came from the inside, from her quirky personality and strength.

But there were some lines you just didn't cross. The quickest way for a man to ruin a friendship with a woman was to have sex with her.

He knew this from experience.

Thankfully, he hadn't done irrevocable damage. As much as he wanted a family, Zoë wanted to stay single and childless just as badly. Unlike other female employees he'd made the mistake of sleeping with—back when he was still young, arrogant and monumentally stupid—she wouldn't expect or want a commitment.

Which was a *good* thing, right?

There was another thump, and what sounded like a gasp of pain, right beside the bed this time. He had two choices, he could continue to pretend he was asleep and let her stumble around in the dark, or he could face what they had done.

He reached over and switched on the lamp, squinting against the sudden bright light, both surprised and pleased to find a completely bare, shapely rear end not twelve inches from his face.

Zoë Simmons let out a shriek and swung around, blinking against the harsh light, clutching her crumpled dress to her bare breasts. This was like the dream she frequently had where she was walking through the grocery store naked. Only this was worse, because she was awake.

And honestly, right now, she would rather be caught naked in a room full of strangers than with Nick.

"You scared me," she admonished. So much for sneaking out before he woke up. Call her a chicken, but she hadn't been ready to face what they'd done. How many times they had done it.

How many different positions they had done it in...

The bed was in shambles and there were discarded condom wrappers on the bedside table and floor. She winced when she thought of the way they'd touched each other, the places they had touched. How incredibly, shockingly, mind-meltingly *fantastic* it had been.

And how it could never, *ever* happen again.

"Going somewhere?" he asked.

"'Fraid so."

He looked over at the digital clock beside the bed. "It's the middle of the night."

Exactly.

"I thought it would be best if I leave." But God help her, he wasn't making it easy. He sat there naked from the waist up, looking like a Greek god, a picture of bulging muscle and golden skin, and all she wanted to do was climb back into bed with him.

No. *Bad* Zoë.

This had to end, and it had to end *now*.

She edged toward the bathroom, snagging her purse from the floor. "I'm going to go get dressed, then we'll...talk."

She backed into the bathroom, his eyes never

leaving her face. She shut and locked the door, then switched on the light, saw her reflection and let out a sound that ranked somewhere between a horrified gasp and a gurgle of surprise.

Just when she thought this night couldn't get any worse.

Her hair was smashed flat on one side of her head and sticking up on the other, last night's eyeliner was smeared under her red, puffy eyes, and she had pillow indentations all over her left cheek. Unlike Nick who woke up looking like a Playgirl centerfold. It's a miracle he hadn't run screaming from the room when he saw her.

Had there been a window in the bathroom, she would have climbed through it.

She splashed water on her face, used a tissue to wipe away the smudges under her eyes, then dug through her purse for a hair band. Finger combing her hair with damp hands, she pulled it taut and fastened it into a ponytail. She had no clue where her bra and panties had disappeared to, and there was no way in hell she was going to go hunting for them. She would just have to go commando until she got home.

She tugged on her battered dress, smoothing out the wrinkles as best she could. In his haste to undress her, Nick had torn one of the spaghetti straps loose. One side of the bodice hung dangerously low. The form-fitting silk skirt was still a little damp and stained from the glass of champagne she'd spilled on herself.

It was the dress she'd worn to both of Nick's weddings. It looked as if maybe it was time to retire it. Or incinerate it.

Zoë studied her reflection, hiking the bodice up over her half exposed breast. Not great, but passable. Maybe everyone wouldn't look at her and automatically think, *tramp*, as she traipsed through the five-star hotel lobby. Not that she would run into too many people at three-thirty in the morning.

She heard movement from the other room, and fearing she would catch him as naked and exposed as he had caught her—she cringed at the thought of her big rear end in his face when he turned the light on—she called, "I'm coming out now!"

When he didn't respond, she unlocked the door and edged it open, peeking out. He sat on the bed wearing only the slacks from last night, his chest bare.

And boy what a chest it was. It's not as if she'd never seen it before. But after touching it…and oh my, was that a bite mark on his left shoulder? She also seemed to recall giving him a hickey somewhere south of his belt, not to mention the other things she'd done with her mouth…

Shame seared her inside and out. What had they done?

As she stepped toward him, she noticed the gaping hole in the front of his pants. She was about to point out that the barn door was open, then remembered that in her haste to get his slacks off last night, she'd broken the zipper. They'd torn at each other's clothes, unable to get naked fast enough, as if they'd been working up to that moment for ten long years and couldn't bear to wait a second longer. She would never forget the way he'd plunged inside her, hard and fast and deep. The way she'd wrapped her legs around his hips and ground herself against him, how she'd moaned and begged for more…

Oh God, what had they done?

She clutched her purse to her chest, searching the floor for her shoes. She needed to get out of there pronto, before she did something even stupider, like whip her dress off and jump him.

"I think these belong to you." Nick was holding up her black lace bra and matching thong. "I found them under the covers."

Swell.

"Thanks." She snatched them from him and stuffed both in her tiny purse.

"Should we talk about this?" he asked.

"If it's all the same to you, I'd rather leave and pretend it never happened."

He raked a hand through his short blue-black hair. Thick dark stubble shadowed his jaw, which explained the chafing on her inner thighs.

"That is one way to handle it," he said, sounding almost disappointed.

He had to know as well as she did that this was a fluke. It never should have happened. And it sure as hell would never, *ever* happen again.

Not that he was a bad guy. Nick was rich,

gorgeous and genuinely nice—and okay, a touch stubborn and overbearing at times. And there were occasional moments when she wanted to smack him upside the head. But he was sweet when he wanted to be and generous to a fault.

How he hadn't found the right woman yet, she would never understand. Maybe he was just trying too hard. Either that or he had really bad luck. When it came to finding the wrong woman, he was like a magnet.

Personally, she liked her life just the way it was. No commitments. No accountability to anyone but herself and Dexter, her cat. She'd already done the mommy-caregiver gig back home. While both her parents worked full time jobs she'd been responsible for her eight younger brothers and sisters. All Nick had talked about during the past five years was marrying Susie homemaker and having a brood of children. The closest she was going to get to a diaper was in the grocery store, and that was only because it was across the aisle from the cat food.

The day Zoë turned eighteen she'd run like hell, clear across Michigan, from Petoskey to Detroit. And if it hadn't been for Nick, she wouldn't have lasted a month on her own. Despite having just started his construction company, or maybe because of it, he hadn't fired her when he found out she'd lied on her application about having office experience.

The truth was, she couldn't even type and her phone skills were questionable. Instead of kicking her out the door, which she admittedly deserved, his alpha male gene had gone into overdrive and he'd set out to save her. He'd helped put her through college, trained her in the business—in life. She'd been more than a tad sheltered and naïve.

To this day Zoë didn't know why he'd been so good to her, why he'd taken her under his wing. When they met, something just clicked.

And, in turn, Zoë had been Nick's only family. The only person he could depend on. He never seemed to expect or want more than that.

No way she would throw it all away on one stupid lapse in judgment, because the truth of the matter was, in a relationship, they wouldn't last. They were too different.

They would kill each other the first week.

"We've obviously made a big mistake," she said. She spotted her brand new Jimmy Choo pumps peeking out from under the bed. She used her big toe to drag them out and shoved her feet in. "We've known each other a long time. I'd hate to see our friendship, our working relationship, screwed up because of this."

"That would suck," he agreed. He sure was taking this well. Not that she'd expected him to be upset. But he didn't have to be so...*agreeable*. He could at least pretend he was sorry it wouldn't happen again.

She hooked a thumb over her shoulder. "I'm going to go now."

He pulled himself to his feet. She was wearing three-inch heels and he was still a head taller. "I'll drive you home."

She held up a hand to stop him. "No, no. That's not necessary. I'll call a cab."

He looked down at the clock. "It's after three."

All the more reason not to let him drive her home. In the middle of the night she felt less…accountable. What if, when they got there, she invited him in? She didn't want him getting the wrong idea, and she wasn't sure if she could trust herself.

Astonishing what a night of incredible sex could do to cloud a girl's judgment. "I'd really rather you didn't. I'll be fine, honest."

"Then take my truck," he said, taking her hand and pressing his keys into it. "I'll catch a cab in the morning."

"You're sure?"

"I'm sure."

He gestured toward the bedroom door and followed her into the dark sitting room. When they got to the door she turned to face him. The light from the bedroom illuminated the right side of his face. The side with the dimple.

But he wasn't smiling. He looked almost sad.

Well, duh, he'd just split up with his fiancée. Of course he was sad.

"I'm really sorry about what happened with Lynn. You'll meet someone else, I promise." Someone unlike fiancée number one, who informed him on their wedding day that she'd decided to put off having kids for ten years so she could focus on her career. Or fiancée number two who'd been a real prize. Lynn had obviously been after Nick's money, but he'd been so desperate to satisfy his driving need to procreate, he'd been blind to what he was getting himself into. Thank goodness he'd come to his senses, let himself see her for what she was.

"I know I will," he said.

"This probably goes without saying, but it would be best if we kept what happened to ourselves. Things could get weird around the office if anyone found out."

"Okay," he agreed. "Not a word."

Huh. That was easy.

Almost *too* easy.

"Well, I should go." She hooked her purse over her shoulder and reached for the doorknob. "I guess I'll see you at work Monday."

He leaned forward and propped a hand above her head on the door, so she couldn't pull it open. "Since this isn't going to happen again, how about one last kiss?"

Oh no, *bad* idea. Nick's kiss is what had gotten them into this mess in the first place. The man could work miracles with his mouth. Had he been a lousy kisser, she never would have slept with him. "I don't think that would be a good idea."

He was giving her that look again, that heavy-lidded hungry look he'd had just before they had attacked each other the first time. And suddenly he seemed to be standing a lot closer. And he smelled so good, *looked* so good in the pale light that her head felt a little swimmy.

"Come on," he coaxed, "one little kiss."

Like a magnet she felt drawn to him. She could feel herself leaning forward even as she told him, "That would be a bad idea."

"Probably," he agreed, easing in to meet her halfway. He caressed her cheek with the tips of his fingers, combed them gently through her hair. The hair band pulled loose and a riot of blond curls sprang free, hanging in damp ringlets around her face.

"Nick, don't," she said. But she didn't do anything to stop him. "We agreed this wouldn't happen again."

"Did we?" His hand slipped down to her shoulder. She felt a tug, and heard the snap of her other spaghetti strap being torn. Her dress was now officially strapless. And in another second it would be lying on the floor.

Oh God, here we go again.

Nick pushed the strap of her purse off the opposite shoulder and it landed with a soft thump on the floor at their feet and his truck keys landed beside it. "We're already here, the damage has been done. Is one more time really going to make that much of a difference?"

It was hard to argue with logic like that, especially when he was nibbling her ear. And he was right. The damage had already been done.

What difference could one more time possibly make?

"Just a quick one," she said, reaching for the fastener on his slacks. She tugged it free and shoved them down his hips. "As long as we agree that what goes on in this room stays in this room."

His lips brushed her shoulder and her knees went weak. "Agreed."

Then he kissed her and she melted.

One more time, she promised herself as he bunched the skirt of her dress up around her waist and lifted her off the floor.

"One more time," she murmured as she locked her legs around his hips and he pinned her body to the wall, entered her with one deep, penetrating thrust.

One more time and they would forget this ever happened...

Two

What difference could one more time *possibly* make? Apparently, more than either she or Nick had anticipated.

Zoë glanced up at the clock above her desk, then down to the bottom drawer of the file cabinet where she'd stashed the bag from the pharmacy behind the employment records. The bag that had been sitting there for four days now because she conveniently kept forgetting to bring it home every night after work. Mostly because she'd been trying to convince herself that she was probably overreacting. She was most likely suffering some funky virus that would clear up on its own. A virus that just happened to zap all of her energy, made her queasy every morning when she rolled out of bed and made her breasts swollen and sore.

And, oh yeah, made her period late.

She was sure there had to be a virus like that, because there was no chance in hell this condition was actually something that would require 2 a.m. feedings and diapers.

She would have a much easier time explaining this away if she wasn't ninety-nine percent sure Nick hadn't been wearing a condom that last time up against the hotel room wall.

It's not as if she could come right out and ask him. Not without him freaking out and things getting really complicated. It had taken several weeks to get past the post-coital weirdness. At first, it had been hard to look him in the eye, knowing he'd seen her naked, had touched her intimately.

Every time she looked at his hands, she remembered the way they felt against her skin. Rough and calloused, but oh so tender. And so big they seemed to swallow up every part of her that he touched.

His slim hips reminded her of the way she'd locked her legs around him as he'd pinned her to the wall. The way he'd entered her, swift and deep. How she'd come apart in his arms.

And his mouth. That wonderfully sinful mouth that melted her like butter in a hot skillet…

No. No. *No.*

Bad Zoë.

She shook away the lingering memory of his lean,

muscular body, of his weight sinking her into the mattress, her body shuddering with pleasure. She'd promised herself at least a hundred times a day that she wasn't going to think about that anymore. Finally things seemed to be getting back to normal. She and Nick could have a conversation without that undertone of awkwardness.

Zoë didn't want to risk rocking the boat.

She hadn't even told her sister Faith, and they told each other almost everything. Although, after their last phone conversation Zoë was under the distinct impression Faith knew something was up. It wouldn't be unlike her sister to drop everything and show up unannounced if she thought there was something that Zoë wasn't telling her.

She took a deep, fortifying breath. She was being ridiculous. She should just take the damned test and get it over with. She'd spent the ten bucks, after all. She might as well get her money's worth. Waiting yet another week wouldn't change the final outcome. Either she was or she wasn't. It would be good to know now, so she could decide what to do.

And decide what she would tell Nick.

As she was reaching for the bottom drawer handle, Shannon from accounting appeared in the doorway and Zoë breathed a sigh of relief.

"Hey, hon, you up for lunch with the girls? We're heading over to Shooters."

Despite being a nervous wreck, she was starving. Though she normally ate a salad for lunch, she would sell her soul for a burger and fries and a gigantic milkshake. And for dessert, a double chocolate sundae. Hold the pickles.

"Lunch sounds wonderful."

She grabbed her purse and jacket and gave the file cabinet one last glance before she followed Shannon into the hall.

As soon as she got back from lunch, she promised herself. She would put the test in her purse so she wouldn't forget it, and tonight when she got home she would get to the bottom of this.

Nick walked down the hall to Zoë's office and popped his head inside, finding it empty and feeling a screwy mix of relief and disappointment. He'd come to her office now, knowing she would probably be on her lunch break. Though they'd promised to pretend it hadn't happened, he couldn't seem to make himself forget every erotic detail of their night together. He'd been doing his best to pretend nothing had changed, but something was still a little…*off*.

Something about Zoë—a thing he couldn't quite put his finger on—seemed different.

He couldn't stop himself from wondering, *what if*? What if he'd told her he didn't want to pretend like it hadn't happened?

He just wasn't sure if that's what he really wanted. Were he and Zoë too different for that kind of relationship?

She was a cat person and he had a dog. He was

faded Levi's and worn leather and she was so prim and...*girly*. His music preferences ranged from classic rock to rich, earthy blues with a little jazz piano thrown in for flavor. Zoë seemed to sway toward eighties pop and any female singer, and she had the annoying habit of blaring Christmas music in July.

He was a meat and potatoes man, and as far as he could tell, Zoë existed on salads and bottled mineral water. He watched reality television and ESPN and she preferred crime dramas and chick flicks.

In fact, he couldn't think of a single thing they had in common. Besides the sex, which frankly they did pretty damned well.

Even if they could get past all of their differences, there was the problem of them wanting completely different things from life. In all the years he'd known her, she'd never once expressed a desire to have children. Not that he could blame her given her family history. But he'd grown up an only child raised by an aunt and uncle who'd had no use for the eight-year-old bastard dumped in their care. He'd spent his childhood in boarding schools and camps.

He wanted a family—at least three kids, maybe more. He just had to find a woman who wanted that, too. One who wasn't more interested in climbing the corporate ladder than having a family. And definitely one who wouldn't insist on a two week European honeymoon followed by mansion hunting in one of Detroit's most exclusive communities.

Material things didn't mean much to him. He was

content with his modest condo and modest vehicle. His modest life. All the money in the world didn't buy happiness. Thousands of dollars in gifts from his aunt and uncle had never made up for a lack of love and affection. His children would always know they were loved. They would never be made to feel like an inconvenience. And he sure as hell would never abandon them.

It had taken him years to realize there wasn't anything wrong with him. That he didn't drive people away. With a long history of mental illness, his mother could barely take care of herself much less a child, and his aunt and uncle simply had no interest in being parents. It would have been easy for them to hand him back over to social services when his mom lost custody. At least they'd taken responsibility for him.

If not for the lack of affection, one might even say he'd been spoiled as a kid. If he wanted or needed something all it took was a phone call to his uncle and it was his.

A convertible sports car the day he got his driver's license? No problem.

An all-expenses-paid trip to Cancún for gradua- tion? It's yours.

The best education money can buy at a first-rate East Coast school? Absolutely.

But no one had handed him his education. He'd worked his tail off to make the dean's list every semester, to graduate at the top of his class. To make his aunt and uncle proud, even if they didn't know how to show it. And when he'd asked his uncle to loan him the money to start his company, the entire astronomical sum had been wired to his account within twenty-four hours.

They wouldn't win any awards for parents of the year, but his aunt and uncle had done the best they could.

He would do better.

There had to be a Ms. Right out there just waiting for him to sweep her off her feet. A woman who wanted the same things he did. And hopefully he would find her before he was too old to play ball with his son, to teach his daughter to Rollerblade.

He stepped into Zoë's office, trying to remember where in the file cabinet she kept the personnel files. Seeing as how she wasn't exactly organized, they could be pretty much anywhere.

Despite the disarray, she somehow managed to keep the office running like a finely tuned watch. She'd become indispensable. He would be lost without her.

He started at the top and worked his way down, finding them, of course, in the bottom drawer. He located the file of a new employee, Mark O'Connell, to see if there was some reason why the guy would be missing so much work. Not to mention showing up late. Nick was particular when he hired new employees. He didn't understand how someone with such impeccable references could be so unpredictable on the job.

He grabbed the file and was about to shut the

drawer when he saw the edge of a brown paper bag poking up from the back.

Huh. What could that be? He didn't remember seeing that the last time he looked in here.

He grabbed the bag and pulled it out. He was about to peek inside, when behind him he heard a gasp.

"What are you doing?"

Nick turned, the pharmacy bag in his hand, and Zoë stood in the office doorway, back from lunch, frozen. If he opened that bag, things were going to get really complicated really fast.

"I found this in the file cabinet," he said.

When she finally found her voice, she did her best to keep it calm and rational. Freaking out would only make things worse. "I don't appreciate you going through my things."

He gave her an annoyed look. "How was I supposed to know it's yours? It was in the file cabinet with the personnel files. The files I need to have access to, to run my company."

He was right. She should have kept it in her car, or her purse. Of course, then what excuse would she have had for not using it? She walked toward him and held out a hand. "You're right, I apologize. Can I have it back please?"

He looked at her, then at the bag. "What is it?"

"Something personal."

She took another step toward him, hand outstretched, and he took a step back.

A devious grin curled his lips, showing off the dent in his right cheek. "How much is it worth to you?"

He hadn't teased her in weeks. Now was not the time to start acting like his pain-in-the-behind old self. "That isn't funny, Nick. Give it to me."

He held the bag behind his back. "Make me."

How could a grown man act so damned juvenile? He didn't have kids, so what, he'd act like one?

She stepped toward him, her temper flaring, and held out her hand. "*Please.*"

He sidestepped out of her way, around her desk, thoroughly enjoying himself if his goofy grin was any indication.

She felt like punching him.

Couldn't he see that she was fuming mad? Didn't he care that he was upsetting her?

Heat climbed up her throat and into her cheeks. "You're acting like an ass, Nick. Give it back to me *now.*"

The angrier she became, the more amused he looked. "Must be something pretty important to get your panties in such a twist," he teased, clasping the bag with two fingers and swinging it just out of her reach. Why did he have to be so darned tall? "If you want it so badly, come and get it."

She slung her hands up in defeat. "Fine, look if you have to. If you find tampons so thoroughly interesting."

Tampons. Didn't she wish.

He raised a brow at her, as if he wasn't sure he should believe her or not. As he lowered the bag, uncurling the edge to take a peek, she lunged for him. Her fingers skimmed the bag and he jerked his arm back, inadvertently flinging the test box out. In slow motion it spiraled across the room, hit the wall with a smack and landed label side up on the carpet.

Uh-oh.

For several long seconds time seemed to stand still, then it surged forward with a force that nearly gave her whiplash.

Nick looked at the box, then at her, then back at the box and all the amusement evaporated from his face. "What the hell is this?"

She closed her eyes. Damn, damn, damn.

"*Zoë?*"

She opened her eyes and glared at him. "What, you can't read?"

She grabbed the bag from his slack fingers then marched over and snatched the box from the floor.

"Zoë, do you think you're—"

"Of course not!" More like, God, she hoped not.

"Are you late?"

She gave him a *duh* look.

"Of course you are, or you wouldn't need the test." He raked a hand through his hair. "How late are you exactly?"

"I'm just a little late. I'm sure it's nothing."

"We slept together over a month ago. How late is a *little* late?"

She shrugged. "Two weeks, maybe three."

"Which is it, two or three?"

Oh, hell. She slumped into her desk chair. "Probably closer to three."

He took a long deep breath and blew it out. She could tell he was fighting to stay calm. "And why am I just hearing about this now?"

"I thought maybe it was a virus or an infection or something," she said, and he gave her an incredulous look. "I was in *denial,* okay?"

"Missed periods can happen for lots of reasons, right? Like stress?"

She flicked her thumbnail nervously back and forth, fraying the edge of the box. Stressed? Who me? "Sure, I guess."

"Besides, we used protection."

"Did we?"

He shot back an indignant, "You know we did."

She felt a glimmer of hope. Condoms could fail, but the odds were slim. Maybe she really wasn't pregnant. Maybe this was all in her head. "Even the last time?"

There was a pause, then he asked, "The last time?"

Suddenly he didn't sound so confident. Suddenly he had an, *Oh-damn-what-have-I-done?* look on his face.

Her stomach began to slither down from her abdomen. "You know, against the wall, by the door. We used a condom then too, right?" she asked hopefully, as if wishing it were true would actually make it true.

He scratched the coarse stubble on his chin. The guy could shave ten times a day but he was so dark he almost always had a five o'clock shadow. "Honestly, I can't remember."

Oh, this was not good. She could feel her control slipping, panic squeezing the air from her lungs. "You can't *remember?*"

He sat on the corner of her desk. "Apparently, you can't either."

He was right. That wasn't fair. This was in no way his fault. "I'm sorry. I'm just…edgy."

"If I had to guess, I would say that since I have no memory of using one, and my wallet was in the other room, we probably didn't."

At least he was being honest. Obviously they had both been too swept away by passion to think about contraceptives. But that had been what, their fourth time? Didn't a man's body take a certain amount of time to…*reinforce the troops*. Were there even any little swimmers left by then?

Leave it to her to have unprotected sex with a guy who had super sperm.

"I guess there's only one way to find out for sure," he said. "Taking the test here would probably be a bad idea, seeing as how anyone could walk into the bathroom. So would you be more comfortable taking it at your place or mine?"

This was really happening. With *Nick* of all people.

When she didn't answer right away he asked, "Or is this something you need to be alone for?"

Being alone was the last thing she wanted. They were in this together. She didn't doubt for an instant that he would be there for her, whatever the outcome. "We'll do it at my house."

He rose to his feet. "Okay, let's go."

Her eyes went wide. "You want to go *now?* It's the middle of the workday."

"It's not like we're going to get fired. I own the company. Besides, you know what they say."

She thought about it for a second then said, "Curiosity killed the cat?"

He grinned. "There's no time like the present."

Three

Nick drove them the ten minutes to Zoë's house in Birmingham. They didn't say much. What could they say? Zoë spent the majority of her time praying, Please, God, let it be negative.

How had she gotten herself into this mess?

Her devout Catholic parents still believed that at the age of twenty-eight she was as pure as the driven snow. If the test was positive, what would she tell them? Well, Mom and Dad, I was snow-white, but I drifted.

They were going to kill her. Or disown her.

Or both.

And this would surely be enough to send her fragile, ailing grandmother hurtling through death's door. She would instantly be labeled the family black sheep.

It didn't matter that her parents had been nagging her to settle down for years.

When are you going to find a nice man? When are you going to have babies?

How about never?

And if the man she settled down with was Nick they would be ecstatic. Despite the fact that he wasn't Catholic, they adored him. Since the first time she'd brought him home for Thanksgiving dinner they'd adopted him into the fold. And Nick had been swept up into the total chaos and craziness that was her family. He loved it almost as much as it drove her nuts.

So, if she were to call home and tell them she and Nick were getting hitched, she'd be daughter of the year. But the premarital sex thing would still be a major issue. In her parents' eyes, what they had done was a sin.

She let her head fall back against the seat and closed her eyes. Maybe this was just a bad dream. Maybe all she needed to do was pinch herself real hard and she would wake up.

She caught a hunk of skin between her thumb and forefinger, the fleshy part under her upper arm that the self-defense people claim is the most sensitive, and gave it a good hard squeeze.

"Ow!"

"What's wrong?"

She opened her eyes and looked around. Still in Nick's monster truck, rumbling down the street, and he was shooting her a concerned look.

She sighed. So much for her dream theory.

"Nothing. I'm just swell," she said, turning to look out the window, barely seeing the houses of her street whizzing past.

"Don't get upset until we know for sure," he said, but she was pretty sure he, like her, already knew what the result would be. They'd had unprotected sex and her period was late. The test was going to be positive.

She was going to have Nick's baby.

When they got to her house, he took her keys from her and opened the door. He'd been inside her house a thousand times, but today it felt so…*surreal*. As if she'd stepped onto the set of film.

A horror film.

She and Nick were the stars, and any second some lunatic was going to pop out of the kitchen wielding a knife and hack them to pieces.

She slipped her jacket off and tossed it over the back of the couch while Nick took in her cluttered living room.

Last night's dinner dishes still sat on the coffee table, the plate covered with little kitty lick marks from Dexter her cat. Newspapers from the past two weeks lay in a messy pile at one end of the couch.

She looked down at the rug, at the tufts of white cat fur poking out from the Berber and realized it had been too long since she'd last vacuumed. Her entire house—entire life—was more than a little chaotic right now. As if acting irresponsibly would somehow prove what a lousy parent she would be.

Nick looked around and made a face. "You really need to hire a maid."

She tossed her purse down on the cluttered coffee table. "I am *so* not in the mood for a lecture on my domestic shortcomings."

He had the decency to look apologetic.

"Sorry." He reached inside his leather bomber jacket and pulled out the test kit. "I guess we should just get this over with, huh?"

"We?" Like he had to go in the bathroom and pee on a stick. Like he had to endure months of torture if it was positive. A guy like him wouldn't last a week on the nest. He may have been tough, may have been able to bench press a compact car, but five minutes of hard labor and he would be toast.

Her mother had done home births for Zoë's three youngest siblings and Zoë had had the misfortune of being stuck in the room with her for the last one. She had witnessed the horror. Going through it once seemed like torture enough, but understandable since most women probably didn't realize what they were getting themselves into. But *nine* times. That was just crazy.

"I'm afraid to go in there," she said.

Nick reached up and dropped one big, work-roughened hand on her shoulder, giving it a gentle squeeze. "We're in this together, Zoë. Whatever the outcome. We'll get through it."

It amazed her at times, how such a big, burly guy who oozed testosterone could be so damned tender and sweet. Not that the stubborn, overbearing alpha male gene had passed him by. He could be a major pain in the behind, too. But he'd never let her down in a time of need and she didn't believe for a second that he would now.

"Okay, here goes." She took the test kit from him and walked to the bathroom, closing and locking the door behind her, her stomach tangled in knots. She opened the box and with a trembling hand spilled the contents out onto the vanity.

"Please, God," she whispered, "let it be negative."

She read the instructions three times, just to be sure she was doing it right, then followed them word for word. It was amazingly quick and simple for such a life-altering procedure. *Too simple.*

Less than five minutes later, after rereading the instructions one more time just to be sure, she had her answer.

Nick paced the living room rug, his eye on the bathroom door, wondering what in the heck was taking Zoë so long. She'd been in there almost twenty minutes now and he hadn't heard a peep out of her. No curdling screams, no thud to indicate she'd hit the floor in a dead faint. And no whoops of joy.

It was ironic that not five minutes before she stepped into her office he'd been thinking about having children. Just not with her, and not quite so soon. Ideally he would like to be married, but life had a way of throwing a curve ball.

At least, his life did.

He let out a thundering sneeze and glanced with disdain at the fluffy white ball of fur sunbathing on the front windowsill. It stared back at him with scornful green eyes.

He was so not a cat person.

He sat on the couch, propped his elbows on his knees and rested his chin on his fisted hands.

So what if she was pregnant?

The truth was, this was all happening so fast, he wasn't sure how he felt about it. What he did know is that if she didn't come out of the damned bathroom soon, he was going to pound the door down. It couldn't possibly take this long. He remembered the box specifically stating something about results in only minutes.

As if conjuring her through sheer will, the bathroom door swung open and Zoë stepped out. Nick shot to his feet. He didn't have to ask what the results were, he could see it in her waxy, pasty-white pallor. Her wide, glassy-eyed disbelief.

"Oh boy," he breathed. Zoë was pregnant.

He was going to be a father. They were going to be parents.

Together.

She looked about two seconds from passing out cold, so he walked over to where she stood and pulled her into his arms. She collapsed against him, her entire body trembling.

She rested her forehead on his chest, wrapped her

arms around him, and he buried his nose in her hair. She smelled spicy and sweet, like cinnamon and apples. He realized, he'd missed this. Since that night in the hotel, he'd been itching to get his arms around her again.

He'd almost forgotten just how good it felt to be close to her, how perfectly she fit in his arms. Something had definitely changed between them that night in the hotel. Something that he doubted would ever change back.

For a while they only held each other, until she'd stopped shaking and she wasn't breathing so hard. Until she had gone from cold and rigid to warm and relaxed in his arms.

He cupped her chin and tilted her face up. "It's going to be okay."

"What are we going to do?" she asked.

"Well, I guess we're going to have a baby," he said, and felt the corners of his mouth begin to tip up.

Zoë gaped at him, her look going from bewilderment to abject horror. She broke from his grasp and took a step back. "Oh my God."

"What?"

"You're smiling. You're *happy* about this."

Was he?

The smile spread to encompass his entire face. He tried to stop it, then realized it was impossible. He really *was* happy. For five years now he'd felt it was time to settle down and start a family. True, this wasn't exactly how he planned it, and he sure as hell hadn't planned on doing it with Zoë, but that didn't mean it wouldn't work. That didn't mean they shouldn't at least give it a shot.

He gave her a shrug. "Yeah, I guess I am. Would you feel better if I was angry?"

"Of course not. But do you have even the slightest clue what we're getting into? What *I'll* have to go through?"

She made it sound as though he was making her remove an appendage. "You're having a baby, Zoë. It's not as if it's never been done before."

"Of course it has, but have you ever actually witnessed a baby being born?"

No, but he definitely wanted to be in the delivery room. He wouldn't miss that for anything. "I'm sure it will be fascinating."

"*Fascinating*? I was there when my mom had Jonah, my youngest brother."

"And?"

"Have you ever seen the movie, *The Thing?*" she asked, and he nodded. "You remember the scene where the alien bursts out of the guy and there is this huge spray of blood and guts? Well, it's kinda' like that. Only it goes on for *hours*. And hurts twice as much.

"And that's only the beginning," she went on, in full rant. "After it's born there are sleepless nights to look forward to and endless dirty diapers. Never having a second to yourself…a *moment's* silence. They cry and whine and demand and smother. Not to mention that they cost a fortune. Then they get older and there's school and homework and rebellion. It never ends. They're yours to worry about and pull your hair out over until the day you *die*."

Wow. He knew she was jaded by her past, but he'd never expected her to be this traumatized.

"Zoë, you were just a kid when you had to take care of your brothers and sisters. It wasn't fair for your parents to burden you with that much responsibility." He rubbed a hand down her arm, trying to get her to relax and see things rationally. "Right now you're still in shock. I know that when you take some time to digest it, you'll be happy."

She closed her eyes and shook her head. "I'm not ready for this. I don't know if I'll *ever* be ready for it."

A startling, disturbing thought occurred to him. What if she didn't want to have the baby? What if she was thinking about terminating the pregnancy? It was her body so, of course, the choice was up to her, but he'd do whatever he could to talk her out of it, to rationalize with her.

"Are you saying you don't want to have the baby?" he asked.

She looked up at him, confused. "It's not like I have a choice."

"Every woman has a choice, Zoë."

She gave him another one of those horrified looks and folded a hand protectively over her stomach. He didn't think she even realized she was doing it. "I'm not going to get rid of it if that's what you mean. What kind of person do you think I am?"

Thankfully, not that kind. "I've never consid-ered raising a baby on my own, but I will if that's what you want."

"Of course that's not what I want! I could never give a baby up. Once you have it, it's yours. My brothers and sisters may have driven me crazy but I love them to death. I wouldn't trade them in for anything."

He rubbed a hand across the stubble on his jaw. "You're confusing the hell out of me."

"I'm keeping the baby," she said firmly. "I'm just…I guess I'm still in shock. This was not a part of my master plan. And you're the last man on earth I saw myself doing it with. No offense."

"None taken." How could he be offended when he'd been thinking the same thing earlier. Although maybe not the *last on earth* part.

She walked over to the couch and crumpled onto the cushions. "My parents are going to kill me. They think I'm still a good Catholic girl. A twenty-eight-year-old, snow-white virgin who goes to church twice a week. What am I going to tell them?"

Nick sat down beside her. He slipped an arm around her shoulder and she leaned into him, soft and warm.

Yeah, this was nice. It felt…right.

And just like that he knew exactly what he needed to do.

"I guess you only have one choice," he said.

"Live the rest of my life in shame?"

Her pessimism made him grin. "No. I think you should marry me."

* * *

Zoë pulled out of Nick's arms and stared up at him. "Marry you? Are you *crazy?*"

Dumb question, Zoë. Of course he was crazy.

Rather than being angry with her, he smiled, as if he'd been expecting her to question his sanity. "What's so crazy about it?"

If he couldn't figure that out himself, he really was nuts.

"If we get married right away, your parents don't have to know you were already pregnant. Problem solved."

And he thought marrying someone he didn't love *wouldn't* be a problem? Not that kind of love anyway. She didn't doubt that he loved her as a friend, and she him, but that wasn't enough.

"We're both feeling emotional and confused," she said. He more than her, obviously. "Maybe we should take a day or two to process this before we make any kind of life altering decisions."

"We're having a baby together, Zoë. You don't get much more life altering than that."

"My point exactly. We have a lot to consider."

"Look, I know you're not crazy about the idea of getting married to anyone—"

"And you're *too* crazy about it. Did you even stop to think that you would be marrying me for all the wrong reasons? You want Susie homemaker. Someone to squeeze out your babies, keep your house clean and have dinner waiting in the oven when you get home from work. Well, take a look around you, Nick. My life is in shambles. My house is a disaster and if I can't microwave myself a meal in five minutes or less, I don't buy it."

He didn't look hurt by her refusal, which made her that much more certain marrying him would be a bad idea. She could never be the cardboard cutout wife he was looking for. She wouldn't be any kind of a wife at all.

And even if they could get past all of that, it still wouldn't work. He was such a good guy. Perfect in so many ways. Except the one that counted the most.

He didn't love her.

She took his hand between her two. It was rough and slightly calloused from years of working construction with his employees. He may have owned the company, may have had more money than God, but he liked getting his hands dirty. He liked to feel the sun on his back and fresh air in his lungs. One day cooped up in the office and he was climbing the walls.

She didn't doubt that he would put just as much of himself into his marriage. He was going to make some lucky woman one hell of a good husband.

Just not her.

"It was a noble gesture. But I think we both need to take some time and decide what it is we really want."

"How much time?" he asked.

"I'm going to have to make a doctor's appointment. Let's get through that first then we'll worry about the other stuff."

Who knows, maybe she got a false positive from the pregnancy test. Maybe she would get a blood test at the doctor's office and find out they had done all this worrying for nothing.

Four

"**C**ongratulations! Your test was positive! If you haven't yet made a follow-up appointment with Doctor Gordon, please dial one. If you need to speak to a nurse, dial two—"

Zoë hung up the phone in her office, cutting short the obnoxiously perky prerecorded message she'd gotten when she phoned the doctor's office for her blood test results.

It was official. Not that it hadn't been official before. The blood test had just been a formality. She was definitely, without a doubt, having Nick's baby.

Oh boy.

Or girl, she supposed.

She would walk down to his office and tell him,

but he'd been in her office every ten minutes wondering if she'd made the call.

She looked down at her watch. Why get up when he was due back in another six minutes?

"Well?"

She looked up to find him standing in her doorway watching her expectantly. "You're early."

"Early?" His brow knit into a frown. "Did you call yet?"

"I called."

He stepped into her office and shut the door. "And?"

She sighed. "As my mother used to say, 'I'm in the family way.'"

"Wow." He took deep breath and blew it out. "Are you okay?"

She nodded. She really was. She'd had a few days to think about it, and she was definitely warming to the idea. Not that it wouldn't complicate things. But it wasn't the end of the world either. She would have one kid. She could handle that. "I'm okay."

He walked over to her desk and sat on the edge, facing her. She could see that he was happy, even though he was trying to hide it. And why should he? What normal woman wouldn't want the father of her baby to be excited?

"It's okay to be happy," she told him. "I promise I won't freak out again."

The corners of his mouth quirked up. "I guess this means we have things to discuss."

She knew exactly what *things* he was referring to. He looked so genuinely excited, so happy, she didn't doubt for one second that he would be a wonderful father. But a husband? She wasn't sure if she was ready for one of those. She didn't know if she would *ever* be ready. The idea of sharing her life with someone, all the compromise and sacrifice it would take…it just seemed like a lot to ask. She was happy with her life the way it was.

That didn't mean she couldn't possibly be happier with Nick there, but what if she wasn't?

As promised, he hadn't said a word about marriage while they waited for the test results. Now he looked as if he was ready for an answer.

"It's nothing personal, Nick. I just…I'm afraid it wouldn't work between us."

"Why wouldn't it? We're friends. We work well together. We understand each other." He leaned in closer, his eyes locked on hers. "Not to mention that in the sexual chemistry department we're off the charts."

God, she wished he wouldn't look at her that way. It scrambled her brain. And she hated that he was right. But good sex—even fantastic sex—wasn't enough to make a marriage work.

He leaned in even closer and she could smell traces of his musky aftershave, see the dots of brown in his hazel eyes. "Can you honestly say you haven't thought about that night at least a dozen times a day since it happened?"

"It wasn't *that* good." She tried to sound cocky, but her voice came out warm and soft instead. It had been more like a hundred times a day.

Nick grinned and leaned forward, resting his hands on the arms of her chair, caging her in. "Yes, it was. It was the best sex you ever had. Admit it."

Heat and testosterone rolled off his body in waves, making her feel light-headed and tingly all over. "Okay, yeah, maybe it was. But that's not the point. I don't want to jump into anything we might regret. What if we get married and find out a month later that we drive each other crazy?"

"Too late for that, sweetheart." He reached up and touched her cheek and her heart shimmied in her chest. "You already do drive me crazy."

Right now, he was doing the same to her. He looked as if any second he might kiss her. And though she knew it would be a bad idea, she wanted him to anyway. She didn't even care that anyone in the office could walk in and catch them. It would take ten minutes tops for the news to travel through the entire building. For the rumors to start. That was exactly what they *didn't* need right now.

She just wished he would make up his mind, wished he would either kiss her or back off. When he sat so close, his eyes locked with hers, it was difficult to think straight.

Which is probably the exact reason he was doing it. To throw her off balance. To make her agree to things she wasn't ready for.

"I mean drive each other crazy in a bad way," she said.

"So what would you like to do? Date?"

"I think we're a bit past the dating stage, don't you? Socially we get along fine. It's the living together part that worries me."

That grin was back on his face, dimple and all, which usually meant trouble. "That sounds like the perfect solution."

Funny, but she didn't remember mentioning one. "Which solution is that?"

"We could live together."

Live together? "Like in the same house?"

"Sure. What better way to see if we're compatible."

She'd never had a roommate. Not since she left home, anyway. Back then she'd had to share a room with three of her sisters. Three people borrowing her clothes and using her makeup without asking. Although, she doubted that would be a problem with Nick. Her clothes were way too small for him even if he wanted to borrow them and when it came to wearing makeup, well...she *hoped* he didn't.

To get any privacy back home she'd had to lock herself in the bathroom, which would last only a minute or two before someone was pounding on the door to get in.

But she had two bathrooms if she needed a place to escape. A full on the main floor and a half down in the finished part of the basement. Granted her house was barely a thousand square feet, but how much room could one guy take up?

Unless he was thinking she was going to move in with him. His condo was twice the size of her house, but it was in a high-rise in Royal Oak, with people living on every side.

No one should ever live that close to their neighbors. It was too creepy, knowing people could hear you through the walls. She dreamed of one day owning an old farmhouse with acres and acres of property. She wondered how Nick, a born and bred city boy, would feel about that. Despite how well they knew each other, there were still so many things they *didn't* know. So much they had never talked about.

Things they could definitely learn if they were living together.

"And if we are compatible?" she asked.

"Then you marry me."

"Just like that?"

He nodded. "Just like that."

She hated to admit it, but this made sense in a weird way.

My God, was she actually considering this? The only thing worse than premarital sex in her parents' eyes was living in sin without the sanctity of marriage. Of course, what they didn't know wouldn't hurt them. Right?

"If we were to do this, and I'm not saying we are, but *if* we did, logically, I think it would be best if you move in with me," she said. "Your condo can get by without you. I have a yard and a garden to take care of."

"Fine with me," he agreed.

"And we should probably keep this to ourselves."

"Zoë." He shot her a very unconvincing hurt look. "Are you ashamed of me?"

Yeah, right, like it mattered. When it came to self-confidence, Nick had it in bucket loads.

"You know how the people in this building can be. I'm just not ready to deal with the gossip. Not until we've made a decision."

"Which will be when?"

"You mean like a time limit," she asked, and he nodded. "How about a month? If by then it's not working out, we give it a rest."

He sat back, folded his arms across his chest and gave her an assessing look. "A month, huh?"

A month should be plenty of time to tell if they were compatible. In areas other than friendship. And the bedroom.

"And if after a month we haven't killed each other, what then? We set a date?"

The mere idea triggered a wave of anxiety. Her heart rate jumped and her palms began to sweat. "If we can make it one month living together, I promise to give your proposal very serious thought."

"And hey," he said with a casual shrug. "If nothing else, we can save money on gas driving to work together, so it won't be a total loss."

"How can you be so calm about this?" The idea of him moving in was making her a nervous wreck.

"Because I'm confident that after a month of living together, you'll be dying to marry me."

She hoped he was right. "What makes you so sure?"

A devilish grin curled his mouth. "This does."

He leaned toward her and she knew exactly what he was going to do. He was going to kiss her. She knew, and she didn't do a thing to stop him. The crazy thing was, she *wanted* him to kiss her. She didn't care that it would only confuse things more, or that anyone could walk in and catch them.

He didn't work into it either. He just took charge and dove in for the kill. He slipped a hand behind her head, threading his fingers through her hair, planted his lips on hers and proceeded to kiss her stockings off. Her body went limp and her toes curled in her pumps.

She'd almost forgotten how good a kisser he was, how exciting and warm he tasted. The memory lapse was purely a self-defense mechanism. Otherwise there would have been a lot of kissing going on these past weeks.

She could feel herself sinking deeper under his spell, melting into a squishy puddle in her chair. Her fingers curled in his hair, nails raked his scalp. His big, warm hand cupped the back of her head with gentle but steady pressure, as if he wasn't going to let her get away.

Yeah, right, like she would even try.

Hearing her office door open barely fazed her, nor

did the, "Zoë, I need—*whoops!*" of whomever had come in. Or the loud click of the door closing behind them as they left. And the very real possibility of the news reaching everyone in the building by day's end.

Nick broke the kiss and backed away, gazing down at her with heavy-lidded eyes. "So much for keeping this to ourselves."

"Yeah, oops." She should care that their secret was out—well, at least one of their secrets—but for some reason she didn't. In fact, she was wondering if maybe he should kiss her again. Her cheeks felt warm and her scalp tingled where his hand had been. She was sure if she tried to get up and walk her legs wouldn't work right.

One kiss and she was a wreck.

"So, when do you want me to move in?" he asked, his dimple winking at her.

How about right now? she thought. But she didn't want to sound too eager. Then again it *was* Friday. That would give him all weekend to settle in.

Oh what the heck?

She looked up at him and smiled. "How about tonight?"

There was a reindeer standing on Zoë's front porch.

Nick stood beside it holding the reins in one hand, a duffle bag in the other.

Okay, it was actually a leash he was holding, and the deer was really a dog. A very large, skinny dog with a shiny coat the color of sable.

"What is that?" she asked through the safety of the screen. Did he really think he was bringing that thing into her house?

"This is my dog, Tucker." At her completely blank look he added, "You knew I had one."

Yeah, she knew, but it never occurred to her that it would be moving in, too. "This is going to be a problem. I have a cat."

"Tucker has a low prey drive, so it shouldn't be an issue."

"Prey drive?" She snapped the lock on the storm door. "Dexter is not prey."

"Tucker is a retired racing greyhound. They use lures to get them to run. Some have higher prey drives than others. Tucker has a low enough drive that he's considered cat safe."

"Cat safe?" She narrowed her eyes at him. "You're sure?"

"He'll probably just ignore the cat." He stood there waiting for her to open the door, but she wasn't convinced yet.

"Will he chew on my shoes?" she asked.

"He's not a chewer. He's a collector."

"What, like stamps?"

Nick grinned. "Cell phones, remote controls, sometimes car keys, but his favorite is slippers. The smellier the better. He's also been known to take the salt and pepper shakers off the table. If anything is missing, his bed is the first place I look."

She looked down at the dog. He looked back up

at her with forlorn brown eyes that begged, "Please love me."

"He won't pee on my rug?"

"He's housebroken. He also doesn't bark, barely sheds and he sleeps twenty-three hours of the day. He's not going to be a problem. In fact, he'll love having a fenced yard to run around."

She looked at the dog, then back at Nick.

"Are you going to let us in? I'm on excessive doses of allergy medication so I can be around your cat. You can at least give Tucker a chance."

He was right. How much trouble could one over-sized dog be?

Scratch that. She probably didn't want to know.

She unlocked the door and opened it. "Sorry about the mess. I didn't have time to clean."

Nick and Tucker stepped inside and the room suddenly felt an awful lot smaller. He unsnapped the leash and hung it on the coat tree and Tucker, being a dog, went straight for Zoë's crotch. He gave her a sniff, then looked up, as if he were expecting something. He was even bigger than he looked standing on the porch.

"He's enormous."

"He's an extra large." Nick shrugged out of his leather jacket and hung it over the leash.

"Why is he staring at me?"

"He wants you to pet him."

"Oh." She patted the top of his head gingerly. "Nice doggie."

Satisfied that he'd been adequately welcomed, Tucker trotted off to explore, his nails click-clicking on the hardwood floor. "Will he be okay by himself?"

"Yeah, he won't get into anything."

She gestured to Nick's lone bag. "Is that all you brought?"

"I have a few more things in the truck. I figure as I need stuff I can run over to my place and pick it up."

"I'm giving you the spare bedroom," she told him.

He flashed her a curious look. "I don't remember agreeing to that."

"I think at this point sex will only complicate things." He'd proven that this afternoon when he had kissed her. Her brain had been so overdrenched in pheromones she would have agreed to practically anything. "We should ease into this slowly. We need to get used to living together. We need to be sure this relationship isn't just physical."

That sexy grin curled his mouth. The guy was un-believably smug. "You really think you can resist me?"

She hoped so, but she could see by the devious glint in his eye he wasn't going to make it easy. "I'll manage."

From the kitchen Zoë heard a hiss, then an ear-splitting canine yip, and Tucker darted into the living room, skidding clumsily across the floor, long gangly legs flailing. Whining like a big baby, he scurried over to Nick and hid behind him. In the kitchen doorway sat Dexter, all whopping eight pounds of him, casually licking one fluffy white paw as though he didn't have a care in the world.

So much for the dog ignoring the cat.

"He's bleeding," Nick said indignantly, examining Tucker's nose. "Your cat attacked my dog."

"I'm sure he was provoked." She found herself feeling very proud of Dexter for protecting his domain. No big dopey dog was going to push him around. "They probably just need time to get used to each other."

Kind of like her and Nick.

"So," she said, suddenly feeling awkward. "I guess we should get you settled in."

Nick followed her down the hall to one of the two downstairs bedrooms. On the left was her office, and on the right her guest room. He stepped inside, taking in the frilly curtains and lacey spread.

"Pink?" He cringed, as though it was painful to look at. "I can feel my testosterone drying up. Maybe I should just sleep on the couch. Or in a tent in the backyard."

"Don't be such a baby," she said and he tossed his bag on the bed. "I was thinking we could just get carryout for dinner."

He shrugged. "Works for me."

"We can order, and while we're waiting for it to be delivered, we can get the rest of your things out of the truck."

He followed her to the kitchen and she pulled open her junk drawer. It held a menu from every local restaurant within delivering distance. "What are you in the mood for," she asked, and he gave her that simmering, sexy look, so she added, "besides *that*."

He grinned. "I'm not picky. You're the pregnant one. You choose."

She chose pizza. A staple item for her these days. The cheesier and gooier the better.

While they waited for it, they brought in the last of his things, most of which were for the dog who lay snoozing on his bed in the living room, occasionally opening one eye to peek around. Probably to make sure the cat was a safe distance away. Dexter lounged on the front windowsill pretending not to notice him.

It wasn't as if Nick had never been to her house, but showing him around, inviting him into her private domain, was just too weird. He would be using her towels to dry himself, washing his clothes in her washing machine and eating food from her dishes. It was so intimate and invasive. The enormity of it all hadn't really hit her until she'd seen him on the porch. She hadn't realized just how used to living alone she'd become in the past ten years. Most of the single women she knew who were her age or younger were looking for a companion. They wanted Mr. Right. She only wanted Mr. Right Now.

Not that she wasn't going to try to make this work.

The tour ended in the kitchen, and when Nick opened the fridge, he frowned. It was pitifully empty. But the freezer was stuffed wall-to-wall with Lean Cuisine dinners.

He gave her a look, and she shrugged. "There was a good sale so I stocked up."

"There's no real food in here," he said. "Don't you *ever* cook?"

Never. It was one of the few things her mother hadn't made her do. She had this nasty habit of burning things. The last time she attempted to cook herself a real meal, she'd wandered out of the room without shutting off the heat under a greasy frying pan and had set her kitchen on fire. Thank God she had a smoke detector and a good fire extinguisher. "Trust me when I say, we're both a lot safer if I don't cook."

For a second she thought he might ask for an explanation, then he just shook his head. He probably figured he was better off not knowing.

"Besides, who needs real food when you have carryout and prenatal vitamins?" she asked cheerfully.

He began opening cupboards, one by one, taking inventory of their lack of contents, shaking his head. Did he think the real food was going to miraculously appear?

"What are you doing?" she asked.

"Making a mental list so I know what to buy. Which at this point is pretty much everything."

"You can buy all the food you want, as long as you don't expect me to cook it."

"It may surprise you to learn that I'm not half bad when it comes to preparing a meal. It's one of the few things I remember doing with my mom."

Though he tried to hide it, she could see a dash of

wistful sadness flash across his face. The way it always did when he mentioned his mom.

"How old were you?"

"Five or six I guess."

"She was okay then?"

He shrugged. "I don't know if you could ever say she was completely okay. But life would be almost normal for months at a time, then the meds would stop working, or the side effects would be so bad she would stop taking them. Gradually she got so bad, nothing seemed to work. I was eight when social services removed me."

"And you haven't seen her since?"

He shook his head. "Nope."

She couldn't imagine going all those years without seeing her parents. Not knowing where they were or what they were doing.

"I used to get an occasional letter, but not for about six years now. She moved around a lot, going from shelter to shelter. I haven't been able to find her."

"What would you do if you did find her?"

"I'd try to get her in an institution or a group home. Her mental illness is degenerative. She won't ever get better, or even be able to function in society. But the truth is, she's probably dead by now."

He sounded almost cold. If she hadn't known Nick so well, she might have missed the hint of sadness in his tone. It made her want to pull him in her arms and give him a big hug. How could he stand it, not knowing if she was dead or alive? Not knowing if she was out there somewhere suffering. Cold and lonely and hungry.

"Are you worried about the baby?" he asked.

"What do you mean?"

"About the fact that mental illness can be genetic."

Honestly, she'd never even considered that. She didn't know all that much about mental illness, and even less about genetics. "Should I be worried?"

"My mom's illness stems from brain damage she sustained in a car wreck when she was a kid. So no, the baby won't be predisposed to it. Unless it runs on your side."

"My parents had nine kids, which if you ask me is completely nuts. But as far as I know, neither of them are technically mentally ill. Unless it was some big secret, I don't recall *anyone* in my family ever being mentally ill. And it's a big family."

"Speaking of big families, that's something we've never talked about," he said. "If this does work out, and we decide to get married, how will you feel about having more kids?"

Did the phrase, *over my dead body* mean anything to him? And how would he react if she was adamant about not having any more children.

That was something they would worry about later, when it became clear how far they planned to take this.

"I'm not sure," she told him, which wasn't completely untrue. There was a chance, however slim, that she would agree on one more baby.

"It's something I feel strongly about," he added.

She could see that, and she couldn't help feeling they were starting with one strike already against them.

Five

Zoë woke at eleven-thirty Saturday morning with a painfully full bladder and a warm weight resting on her feet. She pried her lids open and looked to the foot of the bed to find a pair of hopeful brown eyes gazing back at her.

"What are you doing in my bed?" Just her luck, Tucker was one of those dogs attracted to humans who didn't like them. She gave him a nudge with her foot. "Shoo. Get lost."

Tucker exhaled a long-suffering sigh and dropped his head down on the comforter, eyes sad. Up on the dresser beside the bed, Dexter watched over them, giving Tucker the evil eye.

"Go sleep in your own bed." She gave him another

gentle shove. He tried one more forlorn look, and she pointed to the door. "Out."

With a sigh he unfolded his lanky body and jumped down from the bed, landing with a thud on the rug, the tags on his collar jingling as he trotted out the door and down the stairs.

She sat up and her stomach did a quick pitch and roll. So far she'd gotten away with negligible morning sickness. A bit of queasiness first thing in the morning that usually settled after she choked down a bagel or muffin.

She eased herself out of bed and shoved her arms into her robe, but when she looked down for her slippers they were no longer on the side of the bed where she was sure she'd left them.

Darn dog.

She shuffled half-asleep across the ice-cold bare floor and down the stairs to the bathroom. She smelled something that resembled food and her stomach gave an empty moan followed by a slightly questionable grumble. She used the facilities and brushed her teeth. She tried to brush her hair into submission and wound up with a head full of blond frizz.

Oh well. If he was going to stay here, he would have to learn to live with the fact that she woke up looking like a beast. It also hadn't escaped her attention that the bathroom smelled decidedly more male than it had the previous morning, and when she opened the medicine chest, she found a shelf full of *guy* things there. Aftershave, cologne, shaving gel and a razor. Along with several other tubes and bottles of various male things.

She shook her head. Weird.

She found her way to the kitchen, doing a double take as she passed through the living room. She blinked and rubbed her eyes, sure that it was an illusion. But no, the clutter was gone. The newspapers and old magazines and dirty dishes. The random tufts of cat fluff had been vacuumed away. He'd even dusted.

A man who did housework? Had she died and gone to heaven, or had she woken up in the twilight zone?

Tucker lay on his bed beside the couch, the tips of two furry pink slippers sticking out from under his belly. *Her* slippers.

"Give my slippers back you mangy thief." Tucker just gazed back at her with innocent brown eyes that said, *Slippers? What slippers?*

Since he didn't seem inclined to move any time soon, she reached down and tugged them out from under him. Lucky for the dog they weren't chewed up and covered with slobber. Regardless, she would have to start keeping them on the top shelf of her closet.

She found Nick in the kitchen standing at the stove, cooking something that looked like an omelet. He wore a red flannel shirt with the sleeves rolled to his elbows, one that accentuated the wide breadth of his shoulders. His perfect behind was tucked into a pair of faded blue jeans that weren't quite tight, but not exactly loose either. On his feet he wore steel-toed leather work boots.

"That smells good."

Nick turned and smiled. "'Morning."

He was showered and shaved and way too cheerful. He looked her up and down and asked, "Rough night?"

"You know those women who wake up looking well-rested and radiant? I'm not one of them."

He only grinned. He probably figured silence was his best defense. To say she didn't look like a troll would be a lie, and to admit it would hurt her feelings.

Smart man.

"Thanks for cleaning up," she said. "You didn't have to do that."

"If I'm going to live here, I'm going to pitch in." He turned back to the stove. "The eggs will be done in a minute and there's juice in the fridge."

Juice?

She had no juice. Just a half gallon of skim milk that went chunky three days ago. Come to think of it, she didn't have eggs, either. Or the bacon that was frying in the skillet beside the nonexistent eggs. Or the hash brown patties sitting in the toaster. "Where did all this food come from?"

"I went shopping."

He shopped, too? She *was* in the twilight zone.

"If you're trying to impress me, it's working." She opened the refrigerator and found it packed with food. Milk, juice and eggs and bags of fresh fruit and vegetables. She wondered if he did windows, too. "What else have you done this morning?"

He grabbed two plates from the cupboard. It sure hadn't taken him long to familiarize himself with her kitchen. "I jogged, showered, cleaned and shopped, and I stopped by my place to pick up a few more things."

"Jeez, when did you get up?"

"Fiveish."

"It's Saturday."

He shrugged. "What can I say—I'm a morning person."

"I'm sorry, but that is just sick and wrong." Not that it wasn't kind of nice waking up and having breakfast ready. She poured herself a glass of organic apple juice—organic?—and sat at the table in the nook. Nick set a plate of food in front of her. Eggs, bacon, hash browns and buttered toast. She wondered if it was real butter. "Looks good. Thanks."

Nick slid into the seat across from her, dwarfing the small table, his booted feet bumping her toes. Invading her space. The man took up so much darned room.

She closed her eyes and said a short, silent, guilt induced blessing. A holdover from her strict Catholic upbringing. Some traditions were just impossible to break.

Nick dug right into his breakfast and, like everything else, ate with enthusiasm and gusto. No doubt about it, the guy enjoyed life to the fullest.

She picked at her food, nibbling tiny bites and chasing it down with sips of juice.

"Not hungry?" he asked.

"Not really." She bit off a wedge of toast. "Mild morning sickness."

"Anything I can do?"

"You could have the baby for me."

He gave her a "yeah, you wish" look.

After a few minutes of nibbling, her stomach gradually began to settle, and she began to feel her appetite returning. Though she didn't typically eat a big breakfast, she stopped just short of picking up her plate and licking it clean. She even reached across the table to nab the last slice of bacon off Nick's plate.

"Not hungry, huh?"

"I guess I was hungrier than I thought."

Nick got up and cleared the dishes from the table. "I was thinking about heading into the office for a few hours. Want to tag along?"

She had enough of the office Monday through Friday. Her weekends were hers. "I don't think so."

Normally she would wait until after dinner to do the day's dishes—sometimes three days later—but out of guilt she took the dirty plates and juice glasses from the sink and stacked them in the dishwasher. "It's supposed to get up in the high fifties today. I was planning on working in the garden. I need to get my gladiola bulbs planted."

"Then I'll stay and help."

She closed the dishwasher and wiped her hands on a towel. "Nick, your living here doesn't mean we'll be attached at the hip. We don't have to spend every second of the day together."

"I'm not asking for every second of your time. But I'm also not looking for a roommate I'll only see in passing." He folded a work-roughened hand over her shoulder. Its warm weight began to do funny things to her insides. "If we're going to do this, we're going to do it right. We're going to be a couple."

A couple of *what,* that was the question.

A couple of idiots for thinking this might actually work? Or a couple of fools for not realizing they were too different for this kind of relationship?

Having a big, strapping man around definitely had its advantages.

It might have taken Zoë two or three weekends to turn over the dirt to create a new flower garden and prepare it for planting. That meant two or three weeks of sore arms, an aching back and dirty fingernails. Nick, macho guy that he was, had nearly the entire area turned over and de-sodded in three hours.

She'd offered to help, but he said he would never let a woman in her condition do a man's job. Normally a comment like that would have gotten him a whack over the head with a shovel, but then he started driving the pitchfork into the soil and she became distracted watching the powerful flex of his thighs against worn denim. The way they cupped his behind just right.

As the temperature climbed up close to sixty, Nick shed first his jacket, then he peeled off his tattered Yale sweatshirt. She found herself increasingly distracted from her chore of picking weeds from the turned soil and dumping them in a bucket to go in the compost pile. She was much more interested in watching the play of muscles under the thin, white, sweat-soaked T-shirt.

What would it feel like to touch him again? What would he do if she got up right now and ran her hand up his back…

She shook away the thought. No. *Bad Zoë*. No touching allowed. Not yet anyway. Not until it was clear this relationship wasn't based solely on sex.

He was just so…*male*. And she was suffering from a serious excess of estrogen or pheromones, or whichever hormone it was that made a woman feel like molesting every man in sight.

One would never guess from the look of him that Nick had been raised among the rich and sophisticated. Not that he gave the impression of being a thug, either. He wore jeans and a flannel shirt the way most other men wore a three piece suit. When Nick entered a room, no matter the size, he filled it. He drew attention with his strength and character. With his unwavering confidence and larger-than-life presence. But he was so easygoing, he could impress without intimidating.

He was also a loyal friend and a fair employer. The kind of man a person could count on.

That didn't mean he was a pushover, though. People didn't mess with Nick. He may have had the patience of a saint, but cross him and watch out. His wick was long, but the impending explosion was catastrophic.

Something bumped Zoë's shoulder and she turned

from watching Nick to find a long snout in her face. Before she could react, Tucker gave her a big sloppy kiss right on the mouth.

"Aaaagh!" She frantically wiped dog slobber off her face with the sleeve of her sweater. "Go away, you disgusting animal!"

Nick turned to see what the problem was. "What's wrong?"

"Your dog just slobbered on my face."

Nick grinned. He probably trained the dog to do that just to annoy her. "That's his way of saying he likes you."

"Couldn't he find a less disgusting way to show affection? One that doesn't involve his spit."

He drove the pitchfork into the ground and leaned on the handle, a bead of sweat running down the side of his face. "I've been thinking about this arrange-ment we have and it occurred to me that we've been out together lots of times, but never as a couple."

"Like a date?"

"Right. So I was wondering if maybe you would like to go out with me tonight."

"As a couple?"

"I was thinking something along the lines of dinner and a movie."

Interesting. "Like a *real* date?"

"Yep."

She hadn't been on *any* kind of date—real or pretend—in longer that she wanted to admit. Her social life had been less than exciting lately. Most men seemed to want one thing, and they expected it on the first date no less. She obviously had no objections to sex before marriage, but even she thought two people should get to know each other before they hopped in the sack together.

"I get pregnant, you move in, *then* you ask me out on a date. Amazing how backward we're doing all of this, isn't it?"

"Is that a yes?"

"Yes. I'd love to go on a date with you."

He surveyed the ground he had yet to turn over. "This should only take me another fifteen or twenty minutes. Then I'll need to shower."

"Me, too. Why don't I hop in first while you finish up."

She hiked herself up, brushing dirt from her gardening gloves and the knees of her jeans. She knew it was something she would have to get used to, but the idea of showering while he was in her house was a little weird. Maybe if she hurried, she could get in and out while he was still outside.

Unless he wanted to conserve water and shower together...

No. *Bad* Zoë.

She gave herself a mental slap. There would be no shower sharing. At least not yet. But that *was* something couples did, right?

"One more thing," Nick called after her as she dashed to the house. She turned and found him flashing her that simmering, sexy smile.

Uh-oh, what was he up to?

"Since this is a real date, I'll be expecting a good-night kiss."

Nick glanced through the darkness at Zoë. She sat beside him in the truck, her head resting against the window, a damp tissue crumpled in her hand. Since they left the theater, her sobs had calmed to an occasional hiccup and sniffle.

On a first date disaster scale of one to ten, they had ranked a solid eleven. But technically the date wouldn't be over until they got home, so he wasn't going to count his chickens. It could get a lot better—or a lot worse.

Agreeing on a movie had been the first hitch. She had wanted to go to some artsy foreign film playing in Birmingham, and he wanted to see the latest martial arts action flick.

After a long debate-argument, they finally compromised—he being the one to do most of the compromising—and agreed on a romantic comedy.

As a trade-off, she'd let him pick the restaurant this time. He chose a four-star Middle Eastern place in Southfield he'd heard fantastic things about. He'd also learned a valuable lesson. Never try to feed a pregnant woman new, exotic food. When the server had set their plates in front of them, the unfamiliar textures and scents had turned her skin a peculiar shade of green. One bite had her bolting to the bathroom.

She'd had to wait outside while he paid the bill and the waitress packed up their uneaten dinner in carryout containers.

Since they were both still hungry, they had stopped at a fast food drive-thru and ate burgers and fries on the way to the theater.

He didn't normally get into chick flicks, but the film hadn't been as boring as he had anticipated, and their experience at the movie theater had been blessedly uneventful. Until the end, that is, when Zoë dissolved into uncontrollable sobs. Which was a little strange considering the movie had a happy ending. She'd been crying so hard he'd practically had to carry her out of the theater.

He'd gotten more than a few evil looks from female moviegoers—as if her emotional breakdown was somehow his fault—and several sympathetic head shakes from their male counterparts.

He wasn't going to pretend he had even the slightest clue what had happened. Or how to fix it. What he did know was that good night kiss he was hoping for seemed unlikely at this point. As did any possibility of seducing his way into her bed.

Beside him, Zoë sniffed and dabbed at her eyes with a tissue.

"You okay?" he asked, giving her shoulder a reassuring pat.

She wiped her nose and said in a wobbly voice, "I ruined our first date."

Ruined was such a strong word. There had been

good points. Given time, he could probably think up a few. "You didn't ruin anything."

"I got sick at dinner then had a breakdown in the movie theater."

He was going to say that it could have been worse, but they were still a few minutes from home. No point tempting fate.

"What if it's a sign?" she hiccupped. "What if this is God's way of telling us our relationship is going to be a disaster? Maybe this is our punishment for the premarital sex."

He'd never spent much time with a pregnant woman, but he was almost one hundred percent sure this was one of those mood swings he'd heard expectant fathers talk about. "Zoë, I think this has more to do with hormones than divine intervention."

"It was our first date. It was supposed to be special."

It was completely off the wall, but despite the fact that her face was all swollen and blotchy and her nose was running, he didn't think he'd ever seen her look more beautiful.

It wasn't often he got the opportunity to take care of Zoë. She was so damned capable and independent. He liked that she needed him. That she had a vulnerable side.

He took her free hand, linking his fingers through hers. "Just being with you made it special."

She looked up at him through the dark, tears welling in her red, puffy eyes and leaking down her cheeks. "That's s-so s-sweet."

But not so sweet that she would be willing to spend the rest of her life with him.

The words sat on the tip of his tongue but he bit them back. He had no interest in trying to guilt her into marriage. If and when they exchanged vows, he wanted her to mean every word she said.

And if that never happened? If she decided she didn't want to marry him?

Well, they would burn that bridge when they came to it.

Six

Sunday—thank goodness—proved to be a quiet and uneventful day. Zoë woke once again to a hot breakfast, and after the kitchen was cleaned, she and Nick had lounged around, chatting and reading the newspaper. Nick had adopted the recliner and Zoë shared the couch with the dog—who in two days had become her shadow. Later Nick watched football and drank beer while she retaught herself to knit, in the hopes of making the baby a blanket.

It felt so…domestic. And though she had never been a big fan of football—or any sport for that matter—it was nice just being in the same room with him, each doing their own thing. It had been…comfortable.

Isn't that how her parents had done it? When they

weren't working that is, which wasn't very often. Her father would park himself in the La-Z-Boy and her mom would grade papers or do needlepoint.

Maybe that was what all real couples did.

Nick fixed authentic, spicy enchiladas for dinner, which as he promised were delicious. And were probably the reason she woke Monday morning feeling as if someone had siphoned battery acid into her stomach.

She didn't manage to drag herself to work until after ten. She knew there was a problem the instant she stepped into her office and saw Shannon sitting at her desk, a determined look on her face.

The kiss.

She'd been so wrapped up in the living together thing, she had completely forgotten someone saw her and Nick kissing on Friday. Obviously, it had gotten around and Shannon was expecting an explanation.

Zoë shrugged out of her jacket and collapsed into her visitor's chair, since her own chair was occupied. "Go ahead, get it over with."

"It isn't bad enough that you don't tell me you're playing hide the salami with the boss—"

"Charming," Zoë interjected.

"—but this morning I take a call from your doctor's office and I'm told your prescription has been called into the pharmacy. Your prescription for *prenatal vitamins.*"

Oh crud. Zoë felt all the blood drain from her face.

Shannon smiled smugly. "Is there by any chance something you neglected to tell me?"

Zoë winced. The kiss getting out was bad enough. She really wasn't ready for everyone to find out about her pregnancy.

"I admit I was deeply hurt."

She didn't look hurt. She looked as if she was preparing to give Zoë a thorough razzing. That was definitely more her style. Zoë and everyone else in the office had learned not to take it personally. Shannon leaned forward, elbows on the desk, fingers steepled under her chin. "But considering you probably just made me five-hundred and thirty-eight dollars richer, I might have to forgive you."

Five-hundred and thirty-eight dollars? "How did I manage that?"

"I won the pool."

"*Pool?*" Why did she get the feeling she didn't want to know what Shannon was talking about?

"Every time Nick skips out on a fiancée there's a betting pool to guess how long it will take him to find a replacement. I said within a week."

"The office has been *betting* on Nick's dating habits?" How is it that she had never heard about this?

"There's been some obvious tension between you guys since the wedding. Lots of long lingering looks when the other isn't watching. I put two and two together." She flashed Zoë a smug smile. "Looks like I was right, huh?"

She so did not need this hassle. There would be

questions that required explanations she just wasn't ready to give.

Zoë blew out a breath. "Who knows?"

"About you and Nick sucking face? Pretty much the whole office. It was Tiffany that walked in on you."

"I should have known, she never knocks." She also had a big mouth, and Zoë was pretty sure she had a crush on Nick.

"What about the baby? How many people know about that?"

Shannon sat back in the chair. "You see, that's tricky. Without telling everyone, I'll have a hard time proving the entire timeline, and the fact that I actually won. I had to ask myself, what's more important to me? Our friendship or being able to buy that forty inch flat screen television I've had my eye on. And as a result, reap the reward of many weeks of fantastic sex from my very grateful spouse."

"So it all boils down to our friendship or good sex?"

"You may not believe this, but after three kids and ten years of marriage, good sex can be pretty hard to come by."

Which probably meant that her secret didn't have a chance of hell in staying that way. "So what did you decide?"

She grinned. "That our friendship means more to me. But, honey, you're going to owe me big time for this one."

"Thank-you," Zoë said softly, close to tears again. Which was so not her. She never cried.

Would this emotional roller-coaster ride never end?

"That doesn't mean I don't want details. So spill."

"We didn't plan this," she told Shannon. "It was supposed to be a one time thing. A drunken mistake."

"But you got a little surprise instead?"

Zoë nodded. "The whole thing is a fluke."

"This was no fluke, Zoë."

She wished she could believe that. "He asked me to marry him."

Shannon didn't look surprised. "That sounds about right for Nick. What did you tell him?"

"That I'm not ready for that. We've decided to try living together for a while first."

"Which sounds about right for you."

Zoë frowned. "What's that supposed to mean?"

"No offense, but you *always* play it safe. You keep everyone at arm's length."

"I do not!" Zoë said, feeling instantly defensive. "You and I have been friends for a long time."

"And you know pretty much everything about me, right?"

"I guess so."

"And what do I know about you? What have you told me about your family?"

She bit her lip, trying to remember what she might have told Shannon, a sinking feeling in her chest. "You, um, know I have a big family."

"I know there are nine of you, but I have no idea how many brothers or sisters you have. I don't know their names. I know you grew up in Petoskey but you never talk about what it was like there. How it was for you growing up. You never talk about school or friends. *Nothing* personal. To get you to open up at all I have to practically drag it out of you. You have a lot of friends here, but besides Nick, I don't think *anyone* really knows you."

She hated to admit it, but Shannon was right. Zoë didn't get personal with too many people. Just her sister and Nick, and Nick hadn't been by choice. He had just sort of insinuated himself into her life, settling in like a pesky houseguest who never left. And there had always been a bit of resistance on her part. There still was. She always held a tiny piece of herself back.

Was Shannon right? Had Zoë been keeping everyone at arm's length?

An uneasy feeling settled in her stomach. Maybe her aversion to marriage had less to do with her family and was instead just a strange quirk in her personality. Maybe she'd never learned how to let herself open up to people. And if she didn't change, what kind of future could she and Nick possibly have? If they had one at all. If she refused to marry him, would it ruin their friendship? Would they wind up resenting each other?

The thought made her heart shudder with fear.

Nick was such a huge part of her life. What would she do without him?

If they were going to make this work, she would have to learn to open up and let him in.

All the way in.

"I'm not saying this to hurt your feelings," Shannon said, looking apologetic. "I think you're a wonderful, kind person. I consider you a good friend. Which is why I'd like to see this thing with Nick work out. You may not realize it now, but you two are perfect for each other."

"I told him no sex," Zoë blurted out, then turned twenty different shades of red. Why had she said that?

Shannon's eyes rounded. "No sex? Ever?"

"Not ever. Just until we're sure our relationship isn't just physical."

"One night of sex in what, ten years of friendship, and you're worried the relationship is only physical?"

Zoë hadn't realized until just now how ridiculous that sounded. And how equally ridiculous it must have sounded to Nick. What he must think of her.

"Do you think denying him sex is my way of keeping him at arm's length?"

"Honey, it doesn't matter what I think. The question is, what do *you* think?"

She was thinking that insisting they live together first had been her roundabout way of putting off making a difficult decision. One that shouldn't have been difficult in the first place. After ten years of friendship, she should know what she was feeling. Either she loved him or she didn't.

And if she didn't, maybe it was only because she hadn't let herself.

Nick had been incredibly patient with her so far, but

at some point he was going to grow tired of chasing her. How could she risk losing the one man she might have been destined to spend the rest of her life with?

She had to make a decision, and she had to make it soon.

"I don't care what his excuse is," Nick barked into the phone. His foreman, John Miglione, had just delivered the news that one of his employees had left for lunch and failed to return—for the fourth time in two weeks. On top of that the man called in sick at least once a week. There was nothing Nick hated more than firing people, but he needed reliable employees. A smart man knew that to survive in business he should surround himself with competent people. The weak links had to go. "Tell him one more time and he's out of a job."

"Will do, Nick. And there's one more thing."

He was silent for a second, as if he were working up to something, and Nick knew exactly what that something was.

"I know you want to ask, so just go ahead and get it over with."

"Is it true about you and Zoë?"

"That depends on what you heard."

"That Tiffany walked in on you two getting down and dirty."

"Tiffany exaggerates. It was just a kiss."

"Does that mean you two are…"

"Possibly. We're giving it a trial run."

"Well, it's about time."

Nick shook his head. "Do you know that you're the third person who said that to me today."

Zoë appeared in his office doorway—speak of the devil. He held up a finger to let her know he would only be a minute.

John laughed. "Then that should tell you something, genius. Give her a big wet one for me. I'll talk to you later."

He shook his head and hung up the phone, turning to Zoë. "What's up?"

"Is this a bad time?" she asked.

"No. John just called about O'Connell. He didn't come back after lunch—again. He seemed like a decent guy when we hired him. Overqualified even, but he can't seem to get his act together."

"That's too bad." She closed and locked the office door.

Did they have a meeting he'd forgotten? And if so, why lock the door?

Without a word she crossed the room and walked around his desk looking very...*determined.*

Determined to do what, he wasn't sure.

There was definitely something up.

"What's going on?" he asked.

With her eyes pinned on his face, she began unbuttoning her blouse.

Huh?

He watched as she slipped the garment off her shoulders and let it drop to the floor. He was too stunned to do anything but sit there as she climbed in his lap. She straddled his legs, her skirt bunching at her upper thighs, wrapped her arms around his neck and kissed him.

No, this wasn't just a kiss. This was a sexual attack. A wet, deep, oral assault. And he was completely defenseless.

He knew she was passionate, but man, he'd never expected this.

She feasted on his mouth, clawing her fingers through his hair, arching her body against him. She rode him like he was her own personal amusement park attraction.

It was hot as hell, the way she was throwing herself at him, still, something wasn't right. Something he couldn't quite put his finger on.

Something was…*missing*.

He felt her tugging his shirt from the waist of his jeans, fumbling with the buckle on his belt.

What the heck was going on?

He wasn't one to turn down sex, even if it was in the middle of the afternoon in his office. In fact, the idea of sex *anywhere* with Zoë was enough to get his engine primed, but something about this just wasn't right. She was kissing him, rubbing her satin and lace-covered breasts against his chest, yet he wasn't feeling a damn thing. He didn't even have a hard-on.

He grabbed Zoë's shoulders, held her at arm's length and asked, "What are you doing?"

"Seducing you," she said, like that should have

been completely obvious, sounding more exasperated than turned on.

"I see that. But why?"

She looked at him as though he was speaking an
alien language. "Why?"

"You said you wanted to wait," he reminded her.

"I'm not allowed to change my mind?"

"Of course you are." But he had a strong feeling
she hadn't changed her mind, or something had
changed it without her consent. It was as if she was
going through the motions, but her heart wasn't
really in it. "Just tell me why."

She blew out an exasperated breath. "Do I need a
reason? Jeez! I thought you would be jumping at the
chance. I thought you would have me naked by now."

"Normally, I would. It just feels like...I don't
know. Like you're doing this because you have to. Or
I'm forcing you or something."

"You're *not* forcing me."

"I'm sorry, but something about this just doesn't
feel right."

A delicate little wrinkle formed between her
brows. "Are you turning me down?"

It was hard for him to believe, too. In fact, he
couldn't think of a single time when he'd turned a
woman down. "At least until you tell me what's up.
Why the sudden change of heart?"

She slid out of his lap, snatched her shirt up from
the floor and covered herself with it. "I thought this
was what you wanted."

He could see that he'd hurt her feelings, but he needed to know what was going on. They had to be honest with each other or this relationship would never have a chance.

"Of course it's what I want. But is it what you want?"

She gave him that confused look again. "I don't understand. I'm here, aren't I?"

"Zoë, why did you come in here?"

She tugged her shirt on and buttoned it. "You know why."

"What I mean is, what *motivated* you?"

Her frown deepened. "I wanted to have sex with you."

He sighed. This was going nowhere. "Let's try this. Let me give you a scenario, and you tell me if I'm right. Okay?"

She nodded and smoothed the creases from her wrinkled skirt.

"You were sitting at your desk thinking about me, remembering that night in the hotel. You became so overcome with lust and passion that you couldn't wait another minute to have me, so you raced down to my office."

She just stared at him, so he asked, "Was it something like that?"

She bit her lip. "Um…"

He was a little disappointed, but not surprised. "Talk to me Zoë. Tell me what's going on."

"I thought that if I didn't have sex with you soon, maybe you were going to get sick of waiting.

Maybe you would find someone else. Someone...
better."

That had to be the dumbest thing he had ever
heard. "Contrary to what you might believe, a man
can go three days living with a woman and not have
sex." He leaned back in the chair and folded his arms
over his chest. "Hell, there have been times I've
lasted a whole week. And if it becomes a problem,
there's no reason why I can't...take matters into my
own hands, so to speak."

Her cheeks flushed pink and she lowered her eyes
to the floor. It amazed him that a woman who so
excelled at talking dirty could possibly be embarrassed by this conversation.

He patted his legs. "Come'ere. Have a seat."

She hesitated—the woman who had just thrown
herself at him with guns blazing—then sat primly on
his knee, tucking her skirt around her legs.

This was definitely not going to cut it.

He wrapped his hands around her waist. She
gasped as he pulled her snug against his chest, her
behind tucked firmly into his lap.

That was much better.

"Okay, now what made you think I would dump
you if you didn't sleep with me?"

She looked up at him, so much conflict and confusion in her eyes. "I keep everyone at arm's length."

"Arm's length?" What was she talking about?

"I'm too private. I don't let people in. You're

going to get sick of me shutting you out and find someone else."

Where was she getting this garbage? How could a woman so intelligent act so dumb? "And sex is supposed to fix that?"

She shrugged. "It's a start."

"Do you honestly think I'm that shallow?"

She shook her head, looking guilty for even thinking it.

"If I thought you were shutting me out emotionally, sex ten times a day wouldn't make a damned bit of difference."

She gnawed at the skin on her lower lip. "I guess I never thought of it like that."

"I guess not." He brushed a few wayward blond curls back and tucked them behind her ear. "You must have had a good reason for wanting to wait, and I respect that. If you're not ready, that's okay. I understand."

The crinkle in her brow grew deeper. "That's just it. I'm not sure if the reason I had was a good one. We've been friends for years and managed not to have sex. So why would I think our relationship would only be physical? And it's not like I don't want to have sex. It's all I think about lately. When I'm not sick, or sobbing my eyes out, that is."

A grin curled his mouth.

"I have this really annoying habit of looking at your butt. I never even used to notice it, and now I can't peel my eyes off of it. And I want to touch it. I want to touch you *everywhere*. So why am I still telling you no?"

He shrugged. She was adorable when she was confused and frustrated.

"I'm afraid I'm doing it because I don't let people close to me."

"Maybe it's just that you're dealing with an awful lot right now and a sexual relationship is more than you're ready for."

"You think?" she asked, a hopeful look in her eyes.

"When I make love to you, Zoë, I want it to be like that night in the hotel. I want you to want me as much as I want you."

Her lips curved in a dreamy smile. "It really was good, wasn't it?"

He couldn't help grinning himself. "Oh, yeah."

She cupped his face in her hands. Her skin was warm and soft and smelled like soap. "You know what? You're a great guy."

Then she kissed him. A sweet, tender kiss packed with so much simple, genuine affection it nearly knocked him out of his chair.

Now, this was definitely more like it. He would rather hold and kiss her this way for five minutes than have an entire night of meaningless sex.

That night in the hotel he knew that there was something more between them. Something they had both buried away. Maybe she just wasn't ready to take that last step. But she would be eventually.

He was certain of it.

Seven

When Zoë pulled into her driveway later that evening there was a car parked there.

"Oh, fudge."

That's what she got for dodging her sister's calls. And giving her a key. She should have known that if she didn't come clean, Faith would pop in for a surprise visit.

Maybe she subconsciously wanted her here. Maybe she needed someone to tell her what to do.

She parked her conservative Volvo beside her sister's flashy little crimson Miata. They had always been polar opposites. Zoë the practical, responsible sister and Faith the wild child.

When they were kids, Faith had always wanted to

loosen Zoë up and teach her to have fun, while Zoë ran herself ragged trying to keep Faith out of trouble. If their parents knew how many times Zoë had covered for her when she'd snuck out after midnight to meet a boyfriend or go to a wild party, they would have strokes.

She gathered her things and headed for the front door. She stepped inside and called, "I'm home."

Faith appeared from the kitchen, her flame-red hair cut stylishly short and gelled into spiky points, a drastic change from the waist-length curls she'd had last time. She was dressed in body-hugging black jeans and a stretchy chenille sweater the exact same green as her eyes.

She clicked across the room in spiked high heels and hugged Zoë fiercely. "Surprise!"

"What are you doing here?" she asked, wrapped up in a scented cloud of perfume and hairspray.

"Don't even pretend you don't know why I'm here. You haven't been returning my calls and that always means something is wrong."

"Nothing is wrong, I promise." She stepped back and looked her sister up and down. She looked perfect, as usual. She wore just enough makeup to look attractive, without being overdone. Her acrylic nails were just the right length and painted a warm shade of pink. Attractive, but not overly flashy. Faith has always been the pretty one. "You look gorgeous! I love the new haircut."

"And you look exhausted. But don't even change the

subject. Why was there an enormous dog in your house and what's with all the guy stuff in the spare bedroom?"

"Those are Nick's things. So is the dog." She looked around, wondering why Tucker hadn't met her at the door. She was kind of getting used to the crotch sniff greetings and sloppy dog kisses. "Where is the dog?"

"I let him out. And why is Nick staying here? Is he getting his place sprayed for bugs or something?"

Before Zoë could explain, the front door opened and Nick walked though, his regular old big gorgeous self. She saw him through different eyes now and couldn't help wondering if it would be obvious to the world what she was feeling. Not that she thought there was a snowball's chance in hell of keeping this from her sister now.

"Pork chop!" Nick said, giving Faith a big hug, lifting her right off her feet.

"Sugar lump!" Faith squealed, hugging him back.

Zoë felt the tiniest twinge of jealousy. Faith had always been so outgoing and friendly. So full of warmth and affection. Why couldn't Zoë be more like that?

Nick set her down and took a good look at her. "Wow. You look great."

"Right back attcha, stud. Zoë was just about to explain why you're staying here. Is something wrong? Did you lose your condo?"

"Um, no," Nick said, looking to Zoë for guidance, like she had the slightest clue how to explain this.

Maybe it would be best to just come right out and say it. "The thing is, I'm pregnant."

Faith's mouth fell open and for about ten seconds she looked too stunned to speak. Maybe just saying it hadn't been the best way to go after all. "You're *what?*"

"Pregnant."

"*Pregnant?* And you didn't *tell* me?"

"Sorry. I was going to call you. I only found out for sure a couple of days ago. I've been a bit... confused."

"Which still doesn't explain what Nick is doing here."

Zoë and Nick looked at each other, then back at Faith. Did they really need to spell it out? Were they so unlikely a couple that Faith would never guess it?

Faith looked from Zoë to Nick, then back to Zoë again. Then she gasped. "It's *Nick's?*"

"You have to swear not to say anything to Mom and Dad," Zoë pleaded. "I haven't decided what to tell them yet."

"How did this happen?" Faith demanded.

"The usual way," Nick said, and Zoë felt her cheeks begin to burn with embarrassment.

"When did you two start seeing each other? And why didn't anyone tell me?"

"Why don't I start dinner while you two talk," Nick said. He beat a path to the kitchen like his pants were in flames and he needed a fire extinguisher.

Coward.

"You and Nick?" Faith said, shaking her head, like she just couldn't believe it.

Zoë felt a jab of annoyance. It's not as if she and

Nick were a different species for God's sake! "Is it really so hard to imagine that Nick would be attracted to someone like me?"

"Of course not. I've always thought you and Nick would be a great couple. I just didn't know you thought so, too."

"I didn't," she admitted. At least not consciously. Maybe all this time the idea had been there, lurking in the back of her mind.

"I want the whole story," Faith said, giving her a pointed look. "And I expect *details*."

Zoë knew exactly what kind of details her sister was referring to.

"Then you had better sit down and get comfortable. This is going to take a while."

Nick, Zoë and Faith sat up until well after midnight chatting. They probably would have stayed up all night if Nick and Zoë hadn't had to go to work the next morning.

Since Nick had the guest room, Faith bunked with Zoë. They took turns in the bathroom, changed into their jammies, then climbed under the covers together, giggling in the dark like they had when they were kids. Back then they'd shared bunk beds. Faith on top and Zoë below.

"Are you sure you can't stay for a few days?" Zoë asked. She didn't see her sister nearly as much as she would have liked to. She wished she lived closer. Especially now that Faith was going to be an aunt.

"I really have to get back. I just had to make sure you were okay. I promised I wouldn't be gone long."

"Promised who?"

Zoë could see the flash of Faith's teeth as she smiled. "I'm seeing someone new. No one really knows about it yet."

"And you accuse me of keeping secrets," Zoë admonished.

"Yeah, well, Mom and Dad aren't exactly going to approve of this, either."

"Let me guess, he's Lutheran."

"Nope."

"Jewish?"

"Atheist."

Zoë cringed. "Ooooh, yikes."

"And he's not a he, he's a she."

For a second Zoë was too surprised to reply. A *she?* "You're dating a *woman?*"

"Are you totally grossed out?" she asked, her voice lacking its usual confidence.

"Of course not! I just…I'm surprised, that's all."

"It kind of surprised me, too."

"What happened? Did you just one day decide, hey, maybe I'll try something new?"

"You know me, I'll try anything once. Her name is Mia. Are you sure it doesn't gross you out?"

She wouldn't lie to herself and not admit it wasn't a little weird to think of her sister in a new way, but all that mattered was that Faith was happy. "I promise, I'm not grossed out."

"That's good, because as strange as it probably sounds, I think I might be in love with her."

It must have been serious, because like Zoë, Faith didn't do love. She didn't let herself get tied down. Didn't talk about having a family. Ever. She just wanted to have fun.

The truth was, Zoë felt jealous. Not about the same sex part. She was firmly rooted in her hetero-sexuality. She liked men, plain and simple.

What she envied was that Faith had clicked with someone and she went for it, no question. Even though she knew it could potentially get compli-cated, she wasn't afraid to take a chance.

Why couldn't Zoë be like that? Why couldn't she just open up and let this thing with Nick happen? Why was he sleeping in the guest room when he should have been in bed with her?

"I'm thinking of telling Mom and Dad," Faith said.

"Wow, it must be serious."

"I swear, I've never felt like this about anyone. I know they're going to freak, and possibly disown me. I guess it's a risk I'm willing to take. I feel I owe it to Mia not to try and hide it. I don't want her to think I'm ashamed of our relationship. I'd like you to meet her, too. Maybe we could come down and stay for a couple days."

"I'd like that," Zoë said, and realized she really meant it. She wanted to meet the person that had captured her sister's heart. "Maybe next weekend."

They talked for a while longer, until Faith drifted

off to sleep. Zoë lay there awake until after one, her mind unable to rest. She couldn't stop thinking about all the things that had changed over the past few weeks. She felt as if her entire life had been flipped upside down, spun around and set back down slightly askew.

But not in a bad way. Things would never be the same, but she was beginning to realize that wasn't necessarily a bad thing.

She tossed and turned for another few minutes, then decided to try a glass of warm milk to help her sleep. Which was kind of weird since she'd never in her life had warm milk and the idea sounded pretty gross. She climbed out of bed and tripped over Tucker who lay sleeping on her rug. She couldn't find her slippers in the dark, and she didn't want to disturb her sister by switching on the light, so she padded across the cold floor in bare feet. She headed down the dark stairway but instead of her feet taking her to the kitchen, she found herself standing in the partially open door of the guest room. Maybe that had been her intention all along, and the warm milk was just her way of convincing herself to walk down the stairs in the first place.

She could tell by his slow and deep breathing that Nick was asleep.

Instead of turning around and going to the kitchen, she tiptoed into the room. She had no idea what she was doing, or even why she was doing it. But it wasn't enough to stop her.

Maybe everything wasn't supposed to make

sense. Maybe it was okay to do things simply because it felt good.

Nick was turned away from her, on his right side, his wide shoulders bare. She felt a deep ache in her heart, a pull of longing that propelled her closer to the bed. Closer to him. She wasn't here for sex, she knew that much. She just wanted to be near him.

Without thinking, or considering the consequences, she pulled back the covers and very quietly slipped in beside him. The sheets were cool and soft and smelled of his aftershave.

She rolled onto her side, facing away from him, carefully tucking the covers around her shoulders. Beside her, Nick stirred.

"Zoë?" he said in a voice rough from sleep and rolled toward her.

"Sorry. I didn't mean to wake you."

"S'okay," he mumbled and curled up behind her, enfolding her in the warmth of his body, wrapping a thick arm around her. He spread one large hand over her belly, easing her closer, burying his nose in her hair.

Oh, this was nice.

She held her breath, waiting to see what he would do next, what he would touch, if he would kiss her. And to her surprise, he didn't do a thing. He just snuggled up to her and fell back to sleep. It was as if he knew exactly what she wanted without her even having to ask.

She sighed and placed her hand over his, twining their fingers together. This was definitely more effective than warm milk. Already her lids were beginning to feel heavy. The heat of his body soothed her, his slow, steady breathing warmed the back of her neck and the deep thud of his beating heart lulled her to sleep.

It was a good thing she was having the boss's baby. In any other situation Zoë's erratic work schedule would surely get her fired. And so much for them saving gas driving together.

It was past eleven when she finally strolled into work. Her sister had already been gone by the time she got out of bed, but Faith left a note saying she would call so they could talk about her and Mia visiting next weekend. Nick, she added, had made her breakfast before he left for work.

Zoë hadn't heard or felt him get out of bed. Typically sharing a mattress meant a restless night's sleep for her. Last night, curled up in Nick's arms, she'd slept like the dead and woke feeling well-rested for the first time in weeks.

One very good reason to invite him upstairs to sleep tonight. In fact, maybe it would be better if he moved *all* of his things up there. Maybe it was time to begin treating this exactly the way they should, as an intimate, monogamous relationship between two people who cared deeply for each other. Maybe even loved each other. And if she wasn't actually in love with him yet, she was darned close.

She dropped her purse and jacket in her office

then took the hall down to Nick's office, getting more than a few curious looks and several knowing smiles along the way. News of the kiss had definitely made the rounds. And instead of feeling ashamed or self-conscious, she found herself holding her head a little higher, her back straighter. She found herself answering their looks with a smile that said she was proud to be with a man of Nick's integrity, a man who was so admired by his peers.

If they only knew the *whole* story.

She *wanted* people to know. She was proud to be having Nick's baby.

The thought nearly blew her away.

The only logical explanation was that for years there had been feelings between them that they had either been denying or stowing away. And now that those feelings had been acknowledged and set free, they were multiplying at an exponential rate.

Nick's office was empty, and she remembered belatedly that he had planned to work on-site today—an inspection had been scheduled that he wanted to be there for. She felt a dash of disappointment that she would have to wait all afternoon to see him.

She turned to leave and plowed into a brick wall of a man coming from the opposite direction.

"Whoa!" He grabbed her arms to keep her from toppling over on her butt. She recognized him as O'Connell, the man they had hired only a few weeks ago. The one who'd been giving Nick so much trouble. "Sorry," he said gruffly.

"No, it was my fault." She backed away from him. "I wasn't looking where I was going."

He was *enormous,* with long sandy brown hair, a bushy beard and craggy, almost harsh features. He wore the typical construction worker's uniform— work-faded, dusty jeans, a quilted flannel shirt and steel toed work boots.

"He's not in?" he asked in a deep rumble of a voice.

"No. He's on-site. He should be back sometime later this afternoon."

He gave her a solemn nod and started to walk away, his heavy footsteps vibrating the floor under her feet.

"Can I give you a bit of advice?"

He stopped and turned back to her.

"Nick is a patient man and a fair employer, but you're pushing him over the line."

He narrowed his eyes at her, looking downright fierce. She might have been intimidated, but she'd spent the last ten years around men like him. They looked big and tough, but deep down most were just big teddy bears.

"Is that supposed to scare me?" he asked.

"Your references from your last job were impeccable. Your work is quality. So what's the problem? Why do you keep screwing up?"

"You wouldn't understand," he said gruffly, a distinct hint of sadness lurking behind a pair of piercing blue deep-set eyes. She couldn't help thinking there was more to this situation than he was letting show. And a damned good reason why he was missing work.

She could read people that way.

She propped her hands on her hips and gave him one of her stubborn looks. "Oh yeah, tough guy? Why don't you try me?"

Eight

It was nearly three by the time Nick got back to the office and the only thing on his mind, the only thing that had been on his mind all day, was stopping in to see Zoë. He barely remembered her climbing into bed with him last night, so waking to find her curled in his arms had been a pleasant surprise. And if he hadn't had an appointment with an inspector, he might not have gotten out of bed.

He wasn't going to pretend to know what had motivated her to do it. She was the one calling the shots, setting the pace. But he felt as if they had taken a giant step forward last night.

They had made progress.

He headed into his office to drop off his briefcase

and jacket, and found Zoë sitting at his desk. O'Connell, his problem employee, was standing by the door, as if he'd just been on his way out.

"Nice of you to show up," Nick told him, feeling his good mood fizzle away.

"Boss." O'Connell nodded Nick's way then shot Zoë a half smile. "Thanks."

Nick felt his hackles go up. What the hell was that all about? Why was he smiling at Nick's woman? And why were her eyes red and puffy? Had she been crying?

She sniffled and returned the smile, which pissed off Nick even more. "No problem. You just have to promise you won't make a move until I talk to Nick."

"I won't." He gave her a nod, and ignoring Nick, walked out.

"What was that all about?" Nick demanded. "Why are you crying? Did he hurt you?"

She chuckled and waved away his concerns. "I'm fine. This is nothing. Just the usual overactive hormones."

"What did you need to talk to me about?"

"Come in and shut the door."

He did as she asked and walked over to his desk. "What's going on? I don't like you being alone in here with him. I don't trust him."

A grin split her face. "Nick, are you *jealous?*"

"Of course not," he said automatically, then frowned. Damn, he *was* jealous. He was behaving like a suspicious spouse. "I'm sorry."

"He came in to quit," Zoë told him.

"That's convenient. It'll save me the trouble of firing him."

"I told him I wouldn't let him. And you're not firing him, either."

Maybe she was forgetting who owned the company. "Why the hell not?" he snapped.

"This guy came highly recommended from his last employer. They couldn't say enough good things about him. I knew something had to be up."

"And?"

"So I asked. Like we should have a week ago."

"*And?*" he repeated impatiently.

"And it took some prying, but I finally got him to admit why he's been missing so much work."

No doubt O'Connell had tried to con his way into keeping the job, pulling on Zoë's heartstrings. She was emotionally unstable enough these days to fall for just about anything.

He folded his arms across his chest. "This should be good."

"He has a sick daughter."

Nick frowned. That he hadn't expected. A drug or alcohol problem maybe, but not a sick kid. He didn't even know O'Connell was married. "How sick?"

"She has a rare form of leukemia."

And what if it was all bull? "You're sure he's not just saying that to—"

"He showed me pictures," she interjected, her voice going wobbly and her eyes welling with tears again. "Taken in the children's ward of the hospital. She looks like such a sweet little girl. Only seven years old." She sniffled and wiped away the tears spilling down her cheeks. "Sorry. It was just so sad. He got misty-eyed when he talked about her. I could see how much he loves her, and how hard it's been for him."

Nick cursed and shook his head. "Why the hell didn't he say anything?"

"Because he's a big burly macho guy who thinks he can carry the weight of the world on his shoulders. He lost his wife three years ago, so it's just the two of them. They moved here from up north to be close to Children's Hospital in Detroit. There's a specialist there who thinks he can help her. Only problem is, she has to go in for treatment several times a week and sometimes he can't find anyone to help him. Some days she's so sick from the chemo and radiation he can't leave her."

"I would have given him the days off."

"It gets worse. Even with insurance, medical bills are eating up all his money and they're about to get evicted from the apartment they're staying in. Although from what he says, it sounds like the place is a dump and it's in a terrible neighborhood. He said they have no choice but to go back up north so he can move in with his parents."

"And what about his daughter?"

"This treatment is her last option. Without it she'll probably die."

Nick leaned forward in his seat. "What can we do to help him?"

A grin split Zoë's face. "I talked to him about the company possibly loaning him some money."

"And?"

"He says he's already too far in debt." She plucked a tissue from the box on his desk and wiped the last of her tears away. "I think he's too proud to take a handout."

"We have to do something." There had to be a way to help this guy. A way that wouldn't bruise his pride.

He looked over at Zoë and saw that she was still smiling at him, her eyes full of warmth and affection. "What?"

"You're a good man, Nick."

He shrugged. "Anyone would want to help him."

"No, they wouldn't. But I knew you wouldn't question helping him. You would do it without a second thought."

She got up from his chair and walked to the door. He thought she was going to leave, instead she snapped the lock.

What was she up to?

She turned and started walking toward him, the weeping gone. Instead she gazed down at him a heavy-lidded, almost sleepy look in her eyes. This was awfully familiar. Where had he seen this before…?

Oh yeah, she'd been wearing an identical expression that night in the hotel, seconds before they pounced on each other.

Oh man, here we go again.

Her cheeks were rosy, her lips damp and full, like

plump, dew covered strawberries. He didn't doubt they would be just as sweet and juicy.

She exhaled a breathy sigh and fanned her face. "Phew, it's getting awfully warm in here, isn't it?"

It didn't feel particularly warm to him, although, if she was going to do what he thought she was going to do, it would be a lot warmer in a minute or two. "If you say so."

She reached up, her eyes pinned on his face, and began unfastening the buttons on her shirt. Very slowly, one by one, inch by luscious inch, exposing a narrow strip of pale, creamy skin.

He could see in her eyes, she wanted him. She wasn't doing it because she knew it was what *he* wanted. And she sure wasn't in a hurry.

Well, hell, it *was* getting hot in here.

"I don't want to wait any longer," she said in a husky voice.

"What if someone needs me for something?" he asked, figuring it would be irresponsible to not object at least a little. They were, after all, at work.

"They'll just have to wait their turn."

Well then. He leaned back in his chair to enjoy the show, felt his heart rate skyrocket when she slipped the blouse from her shoulders and let it drop to the floor. Underneath she wore a siren-red transparent lace bra that barely covered the essentials. Her skin looked pale and creamy soft, her nipples taut and nearly as rosy as the fabric that did little to cover them. She wasn't what he would call well-endowed, but what she did have was firm and perfectly shaped. Just enough to fit in his cupped hand with barely any overflow.

And he was so hard that any second he was going to bust out his zipper.

Zoë unfastened her slacks and pushed them down. And when he saw the thong she wore underneath he stopped breathing. In the same vibrant shade as her bra, it was so scandalously brief and transparent it left *nothing* to the imagination.

Had she dressed this way for him or did she always wear sexy underwear to work?

She flashed him a mischievous smile. "See anything you like?"

He lowered his eyes to his crotch, to his very obvious erection. "What do you think?"

He followed the movements of her hand as she stroked a path between the swell of her breasts, trailed it down her taut stomach, stopping briefly to circle her navel, then lower still, brushing her fingers over the itsy bitsy patch of lace.

She leaned forward, resting her hands on the arms of his chair, giving him a beautiful view of her cleavage. "Thinking about stopping me again?"

Oh, hell no. He reached up and hooked a hand behind her neck, pulling her face to his, his fingers tangling through the softness of her pale curls. "Kiss me."

Her lips were soft and warm and so sweet as she brushed them against his own. She slipped into his lap, straddling his thighs, pulling at his clothes—

The knob on his office door rattled, then there was a loud pounding. "Nick! Open up!" John called.

Damn it.

"I'm busy," he shouted in the direction of the door. He had a nearly naked, aroused woman in his lap who seemed intent on getting him naked, too. No way in hell he wasn't going to make love to her.

"It's an emergency."

He closed his eyes, let his head fall back, and cursed.

Zoë let go of the hem of his shirt and called, "What happened?"

There was a brief pause, as Nick was sure his foreman was putting two and two together, then he said, "Sorry to interrupt, but I just got a call that there was an accident at the Troy site."

Zoë sighed and Nick cursed again.

"How bad?" he called.

"I'm not sure. I only know they took one of our guys to the hospital."

He scrubbed his hands across his face and mumbled, "I don't believe this."

"Give us a minute," Zoë said, and he looked up at her apologetically. "I know, you have to go."

She climbed out of his lap and grabbed her clothes from the floor. He stood up and tucked his shirt back in.

He watched her dress, knowing his own face mirrored her look of disappointment. "We have piss-poor timing, don't we?"

She buttoned her blouse and tucked it into her slacks. "No kidding."

As she headed for the door, Nick grabbed her arm and tugged her to him. "Tonight," he said, "you're all mine."

Unfortunately *tonight* never transpired.

Zoë ran home to let the dog out at five, then went back to the office and stayed until eight to make up for some of the time she'd been missing and work she'd been neglecting the past couple of days. She expected Nick to be back home when she pulled in at eight-fifteen, but the driveway was empty and the house dark.

The intense tug of disappointment she felt took her by surprise. Coming home to an empty house had never bothered her before. Well, not usually. Sometimes it sucked being alone, but she always had Dexter to keep her company.

In only a couple of days she'd grown used to having Nick around.

She raided the frozen dinners in the freezer, unable to choose between her two favorites.

"What do you think?" she asked the dog, holding them both up. "Chicken Alfredo or lasagna?"

He looked up at her with a goofy dog smile, his long skinny tail wagging like mad and whacking the table leg.

"You want me to make both?"

He barked, which he almost *never* did, so she took that as a yes. She'd never been much of a dog person, but Tucker wasn't half-bad. She couldn't help growing attached to him, especially when he shadowed her every step, gazing up at her with lovesick puppy eyes.

She nuked both dinners and ate in front of the television, tossing bites to Tucker who gobbled them up enthusiastically. When they were finished eating, Zoë stretched out on the couch with the cat curled up on her feet and the dog sacked out on the rug beside her. She channel surfed, running across a show about babies on the Discovery Channel. She settled in to watch it and the next thing she knew, someone was nudging her awake.

Nine

Zoë pried her eyes open, feeling drugged from sleep. The television was off and Nick stood over her grinning, illuminated only by the light in the hallway.

"What time is it?" she mumbled.

"After midnight."

"I guess I fell asleep." She yawned and stretched. "How did it go at the hospital?"

"Nothing fatal. A couple of cracked ribs and a broken collarbone. He'll be off work for a while, but he'll make a full recovery." He extended a hand toward her. "C'mon, let's get you into bed." At her curious look he added, "To sleep. I think we're both too tired for any fooling around."

He was right. It had been a long eventful day for them both.

He took her hand and hoisted her off the couch.

"Are you coming to bed, too?"

"With you?" he asked, and she nodded. "Do you want me to?"

She really, truly did. "I want you to."

He flashed her that dimpled grin. "Then I will."

"I have to brush my teeth first."

"Me, too. You mind sharing the sink, or do you prefer to take turns?"

It's not as if she had never shared a sink before, and often with three or four other people all rushing to get ready before the school bus honked out front. Besides, that was what couples did, right? "I don't mind."

It was a little weird watching Nick brush his teeth. It was one of those normal everyday things that a person did that she never really thought about, but doing it together felt very personal and intimate. Like learning a secret.

She drew the line at staying in the bathroom while he used the facilities—some secrets should stay secret—and went upstairs to change into her pajamas. In her bedroom she found Tucker and Dexter curled up together on her bed.

She propped her hands on her hips and told Dexter firmly, "You little traitor."

Dexter looked up guiltily.

"Get down," she said, tugging on the covers. Like

new best buddies, both animals jumped off the bed and headed down the stairs together.

It would seem that even Dexter had already adjusted to having them here. That had to be some sort of sign, didn't it?

She stripped down and slipped into an oversized, extra long T-shirt with a Happy Bunny logo on the front. She was already under the covers by the time Nick came upstairs. She curled up on her side and watched as he sat on the edge of the bed and first pulled off his work boots and then his socks. Next he unbuttoned his shirt, tugged it off, and draped it across the footboard.

She sighed with pleasure at the sight of all that beautiful bare skin over ropes of lean muscle. Despite his dark coloring and coarse beard, he wasn't all that hairy. Just a sprinkling on his pecs that trailed down into a narrow path, bisecting his abs and disappearing under the waistband of his jeans.

Looking completely at ease in her bedroom, he rose to his feet and unfastened his jeans. He shoved them down and kicked them off, revealing long powerful legs. Men's legs didn't typically do much for her, but as far as she was concerned Nick's were perfect.

Wearing only his boxers, he slipped into bed beside her. He rolled on his side facing her, leaned close and gave her a brief, but incredibly sweet kiss. His chin felt rough against her skin. He smelled of toothpaste and soap and just a hint of aftershave. "Good night."

"Good night." She reached behind her and

switched off the lamp. As her eyes adjusted to the dark, she could see that Nick had closed his eyes. He must have been pretty tired considering he was typically out of bed before 6 a.m.

Yep, she was tired, too. Absolutely exhausted. Much too tired to finish what they had started in his office this afternoon.

So why couldn't she seem to close her eyes? Why was the urge to touch Nick nagging at her?

She didn't want to wait. She wanted sex now, damn it!

She laid a hand on Nick's arm, rubbing from wrist to shoulder. "Nick, you awake?"

He didn't respond so she gave him a gentle shake. "Nick, wake up."

He answered with a half mumble, half snore.

He was sound asleep.

Swell.

She sighed and rolled onto her back. Two days ago she hadn't been ready for sex, now it was all she could seem to think about. If only they could get their schedules coordinated.

Tomorrow, she decided. Tomorrow they were going to get down and dirty and *nothing* was going to stop them.

"I think I figured out a way to help O'Connell," Nick said the next morning at the breakfast table. He'd fixed them pancakes, sausage patties and freshly squeezed juice from organically grown oranges.

The way she'd been eating lately, she was going to gain a hundred pounds before this baby was done cooking.

"How?" she asked, stabbing her third sausage patty.

"Well, his immediate problem is finding a place to live that he can afford, right? Well, I have a two bedroom condo sitting empty in Royal Oak. They can stay there rent free."

"You're a genius! That's absolutely *perfect*. Do you think he'd go for it?"

"Since it's paid off, and I'm not getting any rent for it now, it's technically not a handout."

"I can't believe we didn't think of it before. And it's even closer to the hospital than the place he's staying in now."

"There's only one possible drawback. Unless I want to kick him and his daughter out at some point, you're going to be stuck with me for God only knows how long."

"And that's okay with you?" she asked.

He nodded. "It really is. How about you?"

She smiled. "It's really okay with me, too."

"You're sure? This is a pretty big step."

A step she honestly felt ready to take. She knew exactly what she wanted, and she was going for it, damn it. "I'm absolutely, and completely sure."

He flashed her that dimpled grin. "Should I talk to O'Connell or do you want to?"

"Since it's your place it would probably be better if you talked to him. It might be easier to accept coming from a guy than me." Then she added, "And you should do it right away."

"Just give me a minute to load the dishwasher," he said, carrying their plates to the sink. "Then we'll get out of here."

Suddenly she couldn't wait to get this settled. After hedging all this time, she was so ready to get Nick moved permanently into her home—into her life—she didn't want to wait another minute.

She followed him to the sink and said, "Nick, look at me."

When he turned to face her, she curled her fingers into the front of his shirt, pulled him down to her level, and gave him a long, deep, wet kiss. One designed to let him know exactly how much she wanted him.

His strong arms circled her, pressing her closer. One big hand plunged through her hair to cup the back of her head while the other traveled downward to fit itself comfortably over her backside.

Zoë pressed her body against him, feeling as if she couldn't get close enough. As if she would *never* be close enough to him.

She knew in that second, without a doubt, she was in love with this man. She was going to marry him, and they were going to have a family. She suddenly understood the appeal of marriage and babies.

Because the babies she had would be Nick's. And it would be his arms she would wake in every morning.

Nick pulled away and flashed her a hungry grin. "Wow, what was that for?"

"It was just a sample of what you have to look forward to later."

He stroked the side of her throat with his thumb, his eyes dark with desire. "I can't wait."

"Me, neither. And the sooner we get to work, the sooner we get to come home."

After only a minimal amount of coercion on Nick's part, and a bit of hedging from O'Connell, he accepted Nick's offer and agreed to move in right away. When O'Connell thanked him, his eyes were filled with such deep gratitude and utter relief, it nearly choked Nick up.

No doubt the guy really loved his little girl. Nick couldn't imagine being in his shoes, the life of his child hanging in the balance. Living with the fear that he couldn't afford the medical treatment needed to save her. Especially after having lost his wife to cancer.

After O'Connell left to pack, Nick sat at his desk thinking about how precious life really was. He tried to imagine it without Zoë. The idea made him sick inside. She was indelibly etched into his life. He had a bond with her that he'd never felt with another woman. That he'd never felt with *anyone*.

"I guess things went well."

Nick looked up to see Zoë standing in his doorway, a big grin on her face. Damn she was pretty. She had that ethereal glow of good health that pregnant women were supposed to have.

She looked…happy.

"What makes you say that?" he asked.

"O'Connell just came up to me in the break room and gave me a bear of a hug and a big kiss." She laughed. "You should have seen the jaws drop. Everyone is going to think I'm cheating on you."

Nick's brow furrowed. "He kissed you?"

"Relax," she said, her grin widening. "It was only on my cheek. And he *smiled*, Nick. Up until that moment I didn't even know he had teeth!"

He didn't like the idea of anyone but him kissing her, but she looked so happy, he felt a grin of his own tugging at the corners of his mouth.

"We really helped him," she said.

He nodded. "We really did."

She crossed the room and slid into his lap, weaving her arms around his neck. "It feels good."

"It certainly does," he growled, tugging her more firmly against him.

She kissed him, drawing his lower lip between her teeth and nibbling. Damn did he love when she did that. She tasted like sweet tea and raspberry-filled donuts.

"Maybe we should lock the door and celebrate," she said, rubbing herself against him. Driving him crazy was more like it. And God it was tempting. After so many near misses, all he had to do lately was look at her and he was instantly hard. He really needed to get this woman into bed. But he wasn't interested in a quickie at the office, when he made love to Zoë, he planned to take his time.

Meaning it would have to wait. *Again*.

"No time," he told her. "We have to get over to my condo and pack up my things. I told him he could move in right away."

She gave him an adorable little pout, then sighed and said, "Well then, I guess we had better hurry. And I don't care if we don't get home until 2 a.m., we are getting naked tonight."

Sounded like a good plan to him.

It was after eight when they finally got Nick's things loaded in the back of his truck and headed home.

Home. The word had a totally different meaning to her now.

While helping him pack, Zoë made a startling and somewhat disturbing discovery. Nick had no pictures from his childhood, no family mementos. Nothing to indicate he even had a family. It was as if he had no past at all, or at least not one he had any desire to look back on.

She had boxes and boxes of photos and old birthday cards, pictures her younger siblings had drawn for her, and even a couple of their baby teeth. She had at least one or two items from each member of her family.

Only then did it truly sink in, did she realize what it must have been like for him growing up. How lonely he must have been, and why having a family was so important to him now.

He'd never truly experienced a *real* family and now she wanted to be the one who gave him that. She wanted to be the one who finally made him feel complete. She planned to spend the rest of her life making up for every lonely day, every isolated minute he had ever spent. Even if that meant having another baby. Or even a third.

Which, of course, would necessitate them getting a bigger house. She wondered if he would mind moving into a more rural setting. Maybe Romeo or Armada. They could have a huge yard for Tucker and the kids to play in. She could have an enormous flower garden, and maybe start growing vegetables. She could can pickles and jam, the way her grandmother used to. Maybe she could even take an extended leave from work and try the stay-at-home-mom thing for a while. Or at the very least work part time from home.

A world of opportunities she'd never even considered had opened up to her and she couldn't wait to see just where life would lead her.

"You're awfully quiet," Nick said, as he backed his truck into the driveway and parked beside her car. "Everything okay?"

She turned to him and smiled. "I'm just conserving my energy for other things."

He put the truck in park and killed the engine. "I want to say to hell with the unloading, but everything I own is sitting back there. I could probably just toss it all into the garage."

"The lock on the door is broken." It wasn't as if she lived in a bad neighborhood. Birmingham was considered upscale by most accounts, but there was no point taking chances. "If we move fast, we can get the boxes unloaded in no time. Consider it foreplay."

"You don't pick up anything heavier than a phone book," he said firmly and she rolled her eyes. He was such a guy.

They climbed out and he opened the tailgate while she unlocked the front door. She could hear Tucker inside, hopping around excitedly like an overgrown rabbit. They had stopped by home only a couple of hours ago to feed him and let him out, but he greeted her as if she'd been gone for days.

"I know, I know," she said, patting his head as she pushed her way through the door. "We missed you, too, you big oaf."

She grabbed Tucker's collar so he wouldn't bolt and held the door open for Nick. He brushed past her with two boxes marked Bedroom. He carried them down the hall and past the stairs.

"Where are you going with those?" she asked.

He turned to her, a puzzled look on his face. "To the bedroom."

"But our bedroom is upstairs."

A slow grin curled his mouth. "*Our* bedroom."

"Our bedroom," she repeated. And because she knew what was coming next, she added, "And yes, I'm sure."

Savoring the mildly stunned, incredibly happy expression on his face, she headed out the door to grab more boxes. If he thought he was happy now, he should just wait until she'd gotten her hands on him.

After she was through with him, a bulldozer couldn't pry the smile from his face.

"That's it," Nick said, closing and locking the front door.

They had hauled everything inside in under twenty minutes and the anticipation was killing her.

Now it was time to get to the good stuff.

"You know what that means," Zoë said, looking up at him from under lids that were already heavy with pent-up lust. Her legs and arms felt warm and weak and her head felt dizzy. She couldn't recall a time in her life when she'd been more turned on by the idea of making love to someone.

She took off her jacket and tossed it over the back of the couch. With a look to match her own, Nick did the same.

As she pulled her shirt up over her head, every inch of her skin buzzed with sexual awareness. The brush of lace from her bra teased her already sensitive nipples. The vee of skin between her thighs ached to be caressed. Even her hair felt alive and tingly.

Nick yanked his shirt over his head and dropped it on the floor. His skin looked deep golden tan in the dim lamplight. Her heart tapped out a wild beat as he walked toward her, unfastening his jeans. She couldn't wait to get her hands on him, touch and taste every inch. How could she have denied herself this? Why hadn't she realized how good it would be?

He stopped in front of her and she felt dizzy with

anticipation, every cell screaming to be touched. He lowered his head to kiss her and she rose up on her toes to meet him halfway. Their lips touched and she went hot all over, as if someone had replaced the blood in her veins with liquid fire.

He unfastened her jeans, shoving them down and she stopped kissing him just long enough to wiggle out of them and kick them into the dark corner beside the couch.

Her heart beat harder, in perfect time with the sudden loud pounding on the front door.

Nick groaned and pressed his forehead to hers, his breath coming hard and fast. "I don't *believe* this."

She didn't have a clue who it could be this time of night, but whatever they wanted couldn't possibly be as important as her getting into Nick's pants this very second.

"They'll go away." She slipped her hand inside his open fly and stroked the firm ridge of his erection through his boxers. He closed his eyes and groaned. He lifted her right off her feet and backed her against the wall separating the kitchen from the living room. She hooked her legs over his hips and gasped as the length of his erection rocked against her, her breasts crushed into his chest.

She kissed him and his mouth tasted hot and tangy. She felt as if she couldn't get enough, as though she could eat him alive and crawl all over him. She clawed at his jeans, shoving them and his boxers down, then cupped his bare behind, digging her nails into his flesh, feeling wild and sexy and completely out of control. No man had ever made her want to let go this way, to give so much of herself.

The pounding on the door persisted for a minute or two, then through a haze of arousal Zoë heard the jingle of keys, and the rattle of the doorknob being turned. Nick must have heard it too because he stopped kissing her and went stone still.

It happened so fast, neither had time to react. One minute they were alone, the next her sister was standing in the open doorway staring at them, mouth agape. Thank goodness there weren't many lights on, but there was no mistaking exactly what was happening.

For several seconds time stood still. No one moved or said a word. Faith looked down at Zoë's hands, still clutching Nick's behind. She said, "Nice ass," then burst into tears and walked back out the door.

Ten

"I'm so sorry," Faith hiccupped for the umpteenth time since Nick and Zoë had yanked their clothes on and tugged her back inside the house. Zoë sat on the couch by Faith. Nick stood across the room wearing a typical male slightly confused, mildly alarmed expression, looking as though any second he might bolt.

Faith was not the crying type, not even when she was a kid, which led Zoë to believe something really awful had happened. At first Faith had been crying too hard to string together a coherent sentence. They were only able to assess that she wasn't in need of medical attention and no one had died.

Faith sniffled and tugged another tissue from the box in her lap. "I can't believe I fell apart like that, and I really can't believe I walked in on you right in the middle of…well, you know."

"Stop apologizing," Zoë told her. "Tell us what happened."

Faith wiped away the mascara smudges under her eyes. "I am such an idiot."

Nick pushed off the wall where he'd been leaning. "Why don't I leave you two alone to talk."

Before Zoë or Faith could answer, he was on his way up the stairs.

"Wow," Faith said. "I sure scared him off."

Zoë shrugged. "What can I say, he's a guy. He's been getting more than his share of emotional stuff from me these days. I think he's suffering from an overload."

Faith sat there for a second, quietly toying with the tissue, then she looked up at Zoë and said, "I got dumped."

"Oh, Faith." Zoë rubbed her sister's shoulder. As if Tucker could sense her unhappiness and wanted to help, he walked over to the couch and laid his head in Faith's lap, gazing up at her with what Zoë could swear was a look of sympathy.

Faith sniffled and scratched him behind the ears. "I told her I loved her, and I wanted us to move in together. I told her I was going to tell my parents the truth, no matter the consequences, and she told me I probably didn't want to do that. Then she said she decided to go back to her husband."

"I didn't know that she was married."

"Neither did I. Long story short, Mia said she had

just been experimenting, and basically trying to make her husband jealous. And I guess it worked. He wants her back." Faith sniffled and wiped away fresh tears. "She was so…*cold*. Like she never cared about me at all. Like I was some high school science experiment."

"Oh, sweetie, I'm so sorry. I know how much you cared about her."

"I feel so stupid. But I can't help thinking I deserved this."

That was just crazy. "How could you possibly deserve to be treated this way?"

"Do you know how many men I've dumped who claimed to 'love' me?"

"Honey, you deserve to be happy just as much as anyone else."

"Speaking of being happy," Faith said, brightening. "It looks like things with you and Nick are going pretty well, huh?"

Zoë felt guilty admitting how happy she was in light of her sister's heartache, but she couldn't contain her joy. "I'm going to tell him yes. I'm going to marry him."

"Oh my gosh!" Faith squealed excitedly and gave her a big hug. "I can't think of a more perfect man for you." She held Zoë at arm's length and grinned. "Not to mention that he has a mighty find rear end."

Zoë grinned. "No kidding."

"Speaking of that, I should go and let you guys get back to business. I can stay in a hotel."

"You're not staying in a hotel. The spare bedroom is free now. Stay as long as you like."

"I don't have to be to work until Monday, so maybe I will hide out here for a couple of days, if you don't mind."

"We would love to have you," Zoë said, rising from the couch, anxious to get upstairs and finish what she and Nick had started. "Maybe we can go shopping tomorrow. Spending money always helps me chase away a bad mood."

"Just so you know, I'll be sleeping with these on." She held up a pair of headphones and an MP3 player, and grinned mischievously. "So be as loud as you like. I won't hear a thing."

When Zoë finally made it upstairs, Tucker on her heel, Nick was sitting in bed, bare-chested and gorgeous, reading a hardcover novel.

"Everything all right?" he asked.

"She got dumped."

"That's kind of what I figured." He closed the book and set it on the nightstand. "Is she okay?"

"Bruised but not broken." She peeled her shirt off and tossed it in the general direction of the hamper, missing her target by several feet. "I hope you don't mind, but she's going to stick around for a couple days. I don't think she wants to be alone."

"Of course I don't mind. But I guess that nixes tonight's scheduled activities, huh?"

She peeled off her jeans and dropped them

where she stood. "I don't care if the house burns down, nothing is going to stop me from getting you naked tonight."

"That's convenient." He flashed her a sexy, dimpled grin, and tossed back the covers. "Because I'm already naked."

Holy moly! Naked and *very* aroused. She raised a brow at him. "Did you start without me?"

"It won't go away. I need you to put me out of my misery."

"It would be my pleasure." She walked around to his side of the bed, dropping her bra and panties along the way. The way his eyes raked over her—she felt as if she were the sexiest, most desirable woman on the planet.

He patted his thighs. "Come'ere."

She climbed in his lap, straddling him. His crisp leg hair tickled her skin as she lowered herself onto his thighs. His body felt warm and solid as he looped an arm around her waist and drew her closer.

"Here we are," he said, tucking her hair back behind her ears.

Finally. "Just you and me."

He stroked her cheek, his eyes searching her face. "I want you to know that there is no one else on earth that I would rather be with right now. That I would *ever* want to be with."

His words warmed her from the inside out. There was no one she would rather be with, either. "Me, too."

She still wanted him, couldn't wait to feel him

inside her again, but that sense of urgency was gone. Now she wanted to take her time, savor every minute. He must have felt the same way, because for the longest time they only played with each other, kissing and stroking and tasting. Exploring each other as if it was the first time, yet she felt as if they had learned each other a hundred years ago.

How could something be exciting and new, yet this comfortable and familiar?

"I love the way this feels," he said, using his thumbs to gently caress the smooth skin at the junction of her thighs. He watched his movements, as if he found the sight of it fascinating. His featherlight strokes made her hot and cold at the same time and her head started getting that dizzy, detached feeling.

She rose up on her knees to give him a better look, gripping the headboard on either side of him and he groaned his appreciation.

He leaned forward, his hair brushing against her stomach and touched her with his tongue. Just one quick flick, but his mouth was so hot, the sensation so shockingly intense, she gasped with surprise and jerked away.

He looked up, a grin on his face, and said, "Delicious."

She might have been embarrassed, but she was too turned on. He cupped her behind in his big, warm hands and pulled her back to his mouth, lapping and tasting while she balanced precariously between torture and bliss. Every slow, deep stroke of his tongue took her higher, until she could hardly stand it. She wanted to grab his head and push him deeper.

She wanted more, and at the same time she was on total sensory overload.

She was aware of the sound of her own voice, but the words were jumbled and incoherent. The wet heat of his tongue, the rasp of his beard stubble on her bare skin—it was too much.

The pleasure started somewhere deep inside, in her soul maybe, and radiated outward. It gripped her with such momentum, time seemed to grind to an abrupt halt. Every muscle in her body clenched tight and her eyes clamped shut. Her hands tangled in his hair, trapping him close as she rode the waves of pleasure. Her body shook and quaked for what felt like forever.

Her heart throbbed in time with the steady pulse between her thighs. She didn't know if it was Nick's incredible skills or the pregnancy hormones, or maybe even a combination of both, but she had never come so hard in her entire life.

She sank down into his lap and rested her forehead against his shoulder, wanting to tell him how out-of-this-world, amazingly and unbelievably sensational he'd just made her feel, how she was pretty sure she'd just had her first out-of-body experience, but she was barely able to breathe much less use her mouth to form words.

So instead, she kissed him, tasting herself on his

lips and finding it unbelievably erotic. She reached down between them and wrapped her fingers around the impressive girth of his erection. He groaned low in his chest and kissed her harder.

She stroked him slowly, felt him pulse in her hand. He was hot to the touch and velvet smooth. She wanted to take him into her mouth, but when she made a move to bend forward he caught her head in his hands, tangling his fingers through her hair. "Don't."

"I want to."

"I want to make love to you."

"Can't we do both."

He shook his head. "I'm so hot for you right now, it's going to have to be one or the other, and I need to be inside of you."

Well, if he put it that way. Besides, what was the rush? They had the rest of their lives to try anything they wanted. And though she had never been particularly creative or adventurous in bed, she wanted to try it all with Nick.

"You know the best thing about pregnant sex?" he asked wrapping his hands around her hips.

"Huh?"

He fed her a mischievous grin. "No need for a condom."

Nick guided her and she lowered herself on top of him. He sank inside her slow and smooth and oh so deep.

He hissed out a breath, his grip on her tightening. For a moment they sat that way, not moving, barely even breathing. It was almost scary what a perfect fit they were, how connected she felt to him. There was no doubt in her mind that Nick was the man she was supposed to spend the rest of her life with. She wanted to have babies with him and grow old with him.

And she wanted him to know exactly how she was feeling. "Nick, I love you."

He smiled, caught her face between his hands and kissed her, tender and sweet. And she couldn't stop her body from moving, from rising and sinking in a slow, steady rhythm. She watched with fascination as a look of pure ecstasy washed over his face. He let her set the pace, let her do most of the work while he kissed and touched her and whispered sexy, exciting things to her. She found herself answering him, using words she never would have expected to come out of a good Catholic girl's mouth. Dirty things he seemed to love hearing.

He reached between them, caressing the sensitive bud he had so skillfully manipulated with his tongue, and the reaction was instantaneous. Pleasure slammed her from all sides, hard, deep and intense. Forget an out-of-body experience. She wasn't even on the same planet. Only when she heard Nick groan her name, when his body rocked up to meet hers, did she realize she'd taken him along for the ride.

They sat there for several minutes afterward, catching their breath. She kept telling herself she should move, but he was still hard and he felt so good inside her. She waited, watching the minutes tick by on the alarm clock, two, then three, then five, but it still didn't go away. In fact, instead of getting soft, she was pretty sure he was getting harder.

Just for fun, she wiggled her hips and he answered her with a rumble of pleasure.

"You weren't kidding about it not going away." She sat up and smiled. "I'm impressed."

"You know what that means," he said, returning her smile. "We'll just have to do it again."

"Do you remember when we first met?" Nick asked. Zoë lay in his arms her head resting against his chest. She smelled so warm and sweet and girly. It was getting late, and they both had to get up and go to work, but his mind was moving a million miles an hour.

"Of course. I came for an interview, and did a pretty fair job of lying through my teeth."

He played with her hair, looping a curl around his index finger then letting it spring free. There were so many places on her body to play with, so many things to touch. He was pretty sure that tonight he'd managed to play with or touch just about every single one. As far as sex went, Zoë didn't seem to have a single reservation or hang-up. He could do or try pretty much anything and she was always ready for more. Things so forbidden and intimate he'd never had the guts to try them so early in a relationship. Of course, they'd had ten years to develop a deep sense of trust.

It had just taken them a while to get to the good stuff.

"I knew an eighteen-year-old couldn't possibly

have the experience you listed on your application, but you looked so young and vulnerable. I couldn't turn you away."

She looked up at him. "Are you saying you took pity on me?"

He grinned. "Pretty much, yeah."

She propped her chin on his chest. "As much as I wanted to get away from my family, those first few months were hard. I never anticipated how lonely I would be. You were incredibly patient with me considering how bad I stunk as a secretary."

He chuckled. "But you tried so hard, I didn't have the heart to fire you. I knew deep down that you were special. And you were cute."

"I never told you this, but I had a major crush on you for the first year."

"I could kind of tell."

She looked surprised. "Really?"

"Yeah, and I was tempted, believe me. But at the time I wasn't looking for a relationship, and I didn't want to risk killing our friendship with a one-night stand. I liked you too much."

"Want to hear something weird. Almost every boyfriend I've had over the years has felt threatened by my relationship with you."

"Want to hear something even weirder? I've had the same problem with *every* one of my girlfriends. It was as if they couldn't believe a guy like me could have a woman as a good friend."

"Maybe they were seeing something we didn't."

"Maybe." He stroked the wispy curls back from her face. "I never told you what Lynn said right before our wedding, the real reason she decked me."

"What did she say?"

"As we were getting out of the car in the courthouse parking lot, she told me that she would only marry me if I fired you."

Zoë's eyes widened. "You're kidding!"

"She didn't want me seeing you anymore, either. I had to break all ties with you."

"That's crazy. What did you say?"

"At first I thought she was joking, and when I realized she was serious, I was too stunned to say anything. It's not as if I wasn't already having major doubts, but up until that moment I had really planned to go through with it."

"Yet, you waited until the last minute to dump her."

"She was so…manipulative. I guess I wanted to punish her, or knock her down a few pegs at least. You should have seen the smug look on her face when we were standing there. When I backed out, I was more or less saying that I was choosing you over her."

"That had to sting." She sounded sympathetic, but he could tell she was getting a lot of satisfaction from this. She liked hearing that he'd picked her over the woman he'd asked to marry him.

"I'm ashamed to admit it, but I actually enjoyed dumping her."

"That makes two of us, because I enjoyed it, too."

"Now I'm exactly where I'm supposed to be." He

spread his hand over her flat belly, where their child was growing. "Here with you and the baby."

Zoë sighed and rested her head on Nick's chest, cupping her hand over his. So was she, exactly where she belonged. And she wanted to tell him so, right now. But after making him wait for an answer to his marriage proposal, somehow just saying yes didn't seem good enough.

Nick," she said, stroking the tops of his fingers.

"Huh?"

"Would you marry me?"

He was silent, so she looked up and saw that he was grinning. A great big dimpled grin full of love and affection. He had gotten the message loud and clear. He leaned forward, caught her face in his hands and kissed her. *"Absolutely."*

A part of her sighed with relief. Not that she thought he was going to say no. Maybe it was because things were finally settled, it felt as though her life was back on track.

Yet there was something else. A niggling in the back of her mind. A tiny seed of doubt. "I think we should do it soon," She said, feeling a sudden urgency to get this settled. To get on with their life together. Like maybe deep down she thought he might change her mind. "You know, because of the baby."

"How soon?"

"How does next Friday work for you?"

His smile got even bigger. "Friday would be perfect."

"Something really small, like the justice of the peace?"

"Whatever you want."

She settled into his arms and snuggled against him, knowing deep down to her soul that she was doing the right thing, and hoping he felt the same way.

He was quiet for several minutes then asked, "Can I tell you a secret?"

"You can tell me anything."

"I've never once told anyone I love them."

She propped herself up on her elbow to look at him. His eyes were so...*sad*. "How is that possible? You were engaged two times."

"Weird huh?"

"You didn't love them?" A part of her wanted him to say he hadn't. The selfish part that wanted him to love only her.

"I don't know. Maybe I did in my own way. Maybe I'm not physically capable."

Maybe growing up the way he had, had damaged him somehow. How terribly sad that a person could go through their entire life never feeling real love.

"I'm a different person with you, Zoë. We're going to be a family."

She let her head drop back down, breathed in the scent of him, felt his heart thump against her ear.

A family. Her and Nick.

Did that mean he loved her? And if he did, why didn't he say the words? Was he really not capable?

Or was admitting that to her just the first step? And

if it had been, at least it was a step in the right direction.

He was quiet for a while, then his breathing became slow and steady and she knew he had fallen asleep.

He did love her. And it wasn't just wishful thinking. She knew it in her heart. She sensed it when he looked at her, could feel it when he touched her. When he was ready, he would tell her.

She would just have to be patient.

Eleven

Zoë felt like death warmed over the next morning at seven when Nick nudged her awake. She managed to pry one eye open far enough to see that he was already showered and dressed and far too awake considering how late they had fallen asleep. And it must have been pretty obvious that she was in no shape to go to work, because he just kissed her, tucked the covers up over her shoulders and said he would see her later.

She fell back to sleep and had strange, disturbing dreams. She dreamed it was her wedding day, and she was walking down the aisle, her arm looped in her father's. Instead of a white gown, she wore the dress she'd worn to both of Nick's weddings, complete with broken straps and stains, and it had been dyed crimson—the same shade as her sister's car.

Not that anyone seemed to think that was out of the ordinary. Row upon row of people dressed in white sat on either side smiling and nodding. Bunches of blood-red roses decorated the aisle, giving everyone a pale, ethereal look.

Her mind kept telling her that everything was normal, but something didn't feel right.

She could see Nick waiting for her by the altar, wearing the same suit he'd worn at his last wedding. He was smiling, but it looked unnatural and plastic, as if he was being forced to stand there against his will. She kept walking toward him, telling herself everything was going to be okay, but instead of getting closer, the longer she walked, the farther away he was getting. The cloying scent of roses crowded the air. But instead of smelling like flowers, it smelled metallic, like blood. It burned her nose and made her stomach ache.

Something definitely wasn't right.

She started walking faster, trying desperately to reach him, but Nick was fading from her vision. Disappearing. She called out to him, but he didn't seem to hear her.

She broke into a run but her legs felt heavy and weak and cramps knotted her insides, doubling her over. The fog grew thicker, closing in around her like wet paper. She clawed her way through it, felt it filling her lungs, constricting her air. She couldn't see, couldn't breathe, could hear nothing but the frantic pounding of her heart.

She called for him again but it was no use. Nick and her father, the smiling people, they were all gone. She was all alone with the sick feeling that she'd just become number three. Nick had left her at the altar, just like the others.

She felt a firm hand on her shoulder and someone called her name.

Zoë shot up in bed, disoriented and out of breath.

"Hey, you okay?" Faith stood beside the bed, a look of concern on her face.

"Bad dream." Her voice sounded weak and scratchy.

"You called for Nick. He already left for work." She touched Zoë's forehead. "You're all sweaty."

Faith was right. The sheet was clinging to her damp skin and her hair felt wet. She felt hot and cold at the same time and everything was fuzzy and surreal.

Zoë blinked several times and fought to pull herself awake, but couldn't shake the sensation of being caught somewhere between sleep and consciousness. It took a minute to realize that the cramps in her stomach hadn't faded with the dream.

It wasn't real, she told herself. She was fine. But the pain was very real and too intense.

Fear skittered across her spine, and her heart gave a violent jolt in her chest.

Faith looked downright scared now. "Zoë, what's wrong? You're white as a sheet."

Everything was fine. The baby was fine, she assured herself, but the tips of her fingers had begun to go numb with fear. She felt as if she couldn't pull in a full breath.

That was when Zoë felt it. The warm gush between her legs.

No, this was not happening.

She and Nick were going to get married. They were going to have a baby together.

"Zoë?" Faith's hand was on her shoulder again and there was real fear in her voice. "Talk to me."

The pain intensified, cramps gripped deeper.

No, no, no, this couldn't be happening. She had to find a way to stop it. She had to *do* something.

She looked up at her sister, tears welling in her eyes. "I think I'm losing the baby."

Nick stood impatiently waiting for the hospital elevator to reach the third floor. He didn't have a clue what was going on, only a message from Faith telling him to get to Royal Oak Beaumont Hospital.

He'd been out of the office all morning, and because he had forgotten to charge it last night, his cell phone was dead. He was unaware of any problem until twenty minutes ago when Shannon accosted him on his way to his office.

He'd tried both Faith's and Zoë's cell phones before he left but neither was answering.

There had to be some rational explanation, he kept telling himself. Nothing was wrong. He was sure that she was fine.

And still a knot of fear had lodged itself in his gut. What if she wasn't fine? What would he do then?

The elevator dinged and the doors slid open. He

crossed the hall to the nurses' station and gave the nurse, an older woman with a fatigued face, Zoë's name.

"Room thirteen-forty," she said in a voice that mirrored her tired expression. She motioned with a jerk of her thumb. "That way, around the corner."

He started down the hall, his heart beating faster and harder with every step.

She was fine. Everything would be okay.

He rounded the corner and saw Faith standing outside one of the rooms. When she turned and saw him coming, he could see by the expression on her face that everything was *not* okay.

His heart took a sudden dive and landed with a plop in the pit of his stomach.

"What happened," he demanded. "Is Zoë okay?"

"She's fine," Faith said. "They're going to keep her overnight just to be safe."

Relief hit his so hard and swift his knees nearly buckled. He braced a hand against the door frame to steady himself. He hadn't realized until just then how scared he'd been. He didn't know what he would have done if she'd been hurt or sick.

So why was she here?

Then it hit him. He'd been so worried about Zoë, he'd completely forgotten about the pregnancy.

"The baby?" he asked.

Faith paused and bit her lip, looking exactly like Zoë did when something was wrong.

Damn it.

They had lost the baby.

What was this going to do to Zoë? Lately she had really warmed to the idea of becoming a mother. He knew this was going to be tough for her to handle. She would feel so guilty. And what if it had something to do with last night? He would never forgive himself if this was his fault.

Right now, he just needed to see for himself that Zoë was okay. "Can I go in?"

"Of course. She's been waiting for you."

Taking a deep breath, he walked past Faith into the room. Zoë sat in the bed wearing a hospital gown looking so small and vulnerable. So alone and numb.

"Hey," he said, walking over to the bed. As he got closer, he could see that she was holding back tears, fighting to keep it together.

It was just like her to think she had to be strong for everyone else.

She looked up at him, her eyes so full of hurt. "We lost the baby."

He had known, but hearing the words felt like a stab in his gut.

"She told me. I'm so sorry I didn't get here sooner." He sat on the edge of the bed and she sat stiffly beside him. She was so tense, one good poke would probably snap her in half. Did she think he was going to make her go through this alone?

"I'm so sorry," she whispered, her voice trembling.

"Zoë, it's okay. It's not your fault." He put an arm around her and nudged her toward him, and everything in her seemed to let go. A soft sob racked through her and she dissolved into his arms. She cried quietly for several minutes and he just held her. He had no idea what to say, what to do. He didn't even know what had happened.

"I-I thought you might be mad," she finally said, her voice quiet and miserable.

He grabbed a tissue and handed it to her. "Why would I be mad?"

She shrugged and wiped away the tears. "I know how much you wanted this."

"But your being okay means a lot more to me."

"It's so weird. I was so freaked out about being pregnant, now I feel so…empty. I really wanted this baby, Nick."

"I know you did." He stroked back a stray curl that clung to her damp cheek. He didn't even want to know, but he had to ask. "Do they know what caused it? I mean, last night…"

"It wasn't that. They did an ultrasound and I could tell by the look on her face that the technician saw something wrong, but she wouldn't say what. She said the doctor would be in soon to see me. That was like an hour ago."

"I'm so sorry I wasn't here for you." Nick rubbed her back soothingly. Sometimes he forgot how petite she was. How vulnerable. His first instinct was to protect her. To say anything to make her hurt less. "I'm sure everything is fine."

"What if it isn't?" she said, sounding genuinely frightened. "What if something is really wrong? I thought I never wanted kids, but the idea of never being able to—" Her voice hitched.

"There's no point in worrying until we know what's going on."

But that got Nick thinking, what if she couldn't have kids? What if they could *never* have a child together? After all these years of longing for a family, waiting for just the right time, could he marry a woman who was infertile?

The answer surprised him.

The truth was, it didn't make a damned bit of difference, if the woman he was marrying was Zoë. Maybe at first his desire to marry her was partially due to the pregnancy, but not any longer. He wanted her.

Baby or no baby.

Before he could tell her that, Doctor Gordon walked in, Faith on his heels. Zoë wrapped her hand around his and squeezed. He could feel her trembling.

"First, I just went over the results of the ultra-sound. I want to assure you that neither of you is in any way at fault. There is a thin membrane that has separated Zoë's uterus into two sections. This constricted the baby's growth, causing the miscarriage."

He went on to explain that she was actually lucky that the egg had implanted itself on the smaller side. Had it been on the other side it's quite possible she could have progressed well into the fourth or even fifth month before miscarrying, which would have been a much more devastating loss.

Nick found it tough to think of losing a baby as a good thing, but what the doctor said made sense.

Zoë didn't say anything, just kept a death grip on his hand, so Nick asked what he knew she was probably afraid to. "Is this something you can fix?"

"I can perform a simple outpatient procedure to remove the membrane," he said. "With no complications, recovery time is usually only a week or two."

"And then she'll be okay? She'll be able to get pregnant?" He wanted to know more for Zoë's sake than his own. He didn't want any question in her mind.

"Did you have any difficulty conceiving?"

"Nope," Zoë and Nick said in unison and the doctor cracked a smile. Getting pregnant had been the easy part.

"Then I see no reason why, with the surgery, she wouldn't be able to conceive and carry a baby to term." He flashed Zoë a reassuring smile. "I think you're going to be just fine."

The grip on Nick's hand eased. He could almost feel the relief pouring through her. He knew how doctors worked. In this litigious society they didn't give false hope. Zoë would be okay. They would get past this. She would have the surgery and they could try again.

"I'd like to see you in the office in two weeks," Doctor Gordon told Zoë. "If everything looks good we can schedule the procedure."

Zoë and Nick each asked a few more questions, then thanked him. When he was gone, Faith walked around the bed and gave Zoë a big hug and a kiss on the cheek. "I'm glad everything is okay."

"Thanks," Zoë said, and some unspoken under-standing seemed to pass between them.

She had no idea how lucky she was to have that kind of bond with someone. To have family. Now he would know, too. When they got married, her family would be his.

"I'm going to run down to the cafeteria and give you guys some time alone," Faith told them. "I'll see you in a bit."

After she left, Zoë said, "So, I guess you're off the hook, huh?"

She couldn't possibly mean what he thought she meant. Nick took her hand and held it. "Which hook would that be?"

"There's no baby. You don't have to marry me now."

"I'm going to pretend you didn't say that."

"What if I can't have another baby, Nick?"

"That's too bad, sweetheart. You're stuck with me." A tear rolled down her cheek and he brushed it away with his thumb. "You heard what the doctor said. There's no reason to worry about that now. You'll have the surgery and everything will be fine."

She nodded, but didn't look completely convinced.

"There is something missing, though," he said.

She frowned. "Missing?"

"We still have to make it official." Enjoying her puzzled look, he reached into his jacket pocket and pulled out the small velvet box. He lifted the lid and watched her jaw drop when she saw the two carat marquee cut platinum diamond engagement ring that had taken him three hours at six different jewelers to choose.

"Oh my God," she breathed, looking genuinely stunned. "You got me a ring?"

"Yeah, and it took me all morning to find the perfect one." He took the ring from its satin bed. She held her breath as he slipped it on the ring finger of her right hand. It was a perfect fit. Feminine but not too flashy.

She held up her hand and the stone shimmered in the fluorescent lights. "How did you know what size?"

"I borrowed a ring from your jewelry box before I left this morning. Do you like it?"

"It's exactly what I would have chosen." Tears welled in her eyes. Happy ones, he hoped. Then she looked up at him with a watery smile. "It's perfect, Nick."

"So now it's official. And since there's no rush, we can wait and plan something nice if you want. Something bigger. I hear most women spend their lives planning their wedding day."

She shook her head. "Not me. I don't need a big wedding. And I don't want to wait. I want to do it next Friday, like we planned."

"Are you sure you'll be feeling up to it? You've been through a lot today—"

"I feel better already knowing everything is going to okay. I want to try again as soon as the doctor says it's safe. I want us to have a baby."

He squeezed her hand. "Whatever you want."

"And I want more than one. At least two, maybe even three."

Wow. When she changed her mind, she really did a complete one-eighty. "We'll never fit a family of five into your house or my condo. I'll have to build us something bigger."

"With a yard big enough for Tucker and the kids to play in? And a huge garden?"

"Whatever you want."

"That's what I want," she said, wrapping her arms around him and hugging him tight. "That's exactly what I want."

She looked happy, and sounded happy, so why did Nick get the feeling something wasn't right?

Twelve

Zoë took the rest of the week off and though Nick thought she needed more time, she was tired of sitting around feeling sorry for herself and went back to work Monday morning.

It had been the right thing to do. Four days later she felt as though she had begun to heal both physically and mentally. She felt ready to move on.

She kept reminding herself what the doctor said, how much worse it would have been if she'd been four or five months along. The baby would have been almost fully developed. A little person. They would have known if it was a boy or a girl.

And they would have spent the days following

the miscarriage not recovering, but planning a funeral. The idca gave her a cold chill.

So really, losing the baby so early, when it was just a speck of life she hadn't even felt move, was a blessing in disguise.

As badly as Nick wanted children, she had expected him to be really upset, but he had seemed more concerned about her health than the fact that they had lost a child. Not that he hadn't made it clear he was concerned about future fertility issues, and he seemed so relieved when the doctor said the surgery would probably fix the problem.

She couldn't help wondering, what if it didn't? Nick hadn't even been willing to discuss it. What if something went wrong and she could never have kids? How would Nick feel about marrying her then?

Of course, by then they would already be married.

Maybe that was why he'd suggested putting the wedding off for a while. Maybe he wanted to be sure she was okay before he tied himself down to her. Maybe he didn't want to marry a woman who couldn't give him children.

She closed her eyes and shook her head.

That was ridiculous. He'd gotten her a beautiful ring and he'd been unbelievably sweet the past few days.

At the hospital, all she had wanted was to come home, but when she got home, it felt as though everything had changed. Getting back to her regular routine had been so difficult. He had stayed beside her the entire first day after it happened. He'd brought her tea and held her when she cried, which was almost constantly.

Why would he do any of that if he didn't want to marry her? If he didn't love her?

And if he did love her, why didn't he say it?

"Hey Zoë, how ya feeling?"

Zoë looked up to find Shannon standing in her office doorway. Again. It was her third time today checking up on Zoë and it was barely three o'clock. She'd been doing this all week, watching over Zoë like a mother hen. "You can stop hovering. I'm fine."

She flashed Zoë a squinty-eyed assessing look. After a few seconds, her face softened, as if she was satisfied that Zoë was being honest. "You know where I am if you need me," she said, then disappeared down the hall.

Word of what happened had traveled through the entire office in record time. She'd received several flower arrangements and sympathy cards over the weekend. They had been addressed to both her and Nick, so that cat was definitely out of the bag. Not that she cared. Everyone would have found out soon enough. They also knew that she and Nick were getting married.

Several men in his crew had wanted to throw him a bachelor party tonight, but he said that in light of what they had just been through, he didn't think it was appropriate. Zoë had said the same thing when the girls in the office had approached her about a trip across the Ambassador Bridge to the male strip club in Windsor.

She just wanted to get this wedding over and done with. Every day she waited she was more anxious, more worried that she would make it all the way to the altar only to have him say he couldn't go through with it.

Or what if he didn't show up at all? They were taking the traditional route and spending the night before their wedding apart. Nick's idea. She was staying home and he was bunking with O'Connell in his condo. Maybe she should have insisted they drive together, so she could at least be sure he would make an appearance.

She nearly groaned out loud.

This was ridiculous. She was being silly and paranoid. Of course he was going to show up. Not only was he going to show up, but he was going to marry her. Even if he hadn't actually said that he loved her.

In less than twenty-four hours she would be Mrs. Nick Bateman. Someone's *wife*. A month ago that fact would have given her hives, but for some reason the idea of getting married didn't seem all that weird to her anymore. She'd changed over the past few weeks. Being with Nick had made her realize that sharing her life with someone didn't mean sacrificing her freedom. It didn't mean compromising herself as a person.

She didn't even mind having his big dumb dog around. In fact, they felt a lot like a family. And someday their little family would grow to include children. A little boy with Nick's dimples and hazel eyes, or maybe a little girl with Zoë's curly hair and stubborn streak.

The possibilities were endless.

Tiffany from accounting barged into her office without knocking—the way she always did—and dropped an invoice on Zoë's desk.

"I need this approved," she snapped.

Nice, Zoë thought. It was common knowledge that Tiffany had been after Nick for the better part of her first six months working here. According to Shannon, Tiffany had been convinced she was next in line after the Lynn relationship had tanked, but Nick had completely blown off her very obvious advances. When she reduced herself to bluntly asking him out, he'd told her very politely—because that was his way—to give it a rest.

She was young, big-breasted and beautiful, and probably not used to men telling her no. Since she had caught Zoë and Nick playing tonsil hockey in the office that day, her panties had been in a serious twist and Zoë had been on the receiving end of a whole lotta attitude.

What Tiffany didn't seem to realize is that Zoë had the authority to fire her jealous little behind—and probably would have if the girl wasn't such a hard worker.

"I'll get this back to you by Monday," Zoë said, hoping Tiffany would take the hint and leave.

She didn't.

"So, tomorrow's the big day, huh?"

"Yup," Zoë replied, pretending to be engrossed by the open file on her computer screen. If you ignored a pest, it was supposed to go away, right?

"Considering Nick's reputation, aren't you nervous?"

Just ignore her, she told herself. She's only trying to get a rise out of you. She looked up, forcing what she hoped passed for a patient smile, but probably looked more like a grimace. "Tiffany, I'm a little busy here."

Tiffany went on as if Zoë hadn't already, in a round about way, told her to get lost. "I'm just worried about you. I'm sure you're feeling vulnerable right now."

Oh please! Now she was going to pretend to be concerned for Zoë's welfare? What an absolute crock.

"I appreciate your concern." *Not.* "But I feel a little uncomfortable discussing personal matters with you."

"You have to be at least a little worried," she persisted. "I mean, before he had a reason to marry you. And now, well…" She trailed off and let the statement hang in the air for Zoë to absorb.

And it did. Zoë had to struggle against the urge to vault over the desk and claw Tiffany's eyes out.

What Tiffany was really saying, was that Zoë was no longer pregnant, so Nick would have no reason to marry her. She couldn't deny the trickle of icy fear that slid through her veins. Because nothing Tiffany said was untrue. Bitchy and rude, yes, but not necessarily inconceivable.

"It would be bad enough being left at the altar, but what if he didn't even show up?"

Zoë's fists clenched tightly in her lap. *Don't kill her. Don't kill her,* she chanted to herself. But oh how good it would feel to blacken one of her pretty blue eyes. Or hell, maybe both of them. Tiffany may have been eight years younger and a head taller, but Zoë was pretty sure she could take her.

"Shut up, Tiffany," Shannon snapped from the doorway, appearing like an angel of mercy. "You're just jealous because you asked Nick out and he turned you down flat."

Tiffany's cheeks blushed a bright crimson and she shot Shannon a nasty look. "My money is on Nick dumping her. I guess we'll just see, won't we?"

She stomped from the room and Shannon mumbled, "What a bitch."

Zoë leaned back in her seat and exhaled deeply. "If you hadn't come in just now, I could see a possible assault charge in my very near future."

"Don't listen to her, Zoë. She has no idea what she's talking about."

"What did she mean by her money?" Zoë asked, even though she already had a pretty good idea.

"Just ignore her."

"What did she mean, Shannon?"

Shannon bit her lip, looking very uncomfortable. "I wasn't going to tell you…"

"It's another pool, isn't it?" Just what she needed, the employees betting on her getting her heart sliced and diced.

Shannon nodded, and Zoë's heart plummeted. She felt like going home, crawling into bed, covering her head and staying there forever.

"What are they betting on exactly this time?" she asked, trying to keep her voice light. Pretending that she didn't feel hurt and betrayed by people she considered her friends.

"They're betting on whether or not Nick will marry you, dump you at the altar, or not show up at all."

Zoë felt physically ill. Her voice shook when she asked, "Where did you put your money? Do you think he's going to dump me?"

"I didn't bet on this one, but if I had, I would have put my money on Nick marrying you. No question. In my life I've never known two people more perfect for each other."

"You don't think he was marrying me because of the baby?"

"As far as I'm concerned, the pregnancy just sped things up a bit. I don't doubt that he wants kids, and maybe that had been a motivating factor before when he asked those other women to marry him, but this is different. I know it is."

Zoë wanted to believe that, but she had to admit, she had doubts. Maybe if he would just tell her he loved her.

If by some miracle he didn't leave her at the altar, if they actually got married, did she want to spend her life with a man who just liked her a lot? Didn't she deserve better than that?

"It's all going to work out," Shannon assured her.

She used to think so, now she wasn't so sure. The question was, what did she plan to do about it?

"Are you sure you don't want me to be there?" Faith asked for the billionth time. "I could hop in the car and if I do ninety all the way I can be there just in time for the wedding."

Three hours, Zoë thought. She was marrying Nick in three hours. It seemed so unreal.

She'd slept in fits and bursts last night and crawled out of bed before the crack of dawn. She was too nervous to eat. Too distracted to do much more than sit at the kitchen table sipping her tea and skimming the newspaper.

According to the *Oakland Press,* the temperature would reach the midsixties with sunny skies all day. She couldn't ask for better weather.

It was her wedding day for heaven's sake! She should be happy. So why couldn't she work up a bit of enthusiasm? She hadn't even managed to drag herself into the shower yet and the dress she and Shannon had spent all day Wednesday shopping for still hung wrapped in plastic in the backseat of her car.

"Zoë?" Faith asked.

"I'm not even sure if I'm going," she admitted.

"Don't even talk like that. I've never seen you so happy. I know you've been through a lot in the past week. Maybe Nick is right, maybe you should wait a while and plan a real wedding. One your family and friends can attend."

And risk being dumped at the altar in front of the entire Simmons clan? Don't think so.

"I've just got prewedding jitters," she told her sister, so she wouldn't actually jump in the car and come down. "Everything will be great."

"Nick loves you."

"I know he does."

But therein lay the problem. She really *didn't* know. Nick hadn't said so, and she'd been too much of a chicken to come right out and ask him.

What if he said no?

Sorry, Zoë, I'm not capable of love, but I sure do like you a lot.

"I have to let you go so I can get ready," Zoë said.

"You're sure you're okay?"

"I'm fine." Lie, lie lie. She was *so* not fine.

"You'll call me later and let me know how it went?"

"I promise."

She hung up the phone and sighed, still not ready to drag herself to the bathroom for a shower. Instead she made herself another cup of tea and sat back down at the table.

Two hours later she was still sitting there, and only then did it sink in that she couldn't do it. She couldn't marry him.

The question now was, what would she tell Nick?

Thirteen

Nick stood in the lobby of the courthouse, alternating between watching the door, checking the time on his watch and pulling his phone from his pocket to make sure it was still on. His starched shirt was stiff and uncomfortable under his suit coat and his new tie was beginning to feel like a noose around his neck.

He'd tried Zoë's house phone and cell but she hadn't answered. He'd even called Faith, then spoke to Shannon in the office, but no one had heard from her for hours.

A smart man, a *realistic* man, would have left a long time ago. Right after he realized his fiancée was, in fact, not going to show up for their wedding.

He should have been at least a little angry at Zoë

for leaving him high and dry, but the truth was, he had it coming.

He deserved this.

In fact, he was glad she'd done it. It was the push he'd needed to realize just how much of an ass he'd been.

What reason had he given Zoë for believing he would marry her? Hell, as far as she knew, he might not have even shown up. Sure he'd said he wanted to marry her, but he'd fed the same line to two other women.

What he had failed to do was prove to Zoë that she was different. That she was the *one*.

He loved her, and he should have told her so.

And it's not as if he hadn't had chances. That night when they had made love and she had told him she loved him, he could have said he loved her, too. And later, when he'd admitted to her that he'd never said the words. He could have told her then.

He could have said it in the hospital, or any time the entire next day they had spent side-by-side, mourning their loss. So many times the words had been balanced on the tip of his tongue, ready to be spoken, but something always stopped him. He had always held back.

Maybe that was simply what he had taught himself to do. His mother had been the only one who loved him and she'd left. By no fault of her own, but that hadn't made it hurt any less.

His aunt and uncle might have loved him, but if they had, they never said so. As he grew up, it was just easier not letting anyone get too close. Not letting himself fall in love.

Talk about a cliché. But clichés were born for a reason, weren't they? Maybe deep down he was still that little boy who was afraid to get his heart broken again.

But it was too late, he was in love with Zoë. The only thing he'd accomplished by keeping that to himself was hurting her.

"I love her," he said to himself, surprised to find that it wasn't that hard to say at all. In fact, he liked the sound of it, the feel of the words forming in his mouth.

It felt…natural.

He pushed off the wall and headed for the stairs, knowing exactly what he needed to do.

It was time he said goodbye to the little boy and started acting like a man.

Zoë wasn't sure how long after their scheduled wedding Nick finally showed up. She sat alone on the swing in the backyard, still in her pajamas, with her legs pulled up and her knees tucked under her chin, wondering if he actually *would* show up. Maybe he was so angry he would never speak to her again.

But then the backdoor had opened and Nick walked through, still dressed in his suit. He crossed the lawn to the swing, hands tucked in the pockets of his slacks, looking more tired than angry.

And boy did he look good in a suit. Almost as good as he looked out of it.

What was wrong with her? She just stood the guy up and now she's picturing him naked?

"You seem to have forgotten that we had a date this afternoon."

She cringed and looked up at him apologetically. "I am so sorry, Nick."

"No." He sat beside her on the swing, loosening his tie. "I'm the one who's sorry."

He didn't hate her after all, not that she ever really believed he would. Maybe she thought she deserved it. "This is completely my fault. I guess I just…got scared."

"Scared that I would back out at the last minute. Or possibly not show up at all?"

She nodded, thankful that he said it for her. And even more thankful that he understood.

"I gave you no reason to believe otherwise." He took her hand and held it, lacing his fingers through hers. "Which makes this entire mess very much my fault."

"I should have trusted you."

He laughed, but there wasn't a trace of humor in the sound. "What did I ever do to earn your trust? Ask you to marry me? Stick a ring on your finger? Well, so what? I did the same thing with two other women and I'm not married to either of them, am I?"

Jeez, twist the knife a little deeper why don't you? Was he *trying* to make her feel worse?

"Um, I'm not quite sure what your point is, but for the record, this isn't helping."

"My point is, I knew exactly what you needed

from me, but I was too much of a coward to give it to you. That line I fed you about the ring making it official was bull. The only way to make this relationship official is for me to stop acting like an ass and tell you how I feel."

"I could have asked," she said.

He shot her a look. "You shouldn't have to."

No, she shouldn't, which is probably why she hadn't. Call her stubborn and a little old-fashioned, but she believed that when you felt a certain way about someone, you told them so.

He cupped her chin in his hand and lifted her face to his. "I never thought it was possible to love someone as much as I love you. Maybe that's why I didn't let myself trust it."

She could feel tears welling in her eyes and burning her nose, and she didn't even have those pesky hormones as an excuse this time.

He kissed her gently. "I love you, Zoë. With all my heart."

She closed her eyes and sighed. No words had ever sounded sweeter or meant so much. Because she knew they came directly from his heart. "I love you too, Nick."

"I have a favor to ask. This is going to sound a little strange, but I'm asking you to trust me."

"Okay."

"Could I possibly have that ring back for a minute?"

It was a little strange, but she trusted him. She slipped it off her finger and set it in his hand.

"I figured it was about time I do this right." He slid off the swing and got down on one knee in front of her. Zoë held her breath and the tears that had been hovering inside her lids began to spill over. "Zoë Simmons, would you do me the honor of becoming my wife?"

"Absolutely," she said. He slipped the ring back on her finger and she threw her arms around his neck and hugged him.

"I know you didn't want a big wedding, but I don't think you have much choice now."

She pulled back and looked at him. He had a very sly, devious grin on that gorgeous face. "Why?"

"Because when I hung up the phone after asking your parents' permission to marry you, they were already working on the guest list."

Her mouth fell open. "You called and asked their *permission?*"

He grinned. "I told you, I wanted to do it right this time."

Oh my gosh, she was now officially daughter of the year. And only a couple of weeks ago she'd been worried about excommunication. "So what did you say?"

"I told them I was in love with you, and I wanted their permission to marry you."

She couldn't believe he'd actually asked permission. "What did they say?"

He grinned. "They both said, it's about time."

Epilogue

Nick trudged down the stairs to the first floor, side-stepping to avoid the half-naked Barbie doll lying in the hallway and kicking aside a handful of Matchbox cars in the den doorway. This all should have been picked up by now.

When he saw the video game on the television screen, he knew why it wasn't.

He crossed the room and shut the television off and received a collective, *"Daaaaaaad!"* from their oldest children, nine-year-old Steven and eight-year-old Lila.

"Don't dad me. You're supposed to be cleaning up your toys. It's almost bedtime."

Six-year-old Nathan, who had inherited not only his father's dark hair and hazel eyes, but also his clean gene, was already working diligently to get all the LEGOS put back in their bin.

"Jenny burped," he said, pointing to the six-month-old tucked under Nick's left arm. The one struggling and squirming to get down and practice the new crawling thing she'd mastered just yesterday.

He didn't have a burp cloth handy, so he wiped away the spit-up with the hem of his shirt, wondering if a day had passed in the last nine years when he hadn't walked around with the remains of someone else's dinner on his clothes.

"Daddy!" four-year-old Olivia, the outspoken one of the bunch, screeched from the doorway, not three feet away. She had two volumes. Loud, and *really* loud. "Mommy is in the kitchen eating cookies again."

He crouched down in front of her, and being closer to the floor and freedom, Jenny let out an earsplitting squeal and struggled to get loose. "Liv' honey, what did Mommy and Daddy tell you about tattling?"

Olivia's lower lip curled into her signature pout. "I want cookies, too."

"Not before bed."

"Then why does Mommy get to eat cookies before bed?" Nathan asked.

"Because she's a grown-up," Lila said, giving him a shove as she walked past him. "She can eat cookies whenever she wants."

"You can have cookies tomorrow," Nick told her.

"She ate like the whole box," Steven mumbled. "There won't be any left tomorrow."

"Hey, mister, I heard that." Zoë stood in the den doorway, hands on her hips. Her hair hung in damp tendrils from a recent bath and her pink robe was conspicuously dotted with cookie crumbs. "Lila, can you please watch your sister for a minute? Daddy and I need to have a quick meeting."

"Sure, Mom!" she said, brightly, taking her baby sister from Nick's arms. Watching Jenny meant she didn't have to clean.

Zoë motioned him out of the room, mumbling, "Five kids. Whose bright idea was that?"

It hadn't actually been anyone's *idea*. After Steven and Lila, who were both carefully planned, they figured they had their boy and girl, so they were all set. But then Lila had started getting a little bit older and Zoë started having those baby cravings again.

They were a little lax with the contraceptives thinking that if it was meant to be, it was meant to be, and along came Nathan nine months later. Olivia was their first real oops baby, and the result of a bit too much champagne on New Year's Eve.

Jenny, oops baby number two, had been conceived when they thought they were being careful. Obviously not careful enough, her doctor had said when the test came back positive.

After Jenny was born, to avoid any further oopses, her doctor had finally put her on the pill. It was wreaking havoc on her menstrual cycle, and she'd been awfully weepy lately, but thank God it appeared to be working. Their only other option had been a vasectomy. Either that or he would have to move into an apartment down the street since after almost eleven years of marriage he still couldn't seem to keep his hands off her.

She led him to the first floor meeting room—the half bath next to the kitchen. One of the few places besides their bedroom that they could truly be alone.

She turned to him, her cheeks rosy from her bath, her eyes bright. It amazed him sometimes how much he loved her. It was as if, once he opened up his heart to her, it went a little crazy making up for lost time.

Each time he thought he couldn't possibly love her more than he already did, he would hear her reading Olivia a bedtime story, changing her voice for all the different characters, or he would catch her blowing raspberries on Jenny's belly while she changed her diaper. There were a million little things she did that made him love her more every day.

He might have been worried that he loved her too much, but she felt the exact same way about him.

"What's up?" he asked.

She blew out a big breath and said, "We have a problem."

He frowned. "What kind of problem?"

"Well, not a problem exactly, more like a slight inconvenience."

He folded his arms across his chest and sighed. "What did they break this time?"

"Nothing was broken. You know how my periods have been screwy since Jenny was born."

"Yeah?"

She bit her lip. "And, um, how I've been feeling a little yucky lately? Really tired and kinda nauseous."

Uh-oh, he had a feeling he knew where this was going. "I thought that was from the birth control."

"So did I. At first."

"But?"

"But then I noticed that it had been a while since I had my period."

"So what you're saying is, you're late."

She nodded. "I'm late."

He took a big breath and blew it out. Here we go again. "How late?"

"Two weeks, maybe three."

He raised an eyebrow at her. "Which is it, two or three?"

She bit her lip again. "Um, probably closer to three."

"Does this mean I need to make a trip to the pharmacy and get a test?"

"I went four days ago before I picked the kids up from school."

"*Four* days?"

She shrugged. "Denial. I finally worked up the courage to take it tonight after my bath."

Asking was merely a formality at this point. "And?"

She sighed. "Oops."

He tried not to smile, but he could feel a grin tugging at the corners of his mouth.

She rolled her eyes. "I know you're happy about this so you might as well just go ahead and smile."

He gripped the lapels of her robe and tugged her to him, brushing a kiss across her lips. "I love you."

"Six kids," she said, shaking her head. She looked a little shell-shocked, but he could tell she was happy, too.

The truth was, they could have six more and she wouldn't hear a complaint from him. He had plenty of love in his heart to go around.

"Not bad for a woman who once said she never wanted kids."

"Steven will be barely ten when the baby's born meaning we will have six kids under the age of eleven." She ran her fingers through the hair at his temples that had just begun to turn gray. "We must be completely nuts."

"Probably," he agreed, but insanity was highly underrated.

"I guess this is what I get for marrying a man who wanted a big family, huh?"

"Yeah, because you know what they say."

She thought about it for a second then said, "Fools rush in where angels fear to tread?"

He grinned. "Be careful what you wish for, you just might get it."

* * * * *

MILLS & BOON

MODERN

Power and Passion

Prepare to be swept off your feet by sophisticated, sexy and seductive heroes, in some of the world's most glamourous and romantic locations, where power and passion collide.

Julia James
Heiress's
PREGNANCY SCANDAL
MILLS & BOON

Jennie Lucas
Chosen as the
SHEIKH'S ROYAL BRIDE
MILLS & BOON

Kim Lawrence
A WEDDING at the ITALIAN'S DEMAND
MILLS & BOON

Sharon Kendrick
The
SHEIKH'S SECRET BABY
MILLS & BOON

Eight Modern stories published every month, find them all at

millsandboon.co.uk/Modern